WE MEN OF ASH AND SHADOW

The Vanguard Chronicles – Book 1

HL TINSLEY

We Men of Ash and Shadow

HL Tinsley

(nevercity.co.uk)

ISBN-13: **978-1-5272-8894-2**

This book is for my dad, who would, even in a round room, still find a way to be in my corner.

CONTENTS

CHAPTER 1
THE RING O' BASTARDS

It was the most highly recommended venue the city had to offer. It was called the Ring O' Bastards and it had the lowest patron-to-murder-victim rate in a five mile radius.

Inevitably, as within any bar, there would be the occasional spot of trouble. An unwitting stranger would wander in from another part of town looking for a drink and a good time, and instead find a fight and a broken nose. They didn't know the rules. People had to learn fast. If they couldn't, they didn't come back and quite often left with one or two fingers less than they had when they arrived.

For the most part Ludnor managed to keep the chaos to a minimum. He also kept a cleaver under the counter next to the pumps. Nobody argued with the old barkeeper, or at least they never did it more than once.

If you were feeling adventurous you could try the food which was always guaranteed to draw a crowd. The menu changed nightly and was largely dependent on whatever had been foolish enough to walk past the back door at the wrong moment that afternoon. There was profit to be made wagering how long a meal would stay down. Any gains would usually be collected by the victor in liquid form. Nobody was foolish enough to actually bring coins into the Ring. Instead they used the counters. The blue counters were for drinks. Red counters were for girls. The black ones were for whatever it was that Ludnor kept under the bar, twisted up in little paper bags.

You made your mark on the counters and used them to fund your evening. The next day one of Ludnor's cousins would come to collect. Nobody ever questioned their tally. Nor did they ever ask how it was that Ludnor seemed to have so many cousins, yet no-one ever saw the same one twice. It was all just part of the system.

Each day passed the same way. The whistles would blow. The doors of the warehouses and foundries would groan open and the masses would flood out.

They would trudge in at seven, and by eleven they were kings of the world. They would make plans, sing songs and vow fervently that this would be their last night in the Ring. The next night they would be back, the cycle would begin again and nobody ever left.

Any hope of leaving had been obliterated the day the walls went up. They lived, trapped in a city divided according to rank and status. Everyone had their place. Captain Felix Sanquain was the man who made sure they knew it. This was the man who paid John Vanguard a living. Not that it was an arrangement Vanguard was happy with. He was mulling over this very fact as he sat on his usual stool facing the evening crowd.

Ludnor stood behind the bar, wiping a rag around a glass as if it would make a difference. They didn't make much conversation. Vanguard was not much of a talker.

There was, however, an unspoken mutual respect between them. They were both relics of the past trying to live in the new world.

Vanguard kept one hand on his drink. That was another one of the rules. Hands on your cup at all times. Management accepted no liability for theft, loss or poisoning as a result of unattended beverages. He watched the card game unfolding on the table to his left. A small pile of counters had begun to build in the middle of the four players. The man closest to the door was cheating. Vanguard could tell by the flickering of his eyeball.

The counters were of little interest to Vanguard. Sometimes it felt as though he was the only sober man still left on earth. Being teetotal meant he had no use for blue. He was not averse to the paper bags now and again, so if a black came his way it would get pocketed for later. The powder seemed to help with aches and pains, but invariably one part of him or another was always hurting. It would be easy to get carried away and he had no intention of becoming just another addict. It seemed better to live with it for the most part.

As for the red, he certainly wasn't celibate but sex was a game for younger men. Not that he would turn it down given a reasonable offer. However, the longer time went on, the less it seemed to matter and he got used to going without. Besides, there were five girls that worked the Ring and they only had six legs between them. Vanguard valued his manhood. It was one of the few things he had left that was still his.

Nobody paid him much attention. The Ring was neutral ground, thanks to the most fervently upheld rule of them all; if you were going to kill a man you let him finish his drink first. Ale spilled on the floor inside. Blood spilled on the floor outside. No exceptions. Ludnor had a zero tolerance policy on that one.

A ginger cat slunk amongst the table legs looking for scraps. It had one front tooth that stuck out, curling up from under its bottom lip like a sabre. Every few minutes someone would stamp on its tail. It would mewl angrily before returning a moment later. Vanguard shooed it away. He had no quarrel with the animal; he just didn't want it to end up on tomorrow nights menu. It ignored the warning. Like the rest of the population, it chose to ignore its fate. Leaning down, he gave it a scratch behind the ears. Vanguard liked cats. In another life, he would have chosen to have a few of them for the company. In another life, he would have made a lot of different choices.

Vanguard was a hard man to describe. People didn't like to look at his face long enough to notice any real detail. If they had looked, they would have noticed the tell-tale signs of a long career in service. They would have seen the scars and the tattoos, the patch on the side of his jaw where the skin had been burnt away. He reached up and ran one finger over the scars, feeling the coarse hairs that half masked the puckered skin. The scars didn't make him any less attractive. Time had done a good enough job of that. At a guess, you might have thought that he was older than fifty. Nobody was sure of his actual age, Vanguard included.

The Ring was one of the few places that Vanguard could go to think. At least here nobody was trying to kill him. He could keep one foot in the past. He could remember. He needed that.

There was a thin line between mercenary and soldier, and an even thinner one between mercenary and murderer. Legitimate killing was a complex business. Truth be told, he had never really been sure at what point one thing had become the other.

Vanguard had begun practicing his trade at the age of fourteen. His entire life had been dedicated to the art. The first kill had been messy. It was another five years before anyone taught him how to do it properly. The army had been good to him. Those years had been the best of his life.

The card game was drawing to a close. The cheat pocketed his fistfuls of ill-gotten counters and stood up. Vanguard watched disinterestedly. The man was a liar and a bastard, but it was not for him that Vanguard had come that night. Ludnor rang the bell that hung above the bar, the signal that the doors would soon close. Either you left now or you stayed in for the night. Most people chose the latter.

The door swung open. All heads turned to face the figure that now stood in the doorway.

It was well known that, as long as you got in before the key turned in the lock the Ring was a place you could stay all night. Useful when you had nowhere else to go. Infinitely better than sleeping outside on the streets. Ludnor spat over the side of the bar. "You're not welcome here."

The bearded man scowled. "Everyone is welcome here."

Ludnor took the cleaver from beneath the counter and slammed it against the bar. "Not you."

The barman was well past sixty years old. Living to forty had made him famous. Reaching fifty had made him a legend. At this point most of the locals looked upon him as something strange and unnatural. There had to be something extremely dangerous about a man who could survive for so long in a place like that.

The newcomer's eyes snapped from left to right. Nobody moved. Ludnor didn't allow murder in the bar, but on this one occasion, he looked like he might be willing to make an exception. Taking a few steps back with his hands up, the man turned and went back into the night. The door slammed behind him.

As the patrons turned back to their drinks, Vanguard took his cue. Standing, he fastened his jacket with one hand, placing the other on the canvas bag that sat at his side. He left the cup sitting on the table. As he walked by, he looked over his shoulder towards Ludnor who gave him the slightest of nods.

Vanguard stepped out into the night and paused for a second. There was a scraping of deadbolts. The door locked behind him. It was time to go to work.

CHAPTER 2
A FAVOUR TO THE CITY

A decent criminal will know the streets like the back of his hand. He will know which corners lead to dead ends. He will know which tunnels mark the fastest escape routes and the quickest ways to get from one zone to another without being seen. A decent killer, however, will know a great deal more.

Vanguard knew, for example, that if the wind blew from the north it would smell of the canals. Diesel oil and stagnant water would sting the nostrils. If the wind came from the south it would smell of coal residue and ash from the foundries. He knew which paths the lamplighters took and where they would end their shift, leaning against the iron railings of the old tenements and smoking cigarettes.

He wiped the side of his face with one sleeve. There was a fine rain coming in. It was the sort of weather that you didn't really notice at first. You just knew that you were dry one minute and soaked to the bone the next. Somewhere in the distance, a clock struck midnight. Doors and windows began to close for the night, bolts creaking along the shutters. Vanguard watched the silhouette of a man disappearing into the haze of the gaslight, heading towards the waterfront.

Observing from the shadows, he watched as his mark stamped through the puddles. Dark, churning water from the sewer systems often poured out onto the streets when it rained, and water made a lot of noise. His target may have been a criminal, but he was not a smart one. If he had been, he might have lived to see another day.

Ambition was a dangerous thing to have in D'Orsee. The bearded man ought to have been content with his lot. He could have spent years operating quite successfully without ever becoming subject to Sanquain's attentions. The captain had little interest in low-level traffickers. But when the vendors started sourcing product from outside the slums it became a problem. People tended to notice little girls disappearing in the middle of the night. The last one they found had been four years old. She had been the daughter of a merchant in the Golden Quarter. Sanquain hadn't cared much about the first few they had found – they were nobodies.

The streets were narrow. It gave the neighbourhood a stifling, suffocating atmosphere. The buildings all seemed to slope toward one another, creating an overhanging canopy of poorly constructed brick and tile. When it rained heavily it made it look as though the city were melting. Vanguard followed the mark through the twisting back alleys until the streets spat them both back out along the towpath. It wasn't until they got to the tunnels that the bearded man stopped. Vanguard saw his shoulders tense. The hairs on the back of his neck were prickling.

He spoke without looking. "I know you're there."

Stepping from the shadows, Vanguard idly scratched

the burnt side of his face with the knife handle. "In that case, there's no point pretending otherwise."

"You're making a big mistake."

"That seems unlikely."

Vanguard had heard it all more times than he cared to count. They all tried it. None of it ever worked. Negotiation was out of the question - no amount of begging, bargaining or last minute pleas for mercy could change that. There was not a bribe or threat he had not been offered at one point or another.

"Kill me and you'll answer to Sanquain."

Vanguard was unmoved. "Who do you think sent me?"

The man's face fell. He had played his only card and it had not played well. Vanguard could tell that he was weighing up the options in front of him. Running was one, fighting back the other. He had three inches height on Vanguard. Probably a good twenty pounds too. It wouldn't make a difference.

Sanquain employed Vanguard for a reason. It was an arrangement that neither of them enjoyed but Vanguard had a talent that nobody else in his service possessed. Sanquain needed it for times when matters required more discreet handling. It wasn't always appropriate to send one of his heavy booted thugs to deal with a problem. They were too noisy, too clumsy and for the most part, completely corruptible. The bearded man could see him at that particular moment, but that was because Vanguard wasn't trying to hide.

The moment he wanted to, Vanguard would disappear. They never saw him coming. They never heard him coming. He melted in and out of sight like a phantom. It was a talent developed over decades. His face could blend into a crowd at a whim. Nobody knew how he did it.

The bearded man changed his stance. He had clearly made his choice.

Vanguard melted back, leaving nothing where he had just been but the lingering sense of his presence. The bearded man lurched forward into the vacant space Vanguard had left; the weight of his body propelling him, legs slightly apart. The clenched fist intended for Vanguard's jaw found nothing but the late night smog. A flash of movement caught his eye, drawing his gaze to the right. The blade came unexpectedly from the left. The bearded man clutched at his throat, surprised by how quickly and silently death had actually come. He had not felt a thing. A pair of bright eyes stared up from the ground, whiskers twitching in eager anticipation. It was as though the rats of the city could smell the blood before it hit the cobblestones.

Vanguard took a scrap of cloth from his inside pocket. After wiping the blade, he scrunched up the material and put the knife back inside the satchel. Some men chose to keep their knives in their jackets, but that opened an invitation to pickpockets. Some simply carried them until they were needed, but rain was not good for the blade. You had to respect the tools of your trade. Vanguard clipped the bag shut again.

It was a pretty unassuming looking satchel. It had cost him two days wages and had lasted eighteen years, part of that time buried underground. It had been a good purchase. Nobody would look at it and think its contents were responsible for so many deaths. Waiting for a few minutes, he listened to the dripping water falling from the roof of the tunnel.

The sound reminded him of being in the Hole.

If the time spent in service had been the best years of

his life, the time spent incarcerated had been the worst. People thought life in the city was bad. They wanted to try life underneath it. Three years buried in a box beneath their feet while they went on with their lives. Five paces from top to bottom, five paces from side to side. No sunlight. No fresh air. That dank hole had been Vanguard's home for thirty-six months. One thousand and ninety-five days to the hour.

By the time Sanquain had found him, Vanguard had gone half mad. There was a steady dripping from the sewer pipes above the ceiling. It had been driving him crazy. When they had ridden back to the chambers that Sanquain held in the Golden Quarter, the sunlight had hurt his eyes so badly he thought they would burn away to nothing.

It had taken six months for Sanquain to bring him back from the brink. The act wasn't one of kindness or charity. It was business. The captain was a practical man and he saw an investment opportunity. To the outsider it would have seemed like a bizarre act on Sanquain's part. The captain already had an entire army of men at his command. The Red Badges kept the streets in order. Why he would want to pluck one man from the bowels of the city was a mystery. They did not know what Sanquain knew. Information was power. Secrets were currency.

A delicate balance needed to exist in order for control to reign over D'Orsee. The captain was smart enough to know that a city did not run on the power of its government – it ran on the power of enterprise.

The real power lay in the money that changed hands under the cloak of night. It was in the street windows that showcased their wares bathed in hazy red light. It was in the shadows of the back rooms where men met to smoke cigars and congratulate each other on all their many successes. Sanquain had an informant on every corner. His finger lay firmly on the pulse of the streets. There was nothing that he did not have an interest in, legitimate or otherwise.

Every now and again, a purveyor of less than lawful practices would get too ambitious. Crime was a necessary evil. It was not, however, practical to have thieves, rapists, and murderers running around the city causing problems. Not unless Sanquain authorized it.

A set of footsteps echoed behind him. The scent of cheap cologne was enough to tell him who approached without having to look up. Dispatch was Vanguard's job, clean up belonged to somebody else.

Hacking back the phlegm in his throat, Sanderson spat at the ground. "So what did this shit stain do?"

"Baby killer. Sold them."

"Fuck he do that for?"

Vanguard would have been inclined to agree with Sanderson's reaction, had it been based on genuine disgust. It wasn't. He was just annoyed that now he had to deal with the mess. Sanderson didn't like Vanguard. The feeling was mutual. Neither of them felt inclined to pretend otherwise.

Sanderson lifted one of the dead man's arms and let it drop to the ground. "What am I meant to do with this? Bastard's built like a brick shit house."

Vanguard held out one hand. "That's your problem, not mine."

"Don't you ever get tired of being such a self-righteous prick?"

A small pouch filled with coins was dropped into his upturned palm. Vanguard stuffed it into the bag and turned without responding, before walking back up the tunnel and out onto the path, leaving Sanderson to deal with the job of clearing the body. There would be more Red Badges coming, he had little doubt of that. Sanderson was not the type of man to do work if there was an opportunity to force someone else to do it. Vanguard had no intention of hanging around long enough to still be there when his lackeys arrived.

He pulled his collar up in an attempt to stop the rain from accumulating on the nape of his neck. Sanderson could think what he wanted. There was more justice in Vanguard's work than in what Sanderson's bunch of petty thugs tried to pass off as law and order. Truthfully, this one he would have killed for free. It would have been a favour to the city.

Vanguard lived in a world where the criminals were better protected than the people - or at least, they were until Sanquain said otherwise. The dead girls would never be mentioned again. They had never really had a chance. It was virtually impossible to get into one of the major cities these days. You needed eight different documents, an authorized travel pass and enough money for a healthy bribe just to get through the gates. Getting out was even harder.

That alone was reason enough for the entire population to keep themselves in a near permanent state of intoxication. It was better than waking up sober and realising the truth. They were all inmates in a prison of their own creation.

CHAPTER 3
HENRIETTE

As with many great changes, nobody had really noticed anything happening until it was too late. People went about their business, wilfully ignorant to the suffering of others. The country had found itself in the clutches of economic strife. There was hunger, disease and discontent. Whilst the poor wasted to nothing, the rich remained wholly unconcerned - until the first of the riots began.

The rebellion had spread slowly at first. It is a common misconception that war must begin with a great act of violence. Anyone to have lived through one will know that they often begin quietly, imperceptibly, with the smallest changes in the wind. Tensions had been running high between the classes for years, long before the first shot was ever fired. Everywhere you went the poor outnumbered the rich and the rich outgunned the poor. It was the same for the residents of D'Orsee as it was in any other city. Civil war had raged for five years. In the end it had finished where it had begun. They all reaped the consequences of their actions, nowhere more so than in the capital itself.

The city had been almost at breaking point when a young military officer with a talent for politics stepped up to offer them a solution. He promised them a new sort of government. After years of violence the country longed for resolution. He had promised a place for everyone in the new world.

Before long, Captain Felix Sanquain was the most powerful man in D'Orsee. The old establishment was dead, the war over. Within the first twelve months of his tenure anyone in a position of power with links to the lower classes had been cast out. There was segregation. Sanquain had divided the city. People now lived in zones decided by their status and rank. Anyone who protested had disappeared in the middle of the night. There were a lot of accidents. More than one liberally minded official had washed up on the banks of the canals after a tragic fall from the towpaths.

In a few hours time, Sanderson or one of his squad would find a fresh corpse discarded somewhere downtown. They'd cite it as a robbery victim or a terrible accident. You'd be surprised how many accidental throat cuttings there were. There had always been a thin line between control and chaos. At least the people that Vanguard killed were real criminals. Perverts, rapists, and murderers – nobody would lose any sleep over their deaths. Vanguard never did.

The rain was easing by the time he found himself nearing home. The Tanners was located in the eastern section of the Black Zone. It still stank even though the tannery itself had been closed for a few years. Everything was bathed in a kaleidoscope of grey. Stacks of discarded machinery and metal lay in haphazard piles across the length of the yards.

Right at the back of the neighbourhood, there was a house squeezed so tightly into the space between the buildings that it looked like it was holding its breath. Vanguard pushed open the gate and tried to avoid the puddles as he walked towards the front door.

Vince was standing outside smoking a hand-rolled cigarette. There was a fresh black eye on the left side of his face. Clearly, it had been a busy night.

Once inside, Vanguard unbuttoned his jacket and walked through the hallway. The walls were covered in brightly patterned wallpaper that peeled at the corners. Pictures hung in mahogany frames. Each contained a different photograph of a girl. They were depicted reclining on a plush sofa completely naked. It was a menu, of sorts, that customers could peruse whilst they waited.

There was a light on at the end of the hall. Henriette was sitting at the table in the parlour. There was a young girl sitting next to her Vanguard had not seen before. A china teapot sat between them and Henriette had set several large, scented candles burning. Jasmine was her favourite. She felt it gave the house an exotic feel. She noticed Vanguard lingering in the hall and waved him in.

Henriette was a thick set, heavy busted woman with a huge amount of curly black hair permanently pinned up on the top of her head. The word most commonly used to describe her was 'sturdy'. It always looked as though her clothes were fighting a losing battle. She ran the house and gave no quarter to any customers who stepped out of line. Given the choice of spending time with anyone in the entire city, Vanguard would have chosen Henriette every time.

"John, come here and see my new girl." She gestured proudly towards her companion.

The girl looked less enthusiastic. She didn't speak but did glance up furtively. She obviously couldn't have been there more than a few hours. She still had that look on her face that suggested she had other options. It wouldn't take long for her to realise there were far worse places to work.

Vanguard pulled out a seat at the table and poured himself a cup of tea. Henriette cleared her throat loudly. The girl obediently offered him a small cake from a tea plate. He spoke through a mouthful of crumbs. "Do you have a name?"

"It's Ruth." There was an air of abject disinterest in her reply.

"No, no, no." Henriette shook her head. "We talked about this. It can't be Ruth, not anymore. It has to be alluring; sensual, nobody wants to fuck a Ruth. Your name is Carmen."

The name suited her. She had a dark look to her eyes that didn't quite seem to fit the youthfulness of her face. Vanguard suspected that she knew a lot more about the world than she ought to. There wasn't an awful lot to her. The girl seemed to be made up of overly long eyelashes, overly long limbs and not much more. Henriette reached over and pressed a thumb against the girl's chin, rubbing away a smudge. "Go to bed now, we'll get your picture taken in the morning."

Carmen got up. It was at this point that Vanguard realised she wasn't wearing anything on her bottom half other than underwear. They watched as she walked down the hall, turning at the end and heading up the stairs to the second floor.

"I'm thinking about putting her in the Desert Empress suite."

"She looks like she'd snap in half."

"Oh I'll soon fatten her up."

They made a little conversation. Vanguard ate another cake. Before he went to bed he gave Henriette the pouch he had received from Sanderson. The rooms on the first floor of the house were rented by the half hour. They all had a different theme and corresponding costume. The girls lived on the second floor together. Henriette had the third. The ground floor was made up of the hallway, the parlour, a waiting room, and a defunct second bathroom. That was where Vanguard slept. It was at the back of the house and had rusted pipes lining the walls. Henriette had put a mattress on the floor for him, but most nights he slept in the tub. There was something more familiar about being in an enclosed space.

He had been renting the bathroom for six months and not once had they ever discussed money. Vanguard simply gave Henriette what he made. She never asked him about his work. She never complained if he took food from the pantry. If they had lived in another world, Vanguard could easily have spent his whole life in comfortable companionship with Henriette.

He had asked her once.

About three weeks after he had taken the room, after a particularly busy night, Vince had been knocked out cold by a customer who had snuck a metal pipe into one of the rooms. Apparently that was always a potential occupational hazard. There had been a screaming from the first floor. That particular customer liked the girls to have bruises.

Henriette had shot the customer in the leg with the

pistol she kept tucked into her corset. In his apparent haste to get out of the building, he had left his belongings behind. There had been a bottle of gin, wrapped up in brown paper. Vanguard had arrived home from his business that night to find Henriette waiting for him. They had sat in the parlour and finished most of the bottle before the sun came up. Vanguard remembered it as being one of the most pleasant evenings he had ever had. It was probably the gin talking, but he had asked Henriette to marry him. She had laughed at him. Not because she was cruel, but because the idea was ridiculous.

Another few weeks of living at the house and Vanguard too had come to realise that Henriette was not that sort of woman. She had a business to run. She ran it well. Just as Ludnor had, Henriette had found a way to make the new world work for her.

The next day she had marched into the bathroom and announced that Vanguard could only stay under the provision that he met two conditions. Firstly, he was never to ask Henriette to marry him ever again. Secondly, he was not to drink again as obviously, alcohol turned him stupid and Henriette would not abide stupid lodgers.

Vanguard could stand to give up a lot of things. There were hundreds of rooms across the city and plenty of people looking for a lodger. But Henriette had something that was a rare commodity in their world. It was the will to survive.

Since that day, he had never again asked her to marry him, and not a single drop of alcohol had passed his lips. Surrounded by death, Vanguard looked at Henriette and felt like she might be the only person he knew who was truly still alive.

CHAPTER 4
THE SQUIRREL IN THE JAR

Tarryn had entered the world to great acclaim. His birth had been announced in all the society papers. He had been told, several times over the years that on first introduction many of the highest ranking ladies in the city had proclaimed him to be the most beautiful child they had ever seen.

His mother had carted him around town, taking him to every afternoon tea or ladies club she could find. She delighted in coordinating their outfits. By the time he was two years old, Tarryn was a regular feature in all the most sought-after venues.

For the first few years of his childhood his father had protested. Tarryn was far too pretty for his own good; being perpetually cosseted by simpering women wasn't helping. After a while, his father had stopped paying him any attention. As a teenager, he had grown accustomed to hearing the words his mother used to describe his father. Eventually, he had learned what they meant. With each passing year, he heard them uttered with increasing regularity. He was scum, a wandought, a bastard - those were some of the more charitable terms she would use. He heard worse and heard it often.

Tarryn was no less striking as an adult than he had been as an infant. Just over twenty years had passed, though now people rarely paid him the compliments they once had. The ladies did not fawn over nor admire him any longer. Instead, he began to fade into the background; lingering in the corners of rooms until eventually people simply forgot he was there. As far as society was concerned, the shine had gone from the diamond.

Unfortunately for him, whilst Tarryn may have, over the years, come to accept his descent from grace as unavoidable, his mother was prepared to do no such thing.

It was Saturday night at The Granville Club. The bar area was populated by the usual crowd - vapid women with too much time on their hands, overworked waiters and miserable looking husbands with fat wallets to match their stomachs. They mingled over drinks and gossip. A chandelier hung from the ceiling and velvet draped from every corner, even in places where there were no windows, simply because it could. The lights caught in dripping diamond necklaces, each one winking out as if to motion to its counterparts.

Two women stood next to each other, partly obscured by an ice sculpture which seemed to serve no purpose other than to provide people with something to stand next to. Their voices could be overheard quite clearly, not that they were trying to be quiet. "What *does* she think she is doing?"

The shrill sound of unbridled laughter pierced the low murmur of polite conversation. It was like nails being dragged across a chalkboard. Tarryn watched his mother, beaming like a cat, as she mingled with a group of financiers. One of them flinched, startled by the sudden peal of mirth. He hadn't said anything remotely funny as far as he could tell. Unperturbed, Lady Leersac reached out one hand and placed it lightly on the banker's arm.

The champagne had been flowing liberally all night. As she leaned forward she lost her balance, liquid spilling from her glass and leaving splashes across the front of her dress.

"I don't know how she even has the gall to keep showing her face here. It's quite pathetic."

The taller of the two women made a clicking noise with her tongue and shook her head. "I've heard the money is all gone, nothing left but pennies. It's positively tragic." The tone of her voice did not suggest any sort of sympathy.

Her friend twisted one finger in a string of beads that trailed down her throat and disappeared into her cleavage. The pearls twisted, making a gentle crinkling noise. "*I* heard the husband was an absolute reprobate - more pox in that house than there is in the dock slums."

"Shameful."

There was a squeal from across the room as Lady Leersac recognised a few of the women on the opposite side of the bar. She stumbled towards them, loudly exclaiming and offering pleasantries which were met with haughty sideways glances. The women seemed to band tighter together, creating an impenetrable barrier. The two women standing at the ice sculpture snorted as they watched Tarryn's mother tapping insistently at the shoulders of her former peers.

Tarryn slipped back further into the corner wishing that he could just melt away into the wall. It had been a mistake to let her leave the house, but she had seemed so calm that afternoon. Sooner or later he would have to go and retrieve her. There would be a scene and it would be all Tarryn's fault as usual. She would curse at him and tomorrow the gossips would have something to talk about over breakfast.

Heat from the combination of the lights and bodies had caused the ice sculpture to thaw slightly. A puddle had formed on the floor forcing the women to step back, so as not to dampen their skirts. The shorter one backed into Tarryn who had no space left in which to escape. She turned slightly. Her face puckered. She sniffed. "Oh, it's you. I think it's time you took her home before she humiliates herself any further."

On that at least, Tarryn could agree with them. It was long past the time to leave. He walked across the ballroom floor and touched his mother on the arm. Confused by the interruption, she turned around. Immediately she beamed. "Look who it is! Have you met my boy? He's such a good boy."

The ladies looked at one another, exchanging disapproving grimaces. Most of them were the very same ladies who had been enthralled with him as a child. It was funny how now they found those same striking features distasteful and freakish. Changing fortunes were so often met with a change of attitude. Tarryn took his mother by the shoulders and began to lead her away. "Come on Mother, it's time to leave."

"So soon? But we're having such a wonderful evening!"

"Yes, we should go now."

Lady Leersac pouted like a sullen child. Fortunately, it did not seem to last for long. Her smile soon returned. As people turned their heads to watch them leaving she took it as a mark of their disappointment that she had to retire so early. In her mind she was still, as she had always been, the most desirable and important woman in the room.

She held onto Tarryn, sweeping across the floor as if being escorted around a ball. She waved to the other ladies, calling out gaily. "Thank you so much for a lovely evening! We'll be back again soon!"

Tarryn tried to block out the sounds of laughter as they walked down the stairs and out onto the street. He hailed a carriage and they spent most of the journey home in silence.

The horse came to a halt on a wide street lined with neatly kept rose gardens. Tarryn paid the driver and helped his mother down from the seat. She seemed delighted with the whole thing. The carriage left and Tarryn walked with his mother a little way further down the road.

He didn't like to stop directly outside the house. His mother frowned when she saw that there were no lights on in the windows. There should have at least been a fire burning in preparation for their return. "Why is it so dark?"

They reached the front door. Tarryn searched his pockets for the key. Lady Leersac stood patiently looking at the knocker. As far as she was concerned all doors opened as if by magic. Eventually, he found it, unlocked the door and ferried her inside. She took off her gloves and laid them carefully on the table in the hallway. Her voice echoed in the empty foyer. "Harper? Harper where are you? We had to open the door for ourselves. Come quickly, we need some tea!"

Tarryn let the door close with a soft click. The key went back in the pocket. He knew better than to leave it where she might find it. "Harper isn't here."

"Isn't she? Where is she? Is she sick?"

"She's just not here."

There was no point in explaining it again. They had been through it enough times. Besides she would have forgotten again by the morning. Instead, Tarryn picked her up in his arms and carried her up the stairs.

Lady Leersac leant her head against his shoulder, lamenting once more over the apparent absence of the maid. Harper had been there earlier. She could remember it quite clearly. It didn't do to let the staff take unscheduled evenings off. Harper had been having an extended evening off for some time now. The last time Tarryn had seen her was eight months ago when she handed in her notice.

The door to the bedroom was open. It made it a little easier to manoeuvre. She didn't weigh much, but the bones in her arms stuck out and would bruise easily should they knock against a door frame or wall. Tarryn sat her down on the bed. Both arms automatically lifted into the air.

It had taken some time to get used to the idea of dressing and undressing his mother. By this point it barely registered. She had wandered about the house naked and wailing often enough for it to have stopped being a shock long ago. It didn't take much to do when she was being co-operative. It was far easier than letting her attempt it alone. She watched as he laid the clothes carefully over the back of the screen that divided the room. He had only turned away for a second when he felt something hard hit him just behind his right ear.

He yelped. "What do you think you're doing?" Tarryn touched one hand to the back of his head. There was a little blood where something sharp had broken the skin. His mother stood brandishing the heeled shoe like a weapon.

HL TINSLEY

Her eyes were ablaze. "Don't touch me! Don't ever touch me!"

"Calm down."

"You'll never put your hands on me again, you bastard. I hate you. Do you hear me? I hate you!"

Tarryn leaned back, the expression on his face weary. She slapped at him, nails clawing at his chest. It was not the first time this had happened. Memories got muddled in her mind, faces merging together. He wouldn't have minded except for the fact that they looked nothing alike. Tarryn's pale features had been inherited from his mother's side.

"Mother stop, I'm not him. It's me. I'm Tarryn. Stop it now."

The scratching paused momentarily. There was a flash of recognition in her eyes. Tarryn waited, holding her wrists tightly as the memories faded and she returned to the present. She still seemed sceptical. "Are you sure?"

"Yes. I'm sure. I'm your son."

She lowered her hands and sniffed. "Good. I hate that bastard."

He didn't expect an apology. They never came anyway. The candlestick had been the worst one. She had caught him by surprise in the sitting room after dinner one evening. The brass corner had taken a chunk out of his skull. The mark was still there on his forehead, hidden by a carefully arranged fringe.

Once she was calm it was relatively easy to get her into bed. Walking across the room, Tarryn reached into his pocket. There was a different one sewn into the jacket for each key. It made it easier to tell if one was missing. Once the windows had been locked, he bid his mother goodnight and bolted the door behind him.

Silence filled the house. In truth, there was not much else left to fill it with. The furnishings were sparse. Dark patches dotted the walls where the paper had hidden behind long since discarded picture frames. Some of the rooms were completely empty; the contents sold off or burned. They kept the lights off for the most part. Lighting wasn't cheap and Tarryn was accustomed to the dark.

The sitting room was cold and quiet. He took off his jacket and hung it on the coat stand. There was a mantelpiece over the hearth. In the middle of it, a bell jar containing a stuffed squirrel stood taking pride of place. His mother loved it. Tarryn couldn't stand the thing. Looking into the glass he caught a glimpse of his reflection. The sight made his fingers twitch. The features that looked back at him were those of a being he did not recognise. Pushing back the fringe, he gazed intently at the scar the candlestick had made. It was the only blemish in a sea of perfect skin. Everything else was perfectly proportioned, perfectly symmetrical. In a way, the scar was the only part of him that Tarryn felt was real.

The squirrel stared back at him through the glass jar.

He took a seat in the armchair that faced the door. If left open there was a clear view of the hallway. His mother was unlikely to get out again, but it never hurt to be cautious. He kept his boots on just in case.

It had been twenty-three days since he had last left her alone for longer than an hour. On one of her better days he had slipped a little extra something into her tea and left her passed out in the parlour. The time had been spent roaming the streets, looking for something but not quite knowing what it was. It had done him good to get out of the house.

He knew he wouldn't be able to last much longer without a proper break. The tension was creeping up his spine and knotting in his shoulders. Tomorrow, he would find a way to get out for a few hours. He had to - he was losing his mind. Sitting in the dark, feeling the hours of his life slowly slipping away, he could swear he heard that damned squirrel laughing at him.

CHAPTER 5
SANQUAIN

D'Orsee was a great, sprawling beast – one that required constant and careful observation. Standing on the streets it was impossible to see the city for what it really was. You could catch a snippet here and there but to truly understand it you needed a higher vantage point. There was no greater position from which to watch over the capital than from the window of Felix Sanquain's chambers.

Sometimes he would stand and watch the smog as it billowed across the skyline. The chimneys spitting ash from the foundries, great stacks peppering the horizon like sentries, guarding the secrets that the acrid clouds concealed below.

Prior to his rise to power, the previous administration had held their offices in the city hall. Located in the northern most section of the Golden Quarter, they had removed themselves from reality. Powerful men surrounded by gilded doors who knew nothing about the streets around them – it was one of the reasons they had lost their power.

It was a Sunday morning which meant that the market place below was abuzz with activity. Sanquain watched the lines of people thronging between the canopied stalls. Shouting and yelling, traders clamoured for attention, attempting to sell perishable wares of questionable quality and freshness to world weary mothers as stray children begged for throw away crusts. Men staggered in and out of the taverns walking straight past the open doors of the church without second thought. They chose to worship at a different sort of altar.

If it hadn't been for the profitability in it, Sanquain would have banned the gin houses. Prohibition had always proven to be an effective form of population control. Far fewer babies were produced as a result of sobriety. Fortunately for the masses, the public houses continued to do a healthy trade.

Sanderson sat in the chair opposite Sanquain's own seat at a large mahogany desk. The captain clasped his hands behind his back. "The tenants in Portamot, where do they stand now with the arrears due to Lord Lucian? I assume the matter is resolved?"

Sanderson curled the fingers of his hand, looking at the blistered knuckles. "There was a negotiation; the tenants have now reconsidered their stance on the rental increases."

"Good. That land is valuable. If people are not willing to accept market rates they should look elsewhere for accommodation. Do you have anything else to report?"

"Nothing of importance."

Sanquain turned from the window, casting his eyes downwards. They lingered for a moment at Sanderson's feet. There was a slight down turn to the corner of his mouth. The captain did not appreciate slovenliness in his employees. "Sanderson, your buckle appears to have broken."

The brass buckle of Sanderson's left boot had snapped off, leaving the leather frayed at the ends.

"I'll get it replaced."

"Immediately. And if you ever report to me in a similar state of disarray, I will have your boots removed. Then you will eat them." The captain turned back to the window. "Buckles included." The clock on the wall chimed, indicating the arrival of midday. There was a sudden shift in the atmosphere. Sanquain adjusted his cuffs. "*You* are late."

Sanderson looked up. Vanguard stared back at him, face flushed from the wind. He was sure the door hadn't even opened. Sanderson grimaced. "You're a creepy son of a bitch, you know that?"

"Better than being an arsehole."

The sound of the ticking clock synchronised perfectly with the echo of footsteps across the room. There was a good distance from the window to the desk. The captain did not hurry. Sanquain eventually took his seat. "Sanderson we are done for the day. I have matters to discuss with Vanguard."

It had been years and Vanguard still hadn't quite worked out what Sanderson's role or purpose was in the great scheme of things. He was afforded liberties that other Red Badges were not, yet the man offered no skill or talent that could not be found elsewhere. He seemed to perpetually linger like the smell on dung.

Sanderson cast one last scowl in Vanguard's general direction before rising from his seat. He bowed sharply before vacating the room, presumably in the pursuit of some poor underling who would soon be relieved of his boots.

"I'll say one thing for the war..." Sanquain paused.

He liked to leave prolonged silences between sentences. It was a tactic used to pressure his visitors into letting slip nuggets of information he could later use. Often they would tell him what he wanted to know simply to fill the void. It was an uncomfortable silence. Vanguard could live with it.

"It does leave a sizeable dent in the population regardless of the outcome. Did you know that there are almost twelve thousand more people living in the city today than there was when the war ended?"

"I didn't know that."

"It is putting a considerable strain on our resources."

"Why are you telling me? I'm not contributing."

Sanquain took in a breath. Vanguard often liked to try and press on his nerves. It would seem that today he was not willing to take the bait. Instead he pressed his fingers together, rubbing the underside of his chin. "Your attitude disappoints me. We are working to solve this city's problems."

"They're not my problems."

"You work for me and I work for the city, which makes them your problems." The captain sat back, smoothing down the front of his jacket. "I have a job for you."

"And I had to come all the way here for that?"

"I need you to spend some time in the Splinters."

Vanguard's eyebrow arched. Criminal activity was rife in the city but as far as he knew the occupants of the Splinters were nothing more than what most thought of as grifters and tricksters. A mild irritation made up primarily of those displaced by the war. They were something of a transient community, hocking supposed lucky charms from street corners to people too stupid to know a con when they saw one. More of a camp than a neighbourhood, the Splinters were not fixed in any one place. Hastily constructed wooden buildings would appear suddenly as if from nowhere. They would set up anywhere that they thought they could make a bit of money. Most of the time they stayed for a few months before it was torn down and reappeared somewhere else. People viewed them as a novelty for a while, but the welcome never lasted long. "What am I supposed to be doing in the Splinters?"

"Watching, observing, and bringing me information about anything I might need to know."

A piece of paper emerged from inside Sanquain's jacket pocket, folded in a crisp line down the middle. He handed it over. Unfolded, the paper depicted an image of a garish face twisted into a gurning smile. Vanguard had seen them posted on walls and fences around the city.

"What the hell is this supposed to be?"

"I'm told these *people* have an establishment. They hold boxing matches, card games, the sort of thing you're familiar with I have no doubt." Sanquain did not try to disguise the contempt in his voice. If the lower breeds were like rats, these people were no better than fleas to him. Their continued existence was an affront. "Despite my best efforts to guide them towards more productive endeavours, it would seem that some of the Red Badges have been frequenting this *club*."

Vanguard said nothing.

"Two of my men washed up in the marina a few days ago. The last place anybody saw them was in the Splinters. There is something rotten in that neighbourhood; I can smell it from here."

"Why me? Why not send in Sanderson? It sounds like his sort of place."

It looked like Sanquain was trying to smile. The corners of his mouth moved as though his face didn't understand what it was the muscles were trying to do.

"You know, Vanguard, these exchanges are starting to become tiresome. I did at one point find the candour in your attitude vaguely entertaining. But I'm a busy man. Do your job, or I may forget why it is that I pulled you from that rank shit hole I found you in."

"There are worse places than the Hole."

"I know you want me to think that. But if you imagine that sending you back to prison is the only thing I'd do to you, then I'm afraid you've learnt nothing in my employment."

Vanguard's face twitched.

"I will make sure that everyone knows exactly what you are. I will see you walk the streets from the court-house to the Pits. Rocks and stones will break your bones. When they are done with you, whatever is left will go back in the Hole."

Sanquain was satisfied that the point had been made.

Vanguard didn't want to go back to the Hole. True, the prospect of incarceration didn't scare him the way it might some people. He belonged in prison of that there was no doubt. Any sane jury would have locked him up and thrown away the key. In D'Orsee you were unlikely to see any sort of jury, sane or otherwise.

There were, however, too many things that Vanguard still needed to do before he could go back - things that he could not achieve languishing in a dank cell. He had a slate that he needed to wipe clean.

As it stood there were only two people in the whole

world that knew what had happened in Bellitreaux. Sanquain was one, Vanguard the other.

Vanguard could stand to be known as a criminal, he could even stand to be known as a murderer. As it stood, most people celebrated the work that he did. Their attitudes might not have been quite the same if they had known that the man who took the perverts and murderers from their streets was the same man who had ensured that so many of their sons had never come home. He did not fear death, but shame was a different thing entirely.

It did not matter how many died at his hands that did deserve it. It would never make amends for the two hundred and thirty-six who did not.

Sanquain had his reasons for choosing the marks that Vanguard dispatched. For the most part, Vanguard did not care what they were. Their motivations for wanting the streets rid of particular parties might have differed, but the end results were the same. Each time Vanguard went to work, there would be one less monster in the world.

Vanguard looked at the paper in his hand. Sanquain would not be giving him the task unless there was something happening that he did not want anyone else to know about yet. The deaths of a few insignificant soldiers would usually be of little interest to him. There was an ulterior motive. No doubt sooner or later it would come to light. Until then Vanguard had little choice.

CHAPTER 6
DAISIES ON THE BANK

Ludnor wiped both hands across the front of an apron that should have been incinerated years ago. Smudges of a residue smeared across the material, leaving behind thick daubs of grease. Vanguard didn't ask what it was, figuring that he probably didn't want to know. It was most likely going to be served as dinner later.

Holding the piece of paper, the barkeeper furrowed his brow and stared at the image. The words meant nothing to him. Literacy was not his forte. He did, however, recognise the picture. "What in the hell do you want to go there for?"

"Call it curiosity. What have you heard about it?"

The Ring wasn't open, but Vanguard had chanced the door. Ludnor had always been a valuable resource when it came to finding out what was going on around the city. There was a good chance that if Sanquain had heard about something, Ludnor would have heard about it too.

A pile of counters sat on the bar, Ludnor arranging them into bags according to the mark on each one.

Someone would come and pick them up soon and take them off to arrange payment. Ludnor picked up one with a 'V' scratched into the surface. He tossed it towards Vanguard. "You know you ought to have more than one."

"One is fine."

"You want a lot of information for a man with just one counter."

"Here I was thinking we were friends."

"Bollocks." Ludnor turned and spat the chewed up remnants of his mouthful into a bucket. He brushed a pile of counters across the bar using one hand. They were almost all blue.

Vanguard wondered who had used so many in one night and if they were even still alive to settle the account. "Have you been?"

"Do I look the type to go to the bloody show house?"

Vanguard took the paper back and slipped it into his pocket. Ludnor was a man of particular tastes and ideas. None of those tastes leaned towards the theatrical. He did however like to know what was going on around the city and in particular, anything that might affect his revenue.

The barkeeper pushed two counters towards Vanguard with his finger. Vanguard took them and put them into his pocket. He probably wouldn't use them, and Ludnor knew it. Vanguard also knew that Ludnor didn't want to get a reputation as the kind of man who gave out information for free. The old man moved closer as if it were some sort of conspiracy they were discussing. "I might not have been myself but half my bloody clientele have, traitorous bastards that they are. I can tell you this much, the whole place is crawling with freaks." Ludnor shuddered at the thought. "You'll want to talk to Herveaux."

"Who's that?"

"He owns half the neighbourhood they've set up in, not that it's worth much more than a piss in the wind. Watch your back. He'll stick a knife in it and empty your pockets while some tart waves a bag of peanuts in your face."

Ludnor reached under the bar and pulled out a large sack. The bags of counters were stuffed into it one by one. When it was full, Ludnor leaned across the bar pushing his elbows to the wood. He wiped his nose vigorously with the back of his hand. "I do know one thing for sure; they make a roaring trade from the Golden Quarter. I've heard there are private parties, up-their-arses aristocrats paying through the nose just to get a glimpse of a foreign tit."

Vanguard reached into his pocket and felt around. There was a bit of paper, the counters and a few coins – certainly not enough for a ticket. Asking a friend was out of the question. Vanguard didn't know if what he had were what you'd actually call friends, but even if they were, they weren't the sort of people you borrowed money from.

"There might be a way in, but you won't like it."

"What is it?"

"It involves asking for a favour." The barkeeper leaned in, his voice low as he explained his plan. Vanguard tried not to wince. If Ludnor's demeanour wasn't enough to dissuade someone from getting too close, his breath certainly ought to have been. "Lucien Herveaux doesn't speak to anyone unless it's about business or you've got something he wants to buy."

Vanguard had to admit that his idea would have been a good one had it not been for the fact that it would most likely end up in him losing one or both of his testicles. Unfortunately, he could not see many other options open to him. Herveaux was a man who valued commerce, and there was only one commodity in the Black Zone to which Vanguard had immediate and ample access.

"Just out of interest, how are you still alive?"

Ludnor snorted loudly, hacking back a mouthful of phlegm. "I'm a very charming man; nobody wants to kill a charming man."

The door creaked. A thin man with hair the colour of ash walked in. The three men exchanged looks without speaking. Vanguard noticed the flash of a knife hidden within the folds of his jacket. Ludnor pushed the sack across the bar. "Have you met my cousin?"

"Not this one, no."

Vanguard took the arrival of Ludnor's cousin as his cue to leave. He settled his previous account, purchased one of the paper bags using a counter and put it in his pocket for later. Making his way down the towpaths towards the Tanners he stopped briefly to relieve himself over the side of the bank. When he was done, he noticed a patch of flowers growing amongst the weeds nearby. Something in the back of his mind remembered that women liked flowers.

The door to Henriette's house was always open between the hours of eleven and one. Vince leaned against the wall, hands in his pockets, looking at the floor. He was there daily. Most of his time was spent outside. The only time he ever stepped inside was if there was trouble. The girls teased him mercilessly. When it was open, the doorway gave a direct view up the staircase to the first floor. They would take it in turns to sit on the top step, reclining in a variety of poses and calling his name. It was a long standing joke in the Tanners that Vince had seen more clams than a fish merchant. In the whole time that Vanguard had been there, he couldn't remember the doorman saying more than maybe twenty words in total. Most of them had been 'fuck' and 'off.'

Henriette sauntered out of the waiting room, a lace shawl draped over her shoulders. She held a fan in one hand. She was followed by an apprehensive-looking gentleman with beads of sweat running down the sides of his face. Henriette pointed the fan towards the stairs. "Don't worry; Simone is very good with first timers. The snow queen suite - third on the left. Do enjoy yourself!"

She caught sight of Vanguard and wrinkled her face. He didn't usually come back to the house during the day. They had an agreement. Henriette had worked hard to build up a standard of clientele that Vanguard simply didn't meet. Irritated she shooed him out of the hall and into the parlour, shutting the door behind them. "It's not that I don't like you, but could you fuck off and come back later?"

Vanguard held out his hand. Henriette looked at the pitiful offering. "What on earth are those meant to be?"

The daisies looked even sadder under the glow of the parlour lights than they had on the canal bank. Vanguard put them hastily on the table, conceding that they had been a mistake. Henriette sat down, letting out a sigh. The usual steady, rhythmic creaking sounded from the floor above them. Every now and then it would be interspersed by a low, guttural moan or high pitched giggling. It would stop after a few minutes or so and then start up again.

There was a sudden peal of laughter, followed by the noise of two sets of feet pounding down the stairs. Henriette stood up and marched over to the door. As she opened it, her face flushed red. Vanguard leaned over and caught a glimpse of pale white buttocks jiggling around in the hallway. The girls in question were half dressed like warriors and had engaged in a contest to see who would dare get closest to the open door in order to stab Vince with their spears first. Fortunately Felicia and Annabelle were too amused by their own joke to get particularly close. They held onto each other, shaking with laughter almost to the point of tears and unable to stand.

"Get back up those stairs at once and leave the poor man alone!"

Paulette appeared at the bottom of the stairs a moment later, one arm reaching out and pulling her unruly colleagues back towards the first floor. The two girls squealed in protest before scurrying back up the stairs, taking their weaponry with them.

Henriette fanned herself dramatically, rolling her eyes. "Absolutely brainless, the lot of them..."

Vanguard shifted uncomfortably. "I need a favour."

"What sort of favour?"

"I need to borrow one of the girls."

"*Borrow* one? For how long?"

"Just for a night."

Henriette's body shook with laughter. "Are you trying to be funny? You want to borrow a whore? When?"

"Tonight."

It took Henriette a moment to realise that it wasn't a joke. Falling silent, Vanguard saw her jaw clench as she held his gaze. When it came to anything that might affect her business or the girls Henriette had all the warmth of an iceberg. "What for, is it dangerous?"

It would have been unfair to Henriette not to disclose the full extent of his plan. That was the bit that Vanguard was most worried about. It was one thing to ask Henriette if he could borrow one of the girls. It was another thing to disclose where it was he would be taking her and why.

Henriette sucked in the air through her front teeth and shook her head as if she couldn't quite understand what he was saying. "You're telling me you want to borrow one of my girls on a Friday night, so you can take her to some club to meet with a competitor? Have you lost your mind?"

"Quite possibly... but I wouldn't ask if it wasn't important. I wouldn't let her out of my sight for a moment - that I promise."

"This club - who goes? A lot of rich people I presume? Plenty of money to spend?"

Vanguard nodded. Expression unwavering, Henriette leaned across the table and lowered her face so that their eyes met. "You bring me in new customers. Better ones. You get one girl for one night and don't ask me again. Do. Not. Lose. Her."

Henriette's hand reached out across the gap between them. Vanguard felt the pointed tip of a meticulously manicured nail pressing upwards into the soft skin beneath his chin. The scent of her perfume did things to him, things that made him instinctively adjust the position of his seating.

"If my girl comes back with so much as a single scratch, I'll chop your balls off."

"Understood."

Henriette straightened up and readjusted the bodice of her dress. The fasteners were straining. There was quite a lot of Henriette to contain. Satisfied that the conditions of their agreement had been made clear, she swept out of the parlour and called up the stairs.

"Carmen!" There was the sound of footsteps across the landing. "Good news! John is taking you out tonight. Now be a dear and go wipe yourself down, you're dripping almond oil on the carpet."

With an escort for the evening secured, Vanguard had other places to be. Part of him was quite glad that Henriette did not want him lingering around during trading time. It wasn't that he objected to being in the house during peak business hours, but it did rather feel like being the only man not dining at the buffet.

He walked back out of the house into the sunshine, pausing for a moment just outside the door. Vince did not appear to have moved an inch. If you didn't know better, you could have mistaken him for a statue, albeit a flat nosed, unattractive one. Vanguard liked the doorman. He didn't have much to say for himself, which was a rarity in a house where everyone had something to say about everything. Vanguard gestured towards the open door. "Just out of curiosity, have you ever...?"

Vince said nothing. He simply pulled a hand from his pocket and held up one finger. A slightly scuffed looking golden wedding band glinted in the sunlight.

"Fair enough."

Vanguard didn't return to the house until almost eight that evening. He stood with Henriette in the hallway, waiting. It would seem that Carmen was taking her time getting ready. After a while he began to suspect she might have climbed out of the bedroom window in an attempt to escape. He wouldn't have blamed her. Eventually she descended the stairs looking decidedly disinterested in the whole affair. "Am I still getting paid for this?"

The skin on the back of Vanguard's neck prickled slightly. He had asked Henriette for Carmen's time as a favour, it hadn't occurred to him that she might be expecting him to pay for it. He wasn't sure what made him feel more uncomfortable, the idea of paying for her or the idea of not.

Henriette snorted. "Certainly not, I'm not paying you to go gallivanting around the city all night. This is a business not a half way house."

Carmen rolled her eyes but offered no further argument. Vanguard held out one arm. She looked at it as if it were a tentacle. After a moment she lightly placed a gloved hand on it and he opened the door. The pair of them walked out of the house and into the night together.

As they walked towards the Splinters Vanguard glanced down at Carmen. There was a youthful, dewy glow to her skin. He wondered how long it would be before it would become dull and lifeless. If she was lucky, it would last maybe another year. For some reason, it made him think of the daisies on the canal bank. How once they had been plucked, it didn't usually take long for them to wither and die.

CHAPTER 7
ASK FOR KOSIC

V anguard was not a person adept in the fine art of casual conversation. Carmen was not a person accustomed to men trying to make much conversation with her of any kind, casual or otherwise. It made for an awkward, silent journey towards the Splinters.

Carmen wasn't entirely sure where they were going or what kind of occasion the evening was meant to be, and so was suspicious of everything. Any slight change of direction or movement from Vanguard and she flinched – it would have been almost imperceptible to the untrained eye, yet he couldn't help but feel insulted. The girl spent virtually all her time lying on her back yet she spooked at the proffering of an arm intended as little more than something to balance on.

It took much longer than anticipated to get to the right part of the Black Zone. Carmen shuffled with each step. Eventually Vanguard realised it was because the shoes she wore were too big for her feet; she didn't dare lift them up too high in case they fell off. "So, how do you like living at Henriette's?"

"It's alright." Carmen kept her eyes forward, clearly either too disinterested or not yet ready to engage in anything more than short, almost monosyllabic answers.

Vanguard didn't make a habit of engaging in small talk with anyone, least of all sullen teenage prostitutes. He didn't know what sort of thing they liked to talk about. It took a while for him to come up with something that might have resembled common ground. "Do you like the food?"

Carmen suddenly twisted so that the upper half of her body faced him. They continued walking along while she studied him. Her nose wrinkled up as she tried to work something out. "What happened to your face?"

"It got burnt."

"I can see that. I'm not stupid. How did it get burnt?"

"In a fire during the war."

"Did it hurt?"

"I don't know, I was unconscious at the time. Hurt after though."

A group of youths barrelled towards them, the stench of gin and stolen cologne clouding the air. The gang dispersed, spreading out as they walked by. Buoyed by alcohol and bravado they made a few lewd, bawdy comments. Vanguard ignored them. Carmen scowled. One of them, presumably in an attempt to impress his companions, threw a coin at her feet. She looked down at it lying in the mud. He gave her a wide grin, gaps where his teeth used to be showing. "Ditch your granddad sweetheart, we'll show you a good time. What do you say lads?"

One of his friends sniggered. "Nah, I like tits on mine."

Instinctively, Carmen stepped back. Vanguard could have sworn that if she'd had hackles, they'd have been up. Vanguard kept a firm grip on her arm. Bending down, he retrieved the coin from the puddle, wiped it on his jacket and put it in his pocket. Without saying a word, he glanced up at the boy who was looking to his friends for approval. Their eyes met.

The boy went pale. "Shit. Shit. Sorry, I didn't realise who you were. I didn't mean nothing by it."

Vanguard kept quiet. The crowd of young revellers began to back off down the road. There were a few more mumbled apologies before they turned tail and hot footed it into the nearest gin house. Carmen pouted, looking down at the gap between her chest and the lapels of the coat. It was true; there wasn't an awful lot to fill it out with.

"What's wrong with my tits?"

"Nothing's wrong with them, stop staring at them."

"You could have said something, you know – defended my honour and all that."

"Why is that my job? It's not like you haven't heard worse. Besides, we've got money now and you didn't need to bend over for it for once."

She mulled it over for a moment, head bobbing back and forth like it was trying to rattle the thought around. In the end, she shrugged again. "I suppose so."

The streets began to open up. There were a lot more people about in this part of town. A few of them gave the pair furtive sideways glances. Vanguard was aware they were not the most obvious coupling, which was saying a lot given the diverse nature of the Splinters. Eventually, the buildings began to give way to a sort of roughly constructed shanty town.

A one horse shay pulled by a grey mare had stopped at the last point on the road where there was still enough room for it to turn. Two men, their faces half covered by scarves, vacated the vehicle just as the horse unloaded its bowels onto the cobblestones. Vanguard promptly redirected Carmen out of the path of the oncoming dung. For a split second he locked eyes with the taller of the two men. What Ludnor had told him was true. They might not have been willing to admit it in high society, but the Splinters were definitely a destination discreetly frequented by the Golden Quarter elite. Vanguard knew good silk when he saw it.

Beyond the end of the road, Herveaux's club provided the focal point for a large open square flanked by two or three storey buildings that were a bohemian medley of wood, brick and open alcoves. A man on stilts teetered past them, throwing flyers to the floor and calling out to the passing crowds. Balconies that looked as though they had no business supporting the weight of a resting bird, let alone anything else, groaned under the weight of small bands of women looking down on the street. Some of them wore masks, twisted expressions that mimicked the image on the flyers. They didn't so much wear costumes as they did swathes of brightly coloured material, bundled and bunched and twisted around them until it was impossible to work out where it ended or began.

There was a gathering of people at the other end of the street, standing near the entrance of the club. The wall was covered from end to end in posters depicting cartoonish images of dancing girls and circus acts. They could hear music coming from inside. A pair of large wooden doors coated in a deep green paint that flaked and cracked provided a barrier between the gathering crowd and the promised decadence within. Carmen glanced up, head craning back. The club stood one storey higher than the other buildings. Vanguard watched as her lips moved silently, counting the decorative finials that had been indiscriminately placed along the line of the rooftop.

He didn't bother counting them, but would have been willing to guarantee there wasn't a church steeple in the whole of the Black Zone that hadn't contributed to the collection.

Carmen looked at them wistfully. "I won't be there forever, you know, at Henriette's."

"Why? Where are you planning on going?"

"I don't know yet, somewhere out of the city, once I've saved enough money for a bribe."

"How long do you think that's going to take?"

"I don't know. I haven't started yet. Why have we come here?" Carmen sounded curious. "It's not a kinky thing is it?"

"Not for me. I just want to find out what happens."

"You're odd, has anyone ever told you that before?"

"Once or twice."

They came to a stop at the edge of the crowd. There was a man at the door checking hats and coats, hanging them over his arm and passing them back to another who was putting them all onto a cart. A young girl flitted between the people, a tray hanging around her neck. It was filled with bags of boiled sweets that smelled like violets.

"Do you want some?"

"What for?"

"To eat."

Carmen nodded less enthusiastically than Vanguard would have expected. She wasn't used to having things given to her for free. It would probably serve her well in the long run, to have a healthy dose of skepticism about her. The coin that the boy had dropped at their feet earlier found its way into the outstretched palm of the sweet seller. Vanguard handed Carmen the bag. She took one out and sniffed it before putting it in her mouth. She sucked vigorously, puffing her cheeks out.

"What do you think?"

"You're alright. You're definitely weird, but you're not terrible."

"I meant about the sweet."

"Oh...it's quite nice."

They were stopped at the door. The man taking the coats held out one arm expectantly and looked at Vanguard. Carmen began fumbling at her top button. Vanguard placed a hand over hers. The man at the door seemed confused. "Coat check?"

"We're not here for a show. I'm here to talk with Herveaux."

"Do you have an appointment?"

"Who are you, his secretary?"

There was a disgruntled shuffling, the crowds parting to make way for an excessively large man with tattoos covering both arms from shoulder to elbow. There was a rash of stubble across his jaw and he had chalk dust on his palms.

"What's going on? Why has the queue stopped moving?"

There was a drawl to his voice. Wherever he was from he hadn't been born in the city. Vanguard doubted he had even been born in the country. It sounded like the words were melting together.

The doorman nodded towards Vanguard. "He wants to speak to Herveaux."

The larger man looked Vanguard up and down. "Any weapons?"

"No. I'm here to talk business."

From what little Vanguard knew of Lucien Herveaux, it seemed unlikely that he would be eager to share the details of the comings and goings of his clientele without first striking some sort of bargain. Vanguard did not feel particularly comfortable with the thought of thrashing out deals over flesh, but flesh was all he had to barter with. Or at least that was what he needed Herveaux to think. He pulled Carmen forward. Without having to be told she began to flutter her eyelashes, pouting slightly and breathing through her mouth. She looked both utterly disdainful and yet at the same time completely desperate for excitement. Henriette was a good teacher. The tattooed man looked unimpressed.

Vanguard decided to cut to the chase. "Like I said, I'm here to discuss business with Herveaux."

Top lip curling into a sneer, the large man disappeared back into the building. Carmen turned and narrowed her eyes slightly. She did not look happy with what she now assumed was the arrangement for the evening.

"I thought I was spending the night with you?"

"I never said that."

"Then who am I spending the night with?"

"Hopefully no-one, now try and be quiet."

A moment later the tattooed man reappeared with what Vanguard presumed was Herveaux. There was an air of pomposity about the club owner. His features were rat-like and pinched. His whole stance oozed with misplaced self-importance. He stopped short of them, considering Carmen carefully. One hand went up to his face, the finger and thumb rubbing the jaw. Using the other hand he made a spinning gesture with one finger.

The tattooed man leaned towards Carmen slightly. "Turn please."

She turned around, lifting her arms into the air with a flourish and giving Herveaux a smile.

He clapped his hands together, seemingly delighted. "Yes, very good, very good. Come!"

Carmen was ushered towards the door. Vanguard made to follow but was stopped short. He looked down at an oversized hand pressing firmly against the flat of his chest.

"Girl only, you come back in four hours, ask for Kosic."

Vanguard glanced at Carmen. "If she goes, I go."

Kosic scowled. "The only place you go is away, before I break your face."

Herveaux had already disappeared into the building. Clearly he had no interest in discussing business or anything else before he'd had chance to see Carmen at work.

Raising both hands as if conceding to the arrangement, Vanguard backed away. Once the crowd started moving again, he melted into the hordes of people. After a minute or two, he walked straight through the open door. Nobody tried to stop him. He might not have been able to spend the evening digging information out of Herveaux and his guests, but at least he could linger unseen and close enough to Carmen to pick up any conversation that might have been of use. More importantly he could ensure nothing happened to her that would cause Henriette to throw him out of the house and back into the gutter.

Inside the club he found himself confronted by a mass of bodies standing shoulder to shoulder. A thick cloud of sweet smelling smoke hung in the air. The room opened up into a large hall, the floor punctuated by platforms standing several feet above the crowds. They were each populated by golden faced flame eaters. Periodically one of them would spit fire into the air and the crowd would reel back before applauding emphatically.

In the middle of it all was a large circular stage with a long platform leading to a curtained off area. Above that were several balconies on which people stood looking out over the expanse of the club. Close to the far end, a selection of circular tables accommodated card games and cigars.

Vanguard scanned the crowds for Carmen. It soon became apparent it was pointless. She was very small and the room was packed with people. Shouldering his way through the bodies, Vanguard looked instead for Kosic. He would be easier to spot and chances were he would be close to Herveaux.

After a few moments, he caught sight of them. There was a good thirty feet between them. Herveaux was fiddling with a large set of keys, trying to unlock a side door. Carmen was standing with them, looking from left to right. This was not part of the plan. Vanguard's agreement with Henriette was that Carmen could accompany him to the club in order that he might showcase her talents to Herveaux's prestigious clients, not so that he could lose her completely.

"Fuck." Vanguard tried to push through the crowds but the path was blocked. Carmen was taken through the door into another room. It shut behind them. When he finally managed to reach it, Vanguard rattled the handle. It had been locked. Henriette was going to kill him.

Unsure as to the best course of action, Vanguard walked away and began making a route around the stage, taking note of his surroundings. There were a few more recognisable faces in attendance. A lot of them were regulars at Sanquain's chambers in the Golden Quarter. It was unlikely they'd want their presence acknowledged. It was hardly illegal to go to a club but Sanquain had made his feelings about mingling with the lower classes well known. If you lived in the Golden Quarter or anywhere nearby you knew better than to admit to any trips to the Black Zone.

So far Vanguard could not see anything worthy of his attention. There were a few Red Badges around, most of them already drunk out of their skulls. Nobody spoke to them. As for Herveaux, he was clearly a con man and a bastard, but they were ten a penny in the Black Zone. It didn't make him a murderer.

After about two and a half hours it became apparent the door would not be opening again until the end of the night. Figuring it would be best to figure out how to avoid getting his balls chopped off by an angry madam, Vanguard decided to get some air.

The smell of the smoke was stifling. A line of dancers were high kicking their way across the stage, overloaded with feathers and beads. He had almost reached the door when the hairs on the back of his neck stood on end. A cold shiver ran down his spine. There was something strange lingering not far away. Vanguard turned and looked back over his shoulder.

Everyone else was looking at the stage, engrossed in what they were doing. They jeered and elbowed each other, laughing and shouting. The room was filled with the sounds of exuberance and intoxication. It smelt of sweat, vomit and sawdust. It was loud and chaotic, everything blurring into a discordant mess of excessive colour. Yet standing in the midst of it all, quietly observing every-thing, was a young man.

Vanguard had never seen him before. The features of his face were sharp and deliberate, cheekbones jutting high. Slowly his head turned, eyes taking in everything that was happening across every inch of the room until finally, they came to rest on Vanguard. In one short, disconcerting moment, Vanguard realised the boy was looking back at him. Not staring straight through him, not questioningly looking at the space around him as if something should be there but wasn't. Whoever he was, he was looking directly at him.

There were at least two hundred people surrounding Vanguard and only one who could see him.

The person to the left of Vanguard moved slightly and obscured the boy from view. When they moved back again, he was gone. Vanguard looked around, seeing nothing but slavering drunks. Focusing on the task in hand, he shook the unsettling feeling from his bones and continued back out onto the street.

Carmen reappeared sometime shortly before one in the morning. Vanguard was sitting on a wall, waiting for her. Kosic escorted her across the street and delivered her back as promised. "Herveaux says you bring her back next week. He says you will talk business then."

"What happened in there?"

"What do you think?"

"Is she alright?"

"What do you care? Next week, you come back. Ask for Kosic."

Vanguard got down from the wall and took Carmen's face with one hand. He turned her head first one way and then the other, squinting in the light and checking for signs of damage. There didn't appear to be any. Carmen batted the hand away.

"Stop it, I'm not a horse." She appeared reasonably unscathed.

"What was behind the door?"

Carmen shrugged. Vanguard wondered if perhaps it was some sort of ailment that caused her to respond that way to everything. There didn't seem to be any question that he could ask that wasn't immediately answered with a slight movement of the shoulders. "Not much, just more people and some rooms."

"What sort of people?"

"Rich ones, I guess. There were other girls. They were nice to me."

"Did you talk to anyone else?"

Carmen scrunched her face up and stuck her tongue out like she was trying to get rid of a horrible taste. "Some old man. Not old like you but really properly old."

Vanguard found little comfort in the idea that he might have been old, but he was at least, not properly old. He got the feeling that Carmen considered anyone over the age of thirty to be practically half dead already. "What did he say?"

"Nothing, he had my foot in his mouth most of the time." She smiled brightly. "He did give me this though..." She held out her hand. There was a small silver pin sitting in her palm. It was topped with a dainty white pearl. Vanguard closed her fingers back around it before anybody saw. Carmen would have to spend a month on her back before she would be able to buy herself a pin like that. She slipped it into her pocket.

"What are you going to say to Henriette?" She asked with a lilting, almost playful tone.

Vanguard sensed a deal was about to be brokered. "What are *you* going to say to Henriette?"

Carmen grinned. "That all depends on whether or not I can keep the pin."

By the time they returned to the house it was the early hours of the morning. Carmen flicked her hair behind her shoulder and put her hat on the side table next to the coat stand. Henriette appeared from the parlour dressed in a nightgown and robe.

"How was your evening?"

"It was lovely. I had a bag of sweets."

Henriette looked from Carmen to Vanguard and back again. Finally she nodded. "All right then, you better come and have some food."

They watched as Carmen devoured the eggs and toast that Henriette had made. Vanguard was impressed. Henriette wished she would take smaller bites. She let it slide for the time being. Dining etiquette was way down the list of priorities when it came to training up new girls. Carmen looked like she could do with a few good meals. Vanguard had a cup of tea which he loaded up with sugar. Once she had finished eating, Henriette packed Carmen off up to bed. Before leaving, she turned to Vanguard. "Thank you for taking me to the club. Can we go again?"

Henriette pointed to the stairs. "Get to bed. Now."

Carmen flounced away. Henriette rubbed the handle of the teacup between her fingers. They sat quietly for a bit. Eventually, she spoke again.

"I don't like the girls being out of the house. Carmen is young and stupid. I don't pretend that this is the best life for them but at least here they eat every day, they have a roof over their heads and nobody beats them, not if I can put a stop it."

Henriette stood. As she went to leave she placed a hand on Vanguard's shoulder. "Be careful what you show her. She will see the world through rose-tinted glass and throw herself into a pit of snakes thinking it is a flower bed. Girls like her die outside these walls. I should hate to have to kill you." Warning issued, she bid him goodnight.

Vanguard went to the bathroom and locked the door. Coat and boots removed, he climbed into the tub. The muscles in his back ached. There were blisters on his feet. He took the paper bag out of his pocket along with a couple of cigarette papers and some tobacco acquired from Vince earlier that afternoon. Vanguard wasn't much of a smoker, so rarely had any on him.

He lit the roll-up with a match and flicked it onto the floor. Finally, he leaned back against the curved lip of the bathtub and blew a plume of smoke up to the ceiling. After a minute or two, the walls started to melt away and Vanguard found himself once more, floating in a great black nowhere.

CHAPTER 8
WELCOME TO THE PITS

V anguard woke up later than usual the next morning. His mouth was dry and there was a pounding in his head that only seemed to get worse the more he moved around. Unfortunately, getting up was unavoidable. There were things that he needed to do.

The house was quiet. Henriette had gone into town, or at least that was what he presumed by the array of teacups and wet stockings that were littered about the parlour. Henriette had specific rules about domestic chores in the house and who should do them.

Paulette was standing at the table, hands hovering over a large bowl of warm water into which she was wringing the sodden garments. She looked like she had been up for a good hour or so. Vanguard enquired as to where everyone else was.

"They're still in bed. Henriette went to the Golden Quarter with Carmen. She wants to get her registered. I couldn't sleep."

"Does Henriette know you're doing that?"

"She won't mind."

Henriette most definitely would mind. The girls all knew they were to do their own washing and mending. Vanguard had often seen Paulette creeping down the stairs in the early hours with a small collection of soiled garments taken from beneath the other girl's beds. It was quite clear the rest of them took advantage of her willingness, but Paulette seemed to like having something to do and so it remained their secret.

Shaking the water from her fingers, Paulette pointed to a small package that was lying on the other end of the table about half an inch from a pile of still-to-be soaked hosiery. It contained a jam roll and an apple. Henriette allowed Vanguard to eat whatever food he wanted while he was in the house – mainly because he ate very little and certainly wasn't fussy about what was offered when he did, but she refused point blank to ever cook for him. He always appreciated that, if Paulette was around, quite often there would be a little packet of something waiting for him.

Aside from Henriette, Vanguard liked Paulette the most. At around twenty she was a little older than the other girls and had something gentle about her. She was delicate and softly spoken. Paulette seemed the type of girl that would have made a good mother one day. It was a shame that she hadn't been dealt a better hand in life.

"Are you alone?"

She shook her head. "Vince is here."

Outside there was a noticeable pile of cigarette butts gathering on the ground at Vince's feet. The morning fog had begun to lift. Each day there was a narrow window of time in between which the fog dissipated and the smog descended. It was the only time you could see the true colour of the city. Most people tried to avoid it if possible.

The Black Zone was the collective term for anything that existed below the canals. It was made up of several neighbourhoods, none of which were considered desirable. Vanguard turned left as he walked out of the Tanners. There was a church steeple in the distance, the spire jutting out above the rooftops. It marked the centre of the area known as the Pits, so called because of its tendency to be occupied by former residents of the prison cells below the city streets. There was a long standing joke in D'Orsee that if you ever got out of the Hole, you simply went straight to the Pits.

Vanguard wasn't interested in the former inmates. It was one of the guards that had caught his attention, or more accurately, a former guard. O'Keefe was a large, doughy man with a red ape-like face. He had quit his job as a guard a few months ago and had been working as an enforcer for one of the foundry owners ever since. The man had a nice side racket in extortion and blackmail going.

It was a simple scam. O'Keefe would find the former inmates work at the foundry and keep the details of their criminal past a secret from their new employer. Something they would be grateful for, up until the point where O'Keefe would turn up looking for a payoff. If they refused, O'Keefe took the money anyway - along with their wives or daughters. The women would be sent back after a few hours, bow legged and sporting fat lips. The wages would be gone.

Standing at the edge of the church gates, Vanguard glanced up. A stone angel with outspread wings looked down at him. Blank grey eyes stared vacantly at nothing.

Vanguard turned away. If there had ever been any angels at the Pits they had packed up and moved out long ago. A drunk was asleep, passed out at the bottom of the steps outside. Nobody bothered to move him. The church only opened on a Sunday and even then people only went for the free bread.

After an hour, O'Keefe appeared on the opposite side of the square. Vanguard watched him walk straight into the first of the buildings. There was a heavy wooden club hanging down the side of his leg, tucked into a belt.

Almost all of the houses in the Pits were shared by multiple families. It meant that O'Keefe had several people in each building to call upon. He was out of sight for a while. Vanguard used the time to bite at his nails. When O'Keefe reappeared, Vanguard watched him tucking something into the coat that he wore. It had deep pockets.

Sanquain was well aware of the racket. As usual, he had been taking his cut. It had all been working out nicely but recently O'Keefe had been getting too liberal with the beatings. The foundry owners were concerned about a decline in employee attendance. It was hard to work with broken ribs. Naturally, they had complained to Sanquain who had assured them fervently that he would see to it that this thug was taken off the streets. They were firmly reassured that Sanquain had it all in hand. The captain would not tolerate this kind of criminal activity.

The streets around the Pits were always full of children running feral through the buildings. Dirty, wire-haired little creatures, nobody really knew which child belonged to which person so they kept a wary eye on them all. Once or twice an hour a head would appear from out of one of the doors. It would catch sight of the gang and yell out. "You lot, stop that!"

The group would disperse like a flock of startled birds only to regroup seconds later. Vanguard watched them scrabbling in the junk piles, picking at scraps from the factories. They had bare feet and bony elbows. It was virtually impossible to distinguish the boys from the girls. One of them ran towards Vanguard as though she would barrel right into his legs. Instead the child went past him, skirting around instinctively.

It was strange. He had never known why it was that people so often didn't realise that he was there. When he had first discovered the talent, he had been concerned. Vanguard didn't believe in magic, but even he had found himself staring into a mirror just to make sure he still saw a reflection. As far as he could make out, he wasn't turning invisible.

There seemed to be a difference between being invisible and just being unnoticeable.

Vanguard had the ability to become part of the background.

It was like natural camouflage. He was made up of shadows and movements. The more that he had around him, the easier it was. You might see him one moment, but then a bird would fly over your head - your eyes would flick upwards for a fraction of a second and by the time you looked back, Vanguard would be gone.

"You, come over here."

The girl jumped.

Vanguard rummaged around in the bag and pulled out the sandwich. Suddenly aware of his presence, the girl watched intently. The food lingered in the air in front of her.

"The man with the stick, where does he go after this? What does he do?"

Two little hands reached up and grabbed at the air around the paper package. Vanguard lifted the sandwich higher, out of reach. She pouted. "You mean O'Keefe? He's a sack of shit."

The girl couldn't have been more than six or seven.

"Where'd you learn to say a word like that?"

"This shit-hole. Welcome to the Pits."

"So where does O'Keefe go?"

"Most days he goes to the Rabbit. Can I have that now?"

Vanguard lowered the sandwich. In an instant it was gone. The girl and her friend scrambled away before the others could see. They each took a lump of bread, cramming the food into their mouths. The roll was too big for them to swallow whole. Instead they sat on the floor happily sucking on it until it dissolved.

The sun was at its highest point. There were a few hours to kill until O'Keefe would head for the Rabbit, the closest tavern to the Pits. Turning away from the church, Vanguard headed towards the canals. If he followed them far enough it would take him to a square patch of dried out grass that was somewhere between a very pale yellow and a muddy green. It was just about the last bit of nature you could find inside the walls. There was nothing to do there but sit and think, so that was what he did.

ON THE OTHER SIDE OF TOWN, TARRYN WAS CARRYING A wooden tray up the stairs. The teacup slid across the surface a fraction. Using one hand, he carefully rearranged it so that it was just the way his mother liked it. It was amazing what you learnt when there was nobody else to do a job.

For instance, he had learnt that the jam spoon could not touch the teapot. If it did the spoon would get warm and the conserve would be too sticky. Initially, he hadn't realised that it made so much of a difference whether or not jam was served slightly warm. Apparently it was the difference between a pleasant morning and a plate being smashed against the wall.

Lady Leersac was sitting up in bed. Her face creased. "What are you doing in here? I'm not dressed yet."

"I've brought you breakfast."

"Why?"

The clock on the mantel told them it was half past eleven. Lady Leersac was rarely awake before ten. Tarryn placed the tray over her lap and turned the tea cup so that the handle faced towards her. "Because it's time for breakfast."

The more he tried to explain things to her the more confusing she found them, so it was best to keep it simple. It was often like talking to a child. Once the curtains had been opened and the shutters unlocked, light streamed into the bedroom. "What do you want to do today?"

Lady Leersac looked perplexed. "Don't ask stupid questions. I'm taking the carriage down to the docks with your father to see the new ship. It's supposed to be quite the spectacle. Everyone is talking about it."

Tarryn felt the tension rising between his shoulder blades. "We don't have any ships left at the dock, they've all gone."

"Does your father know about this?"

"He's dead."

"Good. I always hated him."

Tarryn watched her sip on the tea, before placing the cup back on the saucer. There was a look of concentration on her face. A moment later the smell of urine began to drift around the room. "Whoops, sorry."

"Never mind, it doesn't matter."

Tarryn helped his mother out of bed, depositing her in front of the mirror in the dressing room. She liked to apply makeup each day just in case guests came to call on them. They never did. The routine could take anywhere between fifteen minutes and four hours depending on her mood.

Whilst she was otherwise occupied, Tarryn stripped down the bed and replaced the sheets. He paused for a moment, both hands pressed into the dirty mattress. The pillow on the floor caught his eye. It wouldn't be difficult - a few minutes and it could all be over. She wouldn't feel a thing. His fists clenched and unclenched against the material.

It wasn't the first time the thought had crept into his head. Every so often, usually after a succession of difficult nights, Tarryn would imagine what life might be like if he was alone. He wondered in what way it might be better. After a while the thoughts would fade.

Bunching the linens into a pile, he took them downstairs. At the back of the house there was a wash room. Years ago it had been used by the staff. They were all long since gone. There were boxes of soap and soda lined up on a shelf just above a large chest of drawers. It would not be economical to throw the sheets away. If they could not be salvaged, they would be burned.

After his father had died, Tarryn had approached the investors in the hopes of taking the helm of the family business. They almost threw him out of the building. The previous Leersac had left them on the brink of bankruptcy. They weren't about to let another take control.

Placing the pile of sheets to one side, Tarryn knelt down and reached one hand under the chest. He retrieved a wooden box from beneath it, a small but indignant spider scurrying across the lid. Inside was a stack of documents, letters and a single photograph.

The picture was of a man with a wide face and greying whiskers. There was a glow to his nose induced by many years of alcohol and indulgent living. He was standing in front of a large ship, the deck stacked high with crates. The name Leersac was emblazoned across the side of each box. It was the last vessel they had ever owned.

Tarryn wondered if the man in the photo would have been smiling quite so broadly had he known the manner by which he would eventually meet his end. He doubted he would have believed it possible. As far as his father had been concerned, Tarryn was and always had been a waste of good organs.

That was why it had come as something of a surprise when Tarryn had received the message asking him to come to the docks. The company had been in trouble for a while, but he had never been asked to go there personally.

Part of him had hoped it was an olive branch extended - a way that they could connect, father and son working together to salvage the remnants of their empire. When he had arrived at the docks, Tarryn had looked for his father. He hadn't needed to look far. The man was leaning over the edge of the ship railing, balls deep in a whore who was squealing like a pig. His father looked over, locked eyes with him and grinned.

It was at that moment that Tarryn had realised the

truth. The man was the devil. There was an evil inside him that poisoned and infected everything he touched. When it was over, his father had walked down the gang plank and over to his son. The prostitute waddled like a birthing sow across the docks grasping her warm coins until she was out of sight.

Sometimes Tarryn wished that he could remember the final words that he and his father had exchanged that night. They were lost in a haze. The sides of the path had been slippery. Tarryn remembered the look of surprise on Lord Leersac's face. He had only intended to push him at first. But as the man who had tormented him all his life lay splayed out on the ground, Tarryn found himself kneeling at the canal's edge.

There had been a great deal of thrashing. The water was high but Tarryn had held him down. Eventually, the bubbles stopped. A few days later they fished his fat, bloated body out of the water. The death was announced in the society papers. It was concluded that the death was yet another tragic accident. Tarryn had watched his mother, weeping and drinking champagne after the news had reached her. Her decline after that had been rapid.

Replacing the picture, Tarryn slid the box back under the chest. Locating the soap, he tipped a load into the barrel along with the dirty sheets. Sleeves rolled up to the elbows, he plunged both hands into the water. It slopped around, the bubbles rising and foaming at the surface. Wringing the sheets, Tarryn squeezed them into a ball, pushing them deeper. The sheets absorbed the liquid. It consumed them. His knuckles turned white, fingers sore from the harsh detergent. They began to redden, the tips getting scoured away. Pulling his hands from the barrel,

Tarryn watched the sheets sink to the bottom and disappear.

"I'm ready." Lady Leersac regally descended the stairs, face smeared with rouge. It had been applied liberally all over her cheeks. With a spring in her step, she went into the drawing room to sit and look out of the window at the street. There, she would wait patiently for guests that would never arrive.

There were a few vials of the powder he used to keep her calm still left in the pantry. One of those would put her into a deep sleep for a good few hours. Later on he would slip one into her teapot.

They both needed some time apart.

CHAPTER 9
YOU CAN SEE ME

I t was late in the afternoon. The Rabbit was already occupied by a sizeable crowd. Vanguard had been there for less than an hour and had already counted seven teeth on the floor, three of which were fresh from the gums.

Gesticulating wildly in order to illustrate the anecdote he was recounting, the man to his left caught Vanguard's forearm with one hand. Brown ale sloshed over the sides of the cup that Vanguard was holding. There was a half hearted apology mumbled, the man turning quickly back to his friends.

Vanguard said nothing. It didn't matter about the ale. He wasn't drinking it anyway. The girl behind the bar had been confused when he had asked for tea. It had seemed better to pretend like it was a joke and order a pint. The barmaid hadn't laughed, because she didn't really understand what was funny about it.

Groups of girls made up to look like porcelain dolls flitted between the tables. They flicked their hair from their shoulders and bent over far more than was necessary.

They were neither clever nor subtle. Smart women knew to avoid the Rabbit, or at the very least to keep a low profile.

O'Keefe was playing dominoes with a couple of regulars. As one of the girls walked past he reached out and gave her backside a hard pinch. The action was met with a swift slap to the face. O'Keefe's fellow players laughed uproariously as his cheek turned a violent shade of red. "Stupid bitch."

The girl stalked off haughtily to rejoin her friends. There was a smattering of laughter as she relayed the incident to her companions. They peered over their shoulders at the domino game. Too much gin and attention had made them bolder than they ought to be.

Vanguard was about to turn back when something caught his eye. She had her back to him, but there was something distinctly familiar about one of the girls. With the uneasy feeling that there was trouble ahead, Vanguard vacated the stool and made his way towards them. Smiling, the girl turned around. She locked eyes with him and her jaw went slack. "Oh, bloody hell."

Without hesitation, Vanguard reached out and took Carmen by the wrist, pulling her back towards the bar. "What the fuck are you doing here?"

Puffing her chest up, Carmen flicked one hand into the air dismissively. "I've run away."

"You haven't gotten very far."

"Well, I'm not going back. I've got friends here."

"No one has friends in the Pits - just people they owe money to."

From across the bar Tarryn watched the exchange with mounting interest. The Rabbit was not his usual venue of choice. He had visited the Black Zone on a number of occasions but tended to stick close to the canals. This particular establishment had a reputation for attracting trouble. Trouble was exactly what he was looking for.

The old man and the girl knew each other, that much was obvious. The nature of their relationship, however, was not as clear. He suspected it was more likely a business relationship than anything familial. The girl did not look pleased to see him either way.

The group of girls that Carmen had been with began to inch away, keen to distance themselves from whatever was happening. Vanguard suspected most of them were there without permission and certainly without any real under-standing of the consequences of their actions. One or two of them didn't look like they could be more than thirteen.

It was a rule that all girls working in the city houses were required to attend the Golden Quarter to obtain registration. The process cost what Carmen would have to spend a month working to earn. Henriette never asked the girls to pay back a penny of the fee. Registration tied the girls not only to the house but to the house's owner as well. Henriette was now completely responsible for Carmen. Allowing her to run amok around the city carried a hefty fine, which only got worse the more trouble Carmen got into.

"I told you I've got my own plans; I just need to find a what-do-you-call-it, a benefactor."

Vanguard tried to count to ten in his head. On the one hand, this was not his business. On the other hand, Henri-ette would be going out of her mind. There were fights, tears and screaming matches between the girls on a regular basis but none of them would dare insult her like this.

Vanguard scoffed. "So you thought you'd look for one in the Pits?"

"Of course not, I'm not an idiot. I'm just here to see my friends."

"The ones that did you up like a clown?"

Vanguard had little to no experience of the kinds of things women liked to put on their faces. Carmen's lips were a bright shade of pink. He wasn't sure what was smeared on her eyelids but it looked ridiculous. Henriette didn't allow the girls to wear makeup in the house. Powder clogged the skin and masked the scars left by pox and disease. A clean face was an easier sell than a painted one.

"Piss off, I didn't ask you to come here."

Whilst their conversation had been unfolding, the dominoes game had come to an end. Vanguard watched from the corner of his eye as O'Keefe got to his feet. He was calling it a night already. With Carmen to the left and O'Keefe to the right, he tried to figure out which was the lesser evil of the two options open to him. Losing O'Keefe would cause no end of trouble with Sanquain. Losing Carmen would cause no end of trouble with Henriette.

From his vantage point across the room Tarryn saw Vanguard turn and look over the now empty tables. He knew the scarred jaw the moment he saw it. There was, however, something else about the man's face, something in his eyes that he recognised. It was more than just a passing familiarity from having caught sight of him in Herveaux's club. Something was stirring in Tarryn's gut - an instinct that told him he had found what he was looking for.

O'Keefe was already half way out the door. Instructing Carmen to stay exactly where she was, Vanguard turned and reached across the bar to pay for the drink. If he moved quickly there was a chance he could still salvage the evening. There was a rattling of bar stools. He looked back just in time to see Carmen bolt out of the door.

"Shit!"

It was supposed to have been an easy job – a quiet night. Clamping the bag close to his chest, Vanguard pushed through the revellers and out into the road. The street was packed. Vanguard scanned the crowds, looking left and right. There was no sign of Carmen. He marched down the cobbles, hoping that by chance it was in the right direction. At the end of the street the crowds began to thin. He was about to turn around and go back the other way when a muffled scream echoed out from one of the side passages.

Instinctively Vanguard slipped one hand into the bag, fingers finding the handle of the knife. The alley was narrow. Shadows lengthened across the bricks. He saw Carmen at the far end, back pressed against the wall, thrashing wildly against O'Keefe.

Wedging one hand against her face, O'Keefe was using the other to pull at the fasteners of her blouse. Carmen stamped at the ground, trying unsuccessfully to find his feet. "Stop squealing, you stupid tart." Carmen's struggling caused him to lose grip slightly, two fingers slipping down her face. She took the opportunity to clamp down on them with her teeth.

"Bitch!" A heavy fist caused the bones in Carmen's nose to crunch. She crumpled to the floor, sliding down the wall. Vanguard stalked forward, knife in hand.

Before he could draw level with O'Keefe, something darted past, moving swiftly and silently forwards. It was impossible to see which direction it had come from. There was a flash of a black dovetailed coat amongst the shadows. Vanguard focused and the shape of another man began to take form against the backdrop of darkness. At first he saw nothing but a faceless blur of pale skin. As Vanguard's eyes grew accustomed to the light he realised he had seen the man before. Or more accurately, the man had seen him.

Things were moving from complicated to dangerous. Vanguard could not afford to have someone else interfering with his work. Now it was likely two men would have to die.

O'Keefe staggered back, reeling from the fist that had landed square in the centre of his face. Pain spread across the bridge of his nose. There didn't seem to be anyone else in the alley. Confused, he lashed out at thin air. "Who's there? Come out and fight me like a man." There was a slight noise, no louder than a gentle breeze passing by. O'Keefe turned towards the sound, eyes blazing.

Tarryn punched him in the gut, feeling the soft paunch of his stomach as he bent double. The sounds and smells of the alley began to fade away, Tarryn's body seemingly moving of its own volition. It was as though he stood outside of himself, a casual observer as his fists launched a barrage of strikes.

Each time that his knuckles buried themselves into the folds of O'Keefe's flesh he felt further from the world, further from the baying howls of his mother and the images of his father that so often haunted his thoughts. It felt as though the weights that held him down were being lifted, each one peeled away.

Vanguard watched, taking in each movement. The more he saw, the less he felt inclined to intervene. The younger man moved like a predator, melting in and out of the night. Each blow connected to its target with a fervour and passion that went beyond a simple desire to pick a back alley street fight. It was violent, untamed and raw. There was skill in it but a distinct lack of control. The blood rushing through his veins was almost audible. Vanguard had met enough of them to know a killer when he saw one.

Tarryn felt his energy surging with each strike. It was singing in his veins, bringing him back to life. In the fine establishments of the Golden Quarter, amongst his peers and even in his own home, Tarryn was rendered incapable of any form of release. There in the dirt and squalor of the alley, he was finally free from restraint.

O'Keefe was still swinging blindly, cursing and spitting blood at the ground. Not a single blow found their target. Tarryn felt his body buzzing. His skin was vibrating.

O'Keefe lost his footing, stumbling forward. Vanguard watched the young man launch himself onto his back. O'Keefe crashed to the ground, one cheek pressed hard against the wet cobblestones. Tarryn was smaller, but agile and fast. As it was the fight was not a fair one. Experience had taught Tarryn that life was not fair.

Pushing his weight against the writhing mass of flesh beneath him, Tarryn dug his fingers into O'Keefe's hair. Driving his head down towards the ground, there was the distinctive sound of flesh tearing. O'Keefe groaned. Again the floor came rushing up to meet the soft mass of his face. It was no longer possible to distinguish any of his features. One more strike and he would be dead. A normal person might have stepped in long ago. Vanguard was not a normal person.

With one final blow, O'Keefe's brains splattered across the ground. Tarryn sat back on his haunches. There was sweat beading on his brow, his lungs burning. Lifting one hand, he wiped a sleeve over his face, spatters of blood smudging across the material. There was hair underneath his finger nails. All he could hear was the beating of his own heart echoing in his ears. Slowly, the world came back into focus.

There was a movement from the corner. Carmen, still disorientated from the punch to the face, looked up. She blinked a few times trying to comprehend what was happening around her. Vanguard moved towards them, stepping out of the shadows. Tarryn got to his feet, fists clenched. The old man looked like he had seen a few fights but Tarryn had the advantage. As far as he was concerned, the only thing Vanguard could see was Carmen slowly coming around. He would let the old man get a little closer.

When the two men were almost upon each other, Tarryn pulled a fist back before sending it hurtling towards Vanguard's face. It was countered in mid-air. A shockwave ran through his arm. Vanguard wrapped his fingers around the fist and held tightly. "I wouldn't do that if I were you."

Tarryn's mouth dropped open. "You can see me."

"Yes."

"How can you see me? *Nobody* can see me."

"What's going on?" Carmen was beginning to regain her senses. Unsteadily she got to her feet. She took in the sight of O'Keefe sprawled across the ground, the pieces of skull and sinew floating in the puddles. She saw Vanguard standing nearby, the knife still in his hand. "Did you do that?"

Tarryn was less than ten feet away. Carmen did not notice him at all. Instead, she pressed a hand to her stomach. She tried to swallow it back down but there was no stopping it. She lurched forward and vomited. Vanguard reached out cautiously. "It's alright. You don't need to be scared."

Carmen took one more look at O'Keefe and another at Vanguard before bolting down the alley and out of sight. He turned back to Tarryn, levelling the knife at his throat. "What the fuck was that? You realise you've completely fucked up my night? Give me one good reason not to stick this in your neck."

"You can *see* me."

"I said a good reason."

Vanguard craned his head back. The sensible thing would be to slit the young man's throat, alert Sanderson and have done with it. Sanquain was always very clear that the work Vanguard carried out should be as discreet as possible. This was far from discreet.

Tarryn looked at the blood on his hands. After years of walking unnoticed through the streets, he had simply assumed that his affliction was exclusive only to him. Now someone was standing before him with the same curse. He couldn't just walk away. Not when there was a chance that the old man held answers he could not find elsewhere.

It was a difficult situation for Vanguard. On the one hand, it was his job to hunt down criminals and monsters. The boy might have been dressed a little better than the usual quarry but he was a killer all the same. The shards of O'Keefe's skull at his feet were proof of that. On the other hand, his actions had saved Vanguard a lot of effort. Carmen was, as far as could be told, relatively unscathed for her ordeal. The job was done. Vigilante justice was still justice of a sort. After a moment, he lowered the knife. He had the feeling he was going to regret what he was about to do.

"Leave. Now. You were never here, none of this ever happened."

"But you need to tell me how you can see me. I need to know how this all works."

"Are you listening to me? You need to walk away. Don't follow me. Don't talk about this to anyone, if you do, I will find you and I will kill you."

The knife remained level with Tarryn's chest as Vanguard backed carefully down the alleyway. Tarryn did not try to follow him. There was nothing about the tone of his voice that suggested he would not follow through on his threat. It would be better to step back, for now, to a safe distance.

Out on the street Vanguard scratched at his jaw. The night had taken a serious turn for the unexpected. He needed to get word to Sanderson. What was left of O'Keefe would need to be removed from the alley before morning. Carmen would be halfway across the city by now. It would take hours to find her and that was if he got really lucky. As fortune would have it, fate had decided that Vanguard had already suffered enough for one night. He hadn't gotten far when he rounded a corner and walked smack into a wall of solid muscle.

"I think you are looking for this?" Kosic stood towering over the dejected figure next to him. Carmen pulled at her arm. She was in a sorry state. There was a purple bruise developing across the bridge of her nose. Kosic placed a hand on her shoulder. "I tell her this is very dangerous place for pretty girls."

Carmen sniffed.

Peering at her nose, Vanguard shook his head. "It doesn't look like anything is broken. It'll hurt like a bastard tomorrow though."

Kosic nodded sympathetically. "When we meet last, I have wrong idea about you. Carmen tells me you are a friend."

"More of an acquaintance."

"I thought you are pimp. But now I know that you are not. I'm happy to be wrong." Kosic removed the hand from Carmen's shoulder and thrust it forward. Vanguard couldn't remember the last time he had shaken another man's hand.

Carmen shivered. It was way past the time to go. Kosic gave them an amiable wave as he left. They watched as he lumbered down the road looking completely out of place.

Carmen reached out and slipped a hand around Vanguard's arm. "Take me home, please."

Watching from the shadows, Tarryn felt the beating of his heart slowing. He had gone out that night with the intention of seeking trouble. It was never hard to find in the Black Zone. Instead he had found more than he had dared hope for.

Once, when he was younger, Tarryn had been in his mother's dressing room. He had been looking for something. As he had moved things on the dresser, a mirror had fallen onto the floor. When he lifted it up, pieces of the glass had fallen away. Worried that his mother would be upset he had tried to put it back together again. It was chipped and broken. There were fragments missing. He remembered running his fingers along the bumpy surface. The pieces did not fit. No matter how hard he tried, the reflection was distorted. It was all wrong.

When Tarryn had locked eyes with Vanguard in the alley, all he could think was how it felt exactly the way that it had felt when he looked into the broken mirror that day.

CHAPTER 10
ARE PEOPLE AFRAID OF YOU?

There was no welcoming fire burning in the hearth on his return. The house was silent. Tarryn stepped into the hall. Everything was washed in shades of grey. When he turned the key in the lock, the sound of the mechanism echoed along the walls. He exhaled, shoulders slumping downward.

Somehow the house felt even more foreign than it had when he left earlier that evening. It had ceased to feel like a home many years ago, if in fact it ever had. Now it was little more than a prison. There were bars on the windows to prove it.

It was a strange sort of quiet, a weight that hung in the air. The walls seemed to groan with it. Tarryn placed the key back into his pocket and ran a hand through his hair. When he glanced down, there was blood still on his fingers.

The corridor to the bathroom at the back of the house seemed to stretch out into the distance. Focusing his eyes, he walked towards the door at the far end of the hall. The world seemed foggy, different. Each step was careful, deliberate. It was like he was underwater, holding his breath.

He passed the open door of the sitting room, noting Lady Leersac still lying exactly where he had left her. A trail of saliva had dried to the side of her cheek. The oil lamp next to her emitted a soft orange glow. He needed to get cleaned up before she woke up again. The drugs always made her groggy and confused. It would be difficult enough to get her upstairs.

A mirror hung in the bathroom above the basin, on which a bar of soap and a folded hand towel sat. He looked curiously at his reflection. There were speckles of red across his nose and forehead. His eyelashes, which were unusually long, had acted as a net for the droplets of blood. They clung to his eyes, like rain drops on a spider's web. He blinked a few times. Turning on the tap, Tarryn stripped down to the waist. Water began to fill the basin, steam rising up and clouding the glass. The reflection began to disappear. The features of his face fading away to a blur. After a few minutes, he was gone, nothing but fog in the mirror.

Rubbing his hands together, Tarryn watched the contents of the bowl change colour. It slowly turned red as he scoured more of O'Keefe away. Using a wire brush he scrubbed at his nails. Some of the water splashed against the floor, drops rolling across the linoleum. The towel scratched as he dried his hands. They looked clean again. Reaching up he used one palm to smear away the condensation from the mirror.

He had hoped that perhaps he might have seen something different this time. Frustrated, he slammed his hands against the rim of the sink. Nothing had changed.

Tarryn needed answers before it was too late. For too

many years, he had lived his life without anyone else noticing his presence at all. People barely remembered that he had ever existed. He needed to know what it was that the old man saw. He needed to see it too. Instead he was melting away to nothing. Maybe it wasn't his mother who was the mad one. Maybe it was him. Perhaps it was both of them. They both had cause enough for madness.

When Tarryn had killed O'Keefe, the soft skin of his face splitting, he had felt nothing. There was no regret, no sorrow for what he had done. The thug had deserved it just as his father had. When the old man had seen what Tarryn had done there was no fear, no judgement. He just saw.

There was a noise from the other side of the wall, the sounds of a person stirring from a deep sleep. Something clattered to the floor in the sitting room. His mother was waking up. Tarryn hastily piled all of the soiled clothes he had taken off, hiding them beneath the bathtub.

"Who's in there?"

"It's just me."

"Henry... is that you?"

Tarryn closed his eyes, squeezing them together. Not this again. The silence of the house was punctured by the sounds of his mother making her way clumsily down the hall. She was calling out once again for her dead husband. Not for Tarryn, the one who cared for her. Not for her son, the one that fed and bathed and dressed her. She barely remembered he existed.

The ghost of his father still followed Tarryn wherever he went. Even in his own home he could not escape it. The man had infected his mother's brain, both literally and entirely. The memory of him consumed her. It would never let either of them go. Bitterness surged through every fibre of his skin. Once - just once - he wanted her to remember who he was.

There was a gentle knock at the door. "Henry?"

Tarryn burst out of the bathroom, the force of his exit almost tearing the door from its hinges. He found the lace collar of her dress; eyes furious as he pushed his mother against the wall. Lady Leersac felt the hard surface against her back, fingers sliding around her throat. Tears rolled down her cheeks. Watching her eyes widen, Tarryn felt the veins in her neck. The blood was pumping through them. Words caught in her throat, unable to find their way out as his grip tightened.

"No! NO! I keep telling you he's dead. HE'S DEAD. Get it into your head, I'm not him."

Lady Leersac's lips began to pale, her eyes rolling back in their sockets. Tarryn didn't want to kill her. He didn't want to hurt her. All he wanted was for her to look at him and know who he was. "Why don't you know me?"

"I-I-"

"Tell me, tell me who I am."

There was the faintest flickering of recognition in her otherwise usually vacant expression. Relinquishing his grip, Tarryn pulled his hands away. Shaking, his mother reached up and touched her throat. He stepped back, ashamed at what he had done. "I'm sorry; I just wanted you to know me."

In the soft light, Lady Leersac stepped forward. She reached up and stroked the side of his face. The touch of her skin calmed him. It had been such a long time since she had comforted him. Knees buckling, Tarryn sank to the floor. His mother knelt beside him, stroking his hair. "Of course I know you. You're my boy. You're my wonderful boy."

Despite everything that he had endured over the years, even on the worst of days, Tarryn had never shed a single tear over the loss of his mother. The woman might have been alive in body but she had been gone a long time. She had fallen away so gradually that there had never been a time to grieve. For a few precious moments, she came back to him. They sat on the floor, her arms wrapped around him as he cried out. His shoulders shook and his chest ached. She shushed him, whispering soothing words into his ears. Her voice sounded like sunshine. "My poor darling boy, what have they done to you?"

When it was over, he took his mother upstairs and put her to bed. She fell asleep almost instantly. Tarryn stood in her room for a little while, watching her sleep, noting the lines and cracks on her face. Tomorrow she would be back to normal and the likelihood was that she would once again not know who he was. The thought of it merely confirmed to Tarryn that what had occurred in the Splinters had not only been necessary, it had been imperative.

Without it, he feared he would not have been able to stop himself from squeezing the life from her that night in the hallway. That could not happen. For all that they put each other through; she remained, after all, the only person who had ever really loved him. They could not lose each other, not now.

BACK AT HENRIETTE'S THE AIR WAS BLUE. VANGUARD had done the safest thing he could and retreated to the bathroom to wait until things calmed down. He had been staying at the house long enough to learn that no good could come from getting involved in arguments between the girls. The screaming and shouting had been going on for a good hour.

Fortunately most of the customers had already been and gone for the night. Half of the house had hailed Carmen like a conquering hero on her return. The other half had wanted her beaten up and down the staircase with a stick.

"I *said* I'm sorry."

"It was meant to be my night off and I had to work all night in the convent suite. I'll be rubbing witch hazel onto my bum for a week because of you!"

"What do you want from me?"

"I want an arse I can sit down on!" Annabelle was not happy. Carmen's absence had meant someone had to take her place that night and she had drawn the short straw. As far as she was concerned, Carmen owed her more than just an apology.

Vanguard placed a hand over his stomach. It growled at him. The sandwich had been the only proper food he had and he had given that away. A man could not survive on an apple alone. Hunger gnawed at his belly. The parlour was only next door. There was a chance that if he was very quick he could get in without the girls noticing. There was also however, the chance that he might get caught in the crossfire. They might turn on him, or worse, ask for his opinion on the matter. It was far better to stay where he was.

Henriette had retreated to the fourth floor. She had a headache. Carmen would be dealt with in the morning, if the other girls hadn't dealt with it beforehand. The yelling continued for a few more minutes before several pairs of feet stamped noisily up the stairs and there was a chorus of doors slamming. There was a quiet knock. The handle turned. He watched as Carmen slipped into the room. She shut the door behind her.

"Has it calmed down out there yet?"

"They've all gone to bed; none of them are speaking to me anymore." She took a few tentative steps forward and sat on the edge of the tub. The bruise on her face had deepened. It looked like it hurt a lot. He doubted it had helped garner any sympathy from the other girls at all. Scrapes and bruises were ten a penny. Reaching into her pocket, she pulled out an orange and handed it over. It was hardly a meal but it was better than nothing.

Vanguard took it, splitting the peel using his nails. "Where did you get this from?"

"From a bowl in the waiting room. They were Paulette's idea. Some of the customers have terrible bad breath. They help sweeten them up a little bit."

"Aren't they going to be angry that you took one?"

Carmen shrugged. "I think we both know that ship has sailed." She sat picking at her skirt. "Why do you sleep in the bath tub?"

"I just prefer it."

"Did you kill that man?"

"He was dead. Let's say we leave it at that."

She tilted her head to one side. "Are people afraid of you?"

"The smart ones are."

"What's it like? Killing somebody?"

"You ask a lot of questions."

"I suppose I'm curious."

The orange peel collected on the floor with each piece that Vanguard tossed over the side of the bath. It gave the room a pleasant aroma. Aside from all the questions, the sulking and the tendency to wreak havoc around the house, he was starting to find that Carmen was bizarrely good company. There was an absolute bluntness about her that, given the nature of her surroundings, was quite admirable. The world would wear her down eventually but she would not make it easy for them. Vanguard sucked on his fingers. "Where are you from?"

Each of the girls had a different story. There were a few that had been runaways. Some had families that needed the money. Paulette and Felicia had been there the longest. Annabelle could skin a rabbit. Simone had three older brothers who had died in the uprising. Often the girls spent so much time pretending to be nuns, or fairies, or whatever it was that tickled the fancy of their customers they forgot who they had been before they arrived.

Carmen tipped her head to one side, eyes roving over the ceiling. "Not sure really. I don't remember and I never had the mind to ask." She shrugged. "Don't suppose it matters."

Vanguard noticed the slightest hint of tension in her shoulders, the muscles tightening. He doubted even she realised she had done it. None of the girls in the house had been blessed with auspicious starts, but they all found their own way to deal with the past. Some of them cried, some of them were angry and some of them even laughed about it. He suspected that deep down Carmen knew more about where she had come from than she would admit to herself. She didn't want to remember. He spat a pip over the side of the tub. "So how did you end up here?"

"Needed the money, had nowhere else to go. I don't think my family ever wanted a girl much. My stepbrother raised me a bit. He was alright. My dad fucked off and left. Don't remember me mam but she wasn't well liked apparently. I suppose I just wanted to get out on my own. See a bit of the world."

"How's it working out so far?"

"It's too soon to tell."

The trace of a smile flickered across her face. "Do you want to hear something stupid?"

"I have a feeling I'm going to anyway."

"When I was little, my brother Charlie used to take me to the Golden Quarter every once in a while. We never bought anything, just sort of walked around. Anyway, we were there once and I saw this woman. She was very tall and slim."

Carmen stood, lifting one hand into the air as if to demonstrate the height of the woman in question. "She was surrounded by people. They were bringing her gifts and asking her how she was. They all seemed so concerned that she be contented. I asked who she was and my brother told me that she was a famous singer. I thought she must be the happiest woman alive. I decided right then and there that I wanted to be a famous singer too."

"Can you sing?"

"No not a note. The neighbours threw a bucket of water on me to get me to stop trying. Didn't matter anyway, a few weeks later they shut the music hall and I never saw her again."

Carmen bent down and picked the peel up from the floor, placing the pieces into her pocket. She yawned. "If you weren't here, if you lived another life, what do you think you'd be?"

"Never really thought about it."

"I think you'd be a farmer – with cows or maybe pigs."

"Why a farmer?"

"You're not afraid of getting dirty and you don't seem to like people very much."

"I suppose that makes sense."

Carmen walked to the door. Before opening it, she turned and looked over her shoulder. "I know now that I can't be a famous singer, but that doesn't mean I have to be this. There has to be something else out there. If this is all there is, then why are any of us even here?"

With that she left. Vanguard leaned his head back. His eye lids were heavy. They were always heavy. At first he saw only darkness. He did not dream much and when he did the images were always grey.

That night, for the first time in years, he dreamed in colour.

He saw green and blue. He saw open fields. Vanguard had never once given any thought to farming. He had absolutely no desire to take it up. That didn't matter. Carmen could have suggested that he be a pirate and he would have dreamt of the sea and cutlasses instead. Vanguard did not dream of what was. He dreamt of what might have been. She had planted the idea that somehow, there might have been something else.

When he woke again, there was sweat beading on his brow. Vanguard tried to shake the images from his mind. He didn't want them. There was no point in holding onto them. They were too dangerous.

CHAPTER 11
IN THE BEGINNING

Vanguard was well aware that he was being followed.

It had been five days since the events outside of the Rabbit. After giving it some consideration, he had decided not to mention Carmen or the unknown man's involvement in the incident to Sanderson or Sanquain. For one thing, Carmen was in enough trouble as it was. There would be no benefit to anyone in revealing the full details of what had actually taken place. After a while, it would be forgotten about and they could all move on with their lives, as much as possible at least.

Sanderson had not been impressed with the state of Vanguard's latest kill. People died all the time in the Pits, but there wasn't normally quite so much debris left to clear up. He had been quite vocal about it.

Vanguard was more than capable of handling Sanderson's sulking. They both had a job to do. It was of no concern to him if Sanderson's life was temporarily made a little more difficult. As far as Sanquain was concerned the job had been done and that was the end of it.

In the meantime, Sanquain's interest in the Splinters continued unabated. The urgency with which he wanted answers was unusual. It was not like the captain to pay so much attention to something that brought him neither profit nor challenge. The Red Badges were far from popular on the streets. It wasn't unusual for a few of them to turn up dead once in a while. Vanguard couldn't help but feel that his talents would be better employed else-where. It wasn't as if there was a shortage of people waiting to get murdered.

Sanquain however was insistent.

Following their earlier encounter at the club, Vanguard had reconsidered his previous strategy when it came to Herveaux. From what he could make out, Herveaux appeared to be a reprehensible mix of pimp, loan shark, ring master and self-aggrandizing business owner. More than once Vanguard had witnessed the man congratulating himself on the acquisition of some new deal or transaction whilst the girls that entered and left the rooms behind the club door walked the floor with hollow eyes. Vanguard could have made another attempt to get close to him, but Henriette would never forgive him if he had lost one of her girls. Vanguard wasn't sure he would have been able to forgive himself either.

Although he hadn't taken Herveaux up on the offer to discuss business, Vanguard had visited the club on a number of occasions. Each time he was there he caught a glimpse of some merchant or aristocrat making a poor attempt to hide amongst the shadows. There was defi-nitely more to it all than met the eye. As far as he could make out, the rooms beyond the locked door remained off-limits to those outside of the Golden Quarter social elite. The only other people who got through were the girls, usually escorted by Kosic across the hall.

Vanguard knew a few of them, having seen them touting their wares in taverns and on the streets. Most of them were pitiful creatures, in need of a good meal and a guiding hand. They all walked the same path, and it was not one that led anywhere good.

Experience had taught him that the offer of a few coins in exchange for whispered words was often met far more enthusiastically than the same price offered for services rendered. This time however, his every question was met with a wall of silence. Either they were afraid, or there was someone behind the door who could afford to buy their silence with a better offer.

His gut was telling Vanguard that there was a larger game in play. It would reveal itself in time, it always did. He was well versed in being patient.

At first, it had been a touch galling to have someone following him around at all hours of the day. Vanguard had however soon come to the conclusion that, for as long as his stalker was lurking nearby, he at least knew where he was. It was a strange sensation knowing that his every movement was being observed. Vanguard felt eyes in the back of his head wherever he went.

Tarryn had started tailing him two days after they had seen each other in the alley. At first it had been tempting to lead the boy into a dark corner somewhere beyond the sight of prying eyes where the issue could be swiftly dealt with. All it would take was one flick of the knife and normality could resume. Instead, Vanguard watched his watcher. From the corner of one eye, he saw the young man lingering in the background. Tarryn was cautious. He did not try to get too close too soon. If nothing else, the boy seemed to have a reasonable survival instinct.

People passed by, mostly oblivious to his presence. It was clear that nobody noticed him. There was, however, a vast difference in the way that they moved around Tarryn. For instance, whenever they came within a few feet of Vanguard people seemed to automatically move, stepping to the side. Crowds parted around him like a river parts around a stone.

For some reason, they did not see Tarryn, but they did not sense him either. Vanguard watched as the boy was knocked by passing elbows, his stride often broken by people crossing the path right in front of him. Once or twice Vanguard saw an innocent bystander tread on his foot.

It was as though the boy was not a part of the world anymore. He stood just outside of it. Long-limbed and slightly built, each movement he made seemed fluid. The clothes that he wore suggested a life of wealth and privilege. The state they were in suggested a decline in circumstances. He was young, little more than twenty, but lacked the arrogance and undeserved self-assurance that most men his age had. Rather than announce his existence to the world, Tarryn merely seemed to whisper it. Vanguard was not sure anyone was listening.

Other young men looking for trouble walked with a certain gait. Vanguard could sense it from a mile away. The tensed muscles, the shoulders held high - they anticipated blood and glory. They were idiots. The majority of men in the Black Zone were like rabid dogs, chomping at each other. Tarryn moved like a wolf. There was never a moment where Vanguard felt as though he was not being studied intently. The boy was absorbing everything. Tarryn was not a troublemaker. He was a hunter. Vanguard could smell it radiating from his pores.

As weeks went, it had been somewhat mundane. Sanquain was preoccupied with matters of extreme importance elsewhere and sanctioning murders had fallen lower on his list of priorities. Vanguard had mostly been left to his own devices. Sooner or later he would be summoned to the Golden Quarter, until then he was just killing time as opposed to people.

Henriette did not like men in the house during the day unless they were paying for the privilege. The stupid part of Vanguard wanted to argue that seeing as how he gave Henriette all his money, technically, he *was* paying for the privilege. The sensible part of his brain told him that it was never wise to be in your landlady's bad books. Not if you didn't want to sleep outside in the rain.

Most of his week had instead been spent observing the occupants of the Splinters. They lived in small groups, speaking a language of their own and had few interactions with those from outside their ranks.

Lucien Herveaux was not around much. He seemed to periodically appear like an insect crawling from out of the woodwork. Vanguard had met cockroaches with better personalities.

Kosic, on the other hand, seemed universally popular with everybody in the Splinters. He spent most of the time lumbering around, a cumbersome beast of a man, out of place without a forest to roam through. Vanguard had seen many a prisoner in his time. He knew well that not all of them lived behind metal bars. If the accent and mannerisms were not enough to tell him that Kosic did not belong in the Black Zone, the look in his eyes was more than sufficient. The exact terms of his arrangement with

Herveaux were not clear; however it did not take much to work out that in the Splinters, Herveaux sat at the top of the table whilst Kosic was left to mind the door.

At least a quarter of the occupants were young girls. They seemed to be anywhere between twelve and seventeen years old. Many of them shared similarities that suggested a common ancestry, if not a direct bloodline. Vanguard had deduced quickly that those particular girls did not seem to be used in the club's private rooms. For that, Herveaux rented out a selection from the local establishments. They usually only lasted a night or two, although it wasn't clear if that was due to the nature of the work or Herveaux simply wanting to keep his offerings fresh.

Amongst the other residents were a man of very short stature with a thick moustache who appeared to act as a clerk of sorts, a skinny teenage boy and a very large woman who sang as she washed bed sheets in the street. The moustached man scribbled constantly in a journal, a pair of spectacles pushed forward on his nose. Each time he began a new page, he would lick the tip of the pencil before pressing it to the paper. When they spoke it was in a clipped, foreign tongue. Whatever they were talking of, it was for their ears and their ears only. It had become their shield, of sorts, from a world that made it clear they did not belong.

By the time Sanquain concluded his official business and turned his attentions back to less official concerns, Vanguard had managed to pick up a few of the words used in the Splinters. He was almost certain he knew how to say 'yes', 'no', and 'bastard'.

There was a bakers cart with red painted wheels permanently parked on the corner of a cross roads about a mile and a half from the tower. A woman and a small boy manned the cart each day glaring from lowered brows at anyone who passed by. Vanguard approached, ignoring the crowds that surged around them. As he drew level the woman reached beneath the cloth that was draped across the top of a wicker basket and pulled forth a small folded card marked with a V. She handed the card to him without meeting his eyes. No sooner than his fingers had touched it, the boy took off, running through the streets to deliver confirmation to Sanquain that his summons had been received.

Sanderson was already at the chambers when he arrived a short while later. Vanguard grimaced as Sanderson blew a long, drawn out whistle through his two front teeth, for no other reason than he knew it rattled Vanguard's bones.

Some years ago, there had been an altercation between the two of them. It had ended with a whisky bottle cracking Sanderson's top right incisor. He liked to remind Vanguard of that afternoon. Sanderson had lost part of a tooth. Vanguard had lost a lot more.

Sanderson ran one hand over his freshly shaven face. There was a nick in the skin where the razor blade had slipped. Vanguard thought it was a shame it had not slipped a little deeper. "Don't you have citizens to harass?"

"Didn't you used to be better looking?"

"That's more than enough from both of you." The captain sat at the desk, eyes cast down at the stack of papers that had been piled in front of him. They each required signatures. The room was filled with the sound of a chair being slowly and deliberately dragged across the floor. Vanguard let his eyes linger on Sanderson for a moment before taking the vacant seat. Sanquain did not look amused. "What progress have you made, Vanguard?"

"Not a lot. They don't talk much in the Splinters."

"Then you should make them talk."

"That sounds like something more up Sanderson's street."

"Sanderson is occupied with other matters at present."

Sanquain did not care to elaborate. It did not matter. Vanguard was well aware of the rumours that had been circulating. They were the reason for Sanquain's recent distraction. The whole city had been talking about it. It was one thing for a few nameless Red Badges to get washed up on the canal banks; it was another thing entirely for an influential member of a prominent family to go missing.

Whether or not he actually was missing was something of a question mark. Vanguard was not entirely unconvinced that he wasn't just gone, which was something very different entirely. If the man in question had any real sense at all, he would have used his impressive fortune to buy himself a way out of D'Orsee. It was far more likely that he was on some foreign beach somewhere, waves lapping at his toes and the sun on his back.

There had been no body retrieved. No sightings of Argent Cooke had been reported for over a week. However, it would not look good if Sanquain was not seen to be searching for him. The Cooke family had built up half the city. There were libraries and schools bearing their name.

"I will not have low breed scum murdering Red Badges in the streets. Hunt them down. I expect results before the month ends. In the meantime, Sanderson will continue to oversee the search for Cooke."

"Don't hold your breath. He couldn't find his arsehole with both hands."

Sanderson glowered. "Go fuck yourself."

Tempting as it was to spend the whole day trading insults with Sanderson, Vanguard had better things to do. Sanquain scrawled another signature on a document. The ink stopped flowing momentarily and Vanguard listened to the scratching of the dry nib across the paper. "These people are a plague. The *decent* people need to know that murderers and thieves have no place in this city."

"I thought you always said everything had a place."

Vanguard had known the words were a mistake the moment they escaped his lips. Sanquain did not appreciate the opinions of those beneath him, and in particular he did not care for Vanguard's thoughts on the matter. There was a marked drop in the temperature of the room. Sanquain slid the drawer in front of him open. Sanderson shifted slightly in the chair. The captain reached into the tray and pulled out a revolver.

He held Vanguard's gaze. The ticking clock had never seemed so loud. Vanguard could almost hear Sanderson's arsehole clenching. His concern was not for Vanguard's well being. If the captain shot Vanguard, Sanderson would not only be left picking chunks of brains out of his jacket, he would have twice the work to do as well. As far as Vanguard and Sanderson were both concerned, there was no truer saying than better the devil you know.

Slowly, Sanquain levelled the barrel between Vanguard's eyes. The trigger was pulled with a soft click. For a moment he wondered if he was dead or not.

"Go about your business, Vanguard, quickly, quietly and without hesitation. I have many bullets to spare.

There is no man so useful to me that he is not expendable."

Vanguard saw Sanderson's eyes slide furtively towards him, lips pressed together in a thin line. There was a knock. The captain turned his gaze towards the officer who stood at the door. His next appointment had arrived. Sanquain indicated to Sanderson and Vanguard that they should leave.

The man that entered the room behind the guard was short, with a soft face. He could not disguise the bow of his legs as he walked towards the desk. Vanguard didn't need to smell it to know that the man's digestive tract was already working over time. He couldn't blame him. The gun that Sanquain had taunted Vanguard with was meant for him.

A little less than a year ago he had been the city clerk. Now he was about to commit suicide. No wonder the poor bastard had already shit himself.

He should have been more careful to whom he revealed his secrets. In a way, Vanguard was sorry that Sanquain had not asked him to do it. At least he could have provided the man with a dignified death. The clerk was not a criminal, however, nor had he murdered anyone. In fact, he was a popular man whose death would be noted. It didn't change the fact that in about two minutes the captain would go for a walk, the clerk would sit at the desk and his brains would be splattered all over the walls. Sanquain had even loaded the chambers for him.

As they stepped outside, Sanderson took in a lungful of air. The light of the afternoon sun made the ginger tones in his hair stand out. He looked hard at Vanguard. "Well, that was stupid, even for you."

Sanderson did not bother to wait for a response.

Watching him walk away, Vanguard scratched at the top of his head. Sanderson was right, it had been stupid. It was out of character. Vanguard was always focused; he never did anything he did not mean to do. Something had distracted him and he was certain he knew what it was.

Vanguard caught sight of the boy skulking in the shadows close to the florists. The smell of crocuses and peonies hung in the air. Once Vanguard moved, so too did Tarryn. Crossing the street and making his way through the alleyways, he ducked around a corner. The moment Tarryn rounded it, Vanguard grabbed him by the collar. "What do you want? Why are you following me?"

Tarryn met his gaze, hesitant but unafraid. There was something behind his eyes that Vanguard could not quite place. He had seen it before but could not work out where.

"I only want to talk to you; I think you could help me."

"Do I look like the kind of person you'd ask for help?"

"I just want to know what you are, what I am."

Vanguard relinquished his grip. "As far as I can tell you're an idiot with a death wish."

A few feet away people went about their business. There was the sound of chattering and loud voices exchanging insincere pleasantries. The world continued to turn; unaware that anything of interest was happening in the shadows. Vanguard stepped back. "The other night, in the Pits, was that the first time?"

Tarryn shook his head. Vanguard was surprised. The boy's performance outside the Rabbit had been frenetic, barely controlled. It had seemed like a first kill. The first was often messy and not well executed. Generally, people either got better at it or got caught quickly. Vanguard scanned Tarryn from head to toe. "You look like you've got money. You got money?"

"I've got a bit, not that much."

"How much have you got right now?"

The fingers of Tarryn's right hand curled into a fist.

"Oh relax; I'm not going to rob you. How much?"

"Twenty-*ish*."

Tarryn and Vanguard clearly had very different interpretations of not that much. Vanguard was half sure he was about to make a terrible mistake. "Can you get more?"

"If I can will you at least answer my questions?"

Tarryn readjusted his collar. Over the last few days, he had tried to anticipate all the possible outcomes of the conversation they were having. This was definitely not what he had been expecting. Vanguard appeared to be thinking.

"I'm hungry." It seemed more as though he was announcing it to the world than specifically speaking to Tarryn.

There was a stall nearby selling warm pies wrapped in brown paper. They walked over. Vanguard took two. The man looked at Vanguard. Vanguard looked at Tarryn. After a moment Tarryn realised what was supposed to be happening and took the wallet from his coat pocket. Once the food had been paid for, he trailed after Vanguard who had already set off through the winding side streets. Vanguard unwrapped one of the pies and ate half of it with one bite. The gravy burnt the top of his mouth. The other was stuffed into the bag.

"What? Did you think one was for you?"

Tarryn frowned. "Apparently it's not. Where are we going?"

"Somewhere quiet where I can think."

After a while, they came to a stop along the canal bank. There were a few scrappy looking children scrambling in the hedgerows. The branches snagged their sleeves as they searched for treasure. Every now and again they'd emerge with a tin can. It would be flung into a sack to be exchanged later for a few brass coins. Standing with his back to the water, Vanguard looked Tarryn up and down. "So are you going to tell me who you are?"

"My name is Leersac. You might know it?"

"Why, is it important?"

"It was, at one point."

Vanguard looked out across the landscape. Along the other side of the canal was a brick wall that obscured the view beyond. If you had a really good imagination, you could almost convince yourself that behind the wall was a vast expanse of lush rolling countryside. There wasn't. There was an abandoned factory and a couple of slums. There was nothing green beyond the barricade.

His head ached. Life was never simple and questions only ever made it more complicated. The answers you got were rarely the ones that you wanted. The longer that he stood at the side of the canal, the more Vanguard noticed the feeling of the wind on his face. After a moment, Vanguard inhaled through the nose, exhaled through the mouth and looked at the sky. "So, what exactly do you want to know?"

CHAPTER 12
I AM THE BEAR

Unsurprisingly, Vanguard was not the only man in the city having trouble with the nature of his employment. It had not been a good week for Kosic.

The theatre was a large place, but Kosic was a large man, six foot six of olive skinned muscle to be exact. The walls were thin and the ceilings high. They only seemed to drop lower with each passing day.

Having spent much of his early life in a place of endless sky and open fields, he found it strange and unnatural to be surrounded by so much haphazard carpentry. His world had become a cage made from wood and faded velvet. It was a world that he could not bring himself to grow accustomed to.

It had been many years since Kosic had last been in his homeland. It had been a good place. People were happy there, or at least, he had thought they were at the time. He wasn't sure if he could trust the memories of it anymore. Perhaps that was just the way he wanted to remember it. A few years in D'Orsee and it was hard to believe a place like that could exist outside the city walls. Better to convince yourself that it had never really existed at all.

He had been barely thirteen years old when they left. Nobody had told him why, simply that they could no longer stay where they were and had to go. He still remembered the boat crossing, how he wanted to vomit with every wave that crashed against the hull. There had been a lot of them all cramped into one cabin. In the end his father had asked Kosic to stand outside. Even then he had towered above everyone else. There just wasn't room for him inside.

As a boy, the towns and cities that lay beyond the Amidian coast had seemed to Kosic like settlements in another world, separated from him by a vast black sea. Finding themselves aliens foisted into a foreign country, they were forced by circumstance to become a village of sorts, travelling from place to place. They did not fit in anywhere. They were not allowed to. So it seemed better to roam, hoping eventually they would find a place they could settle. By the time he arrived in D'Orsee some years later Kosic had seen more of the country on his travels than most had in a lifetime.

Almost two decades would pass before he would cross through the gates of the capital. By that time there were very few of the people he had arrived to the country with still left.

The war had not left any of them unscathed. They had hoped at first that the violence would pass them by. After all, it was not their fight. Kosic and his people had no interest in taking sides. They only wanted to survive. As it turned out, the soldiers scouring the land for rebels saw very little difference between a revolutionist and a stranger from another land.

They had shot his father without provocation. Soldiers swarmed the countryside, snatching parents from their children and pulling families apart. They had arrived early one morning to their village, before the dew had slid from the grass blades, and marched straight into the camp. Kosic had watched as people he had known since childhood stumbled and fell, falling face first to the ground as the bullets hit them in the back. They had run, grabbing at each other and hoping to find the cover of the trees nearby.

The soldiers had torn the camp apart. They were looking for hidden rebels, or at least, that was what they later claimed. They found a few old people and some women, too pregnant or too frightened to run when they still had the chance. The women they kept for a while, passing them around like chattel. One in particular they had kept in a cage, like the sort used to keep exotic birds. Kosic remembered her. She had large eyes with diamond shaped pupils and a harelip. The soldiers seemed to find her amusing.

Those that survived had hidden in woodlands, watching and waiting. By the time the soldiers had moved on, there was nothing left to salvage. With no money and nowhere else to go, they had banded together and made their way to the capital city. There would be jobs there and the opportunity to rebuild, or at least that was what they told themselves.

The day they arrived, Kosic had seen an organ grinder playing music for pennies. Beside him there had been a great black bear chained to a post. As the music sped up, the man poked at the bear with a metal rod. The beast shuffled and grunted. It had made him sad to watch them. Sometimes Kosic wondered what had happened to the bear.

He wondered if perhaps he was the bear.

The Splinters had been the only place with room for them. Weeks of wandering the streets cold and hungry, and Kosic realised that they had no other choice. Of course he knew now that it would have been better to disband than to have signed Herveaux's damned contracts. It was too late.

Building the club had given Kosic hope. It was to be a place of music and joy; somewhere that people could come and forget about their troubles for a while. Many of the beams had been lifted into place under the sweat of his own back. It was not until later that he had come to realise what it was that he was truly building.

Once the work had been completed, Kosic and his companions had put on their first show. It was to be a glittering spectacular. It would have brought colour into an otherwise grey and lifeless city. Not a single person had come. The hall remained empty. They had sat silently on the side of the stage for hours, waiting and feeling their hopes drain away.

The sound of footsteps had echoed across the floor. Herveaux had looked down at them, moustache twitching. Money did not grow on trees. Timber was not cheap. The losses would need to be recouped. They had signed an agreement. Kosic and his people owed a debt. They belonged to Herveaux now.

The following night Kosic found himself stepping into a hastily constructed ring lined with rope. The floor was strewn with sawdust. He never knew the name of the man who stepped in with him. Kosic had pulled the punches as best he could.

His victory brought no joy, only shame as they hauled his opponent away. More than one hundred people came. Herveaux made all of the money back and then some. And so it began. What started out as a weekly fight soon turned into a regular event. Tickets sold by the dozen. Herveaux knew his audience. They didn't want beauty and grace. They wanted blood.

Cracking his knuckles, Kosic looked at the skin. It was a little rough from the chalk dust but otherwise unmarked. It ought to have been covered in bruises. There had been no shortage of volunteers eager to get into the ring the past few days. Nobody would have ever known that Kosic had been in it at all.

On the stage in front of him, the girls of the chorus line limbered up ready for the evening show. Legs kicked high, arms outstretched. Delicate fingers toyed with the air, curling and moving to the sound of a fiddle. The boy played well. Remy pulled the bow across the string, the notes mournfully pouring from the instrument.

"What are you looking at?"

A voice came from a considerable way below Kosic's line of vision. He found that most people were below his line of vision and Demetrio just scraped past five foot on his best day. There was a sharpened pencil tucked behind his ear.

"I am just thinking about things."

Demetrio sniffed. "A dangerous pastime in my experience."

Kosic turned his hands over and looked at the palms. "I was thinking that we should not be here, any of us. You should not have followed me here."

They watched the rehearsal together. The idea that they would be anywhere else was still an alien concept to Kosic. It was true that they were little more than slaves now, but it was better that they should remain together. There were few enough of them left. Demetrio shrugged. "We didn't have much choice, my friend, a man your size is hard to lose. Believe me, I've tried many times."

Kosic appreciated his companion's attempts at humour.

"Besides, where else would we be but together?"

Kosic lowered his hands, eyes still trained on the stage. The music filled his ears, somehow reminding him of the scent of chicken and potatoes, of campfires and the moonlight between the trees. He wondered if any of them would ever get to go home again.

"Our guest has been asking to speak with you."

"Is he comfortable?"

"As comfortable as one can be in a cell."

"I will come later; there are too many people now."

Demetrio nodded in response and disappeared back into the dark recesses of the club. Kosic rubbed his face, feeling the heat of his skin. Herveaux appeared as if from nowhere. He did not look happy. "If you've got time to stand around here, you've got time to work."

"The club is empty, what do you suppose I will do?"

"You should be preparing. You're in the ring tonight."

"I am in the ring last night."

"And? You'll be in it tomorrow night, and the night after and the night after. Unless you prefer that I make the money it takes to keep you some other way?"

The girls had climbed down from the platform to retrieve their belongings. They laughed and chattered. Remy, the teenage boy with the scrawny torso, propped the fiddle against the side of the stage and sat down, taking a sip of water from a flask. Carefully sizing each one up, Herveaux lifted one arm and pointed. "You, whatever-your-name-is, you're behind the door tonight."

The girl looked panic stricken.

Kosic's fists tightened. "No, not them - that is not in contract."

Herveaux took a single step forward before bringing the black riding crop he carried up to Kosic's chin. The coarse rope dug into his skin. "Then make me my money."

Herveaux stamped away, stopping only to snap the riding crop across the fingers of Demetrio, who had been scribbling in his notepad. The pencil rolled to the floor, forcing its owner to scrabble along the ground in an attempt to catch it.

Kosic spent the remaining hours until the evening fell sitting alone. He tried to remember the land that he had grown up in, to conjure the memory of any small detail that might still linger in the back of his mind. They were all fading.

The hour came. The theatre was packed. People wedged in spilling beer on the floor and shoving at one another. The audience eagerly anticipated the entertainment ahead. He heard them bay like wolves with the smell of blood in their nostrils. There was fresh sawdust on the floor. He heard the thumping of hands together in rowdy applause. Herveaux was already there, goading the crowd as Kosic approached the ring. Remy lingered on the edge of the ropes. He was naked from the waist up, palms pale with dust.

"Remy?"

The boy looked at Kosic and nodded. Kosic felt the weight of his burden double.

Remy shrugged. "Don't worry, I can take a punch. I'm stronger than I look."

At a good foot shorter than Kosic, Remy had never been in a fight in his life. Nineteen years old, the boy had not been in the Splinters long. He had been seeking refuge in the city. Unable to speak much of the language, Remy had been cast out of every place he had been until Demetrio had found him playing arias in the street. He could play music that would make grown men weep. Nobody in the room cared one bit. They did not care for his sharp mind, or skill with illusions and magic. They did not want to hear him play the flute or fiddle.

Kosic shook his head. "I won't do it."

There was never a shortage of volunteers for the fights. Herveaux had an endless supply of criminals and desperate men waiting for their chance. Kosic knew that there had been fighters for the night. Herveaux was reminding Kosic of his place.

"You know what will happen if you don't. I'm not afraid of you."

Remy intended to ease his burden, but it only served to make Kosic feel worse. He did not doubt for one second that Remy was brave. The world would have been a better place had it been filled with people half as decent. Now they would fight. Kosic would win and Remy would forgive him for every blow. The matter would never be spoken of again. Yet Kosic would carry the guilt with him long after the night ended.

The bell rang. Remy pumped his fists, making a show of jabbing at the air and darting from side to side. The crowd jeered and booed. They called out insults and slurs. Herveaux circled the sidelines, watching them from behind the ropes.

Remy ran forward, launching a barrage of punches against Kosic's gut. Remy's arms shuddered with each strike. Kosic did not feel a thing. The boy might as well have been punching a tree.

Kosic glanced up. Demetrio and the others watched from the shadows across the room. They did not look away. They were letting Kosic know that he was not alone.

The boy staggered forward, swinging blindly. Kosic took the wind from his lungs and the food from his guts. The sound of retching was met with the stamping of feet. Kosic looked down at the audience. They cheered. Remy seized the opportunity to reach up and clip Kosic's jaw.

Herveaux scowled. "Stop pissing around and finish him off."

With a heavy heart, Kosic pulled his arm back. Remy flew across the ring, crashing against the ropes. Two teeth bounced across the ground. There was a roar of approval from the audience. Remy's brain rattled, stars flashing before his eyes. Kosic couldn't help it. He had fists made of granite. Blow after blow, Kosic prayed that the next would be the one to knock him unconscious. In his mind, he heard the organ grinder's music. Finally the boy slumped forward and hit the ground.

The crowd roared. Herveaux crawled under the ropes and gave Remy a kick. The boy did not move. Turning to the baying crowd, he lifted the strongman's hand into the air. "Eighty-three wins by knockout and still undefeated; I give you Kosic the Giant!"

The sound of applause muffled in his ears. Faces in the crowd blurred away to nothing. Kosic leant his head back and breathed in deeply. When he finally looked back down again, there was a boy standing in the ring with him. Kosic did not move. Neither of them said a word.

The child was staring at him, eyes wide with disbelief. He had never seen anything as big as Kosic before. He figured it must be true that he was a giant. The boy knelt down, fingers fumbling at the ground. Plucking one of Remy's teeth from the floor, he stuffed it into one of his pockets like it were a souvenir.

"What are you?"

Turning to look at the spot where Remy had fallen, Kosic answered the boy in a whisper.

"I am the bear."

CHAPTER 13
BELLITREAUX

As fate would have it, from the canals, Tarryn and Vanguard would end up heading in the direction of Winifred Beaumont's house. It had not been part of Vanguard's plan to take Tarryn along with him but the boy was there and it would make no difference to the outcome of the evening whether he came or not. For once Vanguard was in the company of someone from whom he did not need to mask the truth. Whether the boy came along or not was of his own choosing. So no invitation was particularly extended to do so either way.

"Where are we going?" Apparently Tarryn did not feel it necessary for Vanguard to invite him. Following along, both hands clasped behind his back, he took on a sort of crab-like walk. It enabled him to hold eye contact longer than was necessary or comfortable.

"Walk like a normal person."

"Alright." Tarryn turned so that he faced forward. "Where are we going?"

"I'm going to work, *you* just happen to be going in the same direction."

"Do you want me to leave?"

"I don't much care either way."

They walked along in silence. The boy had an air of inquisitiveness and curiosity to him. Vanguard had seen it before. He had the look of a boy who poked at dead animals with a stick. Death intrigued him. What the boy lacked in conversational skills, he more than made up for in observational ones. Both eyes darted from one place to another, drinking in everything around them.

"What are you?"

"I told you, I don't know and I don't know what you are either."

"I don't mean that, I mean this? What you do? How did you get to be this?"

Vanguard hunched his shoulders, bracing himself against the wind. Sensing that he would not get an answer, Tarryn ceased his questioning and walked with his head down. The cold air clawed at Vanguard's eyes, bitter and biting. He tried to focus on the stinging on his skin, tried to keep his mind from wandering. He had to keep moving forward. There was nothing to be gained from speaking of the past.

ॐ

WHENEVER VANGUARD THOUGHT OF BELLITREAUX, HE thought of the trees – all of them dead long before they ever arrived. Standing on the battlements and looking out over the landscape you would find nothing but twisting black husks bursting from the frozen ground, stretching out into the distance as far as the eye could see.

It seemed to be a land cursed by endless winter. The further north you got the less summer there was to be had.

Vanguard had been there since October. Each time he opened his mouth a plume of warm breath would curl into the air.

By mid January it was so cold that your hand froze to the stone if you left a finger lingering too long on the balustrades. Bellitreaux was the last place any of them wanted to be. It was as close as you could get to nowhere without being smack in the middle of it.

The men stationed at the castle had quickly found that the best way to keep even slightly warm was to continuously march along the walls. That was why Vanguard always remembered the trees. He had spent nearly ten hours a day for over half a year staring at them. Sometimes he would remember the way that his comrades looked as they passed by, cloaks held tight to their chests. Often they would murmur beneath their breath, the words lost and frozen in the wind. Vanguard would grunt in agreement without ever actually knowing what it was they had said.

By the time Vanguard was at Bellitreaux, it had been over a decade since he had been drafted into the renowned Ninth Company. An earthy collective, there were a little over one hundred and twenty of them in total. Not one of them was what you would call well bred. They were soldiers chosen for their skill in combat, agility or anything deemed advantageous or unusual.

It was also the one company that you couldn't buy your way into. Most of the army at that time was comprised of private yeomanry and hired soldiers working for the upper classes. If you wanted to be a part of the Ninth, you had to earn it. Apparently they had seen something in Vanguard. What it was, he had never quite worked out.

When Arnauld had drafted him into the company, Vanguard had been on a fast track to nowhere. Soldiering was a good life but it didn't pay well. In those days he had not been averse to the odd bit of thieving – not if it meant actually being able to eat. The Ninth Company liked to refer to themselves as 'the Gentry', mostly because they thought it was hilarious when they did.

One thing that a lot of the men had in common was that none of them had ever set foot in such a large house before then. It seemed a huge novelty at first, to sleep in beds that had been occupied by nobles or royalty at one time or another. There were plenty of souvenirs to be taken from cupboards or prised from walls. Once that was over however, it began to seem less and less interesting the longer time went on. Even so, it did not matter how dull it got inside the walls, it was still better than being outside of them.

After years of marching across the country, Vanguard and the men had initially been pleased to stay in one place for a little while. The war was drawing to a close, everyone said so. With little leverage left to use, rebels had been ransacking and taking over properties and houses across the north in one last desperate attempt to topple the aristocracy.

According to rumour, the castle at Bellitreaux had been overrun and despite its lack of strategic importance, the city wanted it back. It seemed to be more about the principal of the matter than anything else. The Ninth had been sent, along with the remnants of a few other companies with nothing better to do.

Finding nothing more than a few scrawny cats hopping about the place on their arrival, the men walked into

Bellitreaux without so much as a whisper of resistance. If Vanguard thought back on it now he should have realised something was amiss. At the time they were too cold, too hungry and too stupid to care.

There had been an officer from the Twentieth with them, a man with little wartime experience and an amiable personality. Fresh to the position and hoping for a chance to prove himself, he had ventured out with a scouting party on the first day leaving the rest of the men behind. They never saw him again.

They waited for a replacement but nobody came. With no orders and no command they simply stayed where they were. Now and again a supply wagon would show up under armed guard. One of them would always ask if there was news from the south, if any orders had been issued. The response was always the same. Instructions to be confirmed, they were to stay where they were.

Outside of the Ninth Company, the majority of the soldiers sent to Bellitreaux were young and inexperienced. They knew little of life, but they knew a lot about the Ninth. They had all heard stories. On more than one occasion, Vanguard found himself the subject of curious glances, the men around him wondering if what they had heard was true. He did nothing to either encourage or dispel the rumours.

Vanguard wasn't the oldest man in residence but he was not far off. The younger men seemed to instinctively gravitate towards him, looking for instruction. He wasn't sure what to tell them. They were decent men, if a little rough around the edges. They had some laughs. Mainly at how ridiculous their situation was.

After a while, Vanguard began to notice that the gap between supply wagons arriving and resources running out was getting longer. It got to the point where the food was starting to run out completely before the next lot arrived.

Then the last wagon came. The driver confirmed the news they had all hoped for. The war was ending, the revolution over. Any rebel who wasn't already out of the cities wouldn't be getting out and anyone who was out had already fled. Bellitreaux was too far away for anyone to care about what happened to it after that. It was time to go home.

Gathering their belongings, they marched alongside the supply wagon. About twenty miles outside of the castle they were met by the fleeing rebels.

The first they knew about it was when Vanguard happened to pass by a dark haired soldier who was holding a silver teaspoon in his hands. It was a gift, a souvenir for his mother. There was a shadow that moved in the distance, a crack splitting the air. The boy looked up and a bullet hit him between the eyes.

They were outnumbered by a considerable margin. The lack of supplies left them with little shot, even less powder. The men had no choice but to retreat back to Bellitreaux. Finding themselves surrounded by a camp of revolutionaries numbering almost a thousand, they had nowhere else to go.

Within a week the wagon had emptied. There were fights over food. Before long there were fights over nothing because nothing was what they had. Hunger became starvation. The first of the men began to wither away. A few of them caught rats if they could. Eventually, it got to the stage where there was none of those left either. There was a well, so the water lasted a little longer. At first, they rationed it, but then fights broke out over that too.

Initially a few tried to escape but they did not get far. Forced by desperation to make a bid for freedom, they ran headlong into a haze of smoke and bullets. The men outside had ammunition by the plenty.

At first, they buried the dead. After a while, they simply pushed them over the wall onto the frozen ground below. They had lost their humanity. It seemed the world had forgotten the men at Bellitreaux.

Vanguard had been standing at the wall one morning watching the trees when he heard the shot fired from within the castle grounds. He knew what it was even before the shouting sounded from below. Arnauld had been the oldest man at Bellitreaux. The shot had remained in his pocket, rolling around on its own until he could take no more. The last of their powder was blown away along with his brains. He had been a good man. One that Vanguard knew well. They had a history together. By that point he had been too hungry even to grieve. He felt nothing but the gnawing pain of his stomach shrinking. Vanguard was, after that, the oldest man at Bellitreaux.

Madness descended. Friend turned on friend, each man reduced to little more than a wide eyed shadow of himself. Vanguard spent a whole day chasing spiders around the cellar, grabbing any he could find and cramming them into his mouth.

Finally, the point came where he too had taken all he could. Vanguard walked to the top of the wall to look at the trees one last time. Standing at the edge of the precipice, he saw the men camped outside the walls. Vanguard was in plain view. Not a single one of them noticed him. Vanguard had always found it easy to go unnoticed. Until that moment it had never seemed like that much of an advantage. Survival instinct kicked in. It drowned out everything else. It wasn't until his feet had carried him back down the steps, across the yard, out of the gates and into the trees that he looked back to see the gate he had left open.

The men huddled inside the building had no apprehension that their enemy could simply walk in. It didn't occur to them because, until that moment, it seemed impossible that anyone could just walk out. That was precisely what Vanguard did. Not because he was their enemy, not because he wished them ill, but because he did not want to die there.

A short distance from the gates he came across an abandoned pack containing some bread and other sundries. Sitting on the frozen ground, Vanguard gorged himself on the food until it felt like his stomach would burst. In the background, he heard the sounds of men dying.

The castle fell, its occupants unjustly abandoned to the vengeful anger of those displaced by Sanquain. Three hundred men had arrived in October. Sixty three succumbed to starvation. Two hundred and thirty-six died that morning - only one man left.

It did not matter how much time passed, nor how far away he was from that place, Vanguard knew that he had left a part of himself in Bellitreaux that day. He would spend the rest of his days afraid that it had been the good part that had been left behind, and that somehow it was still standing there staring out at the gnarled, twisting trees.

TARRYN TRIED TO FOCUS HIS MIND, ATTEMPTING TO quiet the voices in his head. Vanguard was in no mood to talk that much was clear. He tried to still his agitation, to just quietly observe and absorb everything around them. For a while he was able to walk in silence, taking in the sounds of the city at night. In the end he couldn't help himself - there were too many things he wanted to know, questions that had gone without answers for far too long. It was an intolerable itch, one that he could not continue to bear.

"So you're like a Red Badge then?" The look on Vanguard's face told Tarryn that it was not a comparison he found favourable. "Fine, sorry. So what are you exactly? You know, officially?"

Official was not a word that Vanguard would use to describe the terms of his employment. There was no payroll, no ledger or account bearing his name. The only conversation that had ever taken place regarding the matter had been within the walls of Sanquain's office, some years previously.

IT HAD OFTEN BEEN SAID THAT THE SIMPLEST THINGS IN life are all that are required in order to make a person feel like themselves again. The restorative effects of a good wash, a decent meal and clean shaven face were often overlooked. A warm bath could be the difference between feeling like a human and feeling like something else entirely.

Unfortunately for Vanguard, his time spent in the Hole had rendered him into something less than a man. No amount of hot water and soap could remedy that. It would take much more. Sanquain had known that on the day they first met, sitting across the table in the office above the market. He had known that what sat before him was nothing more than a hollowed out husk. That was fine. He had no need for more men. What he needed was something different.

It was the first time that Vanguard had been in the Golden Quarter since the dissolution of the old administration. It was the first time he had been anywhere. A lot had changed in his absence. The world had moved on whilst Vanguard was left to rot beneath the ground. There was a tremor in his left shoulder - a souvenir from the Hole, one that would fade in time. Sanquain could wait. Given a few weeks of recovery Vanguard would be fit for purpose.

With one hand, Vanguard brushed the hair from his face and spoke the first words he had uttered in weeks. "Why am I here?"

Sanquain had been different back then. When his rise to power had first begun he had looked and felt like a younger man. Just a few years later and he had the look of a man who had spent his entire life sleeping with one eye open. He had made many friends and had gained many enemies during his ascension. In many cases the two were one in the same.

"There is something I find interesting about you."

Vanguard remembered the soreness in his throat, dry and scratching. A jug of water was produced. The cold liquid helped a little. It was good to drink something that wasn't fetid. "What's that?"

"I'm interested in how it is that in a castle occupied by over three hundred men, you were the only one that managed to walk out of the doors."

Vanguard said nothing.

"From my point of view it seems like one of two things happened. Either you were in league with the rebels, which makes you a traitor or you somehow escaped without being seen, which makes you a deserter. Which is it?"

Knowing that his response could lead to a swift return to a dank cell, or worse, Vanguard thought carefully about how he would answer. In truth he felt he was both and neither. Desperation had driven him to walk from the castle, nothing more. "From what I can see, there's not much difference."

"So you admit you are both deserter *and* traitor?"

"I'm just someone that's supposed to be dead."

"And now that I have resurrected you, what do you think to the new world?"

Even with the sunlight burning his eyes, Vanguard was not blind to the world around him. The city smelt the same. It sounded the same. As he had sat in the carriage that had brought him to the Golden Quarter, he smelt the sweat and smoke of the Black Zone become the sweet scent of perfume and flowers.

"It seems the same to me."

"Is it not better now? A city divided so that everything can remain in its proper place?"

"It was divided before; all you've changed is geography."

"Then we are agreed. There is a place for everything and everyone, dead men included."

Their exchange lasted for a few more minutes. It seemed much longer. Sensing that their meeting was drawing to a close, Vanguard repeated the question. "Why am I here?"

"Because I know what you are, I know what *they* are and I know what I am."

"And what is that?"

Sanquain leaned back in the chair. "They are the scum of the earth. I am their judgement..." He inhaled deeply. "...and you will be my executioner."

CHAPTER 14
WINIFRED

Winifred Beaumont was not a pleasant woman. Aside from the vile temperament with which she ran her home, she was a cold-blooded murderer. Murder for money was an indiscriminate business; however Vanguard tried not to make a habit of killing women.

It wasn't any sort of aversion to the slaying of the fairer sex that stayed his hand. Most of his victims would have slit his throat with a smile and a flirtatious wink given half the chance. Monsters were monsters no matter their gender. Vanguard was hesitant to kill Winifred because when he did, she would not be the only one to suffer as a consequence.

There was a large dilapidated building in the centre of the Pits. Mrs. Beaumont was the owner and keeper of the house. She had been in the Black Zone for years, gathering a reputation as a woman who would take in unwanted orphans and unfortunates with nowhere else to go. It was far from being a safe and welcoming place for those in need; sitting out on the stoop each day, smoking endless cigarettes and screeching obscenities at her charges seemed to be the limit of Winifred's nurturing.

It was not unusual to see the older children running through the streets, picking the pockets of unfortunate passers-by. They were feral creatures. Of course if they were ever caught, Winifred would deny all knowledge of them.

Suffer as they might, the older children were at least useful to her. The younger ones were not. Children were perpetually hungry. The city paid for each child that crossed the threshold – a donation given for care and safe-keeping. It did not take long for Winifred to learn that it was more profitable to keep space free in the house. No child was turned away. Yet Winifred never seemed to run out of beds.

Babies would be left on her doorstep in a sorry state, weak and malnourished. Infant mortality was tricky. More often than not, the babies would be dead within a week. The rat poison she kept beneath the sink didn't help. At first, people had been dismissive. Some had even been sympathetic. The poor woman had tried her best. Sickness was rife in the city. It could not be helped if some of the weaker ones did not make it. Eventually though, it got to the point where they could not deny the obvious anymore. It took much longer than it ought to have done.

The law stated that there should be a public trial. Sanquain felt however that this course of action would be inappropriate. A trial would raise many questions and, if the question of what happened to the babies arose, so too would the question of where they had come from in the first place. If the true lineage of half the bastards in the Black Zone ever came to light, there would be a mob of angry aristocrats in the town square by dawn. It would be better for everyone if Winifred met with a swift and quiet end.

Better for everyone except the children still living in the house. With a bit of luck, the older boys might find themselves drafted into one of Sanderson's gangs where they would spend the next few years beating money out of debtors. Some of them would make it on the streets. They would have a chance, even if it was not much of one.

Vanguard's concern was that Sanquain might view the children as loose threads. Ones that Sanquain would prefer nobody had the chance to pull at.

Tarryn looked at Winifred. A thin cigarette perched between her bony fingers. Vanguard noticed the twitch in his hand.

Tarryn whispered under his breath. "So how do we do this?"

"There is no 'we'. Only me."

"She can't see us, though. I can help you."

"This isn't some bloody dust up behind a bar. Besides, she can't see *me*. We don't know who can see you. The point is to be discreet. It's not discreet if somebody walks past whilst someone's getting done. They might not see us but they can still see someone getting murdered."

"Won't people know she's been murdered anyway?"

"Not the point. There's a difference between knowing someone's *been* murdered and knowing someone is *getting* murdered."

Given the time of year, it wasn't too chilly. The city only had two seasons and within that, only two types of weather. It was either raining or it wasn't. That night it wasn't. They had about an hour and a half to wait.

Eventually, a bell tolled in the distance. Right on cue, the children emerged from out of the depths of the house, wrapped thick in scarves and hats. The winter clothes were not designed for warmth. They were arranged so as to disguise their faces.

Winifred sent the children out at the same time every night. While the legitimate sons and daughters of the Golden Quarter slept soundly in soft beds, the illegitimate ones were put to work. Drunks were easy targets. In a few hours time, Winifred would have a pile of wallets and pocket watches to rifle through.

Tarryn lurched forward slightly. Vanguard pulled at the back of his jacket with one hand. "You wait here."

Vanguard took the knife from the bag. Pulling it towards him, he held the blade close to his body, not wanting to reveal the flash of the metal.

Tarryn put out one hand. "Let me do it. I'm ready."

Vanguard looked at the hand in disgust. No respectable killer would ask to handle another's weapon. The knife he carried had been in his possession for over a decade. It wasn't a tool for a hapless amateur. "What did I *just* say?"

Creeping forward, Vanguard moved silently. It was no more than the work of a single stroke, the skin of her throat splitting like fruit peel. Winifred gurgled out a few last breaths, lurching forward and reaching out one hand. Vanguard wiped the knife and returned it to the satchel.

Tarryn looked down at the body. "That was faster than I thought."

"It usually is when you're not beating them to death in an alley."

Tarryn was about to respond when they heard the sound of sniffling from behind them. Vanguard turned. A young boy of around twelve years old stood illuminated by the gas light. Purple bruises ran up and down his arms. The pockets of his trousers were stuffed with trinkets and treasures. The boy had obviously had a fruitful night, returning earlier than the others to hand over the bounty to Mrs. Beaumont. Vanguard watched the boy scanning the scene before him, taking in the sight of blood and spilled tobacco. He walked past them both. The boy seemed to be processing what had happened. A grin appeared on his face, spreading from ear to ear. Pulling back one foot, he landed a hard kick to the side of Winifred's head. There would be no tears over their guardian's departure from the world.

The boy looked from left to right, checking to see if anyone else was coming. He bent down, rifling through the pockets of the dead woman's apron. Locating the half-empty tin of tobacco and the rolling papers, he stood up once again.

Thumbing through the powdery brown contents, he held a paper in the other hand. It would have been amusing to watch, had it not at the same time been so pathetic. The boy clearly had not attempted to roll a cigarette before. Trying valiantly to mimic the action he had seen done so many times before, he ended up with what was a thin, soggy, half cigarette that peeled at the ends. Striking a match against the tin, the boy held it up to his face.

Whether it was the flickering of the match, or some subtle movement made without intention, something caused his gaze to snap upward. Vanguard knew from the way the boy simply looked through him, that it was not he who had caused the boy's eyes to widen.

Nausea churned in Tarryn's gut. The boy had seen him. Unlike Vanguard, Tarryn had not yet mastered his natural skills. He could not control them. Meeting Vanguard had at last given him the chance not just to understand them, but to learn how to use them. Now it was all fading away before his eyes. It had been the first and last time Tarryn would get to have a taste of a life amongst the shadows. The boy would ruin everything.

Tarryn moved. Reaching out and grasping at the boy, he held onto him as the child scrambled to escape. Squealing like a piglet, the boy kicked into the air.

Vanguard hissed at him. "What are you doing?"

"He saw me, he saw my face."

The boy lashed out with scrawny legs, worn boots scuffing at the ground. Grabbing the material of Tarryn's coat with one hand, Vanguard pulled the knife from the bag with the other. Tarryn was still trying to keep hold of the boy. With one deft move, Vanguard brought the blade through the air. The tip found its home in the skin and muscle writhing beneath him. There was a piercing howl. The boy darted into the night. Putting one hand to his arm, Tarryn looked down at the blood flowing through the sleeve of his jacket.

"You stabbed me...you stabbed me in the fucking arm. What if he tells someone?"

"He's a boy. He's not going to tell anyone anything. You'll live."

Tarryn held up one blood covered finger to his face. The blood was his but it could so easily have been the boys. In the moment, all he had done was act on instinct. Leaning forward, he placed a hand on each knee and threw up.

Vanguard waited. "Are you done?"

"I would have killed him."

Vanguard let the air hang for a moment. "You're a killer. It's what you are."

"I never meant to be, I didn't mean to kill anybody."

"Oh yeah, and what about the next time?"

"There's not going to be a next time, there was never meant to be a first one..."

"There's always a next one for people like us."

Vanguard reached up and scratched at his armpit. There was a patch of sweat accumulating that had begun to seep through the material of the coat. He ought to try and clean up a bit before going to the house that evening. He was hungry. Although he had only seen her that morning, he had the sudden urge to speak to Henriette. Not about this, about anything but this.

"How can I stop it?"

It would have been nice to tell the boy that it was a simple matter of choice. Vanguard was not in the business of nice. Tarryn was going to kill again, of that there was no doubt. It was inevitable. He needed it even more than he knew. Now he'd had a taste of it, the hunger would only grow.

Left alone, there was no telling what Tarryn might become. Vanguard had been much younger when the army had found him. For better or worse the journey that they had set him on had kept him alive. For as long as he could remember, Vanguard had walked the thin line between monster and man. Now he would need to show someone else how to tread that same path.

CHAPTER 15
THE BALANCE OF DEBT

Vanguard did not like to be in any man's debt. Unfortunately, he needed a favour and there was no way around it. Standing beneath the glow of the street lamp, he blew out a long breath, watching the cloud of warm air slowly dissipating into the evening sky. The night was still young enough for the streets to be relatively quiet. Somewhere in the distance two stray cats were mewling angrily at one another.

Vanguard smelt the aroma of musk and sweat long before Sanderson leaned against the wall next to him. This was not going to be an enjoyable encounter.

"This had better be good. I had plans tonight."

"I need a favour."

A grin spread across Sanderson's face. "Say that again?"

"Believe me if I thought anyone else could get one, I wouldn't ask."

"And what exactly do you need from me?"

"I need a city badge."

Sanderson looked thoughtful. "Tricky. They're not that

easy to get, we don't just give them out to anyone. You need someone with the right connections."

Vanguard sighed. "Can you get one or not?"

"Of course I can get one; it'll take a few days though. You'll owe me."

"I already owe you."

Sanderson's tongue flickered across the broken tooth. "I haven't forgotten."

Vanguard glanced up. Tiny specks of dust and rain danced in the gloomy light. Sanderson was enjoying himself. It had been a while since the balance of debt between them had been tipped one way or another. This time it had tipped in Sanderson's favour.

"And if I should manage to procure such an item, what's to say I won't just tell the captain about it? I'm sure he would be curious as to why his pet mercenary would want a badge."

Vanguard clenched his jaw. "Because I know you'd rather have me in your debt than be in that bastard's good graces."

"You know, in another world we could have been friends."

"In another world we could have been a lot of things."

With an agreement in place, the two men parted. It was getting darker. Vanguard had nowhere particular that he needed to be. For once, his time was his own.

The usual crowd had gathered in the Ring, drinks being liberally poured and spilled as they greeted each other with hearty shoves. Vanguard walked in and took his seat. Ludnor gave him a cursory nod from behind the bar. A moment later, one of the girls brought across a cup of strong dark tea and placed it in front of him. The water was only just warm. Ludnor was not really equipped to provide hot beverages. He didn't see the point in it, being as how he only had one customer who ever wanted them. It didn't taste like tea was supposed to, but it provided Vanguard something with which to warm his cold fingers.

It would have been faster to request a city badge directly from Sanquain but Vanguard knew that it would not have been a smart move. There were a great many things that he needed to learn about Tarryn before deciding whether to reveal their agreement to anyone. Sanquain would want to use the boy. Tarryn was not ready to meet the captain. Vanguard hoped that he would never have to.

All of the Red Badges carried a city badge. It was an insurance policy, a safeguard of sorts. It allowed the holder to operate under the authority of Sanquain's office. Nobody had ever seen Vanguard at work, so he was not concerned for himself but Tarryn's skills were volatile and unpredictable. If the worst should happen, the badge would offer the boy some protection from retribution. There was only so much that Vanguard could do.

There was always the chance that Sanderson would be curious enough to look into why Vanguard had asked the favour of him. If he did, it did not matter. He would not say anything about it, or at least, not until the moment it became most advantageous. Sanderson had always been the type of man who adapted to survive – no matter what it took.

THEY HAD BEEN CAMPED ABOUT THIRTY-SIX MILES FROM Bellitreaux. They were three hundred and fifty or so men, some from the capital but most of them from Leaumond -

the last major borough before the landscape became a frozen wasteland.

For the past few months Vanguard and a significant proportion of the army, the Ninth included, had been dispatched to march up and down the land rounding up dissenters and anarchists.

At that point, Vanguard and his comrades were still in the employment of Captain Jules Piven. It would be less than a year later when the former governor would take a pistol and put it to the roof of his mouth. Many doubted the authenticity of the suicide note later produced by his successor, Felix Sanquain.

Piven had not been an effective leader. He was a man bred from good stock but of poor judgement. Sanquain was an intelligent, decisive man. Where others cowered, he took action. As the lower classes rose up, Sanquain beat them back without remorse. The Governor fell from grace. With little left with which to challenge either Sanquain or subdue the rebels, Piven was eventually forced to concede authority.

It had been in the final year of the conflict that Vanguard had witnessed the arrival of a group of soldiers marching from the west back towards the city. Amongst them was a tight-lipped man with flecks of ginger hair in his beard.

The air around the camp smelt perpetually of soup. A thin, greasy concoction - to call it soup was a generous term. It was boiled water with salt and the trimmings of any unfortunate bird or rabbit that did not move quickly enough. It was hot, though, which meant that a pot never lasted long.

The downside to the soup diet was the speed with which it travelled through the digestive system. Privacy was not something in great supply. A rustling bush was more likely to be a fellow soldier taking care of personal business than it was a rebel attack.

After one particularly potent batch, Vanguard found himself sharing a bush with the red-bearded soldier. He hadn't intentionally chosen that bush, it just happened to be the closest one available. By the time he realised that it was occupied his trousers had already dropped.

Vanguard had not spoken a word to Sanderson since his party arrived at the camp. The first sound he ever heard from him did not come from his lips. For fifteen minutes neither of them spoke. Each man stared intently at the frozen ground directly in front of them. When it was over, Sanderson pulled up his trousers. "Fucking soup."

Vanguard snorted. Sanderson shook his head, grinning at the ridiculous nature of their situation. The aroma around the bush brought tears to their eyes.

"James Sanderson, I'd shake your hand but..."

Vanguard stood up. "Yeah, welcome to shit city."

"Been here long?"

"Too long. It doesn't get any better."

They vacated the bush as quickly as possible. Before long it was occupied again, another soldier pushing past them with a pained look on his face. Sanderson eyed Vanguard carefully. "Do you play dominoes?"

"Not had much chance recently."

"Well then, may as well kill some time. Come on, you know what they say, those who shit together, stick together."

"Not heard that one before."

In the weeks that followed Vanguard came to learn many things about James Sanderson. Firstly, the man had an inexplicable talent for winning at dominoes. Secondly, the man was a bit of a bastard. Even so, he didn't find that he particularly disliked him. They were similar in age and experience. Both of them had travelled. They were both equally as unimpressed with the world. Sanderson also had a skill for acquiring hard to find items. Everything at the time was rationed yet somehow he managed to procure a variety of hard to come by goods on a regular basis. Vanguard didn't ask where they came from. When you spent each day frozen to the bone you didn't question how the liquor came into your possession, you simply drank it.

There was little in the way of fighting left to be done at that point. The rebels had not yet made their way that far north for the most part. Every once in a while there would be a skirmish, the odd few fighters that had travelled that way meeting with soldiers on patrol.

It had been about six weeks since their meeting in the bush. A bottle of whisky had appeared as if from nowhere. Sanderson had been generous with the pours. There had been a buzzing in Vanguard's head, a numbness that spread pleasantly from the fingers to the toes. A few large birds circled overhead. Vanguard looked up, holding one hand across his forehead and squinting. There could have been four birds, there might have been two - he was three drinks past being able to tell.

"I'm bloody starving." Sanderson's announcement was followed by a loud gurgling. He looked down at his stomach. Neither of them had eaten anything since that morning. Vanguard turned away from the birds, looking at the empty ration pack on the floor.

"What do you want me to do about it?"

"You ever ate a black eagle?"

"Oh yeah all the time, practically fucking grew up on it."

"Do you want food? Or do you want to just sit here being an arsehole?"

Sanderson scrambled unsteadily to his feet. Vanguard realised he was being serious. Taking the pistol from inside his jacket, Sanderson checked the chamber. "Twenty says I hit a bird before you do."

All of the men carried pistols at all times. Normally they could at least see half straight when firing them. Neither of them was in any condition to be shooting at things. It was a terrible idea. Vanguard's stomach growled. "Deal."

The floor was uneven and kept moving, or at least it seemed as though it did. Vanguard had to focus just to put one foot in front of the other. Sanderson was a little further ahead. He was in no less an inebriated state yet somehow seemed to have far more control over his legs.

"Move it, before they disappear."

"I *am* moving it."

There was a cry from above their heads, one of the eagles swooping. Sanderson lifted the barrel. The shot went wide. Tears from the wind prickled his eyes, vision blurring. He scowled.

Hands shaking from the cold and the alcohol, Vanguard tried to focus on the black dots spiralling above them. The sound of the pistol cracking was louder than expected. Sanderson laughed, highly amused. "You couldn't hit one if they were on the ground."

Vanguard reloaded. Hands fumbling, the ball rolled around between his fingers. Lifting the gun, the second shot rang out. There was a squawk and a fluttering of feathers in mid-air. The bird plummeted.

Vanguard looked triumphantly at Sanderson who did not look happy. "It wasn't your turn."

"Still hit it. I'll take that money now, thanks."

They found the eagle on the ground not far away. It lay near a rotted log in a cluster of trees that had long since lost their leaves. Vanguard picked it up, shaking the loose feathers free. Sanderson, not pleased at the idea of losing a bet, grabbed at the dead bird.

Whether it was the whisky, the endless mind-numbing days in the cold or the irritation at Sanderson's reluctance to make good on the bet, Vanguard found himself rolling across the ground. Locked in a flurry of fists, the two men exchanged insults and jabs. They traded blows, the pair of them scrabbling amongst the trees. Vanguard swung angrily at Sanderson's nose. A sudden, searing pain shot through Vanguard's body from groin to ears, bringing tears to his eyes.

When he thought back on it later, he did regret his actions. Not because he felt any sense of guilt, but because it would have been stupid and pointless to die in some unknown woodland in the middle of nowhere.

Rolling onto his knees, Sanderson levelled his pistol at Vanguard's chest. His finger twitched on the trigger. It clicked. His face fell as he realised that he had not reloaded the barrel. Grabbing the whisky bottle that had fallen from the pack, Vanguard cracked the bottle across Sanderson's face. It caught him in the mouth, front tooth chipping on impact.

They did not hear the footsteps across the frozen ground until a pair of hands grabbed them roughly by the collars. "You two, what the *hell* do you think you are doing?"

Drunk, dishevelled and skin blistered from the wind,

neither man could offer up any excuse that would allow them to avoid the inevitable flogging. Vanguard spent the night in a prison wagon. Sanderson was sent back to his own company, doubtless to reap the consequences of his actions.

As it transpired, neither of them would be punished for their misdemeanours. Orders arrived from the city. The army was to move again. Sanderson and Vanguard would not cross paths again until many years later.

The morning after their brawl in the woods Vanguard was sent on his way to Bellitreaux. Many months later he heard whispers on the grapevine that a soldier named James Sanderson had returned to the city and found an appointment as a part of a new yeomanry created by Felix Sanquain.

Vanguard had thought of retribution. He had thought of murdering Sanderson on many an occasion. He had no doubt that Sanderson would have killed him that day amongst the trees, had the chamber not been empty.

There was one reason and one reason alone that Vanguard had not sought revenge. Sanderson was a remorseless bastard who would use his own mother as a human shield. He was also the one responsible for Vanguard's liberation from prison.

It was a source of constant conflict to Vanguard that the man who had tried to kill him, was also the one that had saved him. It was unlikely that he could have lasted another year in the Hole. Vanguard had no idea how Sanderson had come to know that Vanguard was in prison, but when Sanquain had been looking for a man to fill a position, Sanderson had been the one to suggest just where he might find one.

Vanguard still had the pistol that had shot the bird

from the sky. He preferred not to use guns anymore unless there was no other choice. It was a lazy weapon, too impersonal. Yet he could not bring himself to get rid of it. Part of him knew that he was saving it.

Up until Vanguard had asked for the badge, he and Sanderson had been square with one another. They could trade insults, come to blows and hate one another but they did not owe each other anything. Now the balance of debt would once again be in Sanderson's favour.

The day would come when Sanderson would gladly and willingly betray him. When that day came, the scales would tip once more. Vanguard had a bullet saved and it carried Sanderson's name. One day their account would be settled in full.

CHAPTER 16
PAULETTE AND THE BISHOP

The second hand wavered momentarily. It looked as though the watch were trying to make up its mind about whether or not it was really eight o'clock.

It wasn't, as it happened. It was actually eight minutes past. The watch had been slow for a long time. Vanguard had thought about getting it fixed a few times but he never did. There was a crack in the glass face that obscured the three. It didn't bother him. It had been like that when he bought it. The watch had been one of the first things that Vanguard had purchased after leaving the Hole. He had got it from a scrap merchant who sold it for a good price.

Underground, there had been nothing to mark the passing of time. A lot of people preferred not to think about the minutes slipping away. Life was a finite thing. Most wished they could deny time altogether. Vanguard, on the other hand, took great comfort in just knowing that it was moving at all. Even if the actual time on the watch was wrong.

He glanced up the street. There were a lot of faces around, none of them the ones that he wanted to see. Tarryn was late. They had agreed to meet at eight outside the club. Vanguard had already been waiting for twenty minutes.

The breeze caught the corner of a scrap of paper to his right. It had been pinned to the wall, along with all the others that had been put up around the city. The disappearance of Argent Cooke was big news in the Golden Quarter. The poster was a good likeness of the man, but it was unlikely anyone would see him. The chances were high that if he wasn't in some other city, by now he was floating around in the canal.

Sanquain had spent much of the last month focusing on the search. Vanguard could not help but notice that the longer Cooke was missing, the more urgently the captain pushed him to hunt down whoever had murdered the Red Badges that had washed up in the marina.

It had been months. Vanguard had asked all the right questions. He had followed all the right people. There was not one scrap of evidence to suggest that anyone in the Splinters had been particularly involved in anyway.

"My friend, you are here again? You are becoming regular."

Arms folded against his chest, Kosic joined Vanguard in leaning against the wall, taking up what was left of the space. Together they surveyed the gathering crowd. They had spoken a few times. Vanguard had begun to suspect that Kosic might have been one of the few decent people living in the city - when he wasn't cracking skulls.

"Night off?"

"No, Herveaux has meeting with investors. I am to go too."

"To what end?"

"Herveaux says the club needs money. If I am there, the investors will be more persuading."

Vanguard didn't bother to correct him. For the most part Kosic made more sense than many of the people he spoke to. If anything he quite enjoyed Kosic's manner of speaking, even if it did sometimes take a moment to process. "I can see how that would work."

The sound of beating drums could be heard from inside the club, the rhythm bleeding through the cracks in the walls. A pair of jugglers stood either side of the door, providing entertainment for those still lingering in the street. The one on the left would periodically fling a ball across the gap towards his counterpart. It would hit the one on the right and cause him to temporarily lose momentum. The juggler would feign annoyance before continuing with the routine. Each time it happened the crowd would roar with laughter.

"Oi, freak..."

Kosic's shoulders slumped. The crowd parted. By comparison to the kind of scrawny specimens usually churned out of the Pits, the challenger who emerged was reasonably well built. Vanguard assumed he was some sort of boxer or pit fighter - the sort of man whose vanity often led to ill-advised confrontations in the pursuit of infamy.

"You think you're big? I'll put you on the ground."

Kosic stood straight, hands raised. "I am not here for fighting. Go back to your friends."

The young man growled. There were many varieties of fighter in the neighbourhood. Vanguard had seen them all – the bruisers, brawlers, backstabbers and cheaters. Kosic didn't fall within any of those categories. The challenger circled, eyes fixed on Kosic. It appeared to be an occupational hazard. Vanguard had seen several young men eyeing him, trying to decide whether or not it was worth it. Kosic seemed more inclined to walk away given the choice.

"Are you a coward?"

Snorting with derision, the man turned as if to walk away. A moment later a thick length of metal connected with the side of Kosic's face. He reeled back, stars in his eyes. Another strike split his lip. Unfortunately, size meant little when someone was beating you about the head with a piece of pipe.

The crowd at the door cheered, excited at the prospect of a free fight. Their applause buoyed the pipe wielder's ill-placed confidence. Kosic wiped the blood from his lip with the back of his hand. There was a disturbance in the crowd, the people stepping aside. Demetrio and a few of the others appeared from inside the club. Vanguard guessed this was not the first time they had witnessed such an altercation. Kosic was shaking his head, trying to stop the ringing in his ears.

Having seen enough, Vanguard stepped forward. "Don't be stupid. You're only going to embarrass yourself."

The pipe froze in mid-air. The man holding it looked hard at Vanguard. Across the street Demetrio watched with interest. Confidence faltering, the assailant hesitated. There were few men in the neighbourhood who would not recognise the scarred jaw and even fewer who would risk getting on the wrong side of it. Two against one were not odds that he was willing to take. Throwing the pipe down, he spat at the ground.

"Fucking freaks, the lot of you." He backed away, turning into the disappointed crowd. Demetrio and his companions gathered around. Kosic stuck one finger in his ear, wriggling it around and shaking his head. Demetrio squinted, trying to get a better look at the side of his face. "That will swell."

"It is not that bad."

"You should come back inside. Mira has an ointment."

Demetrio stared at Vanguard. There was a momentary flicker in the muscles of his face. He had the look of a man with something to say, or at the very least a question to ask. "Did you know that man?"

"Why would I know him?"

He furrowed his brow. "The way he looked at you, it was like he knew you."

"I guess I've just got one of those faces."

A moment later, Herveaux appeared at the entrance of the club. There were crowds to control and an audience to entertain. It was difficult to do that when most of your employees were milling about outside wasting time.

Sensing his own time being squandered, Vanguard came to the conclusion that Tarryn had clearly found something more important to do with the evening. Part of him wanted to cut his losses, head for the Tanners and write off the night as a loss. Another part however, was telling him that something was not right. They had met several times recently and on each occasion Tarryn had been early. Vanguard could feel his presence even before he saw him. The boy was eager to learn. Murder was not an occupation well suited to most. For Tarryn it was a calling.

There had been no more alleyway beatings. He had listened to all of Vanguard's instructions. He was getting better; his ability to blend in and out of his surroundings improving with each time they walked the streets. For the most part he simply watched Vanguard as he worked. Even so, Vanguard could sense his impatience growing. He would not have changed his mind about their agreement.

Not tonight. Not when Vanguard had promised him that he would finally be unleashed. He wanted it too badly.

There were very few things in D'Orsee that could not be found by a man with the right resources and motivation. Vanguard had enough of both at his disposal to make tracking the boy down a pretty straightforward task. Within a few hours of asking all the right questions, Vanguard found himself standing on the front step outside a grand house. It had seen better days.

Vanguard was no fool. He had known from the moment they had met that Tarryn was what people referred to as a 'burner'. A derogatory term, it was used to describe those who had once been at the top of the social ladder. Former aristocrats who struggled to make ends meet yet steadfastly refused to abandon their crumbling empires. Instead, they kept the fires going by burning anything that wasn't nailed down.

He clipped the brass knocker abruptly against the door. It made an echoing sound, the sort that comes from a building half empty. A few minutes passed. He knocked again, this time a little louder. There was the sound of a bolt scraping and the turning of a key in the lock. Tarryn stood at the door holding a blood-stained handkerchief to his nose.

"For fucks sake, am I the only one not getting punched in the face tonight?"

"Darling, who is it?" A female voice sounded from down the hall before Tarryn could answer.

Not wanting Vanguard to witness anymore than he already had, Tarryn slipped outside and pulled the door closed behind him. The blood was starting to cake around his nostrils. Sniffing, he felt the skin tightening. It made his eyes water.

"I know I'm late, I've been dealing with something."

Vanguard looked at him. "I can see that."

Another figure appeared in the doorway. Tarryn cursed. He should have locked the door. Lady Leersac stood in the open frame, looking at the two men standing on the step. Vanguard nodded politely. "Good evening, madam. Sorry to disturb you."

Tarryn's mother beamed. It had been so long since they had received visitors. Tarryn felt the flush of embarrassment creeping up his neck. The side of his face twitched. Lady Leersac was glad she had spent so much time on her makeup that morning. "Darling, why didn't you tell me we had a guest?"

From the way that Tarryn's throat tensed, Vanguard could tell that he didn't so much consider him a guest as an unexpected intrusion. Lady Leersac extended an arm, waving her downturned hand in Vanguard's general direction. He duly shook it, ignoring the soggy crumbs mashed between her fingers.

"John Vanguard, may I present Lady Madeline Leersac. Mother, this is John Vanguard...he's a colleague."

Madeline frowned. "You don't need to tell me who he is, it is perfectly obvious." She gave Vanguard a welcoming smile. "Won't you come in, Bishop?"

They walked into the house together, Lady Leersac looping her arm around his. Tarryn followed behind, a little too closely. Vanguard could feel the breath on the back of his neck. Sitting on the chaise longue, Madeline stretched her arms out and complained about the lack of tea and biscuits.

"I'll go and fetch some." Tarryn looked at Vanguard pointedly.

Plucking one of the cushions from the chair, Lady

Leersac pressed it to her face, rubbing the threadbare velvet against her skin. She seemed to like it. At least that was what Vanguard presumed based on the purring sound she made.

He followed Tarryn into the kitchen. There were a few plates on the side, pieces of discarded chicken left to go cold. Vanguard grabbed a chunk, popping it into his mouth. "Do you live with your mother?"

"Yes, I do. Why did you come here?"

"I thought we had an arrangement, I wanted to know what happened."

There was an unintentional slip in Tarryn's gaze. Vanguard followed it towards the full sink. Amongst the crockery was an ornate silver candlestick. There was still blood on the metal. It explained a lot. Lady Leersac was clearly as mad as a box of frogs.

"She's not well. She's ill."

A number of empty vials sat gathered behind the taps. Picking one up, Vanguard pulled the cork from the bottle and sniffed. Sedatives – potent ones. There were at least six bottles empty. "How much of this have you been giving her?"

"Just enough for a few hours each night."

Tarryn ran a hand through his hair. Vanguard had no right to be there. Nobody had invited him. This was his business and nobody else's. There was a loud crashing from the sitting room. Something else smashed to clear up. "I want you to leave now."

Vanguard placed the vial back down. "You know this stuff will kill her?"

Without warning Tarryn turned and pushed the weight of his body into Vanguard. The shelf above their heads rattled as they met with the wall. Vanguard looked down at the fingers grasping the lapels of his jacket. Tarryn hissed, the words escaping through barely parted teeth. "You don't know anything about it."

"I'm not asking about it."

Relinquishing his grip, Tarryn stepped back. "It doesn't matter anyway, I can't get any more. Nobody will sell it to me, not anymore."

Lady Leersac called out; demanding to know what was taking so long. Tarryn knew he would never hear the end of it if their guest was not allowed to stay. Walking into the next room, he set the tray down on the table. Vanguard sat down.

Mad she might have been, but it was obvious that at one point Madeline Leersac had been an intelligent and articulate woman. Disease had stripped her of that. Life had been cruel to her. It was funny how all of her misfortunes had led her to become the only woman in the Golden Quarter ever to offer Vanguard a biscuit.

The source of Tarryn's impotent rage became clearer with every passing moment. The boy was a hunter who could not hunt. All of his natural instincts were brimming beneath the surface, forced to lay dormant because he could not leave this mad woman alone. If they were left to fester, they would eventually consume him. Madness bred madness. The city did not want Tarryn Leersac to lose his mind. It was too dangerous. The boy needed something to relieve the tension.

Fortunately, Vanguard knew of someone who could offer just such a service. "Can you get a message from here to the Black Zone?"

"Yes, but why?"

"I have a friend I'd like you to meet."

A message was sent with a driver to the house in the

Tanners. Vanguard drank the tea. A short while later there was a knock at the door. Paulette stood on the doorstep, confused as to why she was in the nicer part of town and why Vanguard had specifically requested that she bring a cake. Henriette had been equally as surprised by the request, but more than happy to acquiesce once she saw the money that had been sent.

Tarryn was not happy. The idea of a whore in their home filled him with bile. "What is this?"

"Paulette is a good girl. You speak to her nicely."

"Why is she here?"

Vanguard took Paulette by the hand and led her into the sitting room. Lady Leersac looked surprised. Two visitors in one night were unprecedented. She sat up, hands clasped delicately in her lap. "Your Ladyship, this is my good friend Paulette. She's brought you a cake."

"Oh, what sort?"

Paulette looked down at the tin in her hands, feeling a little embarrassed with the meagre offering that it contained. Had she known where she was bringing it, she would have opted for something a little fancier. "It's a jam sponge."

"My favourite!"

Unconvinced, Tarryn followed Vanguard to the hallway. "Are you sure about this?"

"You need a nurse and you can't afford one. Paulette is sweet and good-natured. She might not have the right schooling but she's got the heart for it. Besides, she's seen enough syphilitics to know how to deal with the madness."

Tarryn opened his mouth. He had hoped it was not as obvious as it seemed.

"Now, I'm leaving. I have business. Are you coming or not?"

Glancing back into the sitting room, Tarryn saw his mother talking animatedly with Paulette. She looked content. Tarryn was far from content. There was an itch beneath his skin that he could not scratch. Not unless he walked out of the front door. "This business you mentioned - what is it?"

Vanguard opened the door and paused momentarily. "We need to see a man about a boat."

CHAPTER 17
A MAN WITH A BOAT

They were very late. Vanguard was concerned they might have missed their opportunity. People dumping bodies didn't tend to hang around to wait for witnesses. It was long after midnight when they arrived at the part of town where the conduit began to widen.

"What are we doing?"

Vanguard lifted a finger to his lips. He pointed across the canal. A dark shadow was out on the water, barely visible against the scrim of a bridge. A man stood at the port side of the vessel, heaving a large object into the murkiness. It was followed quickly by another.

"A mark?"

Vanguard shook his head. "They're bodies alright, but Wick is no killer; hasn't got the stomach for it. You're not here for him."

Crouching down, Tarryn looked over the edge of the bank and caught a glimpse of his reflection. The face that looked back at him now was very different to the one he had seen in the bathroom mirror. Against the backdrop of the night sky, Tarryn felt a little more at peace with what he saw.

"Stop admiring yourself and hurry up."

They followed the boat as it made its way down the canal. After a while, Wick began to steer towards the sides. There was another figure waiting for him on the bank. Vanguard stopped and pointed towards the water's edge. "That's who you're here for."

Squatting low to the ground, Tarryn felt anticipation rolling down the length of his spine. Breathing in, he smelt cold air and excessive body odour. The two men on the bank were distinctly aromatic creatures. Tarryn could have found them with his eyes closed.

Wick stepped out of the boat and held out one hand. There was an exchange between the two men, a bag full of coins slipped from one to the other. Wick held the bag to his ear, shaking the contents. In a few minutes time, one of the two men would be dead. This would be the last money Wick would ever receive from this particular customer.

The two bodies that had been unceremoniously dumped over the side of the boat had belonged to Sister Margaret and Sister Moira. There weren't many places left in the city where the devout could still go to worship. There was, however, a sisterhood that kept a residence in a part of D'Orsee a few miles from the Pits. They lived quietly, administering what little aid they could to the surrounding population. For the most part they were well liked and went unbothered by thugs and criminals.

Unfortunately, the man that ended their lives was known around the area for having very specific carnal desires.

Henriette would not allow him within ten feet of her house. Others who did permit him entry rarely did it more than once. He was instead forced to find satisfaction on the streets. There was a string of prayer beads permanently tucked into the back pocket of his trousers.

It was a good first mark for Tarryn. Vanguard had been careful not to let him off the rope too soon. It wouldn't be good for anyone to unleash the boy too early. He was a decent student, but there was still urgency in him. It needed to be tamed.

The arrangement between them was not one that Vanguard could have foreseen. He had never planned to have an apprentice, although he supposed that was what the boy was now. Tarryn needed money and had a natural talent for killing things. Vanguard was getting older. He wouldn't be around forever. "It's time. Take the path and keep it clean. Don't let anyone see you."

Tarryn looked towards the water. "What are you going to do?"

"I need to speak to our friend Wick there."

"What if he can see me?"

"Make sure he doesn't."

"Thanks, that's helpful."

Vanguard pulled a small item wrapped in brown paper from his bag and handed it over. Tarryn took it. Beneath the paper was a knife, unused and smooth-handled. It was light and had a good feel to it. Tarryn jabbed it into the air. It was a gift that he would not soon forget.

"You know you're paying me back for that right?"

As the two men in front of them parted, Vanguard looked at Tarryn and nodded. "You know what you need to do, don't over think it. This is what we are. It's not a trick, it's all instinct. I'll come and find you when I'm done."

Leaving Tarryn to his work, Vanguard made his way down to the boat where Wick was focusing on the mooring ropes. Startled by the sudden presence of someone behind him, Wick turned. There was a flash of a knife, the blade held close against his throat. "Please, I ain't done nothing. Whatever you want, take it. Don't kill me."

"I'm not going to kill you."

"Then what do you want?"

Lowering the knife, Vanguard kept the tip pointed at the boatman's chest. Wick trembled. It was funny how he had no qualms about disposing of bodies, yet was so hesitant to become one. Life became much more valuable when it was your own in question. "Information. You know anything about the Red Badges they dragged out of here a few weeks ago? Two of them?"

"Red Badges? I don't know anything about no Red Badges."

"I thought you were the man to ask about anything going in or coming out of this canal?"

"Don't know who told you that. I'm just a boatman."

Vanguard didn't know whether to laugh or not. "Look, we can either do this the easy way or the hard way, which do you prefer?"

"I swear to you, I don't know anything about anything."

Realising that they were going to have to do things the hard way, Vanguard reached up and pulled the neckerchief from around Wick's throat. Balling the material with one hand, he forced it into the boatman's mouth. Protests muffled, Wick's eyes widened as Vanguard took his right hand and placed it against the edge of the boat. There was a flash of metal through the air. The scream was stifled by the gag.

Vanguard stepped back and observed his handiwork.

Wick looked in horror at the knife in his mangled hand, stuck fast in the rotten wood. Vanguard looked thoughtfully at the deck of the boat. "I've never tried sailing before, doesn't look that difficult. Shall I have a go?"

Wick shook his head fervently, voice barely audible. "No! No!"

"Can't hear you, but I assume you're saying yes."

Hopping over the side, Vanguard proceeded to stride over to the steering wheel. Wick tugged unsuccessfully at his hand. The boat lurched on the water. The force pulled Wick towards the edge, the boatman groaning as the sinew ripped.

"Sorry, still getting to grips with it."

Wick had no choice but to move along with his hand still stuck to the side of the boat. Vanguard stood at the helm, letting the vessel slowly meander down the side of the bank. It was quite nice being out on the water. Maybe the boating life was for him after all. The boat veered slightly and there was an agonised wail from the bank. Reluctantly, Vanguard brought it to a stop.

Stepping back onto land, he pulled the neckerchief from Wick's mouth. "Sorry, you know, I completely forgot you were there. How's your hand?"

Wick whimpered in response.

"Now, how about I ask you those questions?"

The boatman nodded glumly. Vanguard pulled the knife from the boat. Wick pressed his bloody hand to his chest, face pale. "What do you want to know?"

"Has anyone asked you to dump any Reds recently? Anyone you could describe?"

Wick shook his head. "No, I swear. If they went in it weren't me that put them in."

"You wouldn't lie to me would you Wick?"

"No, I wouldn't lie to you. I'm telling the truth."

As much as Vanguard would have liked to have put a few more well-placed holes in Wick before leaving it was clear that he knew nothing of use. It seemed that the further Vanguard dug into the murders, the less he seemed to find. Either people genuinely didn't know what had happened, or someone was covering something up. A thought occurred to him. "What about Argent Cooke, did you dump him?"

Wick looked genuinely horrified at the idea. "No, never, I would never, I don't know anything. I wasn't there." Wick's eyes darted from left to right. The words trailed off as he realised he had said more than he should have.

Vanguard took him by the scruff of the neck. "Weren't where? What do you know?"

Wick's shoulders slumped. There was no point trying to lie about it. "Not me, I don't know but I might have heard something."

"Heard something from who?"

Wick leaned forward. He whispered a name into Vanguard's ear. Vanguard's face turned ever so slightly greyer. It was not one that anyone wanted to hear.

"Alright, we're done here. Just so you know, if you tell another soul that you saw me tonight, I'll tell everyone in the Pits where they can find Sister Margaret and Sister Moira and who put them there."

"I didn't kill them!"

"I think we both know that they won't care about the details."

"What about my hand? How am I going to explain this?"

Vanguard looked back onto the deck of the boat, the

vessel stacked high with chains and ropes. "Boating is a dangerous business. Accidents happen." Wick was still whimpering when he turned and walked away.

Not far from where Wick stood nursing his injury, Tarryn was making his way along the side of the bank. Coming to the entrance of the docks, the area began to widen. Barges and sail boats gave way to larger vessels. Rusted anchors and spare parts lay scattered and abandoned.

It had been a long time since he had been that far north. The sound of the water lapping against the hulls could have fooled anyone into believing they stood at the edge of an estuary. There was nothing natural about it. It was a junkyard of man's great achievements. What had been a bustling hub by day was now nothing more than a ghost of what once was.

The ships had been left to decay. Tarryn's empire, along with so many others, was reduced to a great metal corpse, drifting alongside a few forlorn survivors. It seemed almost prophetic that he should be in this place at this particular time.

Following the mark, Tarryn held the knife, blade turned towards him so as to conceal it from sight. Vanguard had told him to do what came naturally. It was not as easy as it sounded. Tarryn's instincts were too accustomed to being restrained. His whole life had been spent trying not to kill people.

There was a section of path ahead occupied by several large containers. They created a narrow gorge, blocking everything in from both sides. Tarryn felt his pulse quickening. That was where it had to happen. He hauled himself up onto the top of a nearby crate. With quiet footsteps, Tarryn ran across the wooden tops until he was just a few feet behind the mark.

Looking out over the vast expanse of the water Tarryn realised they were not far from the place that his father had taken his last spluttering breaths. Lifting his head, he saw the pale moon looking back at him. The moment that Tarryn dropped from that roof to the ground, everything would change. Vanguard had shown him a way to put his skills to use, to satiate his desire yet still have a purpose in the world. Tarryn was many things by the light of day. He was an abandoned child, an angry son. He was the subject of scorn and derision. There was no place for him in the daylight. When he dropped down into the darkness, he would be a mercenary and there would be no going back. Without hesitation, he stepped off the crates and dropped down into the gorge.

There was a rustling in the wind. The mark turned and glanced over his shoulder. He saw nothing. A smile spread slowly across Tarryn's face. Vanguard had been right. He could control it. Tarryn began to walk down the pass. Adrenaline surging through his veins, the pace increased. The blade sliced across the air, Tarryn swinging low and bringing the knife across the man's torso.

Grasping at his abdomen, panic crept across his victim's face. Tarryn swung back around, sweeping past and slicing at the air again. The sounds of screaming went unheard. Above the docks, the indifferent moon looked down as Tarryn painted the space between the containers red. It was not quick. It was not clean. Nobody saw anything. By the time Vanguard reached them the job had been done several times over. Tarryn was crouching down, back pressed against the side of one of the crates. The body lay a few feet away, riddled with slices and cuts.

Vanguard looked at it. "You could have reined it in."

"It wasn't my fault, he fought back."

It was a lie. Vanguard would not have been happy with him had he known the truth. Tarryn had fully intended on doing as he had been instructed when it had started. It was meant to have been quick and simple. He had simply gotten lost in the moment. Next time would be better.

"Did he see you?"

"I don't think so, but I don't think he wanted to die either."

"No, they never do."

A few hours later they parted ways. Vanguard went off to do whatever it was that he did when his work was finished for the day. Tarryn walked along the streets, taking in the world at night. Everything was still and quiet.

Arriving home, he pushed the door open. The house was dark. There were no signs of life anywhere. A moment later there was a slight clattering from the floor above.

Heart pounding, Tarryn climbed the stairs two at a time. Rounding the banister he ran straight into an unfamiliar person creeping around near his mother's bedroom. Grabbing the assailant, Tarryn forced them back against the wall.

"No, don't, please, it's me, it's Paulette!"

Eyes adjusting, Tarryn saw Paulette looking back at him. He immediately withdrew his hands. "I'm sorry, did I hurt you? I didn't mean to...I thought...why are you up here?"

"It was getting late and your mother was tired, she wanted to go to bed."

"Where is she now?"

"Asleep. She has been for quite some time now. I didn't

know if you were coming back, I must have fallen asleep. I was sitting in the chair and I dropped the book."

"What book?"

"The one she asked me to read to her."

Tarryn looked down. There was a book in Paulette's hands. It had a leather cover; the pages yellow with age. It was a story for children, one about a robin that came in the winter to wage war on the summer birds. His mother had read it to him as a child. Even he did not know where it had been kept. He had assumed it was lost long ago.

"I'm sorry; this must have been a very unpleasant evening for you."

"I've had worse. She's actually very nice once you talk to her for a while."

Tarryn escorted Paulette back down the stairs so that she could collect her tin and coat. Searching through the sitting room, she huffed. The tin was nowhere to be seen. Prising back the cushions, she checked to see if it had slipped down behind the panel of the chaise. It was impossible to see anything in the darkness. Paulette went to light the lamp.

"No don't!"

The warning came too late. Light flooded the room. Tarryn looked back at Paulette, the angles of his face catching the glow. There was blood splattered across the entirety of his body. Paulette took a step back. "Is that yours?"

Tarryn did not know what to say.

"It isn't, is it?"

Frozen, Tarryn remained silent. He did not know what to do.

Finally, Paulette spoke. "I'll fetch some hot water."

Confused, Tarryn followed her to the kitchen where she set about running the tap.

"I assume whoever it was deserved it?"

"What do you mean?"

"John thinks that nobody knows what he does at night. We know, but we don't say anything because they always deserve it. They're terrible people. He only goes after the bad ones."

"Aren't you afraid of me?"

Paulette shook her head. "No. The way I see it, one more Vanguard in the city can only be a good thing. Besides, I know what he'll do to you if you hurt me."

A short while later, Tarryn saw Paulette to the door. She said goodbye and pulled her coat tighter around herself against the chill.

The sun was coming up over the rooftops. It would be a few hours before Lady Leersac arose, wanting breakfast. It had been a night full of surprises. Tarryn found an odd sense of calm washing over his body. Vanguard had been right. There was a place in the world for him. Vanguard did not see Tarryn as a monster because he too was one. Even Paulette, someone sweet and good-natured, had not shunned him when confronted with the truth of what he was. She had simply accepted it.

All his life, Tarryn had been told he did not belong anywhere. Now he could see that perhaps the world had been wrong. As his head fell against the pillows the thought gave him comfort and, for the first time in many months, he slept soundly.

CHAPTER 18
THE BUTCHERS

The speed at which the unusual becomes usual will vary from person to person. It always depended largely on the history of those experiencing it. Vanguard had, long ago, accepted that the life he led was far outside the parameters of what other men would consider normal.

It had not taken long for him to become accustomed to Tarryn's presence. Adaptability had always been an integral part of survival in the city. At first, he had been concerned that after so many years working in solitude, it would not suit him to have company. Vanguard was not somebody who often enjoyed the companionship of others.

Fortunately, Tarryn was used to being quiet. Because they did not talk much, Vanguard was able to watch his young companion. Tarryn was torn. One half of him was trying to be the man that society expected, the other wanting to give in to the raw, primal instincts that bubbled beneath the surface.

His first mark had given him a confidence that he had

not had before, that much was true. There was a vast difference between killing because the opportunity presented itself, and killing with intent. During the daytime hours, Tarryn was still quiet and reserved. He held himself back. Time and experience had taught him that it was better that way. By night, all his worries began to fall away. Stalking like a cat across the rooftops, Tarryn's true nature came to life. He was learning quickly.

Vanguard walked the streets as Tarryn went from balcony to sloping roof. He preferred a higher vantage point. The days passed quickly. Conveniently, Vanguard found that having someone else to do the grunt work left him with time to conduct his investigations elsewhere.

By this point he was no longer interested in Sanquain's motives for wanting to discover who had killed the Red Badges. Vanguard wanted to find out for himself. He had never come across a death in the city that he could not explain. It was oddly frustrating.

On the nights that they worked, Tarryn would use the money that he kept in reserve to obtain a few hours of Paulette's time. It allowed him to come and go as he pleased. Tarryn found her presence in his home to be both confusing and a comfort in equal measure. It was unusual to be in the company of a woman who did not look down on them. Whenever he said something strange, which seemed to be often, Paulette paid no heed. She simply continued about her business. It had been nice until Tarryn remembered that Paulette was nice to everybody. It made him angry to feel that way. It reminded him that nobody was good for free. No matter how convincingly they made it seem so.

Tarryn's mother on the other hand was delighted with her new companion. There was a change to the atmosphere in the house. Tarryn would arrive home to find silvery laughter echoing through the corridors. In a way it made it feel all the more alien. He had thought it might have given him a sense of freedom. Instead, it made him feel like a ghost in his own home.

Had Lady Leersac been able to comprehend the exact nature of Paulette's social status, it was unlikely that she would have made it across the threshold, let alone into the sitting room. Tarryn found their relationship intriguing. There seemed to be nothing that his mother could say, or do, that could throw Paulette from her stride. The last few years of his life had been spent trying fruitlessly to save the last remnants of his mother's addled mind. Lady Leersac did not recognise her own flesh and blood yet Paulette delighted her. Something about it set his teeth on edge.

The rational part of Tarryn's mind knew that it was not Paulette that had been their ruin. But as she sat in their home, drinking tea and making idle conversation, he could not help but notice the way she smelt of other men, the way their cologne lingered on her skin. It was a reminder of how far the family had fallen.

The longer that time went on, the more Tarryn noticed Vanguard becoming distracted. His attentions were often elsewhere. It was galling. When they had made their agreement, Tarryn had hoped that they would be entering into a partnership. He had hoped that eventually Vanguard would come to think of him as an equal. There was money; Vanguard had at least kept his word on that. The business of death was just about lucrative enough for Tarryn to survive on. But that aside, Vanguard was a lacklustre mentor.

Watching Tarryn stride across the skyline, Vanguard

kept both feet firmly on the floor. There was simplicity to the way that he carried out his business which so far had served him well. Tarryn craved approval. The need for validation seeped out of his pores. Vanguard would not stroke his ego by fawning over the ability to jump from one rooftop to the other. It was unnecessary exhibitionism. Dropping down onto the ground, coattails settling around his legs, Tarryn appeared before him without a sound.

Vanguard grunted. "What do you want a parade?"

Tarryn's smile fell. "A little bit of recognition would be nice."

"Congratulations. You can jump off a roof."

Disappointed, Tarryn pushed his hands into his pockets. This time he stuck to the cobblestones. Eventually, the more familiar parts of the city began to fall away. They were clearly going somewhere specific. Vanguard was walking with vigorous intent.

You would think that in a city were places like the Pits could exist; there was unlikely to be another part of town that people would attempt even more fervently to avoid. That was not the case. Some distance from the centre of the Black Zone, was the place known as the Butchers. It was a place that not even Vanguard went without good reason.

Tarryn kept a close watch on the side streets. Each one was plugged with overturned carts and the like. They had been arranged so as to be as obstructive as possible. They were the barricades, the borders that let a person know they were entering into Hector Mandego's territory. Yellow eyes blinked from between bins and boxes scattered across the pathways.

"Let them see you." Vanguard nodded towards the broken windows. Tarryn looked from house to house.

Long curtains fluttered as dirty faces peered out from behind them. They would disappear as soon as the two men drew level – no doubt to relay some message to a counterpart inside. News travelled fast in the Butchers.

There were several men following them. They kept a short distance back, lingering in the shadows. They were sentries. Vanguard knew well enough that their arrival had already been noted by those in the house at the end of the block.

The Butchers ran in a similar manner to the rest of the city. One man sat at the top and everyone else had their place below him. When D'Orsee had been divided, the crime lords had seized the opportunity to each carve out their own little kingdoms. This was the place over which Mandego presided. A thief, forger, extortionist, and racketeer, had Mandego had the money and status behind him that Sanquain had been privy to since birth; it could well have been him ruling over the city instead.

The Butchers was packed to the hilt with criminals. It was a place where you learnt to sleep with one eye open. There were very few things left on earth that still unnerved Vanguard. Nothing put the fear of God into him like a trip to the Butchers. Three years in the Hole would be nothing in comparison to ten minutes in that place if Mandego gave the order.

Mandego was the only man in the Butchers who could authorise the shedding of blood inside their borders. One word from him and Vanguard would find himself spread-eagled on the ground, each limb attached to a different wagon.

"*Vanguard...*" A petite woman with small, sharp teeth stepped out of one of the houses. She hissed as if the sound of his name caused such offense she could scarcely bring herself to spit it from her lips. Patches of dry scalp showed through hair that had been ripped away. A large purple bruise spread across her jaw.

"Catherine Crass, been getting into fights again? Who won this time?"

The woman smiled. Catherine was Mandego's long term and primary lover, a renowned fighter and had an infamous right hook. Flicking her thumb over her shoulder, she laughed a little. Vanguard followed the direction of the thumb. A little distance away was a much younger woman. Both of her arms had been laid out flat against a fence post, tied at the wrists and elbows. The height of the fence made it so that the woman was forced to bend at the waist, head hanging limply over the other side. On hearing Catherine's voice she lifted her head. Vanguard assumed that at one point, her nose had been in the middle of her face. It wasn't any longer.

Catherine yelled across the street. "Don't fancy yourself quite so much now eh Mary?" The woman whimpered indecipherably. Tarryn shifted from one foot to the other. Catherine's head snapped to the right. "Who the fuck is this pretty boy?"

"This is my associate."

Vanguard felt the flickering tension in the air. The time for small talk was over. Every minute they spent in the Butchers was a risk. Catherine shuffled forward, swaying across the cobblestones like a courtesan across a dance floor. She stopped directly in front of Tarryn, sniffing the air around him. "He smells like death."

"I need to speak with Mandego."

Turning her attention back to Vanguard, Catherine spat at the floor. "You've got big balls, I'll tell you that for nothing. You've either got something really important to say or you've got a fucking death wish. Do you know what we did to the last Red Badge that came here?"

"I can imagine."

Catherine leaned in, eyes gleaming. "No, you can't."

"Anyway, I'm not a Red Badge."

"Might as well be, you've killed enough of ours. We don't like those that betray our own kind."

"I've never been your kind, Catherine. Let's not pretend there's honour between thieves."

Catherine looked from Vanguard to Tarryn to the sentries and back again. Finally, she nodded towards the end of the road. "Fine, you come with me. The other one stays here."

"Will he still be alive when I get back?"

"Depends on what you've got to say."

Those born into wealth and privilege might argue, but Vanguard knew that the most valuable possession any man could have in the city was knowledge. It got you further and allowed you to live longer than gold ever could. Information was priceless and Mandego was loaded with it. Catherine lifted the hem of her skirt so as not to scrape it along the floor. There was a rocking to her hips that would have been tempting on a more attractive woman.

They came to a house with men stationed outside the door. The sentries reluctantly moved for Vanguard. Catherine led him down a long corridor, candlesticks set along the floor lighting the way. They stopped at the far end. Pushing open a large set of wooden doors, Catherine swaggered into the room.

Mandego sat on an ornate ceremonial chair, no doubt misappropriated from one of the old churches, both legs swung over the armrest. There was a skinny girl on her knees in front of the chair. One of Mandego's hands held an apple. The other was held by the girl who was furiously scrubbing at his fingernails with a brush.

Of average build, Mandego was a fraction shorter than Vanguard but there was not much in it. They were of similar age, although Mandego had fared better with the years. Over half the children in the Butchers were his bastards. Stamping over to them, Catherine dug her nails into the girl's hair and dragged her to her feet. "Fuck off."

The girl took the brush and scurried away. Mandego took an exaggerated bite of the apple. It took a few seconds longer than necessary for him to swallow the mouthful.

Vanguard glanced left to right. The room was empty aside from the three of them. It had been lavishly decorated with ill-gotten goods in varying states of disrepair. Battered wooden boxes and mismatching tea sets adorned the long table. There were piles of books everywhere. Between those were wads of paper stuffed between pages or rolled up into scrolls and left in piles. Charcoal smudges and dirty finger marks had turned the once white lace cloth beneath them grey. Mandego was not only one of the few men in the Butchers to be literate, he also fancied himself to be something of an accomplished artist.

"John Vanguard. The killer of killers…" Mandego spoke through another mouthful of fruit, spitting juice and pips into the air. "The hunter in the night, the scourge of the underworld, the scary monster under the bed…"

He turned, smiled broadly and lifted both arms into the air. "What brings you to my castle?"

CHAPTER 19
MANDEGO

The air in Mandego's chamber was stifling. There had been a fire burning recently which had left behind the cloying smell of burnt wood and smoke. Dust clung to curtains that had not been opened in several weeks. Vanguard watched Mandego carefully. The man was a snake - one that would bite without warning or provocation. Hector placed both feet on the floor, leaning forward. "So what news did you come to share with me?"

Mandego had a fast, musical manner of speaking. Every word dripped with scorn and derision, yet at the same time came out oddly lyrical. Mandego liked to think of himself as impish. Vanguard thought of him as dangerous. People underestimated him. They ended up dead. Grinning, Mandego threw the core over one shoulder, pressing a finger to his ear. "I'm all ears."

"I'm looking for a murderer."

Mandego leant back, spreading his arms out at both sides as if welcoming an old friend. "Well, you've come to the right place then, which one would you like?"

Catherine sniggered.

"I'm not here for one of yours, not tonight."

Mandego clapped his hands together as if that concluded their business. "Thank you very much. I appreciate that you came all this way to let me know. We shall all rest easy in our beds now. Cheerio, be careful not to get your throat slit on the way out."

"I need your help."

Mandego's face twitched. Vanguard watched as his shoulders began to shake. Laughter echoed around the room. Amused by her lover's mirth and keen to play a part in the proceedings, Catherine followed suit. Bent double, she clutched at her stomach and slapped the surface of the table. After a few seconds Mandego snapped his fingers together in the air. Catherine quietened immediately.

"Oh God help me, you're a funny fucker, Vanguard. It is a shame I have to kill you because you don't half make me chuckle."

There was a blur of movement. Vanguard felt the tip of a blade pressed to his side. It lingered just between his ribs. Glancing down, he saw Catherine flash a sharp-toothed smile.

Mandego's face changed. "You come into my home, with your hands dripping in the blood of my people and have the gall to insult me by telling me that you need my help?" He stood up and marched across the room until they stood face to face. "I will cut your balls off and eat them."

Mandego snapped his jaw together, teeth biting at the air in front of Vanguard's face. There was a good chance he would not live to see the sun rise again. Mandego had no love for Vanguard. As far as the crime lord was concerned, Vanguard was the rabid mongrel perpetually nipping at his heels. He was even less enamoured however, with the Red Badges.

"I'm looking into the deaths of a couple of Reds that got washed up several weeks back. Can you find out who did it?"

"If I could, I'd shake their hand and wish them well."

"You might not, if you knew why I needed to find out."

"And why is that?"

"I think it might be connected to Argent Cooke."

There was a heavy silence. Mandego's eyes narrowed. They were searching for a sign, a telltale tic or muscle movement in Vanguard's face that would determine whether or not it was a lie. After a moment, Mandego turned to Catherine and flicked his head towards the door. "Get out."

Catherine opened her mouth to protest.

"I said out."

Once she had left Mandego strode back to the chair and sat down. His chin came to rest on his balled fist, lips pursed. He made a strange humming noise as he thought. "You really *don't* bring any good news when you turn up, do you?"

"I heard you might know something about Cooke."

Hector was an intelligent man. The people who surrounded him might have been simple, instinctive creatures, but their leader was as sharp as a knife. Vanguard had found no links, no connection to the dead guards anywhere in the Splinters.

"I don't know anything about what happened to him, but I do know this, Sanquain's sent every man he's got out on the search. They've been looking for weeks and turned up nothing. Want to know what's interesting about that?"

Vanguard didn't bother to answer.

"He's got everyone searching *inside* the city, but not a single one of the fuckers has bothered to look outside. I've got a man at the wall, says Sanquain had some ambassador from Lycroix here the other day and didn't say a word about it. The ambassador is Cooke's second cousin, yet he didn't have a clue." Mandego scratched his chin, fingers pulling at the skin. "Now, isn't that a little bit strange?"

Vanguard's lips flattened. It was strange. It was all very strange.

"There, you see? I've given something to you, now you give something to me."

"Fair enough. My associate is carrying a list that details the names of your sentries who have been selling secrets to the Red Badges. We were planning on killing them all tonight but I thought you might like to deal with it your-self. I'm sure you'll want to have a talk with them."

Born in the gutters to a nobody, Mandego had fought for decades to achieve the status he had. It was a rank that he had held unchallenged for years. That did not mean that everyone who followed his lead would remain loyal. Mandego did not offer mercy to traitors. If he did, he would not survive long. Grinning, he snapped his fingers. The door opened and a sentry appeared. Vanguard watched as the two men exchanged a few quiet words.

"It's been nice seeing you again Vanguard. You know, one of these days we really are going to have to have a proper go at killing one another."

"I'll look forward to it."

Mandego laughed. "See you around, John."

At the other end of the street, Tarryn waited at the barricades for Vanguard to return. He was not alone. A quick scan of the road told him that there were at least nine sentries. There were probably more in the shadows. They did not hide well.

"Don't look so afraid, Flowerpot. We ain't going to kill you unless we have to."

Catherine Crass took a swig from an almost empty gin bottle. Perched on the side of an overturned cart, her right leg hung down as she casually kicked it back and forth. The skirt had hitched up to reveal a thick ankle and bare calf. Tarryn looked away.

Catherine laughed. "What's the matter? You not saw legs before?"

"When is Vanguard coming back?"

"When Hector and him are done with their business."

Catherine went back to her gin, losing interest. Tarryn scanned the barricades. Most of the sentries had improvised weapons. Clubs and mallets rested heavy on the ground. They were not real fighters. He tried to temper the agitation that buzzed in his fingers.

"You don't understand how it works around here do you?" Catherine tipped her head to one side as if sympathising.

"What do you mean?"

"Your friend left you here with us because he knows you don't come here without something worth bringing. Now he's gone off up there and left you here. Why do you think that is?"

"I don't know."

Catherine swung both legs over the side of the cart and jumped down. "Whatever valuable manner of thing your friend has got, he don't want you knowing about it. That's why the men are up in the house doing business, and you're out in the cold with me."

Tarryn looked at the floor. This was not the way that

he had envisioned the evening. They were supposed to be stalking marks and cutting throats. Instead, he was standing in a puddle, talking to a woman with less hair on her head than most of the men nearby.

"Don't like it, do you? When there are more of us than what there is of you."

"You're trying to provoke me."

Catherine ran her tongue across the front of her teeth. "Is it working?"

There was no time to answer. Vanguard was walking down the road towards them, arms held above his head. The barrel of a pistol was pointed directly at the centre of Vanguard's back. He came to a stop twenty feet or so away. The man with the gun indicated to one of his comrades. They exchanged whispers, looking back towards Tarryn. It seemed that everything in the Butchers worked via a murderous chain of whispers. One person whispered to another, who then passed it down along the lines until finally, it reached Catherine.

Taking up position behind Tarryn, she snaked her arms around his waist. Tarryn tensed. Catherine ran her hands along the front of his body, fingers probing and searching in each of the pockets. Finally, they found something. Pulling out a folded piece of paper, she stepped away and examined it.

Catherine gave a nod towards Vanguard. "Lovely doing business with you."

A short while later, Vanguard and Tarryn both emerged from beyond the wrong side of the barricade. Vanguard looked up and down the empty streets. He wanted a drink. He needed to get off his feet for a while.

Back in the Tanners they walked into the Ring O'Bastards. Ludnor was behind the bar, watching the proceedings with a knowing eye. Vanguard ordered his tea and was met with the usual derisive snort.

Ludnor looked at Tarryn. "And you are?"

Vanguard answered before Tarryn could speak. "He's with me."

"Does he know the rules?"

"The important ones, yes."

Ludnor reached behind the bar and brought forth a large glass jug. There was a watery brown liquid sloshing around inside the glass. Tarryn looked at it. There were bits of cork floating in the contents. It was a far cry from champagne at The Granville. Vanguard selected a table and they both sat down. He nursed his drink, letting the mug warm his hands. Tarryn sipped at the acrid liquor. It burned all the way down to his toes. "What was on that piece of paper?"

"Names."

Stretching his legs out under the table, Vanguard leaned back. By now the men whose names had been on the list would be knee deep in their own guts, pleading for their lives and trying to shovel their stomachs back inside. Their words would fall on deaf ears. It was unfortunate, being that they were true. There had been three names on the list. All of them had been guilty of crimes worthy of Vanguard's attention. None of them had sold any secrets to Sanquain. Mandego would not stop to worry about that though.

"Why did you even bother to take me with you tonight?"

"I thought it would be wise to have a second pair of hands."

"Bullshit. If you thought that, I would have gone up to the house with you."

Tarryn ran one finger around the rim of the glass. After a moment he removed his hand, letting it come to rest on the surface of the table. Behind them, the toothless man played the piano.

"I needed someone to wait at the barricades with the list. What's the problem? You're fine. We're both alive so stop sulking and get over it."

"And what if Mandego had just taken the list and shot us both?"

"We'd both be dead and I wouldn't be sat here listening to you whining."

Vanguard turned away. The tempo of the music began to increase, the crowd getting livelier. There was a grin on the toothless old man's face. They cheered and roared at every chord and glissando. Vanguard said nothing more. The lines on his face seemed to be etched deeper than usual. Tarryn started to suspect that they were full of secrets.

There was little doubt that Vanguard had taken them to the Butchers that night knowing there was a chance they would not leave. The thing that bothered Tarryn the most, however, was that he was not at all surprised. Vanguard had not taken Tarryn with him that night because he was confident that Tarryn would survive Mandego and his men. It was because Vanguard did not care if he didn't. Even after following every rule, taking heed of every word, Tarryn was still not equal in Vanguard's eyes. They were not partners. He was completely expendable.

CHAPTER 20
SCARRED WHORES

Nobody could quite put their finger on it, but there was a tension to the air that buzzed like a swarm of wasps. Nervous, flickering energy seemed to permeate across the city. The gossips and scaremongers were hard at work. There were all sorts of rumours. The city had gone bankrupt. There was a plague coming. Murderers lurked on every corner. Only half of what was being said was true and it was hardly news. It was simply being delivered in a more exciting manner than usual.

With nothing left for them to do, Tarryn called it a night and made his way back to the Golden Quarter. It had been a disappointing evening.

When he had first started working with Vanguard he had harboured high hopes. The more time they spent together the more he felt them fading away once more. As Tarryn embraced his new life, Vanguard seemed to be losing interest in his. Whatever bond or common link he had hoped to find between them was getting further away with each passing day. Tarryn felt no less alone now than he had before.

Lady Leersac was asleep in the sitting room, snoring gently. Paulette was watching her from the armchair. She lifted a finger to her lips, bidding him not to wake the old woman. She stood, brushing down her skirt. Tarryn escorted her down the hallway. "I suppose you'd better leave."

"Are you sure? I can stay if you want. I'll make you something to eat."

"Why would you do that?"

"Aren't you hungry? When did you last have something?"

Tarryn couldn't remember. The more he thought about it, the more his stomach gnawed at him. Recently he had been preoccupied with other things. Vanguard didn't seem to eat often and there wasn't much time during the day. Tarryn was used to going without.

Paulette was insistent. "I'll make you something."

"Can you cook?"

"I don't know, I never really tried, but it can't be that hard. I can heat soup, make toast and butter?"

Tarryn followed her to the kitchen. She turned the stove on and rummaged through the cupboards, finding very little that she recognised. Long strands of hair hung across her face. Tarryn noticed that she kept touching it. "What's wrong with your face?"

She hesitated. Angling away, Paulette rearranged her fringe hastily and took a pot from the sink. She turned the tap on, filling it with water for tea. A moment later she felt his breath on her neck. Paulette turned slightly. Tarryn was not accustomed to touching women. He kept a wary distance from most people. It was surprising to feel how warm she was up close.

Paulette flushed. "Don't worry about it, it's nothing."

Tarryn pushed her fringe aside a little more forcefully than was necessary. It was not intentional. He just hadn't had much practise at doing it before. Beneath the hair, carefully concealed, were two deep lines, each the size of a woman's finger nail. There was a little blood, the skin red and welted.

"She didn't mean to."

Tarryn looked blankly at the scratches. "I know that. Does it hurt?"

"A little..."

Before he could stop himself, Tarryn pressed one finger to the mark. Paulette winced, shrinking back against the counter. He retracted his hand. Until that moment, Paulette's face had scarcely registered to him. She was pretty, but he hadn't given it much thought. He wondered if it would make a difference to business, if men would find her less desirable.

The thought was more pleasing than it ought to have been. Paulette had done nothing to wrong him. Yet the idea of her blemished, scarred, somehow made her feel more accessible. It made her feel real. He suddenly realised that he was standing very close. Tarryn drew back, letting Paulette continue with her cooking. The water on the stove came to a gentle boil, the bubbles bursting on the surface.

"Will they take you back? If you get scarred, will that...*place* you came from take you back?"

"That's an odd thing to say."

"I didn't mean it to be, I just thought it might affect

things. You can't sell an apple if it's purple and bruised. Nobody wants it."

"I'm not an apple."

Tarryn felt the side of his jaw twitch just below the ear. He often wondered how Paulette felt about what she was. He wondered if she felt ashamed. In her shoes, he would have taken a hot knife to his own face years ago.

"I don't think it will scar. It should be fine in a few days. Besides, who said I need to go back? I could stay here instead; I could help around the house and look after your mother."

The idea had occurred to Tarryn before. His mother had been much easier to handle since Paulette had come into their lives and it did give him a lot of free time. What had not occurred to him was the notion that Paulette might have been eager to agree. For most people, a few hours in Madeline Leersac's company were more than sufficient.

"I couldn't pay you a nurse's wage."

"I'm not asking for a nurse's wage. I'm happy with just a room and food."

Tarryn wondered if it was perhaps Paulette's lifestyle that had given her the ability to seemingly move through life undaunted. In any other woman it would have come across as resilience. Somehow, in Paulette it seemed more naive. The more that he watched her, the more he noticed little things that he had not seen before. The thing that most caught his attention, however, was the presence of a small scar behind her left ear. A thin line, the sort left by a stick or cane. It looked to be at least a few years old. It occurred to him then the reason Paulette might have been so eager to stay.

She found some bread and cut it into thick slices. He

watched the tremor to her hand as the blade tore through the crust. He took it from her, resuming the slicing while she made tea.

"Doesn't it bother you, knowing what I am?"

She shook her head. "I've seen worse."

Paulette did not want to go back to the Black Zone. She wanted to stay despite knowing what he was and despite knowing what his mother was. She wanted to stay because it was better to live in a house with one monster, than to work in a house frequented by hundreds.

There was no scratch or mark that would stop them coming for her. A scarred whore was still a whore. They just paid a little less for the privilege. It would have made him feel better, had it not been quite so tragic.

CHAPTER 21
BEAUTIFUL THINGS

I t is an unfortunate truth of the world that people will always want to soil beautiful things. They cannot simply let them be. It is why there will always be footprints in the freshly fallen snow. Flowers will grow from the earth and somebody will always want to pluck off the petals.

In a place where beautiful things are rare, the desire for them is all the more urgent. It was for that reason, that Henriette employed beautiful girls. They made her more money, that was true. But it was not for that reason that she chose them.

Henriette took in the girls who would, due to the unfortunate fate of genetics, be the most likely to become ruined by the world. They were the ones over whom the people of the city would fight, lay claim to and use until there was nothing left of the beautiful thing that once was. In her own way, she always tried to protect them. It was better to convince her patrons that Henriette's girls were to be preserved. Their work was unpleasant. There was no getting away from the fact. That was just the way it was. At least under her care, the girls had a better chance of avoiding the fates of those in other houses or on the streets.

Sadly, not even Henriette could control the actions of evil men. All the rules in the world did not matter to someone who was willing to break them.

It did not happen often, but every now and again, a client would come to the house that did not see the girls as things to be treasured and revered, but as things to taint and ruin. They took pleasure in knowing that the next person to look upon them would see something that had been broken.

Carmen sat on the edge of the bed, picking at the scab on her right knee. The blood had dried and started to flake. Gazing down at the angry red mark, she kicked the leg out and felt the skin tightening as it stretched. Carpet burn was the least annoying thing she'd had to deal with that particular evening.

She could try for the rest of her life and would still never work out why anyone would find a wimple alluring. None of the girls liked working in the convent suite. The other rooms were at least comfortable. It was difficult to focus on the task at hand when you were surrounded by crosses and scripture. Carmen shifted slightly, the metal springs poking through the thin material.

She turned and looked over her shoulder at the enormous bulk snoring on the bed. She didn't know his name and didn't care. Sometimes they liked to tell her - half the time they were lying anyway. Whoever he was he had clearly had a full evening of excess before arriving. Carmen had barely removed the habit before he passed out. The booking was for thirty minutes and Henriette did not like the girls to leave the room before time. Carmen flicked at the covers.

After another five minutes had passed Carmen scrambled over the unconscious customer and whispered sweet nothings in his ear. There was no reaction. She pushed down on the mattress, shaking it. When that didn't work she had slapped him in the face. The snoring continued uninterrupted. After a while she clambered down to the end of the bed and sat, cross-legged and biting her fingernails.

There was a gentle knock at the door. "Carmen?"

Henriette was using her work voice. It had a much softer tone to her off-duty voice. It sounded warmer, more nurturing and inviting. Henriette said it made her sound more trustworthy. She also used bigger words. The clients seemed to like it. They liked to think of Henriette as being of a higher class than she truly was. They knew it was a lie, but it gave the house an illusion of stature.

Opening the door, Carmen popped her head around the frame. Henriette was decked out in full evening regalia. A black corset lifted and accentuated her already quite obvious cleavage. There was a tasselled fringe that hung around the top of the bust. She waved an ostrich feather fan across her face. "Come downstairs please, I have someone who would like to meet you."

"I'm with someone."

Henriette peered around the door. On seeing the unconscious man on the bed, she rolled her eyes. Drunks were too predictable. "I'll have one of the others come in and remove his trousers. When he wakes up they can tell him he was wonderful and take the money. He'll go home just as happy as a pigeon."

Taking a robe from the hook on the wall, Carmen took

one last look at her sleeping customer and walked out into the hall. The two women made their way down to the waiting room.

There was a slightly built man sitting on one of the chairs, a hand on each knee. He had a reddish blonde tinge to his hair and beard, a pair of glasses perched on the end of his nose. A small bead of sweat clung to the top of his upper lip.

"This is Mr. Bleath. It's his first time, and he's requested you by name."

Carmen smiled and flicked a lock of hair behind her shoulder. "How nice of him."

Something about his face was familiar but she could not work out from where. It was not until he spoke that Carmen realised where it was they had met. Bleath was a clerk in the offices of Felix Sanquain. That meant that he had money and good connections. It was little wonder that Henriette was so willing to make special arrangements.

Carmen held out a hand. Leading Bleath to the next floor, she noticed that there was dampness to his hands. The man was sweating profusely. She tried not to smile. It was always funnier when they were nervous.

Opening the door to the Desert Empress suite, Carmen sashayed in. Mr. Bleath stood in the doorway, hands at his sides. Carmen looked back over her shoulder; forehead tipped forward and eyes slumberous. "Would you like to come in?"

Mr. Bleath stepped inside and shut the door gently. Carmen watched as he took in the room.

Ornate gold statues stood in each corner. The walls were adorned with plush curtains that draped against shimmering silk hangings depicting eastern languages. There was an outfit hanging from the hook on the wall. It was a sheer white cloth that merely skimmed across the skin.

Carmen walked over and ran a finger down the length of the material. "Shall I put this on?"

There was a slight tremor to Bleath's voice. "No, no, what you have on is fine."

"Well then..." Carmen slipped the top of the robe from her shoulders and let it fall to the floor. "What would you like?"

Bleath took a few steps inside the room, stopping and placing one hand on the head of a golden cat. The sounds of the house echoed around them. Some men found it distracting to hear others at work. Some quite liked it. Carmen was not sure which sort Bleath would be.

"Actually, I'd just like to talk to you first."

"Alright, I like talking. What shall we talk about?"

Bleath glanced up. Carmen suddenly felt strangely exposed.

"I'd like to talk to you about John Vanguard."

"Most men prefer talking about other things. Wouldn't you rather talk about something else?"

A smile spread across Mr. Bleath's face. He shook his head. "I'm not like most men."

"I don't know what you'd like me to say?"

"I'd like to know what sort of things he says, what sort of things he does...who his friends are."

Carmen walked across the room and stood at the window. She stroked the ledge in what she hoped looked like nonchalance. Just below, she could see the yard. The stubbly grey hair of Vince's shaved head was just about visible. "You wouldn't find it very interesting."

Bleath walked back to the door and turned the lock. Carmen looked out of the window and then back again.

Across the room, Bleath removed his glasses and placed them carefully on the table. "I think I would."

"Why did you lock the door?"

Carmen watched, breath catching in her throat as Bleath reached into the inside pocket of his jacket and removed a silver cylinder. There was a quiet noise as he pulled it upwards, stretching it out. When it was fully extended, Bleath ran one finger along the length of the metal cane.

"Unlock the door. Unlock it now or I'll scream. Vince will break the door down. He'll be here in a minute."

Bleath looked up to the ceiling and let out a breath. Carmen felt her stomach turn as she watched his whole body shudder with anticipation. "That's all I need."

After several years of working for Henriette, Vince had become accustomed to the many noises that he would hear coming from the house on any given day. There were the groans, the grunts, the squeals, and the bellowing roars. It was like learning a foreign language. The more you heard, the more you were able to decipher what each one meant.

The cigarette that he had been smoking was almost burnt down to the tip when the screams came from the first floor. They were the kind of screams that took Vince across the threshold. Flicking the stub towards the doorstep, he took the stairs two at a time until reaching the top. Henriette appeared behind him. Vince tried the door handle, rattling it. The sound of pleading brought the girls from the other rooms. Henriette gave Vince a nod. Putting the full weight of his body into his foot, Vince kicked at the panel. It shuddered, the wood splintering.

"Please!" The voice came from inside the room.

Henriette removed the pistol that she kept hidden

beneath her clothes. There was one shot loaded. "Vince, get the fucking door open!"

"*Please...*"

Another firm kick and the panel gave way. Bleath had been right. It had taken less than a minute. It was all the time that he needed to convey the message that Sanquain had given. It was written all over Carmen's body. Henriette levelled the pistol at his head. She felt her finger pressed against the trigger. Bleath grinned, wiping away the sweat from his brow.

"You can't shoot me. You know who I work for. Where are your whores going to go if you're swinging from the gallows?"

The barrel shook, anger surging in Henriette's veins. Bleath snapped the cane back down to its original level and placed it back in his pocket. Vince looked to Henriette for instruction. The side of her jaw tensed. Henriette squeezed the trigger. Bleath looked over at the bullet hole lodged into the wall just to the left of his head. Henriette spat at the floor. There was nothing she could do. Not without risking all of them.

"Get him out of my house."

Vince took Bleath by the collar, dragging him down the stairs and out of the door. The clerk did not protest. The work he had come to do had been completed. The girls quickly cleared the other rooms, appeasing their clients with sweet promises of extra special attentions upon their next visit. Vince turned and went back into the house, shutting the door behind him. There would be no more entry until Henriette opened it.

In the bedroom, Henriette knelt at the floor. Carmen lay against the carpet, naked and quiet. Henriette did not touch her. She knew that it would set her body alight and so they simply stayed still for a while. A few of the girls popped their heads around the door. Henriette waved them away. Carmen stared at the patterns on the rug.

Thin red lines screamed out from every inch of her bare skin. Henriette tried to put a blanket over her, but it stung. It hurt to breathe. Tears fell silently from unblinking eyes. After a little while, Carmen felt the touch of Henriette's hand on her head, softly stroking her hair.

Arriving to find the door shut, Vanguard entered the house to virtual silence. The girls sat on the chairs in the waiting room, eyes damp and red. Vince appeared at the top of the stairs, holding a cloth in his hands that had once been white. They passed each other, neither saying a word.

Vanguard had only ever gone up the stairs once before. The first time had been the night that he had asked Henriette to marry him. Ascending them that night, he knew even before they spoke that this time, it would be Henriette's turn to ask something of him.

Carmen was lying on one of the beds in the girl's room, propped up by pillows. Henriette stood looking out of the window. Simone sat behind Carmen, brushing her hair with a soft bristled brush. There was a blanket draped across both the girls, ensconcing them in a cocoon of warmth. Carmen did not look up. She stared at the bed sheets.

Vanguard did not say anything. There was not much that could be said; nothing that would have helped anyway. Henriette nodded towards the door. They left the room, closing it behind them.

"I have a friend with a house near the docks. I think I'll send her there until she recovers. It'll do her no good to be here. She won't know them, but they'll look after her until the wounds heal. A couple of days away will help."

"She should be with people she knows."

"I know, but..." Henriette paused. Vanguard understood. It was hard enough to find people you felt you could trust with your own life in D'Orsee. Finding people you could trust with those you cared about was even harder.

Vanguard looked back towards the closed door. A thought occurred to him. "I think I know someone else who might help her, someone more familiar."

An hour or so later, there was a knock at the front door. Vince opened it, letting their guest into the hallway. After exchanging a few words with Henriette and Vanguard, he made his way up the stairs and into the bedroom. Carmen did not say anything to Kosic. She simply lifted her arms and put them around his neck. As he carried her down the stairs, Kosic nodded to Henriette. "I will not let anything more happen to her, I promise. We will take care of her."

The girls crept from the waiting room, watching as Carmen was taken away. Argue as they might, they were a family. They took care of one another. Kosic left, taking Carmen into the night. Vanguard followed Henriette to the parlour, shutting the door so that their conversation could not be overheard. "Who did this?"

"Mr. Bleath, the clerk from the chambers. She said he came here to ask about you."

"I've put you in danger; I'm a risk to you all. I should leave."

"You were always a risk. I knew that from day one."

"Then why let me stay?"

"Because we all know what you are, even if we don't say it, and we know that each time you go out at night, there's one less bastard like that walking the streets. We don't want you to leave."

"What do you want?"

Part of him had always known that this day would come. Vanguard looked down at Henriette. Other people didn't always see it, but she was really very attractive, or at least, he thought so.

She craned her face upwards until he could feel her breath on his face. "I want you to kill him, John. I want you to make that bastard pay."

CHAPTER 22
THE WORM TURNS

Mr. Bleath was well aware that there would be consequences when he had agreed to carry out the captain's orders at the whorehouse. It did not concern him. He was well paid and well protected. Sanquain had promised as much. What he did not expect, however, was to see Vanguard quite so soon afterwards.

Sitting at his desk, Bleath used a sheet of blotting paper to daub the ink on his documents. Blowing at the fresh signature, he glanced up. At the other end of the corridor, Vanguard stood arms at his sides. He tried to steady the twitching of his fingers, the digits longing already to curl into a fist that would see Bleath's shiny white teeth expelled out through the back of his skull. Bleath smiled. Not even Vanguard would be so stupid as to do anything within the halls of the chambers. "Good morning, how can I help?"

Vanguard knew that the cheerful manner in which Bleath greeted him was designed to push on the raw nerves that had already been exposed. It was working. Vanguard stared down the length of the corridor, imagining killing Bleath in ways that most normal people could not even fathom.

Instead he walked towards the desk. "I have an appointment."

"Very good, Captain Sanquain is waiting for you. Can I offer you a drink?"

"No."

There were fewer than twenty feet between the desk and the door of Sanquain's office. Vanguard only had to make it that far without killing anybody and the day could continue as planned.

Bleath let the tip of his fountain pen linger in mid-air. "I very much enjoyed my time with your friend. Do pass on my regards, won't you?"

The next thing Bleath felt was the crunch of his spine against the wood as the flat of his back was driven down onto the surface of the desk. The decorative moulding of the ceiling looked down at him. Bleath spluttered and choked as the weight of Vanguard's knee crushed his wind-pipe, knocking the glasses from his nose.

"Vanguard." Sanquain stood in the open doorway, watching the scene unfolding before him. "Release my employee immediately and let him return to his business." Vanguard gritted his teeth, pulling away. There was a smack as the clerk's head hit the desk. Sanquain marched back into the office without acknowledging the mess. It would be cleaned up before he emerged again.

The captain wasted no time in getting straight to the point. "I'm concerned that you've not been focusing on your work."

"So you sent Bleath to my home? What, as some sort of warning?"

"I sent one of my clerks to ascertain whether or not

your living arrangements were causing you to become distracted. I'm told there was an altercation in the pursuit of his duties."

"Your man beat a girl half to death. The law says there should be justice."

"That is not your decision to make."

"She's just a girl."

"She's a whore, one who agreed to a transaction and then tried to rob her customer. Your friends should think themselves lucky that I don't arrest the girl and revoke their licenses."

"You know damn well that isn't what happened."

"Regardless, we all know where we stand now. We can move on, is that understood?"

Vanguard glowered. "You know I'm going to kill him."

"I haven't sanctioned any such act. Should any harm come to Bleath I'll have you arrested."

A short time later, issued with instructions for the week and a new list of marks, Vanguard left the chambers and headed for the towpath. He walked along the canal bank until he came to the patch of grass. Sitting down, Vanguard pulled a clump out of the ground and threw it at the water. It scattered on the wind leaving a single daisy behind, growing from the mud. Reaching out, he ran a finger along the stem.

There were at least six names on the scrap of paper in his pocket, all of them criminals that Sanquain deemed deserving of death. Bleath was not one of them. Vanguard had never fancied himself a vigilante. It wasn't his job to rescue people or avenge them. Those days had been over long ago and even then, nobody had ever cared for what he had done. There might have been a benefit to others in the work he carried out for Sanquain, but it didn't make him a good or righteous man. Nor had it made the world a better place.

It had been a long road to get from Bellitreaux to where he sat. Vanguard had seen a lot of things over the years. He did not, however, ever remember having a dream until Carmen had come along and reminded him what it was to be hopeful. His skills had served the wrong people for too long. It was time for Vanguard to make his own list, starting with Bleath.

When he eventually stood, something caught his attention. Pinned to a tree, fluttering in the wind, was a card with a single V on the front. He walked over and ripped the note from the trunk. It was handwritten. The ones that Sanquain used had a printed V on the front. Turning it in his hands, Vanguard read the words on the back. He did not recognise the handwriting.

Close lies the truth.

Placing one hand against the surface of the tree he felt the rough bark beneath his fingers. Bleath's death would mean great changes. Once it was done, Sanquain would know their agreement had come to an end. There would be no turning back. Vanguard needed a place he could lie low for a while, one far away from Henriette.

LUDNOR WAS IN THE RING O' BASTARDS, GOING ABOUT his usual routine of dividing counters on the bar into piles. He did not look surprised to see Vanguard walk in. The barkeeper carried on counting without looking up.

Vanguard had never sat anywhere in the Ring aside from the bar and his usual table. For some reason, he decided to walk across the room and sit at the piano. He had never learnt to play. Maybe he should have done. A single note rang out, Vanguard's finger pressed to the key.

Ludnor tossed a rag over his shoulder. "Something I can help you with, Maestro?"

"I need a place to stay."

"I need a new kidney and a redhead with massive tits to sit on my face, but life's a bloody disappointment, isn't it?"

"I can pay."

"I don't doubt it, but I don't take lodgers."

Vanguard withdrew his hand from the piano and turned around on the stool. "Do you remember when I asked you before, how you'd managed to live so long?"

Ludnor snorted. "Vaguely."

"I've worked out what it is."

"Do tell?"

"You're alive because I've never wanted to kill you before now."

Ludnor had terrible eyebrows. They began to move, two great hairy slugs twitching away. His eyes creased as the smile spread over his face. Vanguard started to laugh. They enjoyed the moment of levity. They were few and far between.

"Piss off, haven't you heard by now? I'm invincible."

The barkeeper reached into the pockets of the apron. He fished around for a moment before retrieving a key. Ludnor threw it across the bar. Vanguard snatched it before it hit the ground.

"There's a shed in the back. It's got a hole in the roof and you'll have to share with the cat. Keep it locked when you leave and don't stay long, I don't want it getting out around town that I'm opening up a fucking B&B." Ludnor pulled the rag away and started wiping at the counter. "And don't expect me to make your fucking breakfast."

Once Vanguard had inspected the inside of the shed, he locked it up and put the key in the bag. The old ginger cat had been inside, curled up on a sack and purring gently. Vanguard had lived with cellmates before. At least this one would keep the rats out.

There was one more stop that he needed to make. Vanguard was starting on a journey that would not end well for him. Where he was going, he could not take the boy with him. From that moment on, for better or worse, Tarryn was on his own.

Paulette was wearing a large feathered hat that had been lent to her by Lady Leersac. They were playing a game of cards. It was impossible to tell what kind of game they were playing although every now and again Lady Leersac would yell 'snap' with great delight. They were quite obviously not playing snap. Tarryn's mother looked up and grinned. "Bishop, how lovely to see you. Do you play cards?"

"Usually yes, but sadly I can't stay very long. You look very nice though."

Lady Leersac looked pleased at the compliment. She waved a hand towards Paulette who smiled and gave Vanguard a polite nod in greeting. "Have you met the Countess of Briage?"

"Oh yes, many times. Hello Countess, nice to see you again."

"Hello Bishop." Paulette replied, not missing a beat.

Tarryn could sense that something had changed. Vanguard seemed even more tightly wound than usual. The two men went into the kitchen at the back of the house. Tarryn could already feel that whatever Vanguard was about to say, it would not be good news.

"What we've been doing, our arrangement. It has to come to an end."

"What do you mean end come to an end? It can't end; this city is crawling with criminals."

"After tonight it won't be my problem. You're on your own."

Tarryn pressed his hands to the edge of the sink, knuckles turning white. Vanguard saw the resentment in his eyes. Rejection was hard for Tarryn to take. Whatever he had been hoping for from their brief time together, Vanguard could no longer offer it. Tarryn needed to find his own way in the world. It was time for them to separate.

"You know what you're doing now, mostly. You don't need me anymore."

"But I do need you, how the hell else do I find work? Do you know who I am?"

"I'm sorry. Where I'm going next, I can't take you with me."

"So that's it? It was all just a waste of time..."

Vanguard reached into the bag and pulled out a leather pouch. He placed it on the counter next to the sink, a few inches from Tarryn's hand. Tarryn glared down at the bag. Vanguard turned and walked out of the house, leaving Tarryn alone at the kitchen sink. The front door clicked shut. A few moments later Paulette appeared in the door-way. She removed the feathered hat. Lady Leersac called from the sitting room, urging her to return to the game.

"Is everything alright?"

The concern in her voice made his jaw ache. A small hand reached out and touched his. Tarryn snatched it away, shock at her touch reverberating across his body.

Paulette looked startled. Had she thought that they were friends? Tarryn shook the thought away. They weren't friends.

"What can I do to help?"

"Why do you keep trying to help us? What's wrong with you?"

Paulette looked disappointed. "There's nothing wrong with me."

"I can't afford to pay you anymore. You have to leave."

"I don't understand, we're playing a game. I don't mind, I like you. I like both of you."

"Why?"

"I don't know. You don't look at me like other men do."

What Paulette meant as a compliment, Tarryn felt like a slap to the face. "Don't I?"

Lady Leersac was calling once again, lamenting at the lack of tea.

"I like being here. I like taking care of you both."

For a brief moment, Tarryn allowed himself to believe that Paulette might be speaking the truth. She might truly like them, both of them, as they were. It felt comforting. She reached out and took hold of his hand. She was warm. He could feel her pulse against the skin of her wrist. She moved closer, eyes full of softness and whispered in quiet tones. "Aren't you lonely?"

He swore that he could still smell cologne on her skin. There were probably still rug burns on her back. It didn't matter what Paulette wanted to be or what they pretended she was, outside in the real world, Paulette was for sale. Every touch, every whisper was a lie, murmured through well-practised lips.

"You're not a countess. You're not a nurse. You're a...a...."

Paulette snatched her hand away. "I know *exactly* what I am."

"Then no doubt you'll be glad to get back to it."

Her cheeks flushed pink. Tarryn couldn't be sure if the increased redness was due to anger or humiliation. Perhaps it was the fear of going back to the place she had come from and what they would do to her. There was sudden and unexpected warmth radiating from Paulette's being, like she was burning up with a fever.

"You can think what you like. I might not *like* what I am, but I didn't choose it and I won't apologise for it." Paulette was clearly trying to maintain some sort of dignity. She would have sounded quite self-assured had the words not spilled out far too quickly. Plucking the hat from the counter, she placed it back on her head and turned away. "I'm finishing the game and then I'm leaving. Don't worry, I won't come back."

Tarryn watched her stalk back into the other room. Her head was held high but the glow of her cheeks refused to fade. They did not speak again. Instead Paulette engaged in inane chatter with his mother about the state of the city hall, refusing to look up from her cards. She knew there was no point in trying. He couldn't tell if the prospect of never seeing Paulette again was a relief or a disappointment. Eventually he turned and walked back into the kitchen to sit alone.

⚜

A SHORT WHILE LATER, ACROSS TOWN VANGUARD STOOD leaning against a fence. Bleath lived in the part of the city that was reserved for those too high ranking to live in the Black Zone, but who were generally considered not a part of high society. The residents of Malmouth were mostly business owners, high-level administrators and the occasional cleric kept around for show by Sanquain. There was a dim light glowing in the upper window of Bleath's home.

Most people tried to avoid going out after dark. If you couldn't afford to take a carriage from one place to the other, you didn't bother. It was too close to the Black Zone. If anything, the risk of mugging or worse was higher here than in other places, because here people had things actually worth stealing.

The shadows cast across his face. Vanguard kept out of sight. The quiet night air was broken by the sound of a cheerful whistle. Vanguard didn't know the tune, but he knew that it was meant for him.

A lilting voice curled into the air. "John Vanguard, come out, come out, wherever you are."

Vanguard unfolded his arms and stepped out from behind the fence. On the other side, Mandego stood peeling a pear with a small knife. The peel was discarded to the floor. Mandego turned his head, taking a chunk of fruit from the knife and speaking through a mouthful. "What brings you to this fine part of town?"

"I could ask you the same thing."

Mandego chewed the piece of fruit thoughtfully, looking at the floor. Eventually, he looked back up. "Just out for a walk, aren't I?"

"You've walked a long way from The Butchers."

"Been a lot going on. Word has it you're about to go rogue. Didn't want to miss that."

Vanguard didn't ask from which source Mandego had managed to procure that particular snippet of information. The man had a way of finding things out. "How'd you find me?"

Mandego tapped the side of his head with the blade of the knife. He looked quite pleased with himself. "I don't need to know where you are to find you; I just need to know where you're going."

"Care to share the reason why you've found me now?"

"I've been hearing things, rumours and such. You know how much I love a good rumour."

"There seems to be a lot of them around these days."

"Doesn't there just? And do you know what I've discovered?"

"Enlighten me."

Mandego threw the middle part of the pear onto the floor. Vanguard watched as he lifted the knife to his mouth and made a lavish show of sucking the juice from the blade.

Mandego spoke from around the metal. "There's another war coming Vanguard, I can feel it. The air stinks of it. Something's brewing. It wouldn't take much to spark off a riot."

"Whatever you're thinking of starting Hector, it won't end well for you."

Mandego laughed heartily. "Oh, I'm not starting anything. I don't need to. I'm just waiting for the pot to bubble over. When it does, I'll be right in the thick of it." He jabbed the knife into the air, carving the night into pieces. "And you best believe I'm going to take my slice when it does."

Vanguard saw the light in the upstairs window of Bleath's house go out. If he and Mandego were going to kill each other, they would have done it by now. Hector was too smart for that. Their final moment together would not happen until the time came when they could no longer be of use to each other. "Enjoy your walk Hector."

"Enjoy whatever it is you're doing Vanguard. Don't forget when everything starts going to shit that I was the one that warned you first."

"You're a model citizen."

Mandego winked. "Every worm turns eventually. I'll be seeing you then." Turning on his heels, he pursed his lips together and resumed whistling. Vanguard watched him getting further away until he disappeared into the distance. The man knew how the city worked. If there were riots brewing then Mandego would know about them before they even happened.

It didn't matter. Whatever fight Mandego could feel coming, Vanguard had a war of his own to wage. Tugging the collar of his jacket upwards, Vanguard slipped one hand into the bag and made his way across the street.

CHAPTER 23
THANKS FOR THE CAKE

Vanguard did not like to make a habit of killing people in their own homes. It was often more work than necessary and there was always the risk of other people interfering in the process. Out on the streets, it was quicker, less intimate. This one was different. This one was personal.

Bleath was no different to any of the other people that Vanguard had killed over the years. He was a scar on the face of the earth, one that liked to beat girls with a metal cane. If Vince had not broken the door down, Carmen probably would not have survived. In any house other than Henriette's, they would have chosen to save the door instead.

There was no chance that this was the first young woman that Bleath had taken the cane to. A man who enjoyed the experience as fervently as he had done was no amateur. Vanguard wondered how many there had been before. There would not be any more.

The back door was not hard to open, leading into a kitchen with cold tiled floors. A pot sat on the stove, the remnants of supper still slightly warm. It had been prepared by a cook who had left at ten. Vanguard knew that because he had watched her leave.

Inside the house, Vanguard was not surprised to find that Bleath lived well beyond the means of a clerk. The furnishings alone were more the kind one expected to see in the homes of merchants and traders. There was no way that Bleath had furnished it from his own pocket.

Vanguard walked through the hallway. A grandfather clock, far too big for the size of house, provided an unexpected obstacle. Vanguard slipped lightly around it. The sound of ticking was audible throughout the house. He moved into the sitting room. It seemed like every other sitting room that Vanguard had ever seen. There was a large bureau against the back wall, a framed portrait of Bleath and a stern-faced elderly woman above it. The fireplace still smouldered. Vanguard knelt down for a moment and put his hands out to feel the heat. The rug beneath his feet was woven into intricate patterns. Vanguard could not help but wonder what manner of clerical task Bleath had completed for Sanquain to gift him with such fine surroundings.

Climbing the stairs, Vanguard ran one hand along the banister. There was not a speck of dust anywhere. As he walked to the door of the bedroom, Vanguard took the knife from the bag and gripped the handle. He was about to push the door open when he paused.

There was another door on the other side of the hall.

Something about it was calling out to him. The hairs on the back of his neck stood on end. Retracing his steps back, he tried the handle. The door was locked. Vanguard bent down on one knee, lifting the flap of the bag. After a second of digging around, he located a thin piece of wire and inserted it into the lock. There was a bit of resistance and finally, a click.

He walked through the room in the dim moonlight. It took a moment for Vanguard to realise what it was he was looking at.

In the centre was a large oak cross, a number of hooks protruding from out of the wood. Shackles dangled from each end, attached to a long, thin chain. There was a camera on a tripod, set up to face the centre of the room. The entire back wall was a mirror, stretching across the full length of the room. Bleath liked to watch himself from all angles it would seem. A long table stretched out, the surface covered with various tools and instruments.

Vanguard picked up a single item. It was a metal contraption with pincer ends and a mechanised spring. Vanguard had seen traps laid out for rats and foxes before. This reminded him of that. Placing it back on the table, he moved quietly through the room. There were clasps, clamps and a variety of canes - at the end, there was a large wooden box. He did not need to open it to know what it contained. Vanguard opened it anyway. He needed to see it for himself.

The box was full to the brim with photographs.

Carmen had not been the only one, nor had she been the first. It was not just women either. Girls, boys, men - Bleath was indiscriminate. He closed the lid and walked back towards the door. Part of him hoped that it would never be opened again. It was a false hope. Sanquain would send someone to come the next day and clean up the mess. Nobody else would ever know.

Bleath was a snorer. The man had no problems sleeping. Vanguard stood in the corner of the room and watched his chest rise and fall. It was strange. He had never watched one of his marks that way before.

Perhaps it was the difference between having seen the photos and not. Until then, Vanguard had never felt the need to look at the faces of his victims in the actual moment that they died. The pictures had changed that. They would be forever etched into his memory. He saw the fear, the pain and most of all the disappointment that the world had abandoned them to such a horrible fate. It was in their eyes, captured forever in sepia tones.

As Bleath lay blissfully unaware of his presence, body covered in silk sheets and heavy blankets, Vanguard realised what the worst thing about dying was. It was not the pain. It was not the suffering. The worst thing about dying was the moment that you knew it was inevitable. When you felt it coming and thought of all the things you had never done. All the moments in life that you wished had been different.

There was nothing more than a split second between being alive and being dead. That was what Bleath captured with his camera. Vanguard needed to see that look in Bleath's eyes.

Placing the bag on the floor and removing his jacket, Vanguard rolled up his sleeves. A weaker minded man might have taken a few of the instruments laid out in the torture chamber across the hall. They would have made Bleath suffer in ways that could not be imagined. He could have wedged the razor blades beneath his fingernails and forced him to bite down on the iron bar until his teeth shattered in his jaw. That was not what Vanguard was. It was not who he wanted to be.

Vanguard was not pain and torture, he was not suffering. Vanguard was the split second between life and death;

the instant where you saw your life flash before your eyes and you knew, completely and definitively, that you deserved to be where you were right at that moment.

Leaning over the bed, Vanguard took the knife and let it hover over Bleath's chest where his heart ought to have been. He watched it rise and fall. Moving his face closer, Vanguard opened his mouth and spoke. "Wake up, Bleath."

Two eyes snapped open, the realisation of whose voice it was forcing Bleath's mind to hone into focus just long enough to feel the tip of the knife plunge all the way into his body. The dead man's head fell to the side, eyes staring at nothing. Vanguard ripped the knife away.

If he had been expecting to feel some relief, some alleviation from the weight on his shoulders, he would have been disappointed. Fortunately for Vanguard, he was wise enough to know that would not happen. Killing was not a joy or privilege. It was just necessary.

Walking back down the stairs, Vanguard felt his eyelids growing heavy. It had been a long day and he needed sleep. Something was bothering him though, a voice that told him there was still more to be seen. Something he had missed that he could not quite put his finger on. It was pulling him back towards the sitting room, insistently whispering '*look again*'.

The bureau looked innocuous enough. It was a fairly standard thing to see in the home of an administrator. Working in the offices of the Golden Quarter meant a lot of paperwork. They often took work home with them. It struck Vanguard then, what it was that bothered him. It was empty. An inkwell and a pen sat in a holder on the top, but otherwise, it was free of clutter. A clerk's desk ought to have been full of notes. There would be ink smudges and blotting papers. Bleath's desk held none of these.

Taking a seat, Vanguard ran his fingers along the smooth leather padding on the surface. His fingers trailed in the dark, feeling along the length of the desk and down to the drawers. The first slid open easily. It contained, as many drawers in the city did, a single pistol and a number of shots. There was nothing else.

The second was stiff. It contained documents, a folded flyer sitting amongst them. Vanguard opened it and found he was looking at the advertisement for Herveaux's club. His brow furrowed. Glancing down once more, he saw another photograph lying on top of a pile of opened letters still in their envelopes.

This one was not of one of Bleath's victims. The photo was probably a good ten years old if not more. The man to the far right he did not recognise. The one in the middle, he recognised immediately. He was considerably older now, with hair the colour of ash. A woman stood beside him, face fixed to the camera with a determined gaze. Vanguard's eyes came to rest on the final figure in the photograph.

Standing on the left, as clear as the light of day, was Argent Cooke. It was not, however, Cooke that caught Vanguard's attention. It was the woman.

Vanguard did not know who she was, but he recognised what she wore. Just beneath her chin, pinned to the top of her collar was a pin with a pearl top. There was nothing special about it. There were probably a hundred women or more with the same pin. Most people would have cited it as nothing more than a strange coincidence. Vanguard did not believe in coincidence.

HENRIETTE'S HOUSE WAS QUIET. THE GIRLS HAD GONE to bed. Vanguard crept quietly up the stairs. He did not know if the girls would be awake or asleep. It was not clear which would be preferable. As he knocked gently, he heard Annabelle's voice. "John?"

The girls were all sitting on the same bed in their nightgowns. Simone had her knees hitched up and her arms wrapped around them. Annabelle unfurled from beneath the blanket and padded barefoot across the wooden floor. The other girls climbed down from the bed, walking over to join them. Simone wiped her nose with the back of her hand.

She sniffed. "You're leaving us, aren't you?"

"I think its best I go away for a while."

Just a few hours ago, Vanguard had been tearing open the chest of a man who liked to hang girls like Simone and the others from hooks to watch them squirm. Now he was standing in their bedroom, awkwardly looking at the ceiling as the girls wrapped their arms around him and sniffled as though they were saying goodbye to an old friend.

"We'll miss you."

Vanguard searched for something poignant to say. He cared about the girls and Henriette. But he was not their father, or their lover, or their protector. He was just someone who had come into their home and settled in like an old cat.

In the end, he plumped for something simple. "Likewise."

Down in the parlour, Vanguard sat at the table and tried to write a note for Henriette. There were a lot of things that he wanted to say. Words did not come easily to him. He wasn't entirely sure if anything needed to be said at all. He scribbled on a scrap of paper and left it sitting on the table.

It's done. Thanks for the cake. John.

Vanguard stood up, placed the bag over his shoulder and let out a breath. It was time to go back to the Splinters. This time, there would be no more secrets, no more lies.

❦

KOSIC HAD AN APARTMENT ACROSS THE STREET FROM THE club. Carmen was sitting up on a cot, propped in place by a stack of cushions. Her injuries were painful, but Mira had turned out to be something of a pharmacist. The powder that she mixed with water and honey had taken the edge off. When she saw Vanguard approaching, she tried to smile through the pain. As he drew closer, the look on his face forced the smile away. Carmen's mouth went dry. "Is something wrong?"

"You lied to me."

"I don't know what you mean."

Vanguard thrust a hand under Carmen's nose, opening the fingers to reveal the pin sitting in the palm of his hand. She looked up, the guilt etched all over her face. "Who gave this to you? Don't lie to me."

The floorboard behind him creaked. Vanguard turned around. There was a blur of movement. Vanguard felt a blast of intense, burning pain. It was followed by a loud bang. Everything went black.

When he eventually opened his eyes again it became apparent that some time had passed. The room was darker, the light fading. He guessed that he had been unconscious for several hours. It felt as though someone had pointed a shotgun at his temple. Touching his face, he found an angry bruise on his nose. It had not been a bullet that had struck him.

It had been a very large fist.

Carmen was peering over him, a look of genuine remorse on her face. "Is your nose broken?"

Vanguard groaned. "Why? Am I not pretty anymore?" He sat up, turning his attentions to Kosic who was sitting in an armchair. Vanguard frowned. "I thought you didn't like fighting?"

"That was not fighting, that was hitting."

Satisfied that Vanguard was relatively undamaged, Carmen crawled back into bed and pulled the covers tight around her shoulders. Kosic brought another blanket over for her. There was a cold bowl of soup sitting on the table next to the cot. Kosic had told her it had vegetables in it that were good for healing. She had no idea what a beet-root was, but Kosic had been adamant about it.

"I'm not sure why it was necessary?" Vanguard asked.

"I come home and I see strange man creeping in dark. I don't think to ask him questions." Kosic cracked his knuckles. "You are fine now."

Shaking his head, Vanguard stuck one finger in his ear. "Debatable."

Kosic seemed to be thinking for a moment. In the end he shrugged. "Can you walk?"

Vanguard got to his feet. There was a ringing in his ears that he doubted would go away anytime soon. He nodded at Kosic. Leading him down the stairs and back out onto the street, Kosic gestured for Vanguard to follow him into the back of the club. Once inside, they reached a wooden lift, designed to be hauled into the air for use in the rafters. As they stepped into it, Kosic closed the gate behind them.

Vanguard looked up at the ceiling. "This lift doesn't actually move, does it?"

"No, it does not." Crouching down, Kosic pried the floor panel upwards. Beneath the lift was a trapdoor. "Follow please." He disappeared down into the hole. Glancing around, Vanguard dropped down after him, landing about eight feet below. There was a tunnel beneath the club, stretching in both directions. Kosic was forced to stoop slightly in places, the ceiling getting lower as they walked along.

"Did you kill Cooke and the Red Badges?"

"Keep up please."

"What is this?"

"This? This is a tunnel."

"How far does it go?"

"Far enough."

Eventually Kosic stopped. There were glowing lamps placed all along the floor, dotted here and there to give a soft glow of light. There was a door in the side of the wall. Vanguard hesitated. "What is this really?"

"What you have been looking for."

Vanguard walked the last few paces and pushed it open.

The room was starkly furnished with bare walls. There were lamps placed on the floor and another on a desk in the middle of the room. Sitting on a simple wooden chair, with his back turned and body hunched over the desk was a man. He was writing something at great speed. The scratching of the nib stopped, the pen held in mid-air.

Vanguard stood there, the truth finally revealed. All the time that he had spent searching the Splinters for the murderer of the Red Badges, he had been looking for the wrong thing.

Argent Cooke put the pen down on the table and turned his head slightly. "Hello John. I expect you have a lot of questions."

CHAPTER 24
A PULL OF THE STRING

There was enough money left in the kitty to see them through to the end of the week. Beyond that they'd be back to burning the furniture and living off bread and jam. Sitting in the armchair, looking at the squirrel in the jar, Tarryn thought of the promises that had been made and broken. Months of his life gone by and for nothing; he was back to where he started.

Tarryn had done everything that he was supposed to do. He had followed every rule. He had tempered his rage. Vanguard had told him to hone his talents and master his instincts. Then he had pushed him away without as much as an explanation.

He needed to get out of the house. The walls were closing in on him. Lady Leersac had a slight tickly cough. It was nothing to worry about, but acting like it could be would buy him a few hours. Tarryn arranged for a carriage to take them to the hospital in the centre of town. They arrived shortly after nine. Tarryn left her in the capable hands of the nurses and told them that he would be back to collect her at midday. His mother was quite happy basking in the attention.

It was not difficult to get across town. Tarryn could adjust easily between being seen and going unnoticed. Vanguard had at least taught him that.

Before they had met, he had assumed it was some sort of affliction that caused him to disappear into a crowd. Now he was beginning to see the advantages. He walked by a market stall laden with cakes and scones. He picked one up and took a bite. The stall owner reeled around, eyes quickly counting the wares. Turning to the young boy who was sweeping at the floor around the table, the owner clipped him around the ear. The boy denied the theft fervently. Tarryn watched, amused as the smell of orange peel and cinnamon lingered in his nostrils.

Perhaps it was better that he and Vanguard had parted ways. There would not have been much time in it before they began to outgrow one another. They would meet again, Tarryn was certain of that much. They walked the same path. The difference was that now Tarryn could see where the path was leading him. Vanguard had been an interesting interlude, one that had prepared him for a life where others could not tread. But inevitably, he would have only slowed him down.

The stall owner slapped the boy who pouted, cheeks flushing red with indignation. Seeing the boy rubbing the side of his face, Tarryn smirked. It wasn't fair, but the boy had to learn. Life wasn't fair. He ate the last of the cake and melted into the crowds.

There were a few miles of ground to cover between the hospital and the part of town that he was heading for. He had only been there once before but was confident it would not be hard to find again. Meanwhile, there was no reason not to test the extent of his skills. He felt the chilling rush of freedom tingling across his skin. Tarryn had never been out in the city unshackled before, not without something to hold him back. For years it had been his mother; for the last few months it had been Vanguard.

Now, as the people hurried around him, Tarryn stood in the midst of it all unseen and unheard. They kept their heads down, not noticing anything around them. It was the first time that he had truly seen the opportunities that lay before him. It was the first time that he felt that what he was could be a blessing just as much as it could be a curse. Tarryn could do what he wanted.

Stretching out one hand, he gently brushed the shoulder of a woman passing by. She turned, face creased with confusion. Tarryn laughed. The woman shook her head and carried on about her business, convinced it had been the wind.

Tarryn looked at his own hand, turning it over and examining it. Brimming with anticipation, he walked over to one of the stalls and perused the goods. He had no intention of taking anything for himself. He was above petty crime. The people around him, however, were certainly not. It would be an experiment. Tarryn knew what his true nature was, how long would it take for others to show theirs?

Selecting a bottle of tonic, Tarryn dropped it into the bag of a passing woman. He stood back, intrigued as to what might happen next. People were, in his experience, predictable beings. They had the illusion of knowing what was happening around them.

As expected, the stall keeper stepped out from behind the table and took hold of the woman's arm. She cursed at him as she was accused of a crime that she had not committed. The stall keeper was having none of it, delving one hand into the bag and holding the bottle up triumphantly. An interested crowd began to gather, faces craning to see what was happening.

Tarryn tilted his head to one side. The husband of the woman was arguing her innocence whilst the accuser refused to relinquish his grip. Adrenaline rushed through Tarryn's veins. With both hands he pushed a spectator, shoving the unwitting man into the back of the stall holder and sending them both clattering to the floor.

Glass smashed against the cobblestones, the bottle breaking and its contents slipping out onto the ground. The husband of the woman swung a fist around, angrily shouting at the gathered onlookers. Chaos erupted. The people began to descend into petty squabbles. They shoved at one another, the sound of the rabble drifting across the market canopies.

Reaching up, Tarryn hauled his body upwards, climbing up onto a nearby overhanging roof. Standing several feet above them all, he watched. They were like animals. It had taken nothing for them to turn on one another. A smile crept over his face. All it took was a pull of the string and the puppets would dance.

In the distance, the clock chimed twelve times. Tarryn's smile fell. It was already midday and he had not completed the tasks that he had set out to do. There was also a large brawl occurring in the middle of the market-place. What had started as a practical joke had become anarchy.

Tarryn chided himself for being so stupid. Starting fights and picking pockets was childish and ridiculous. Dropping down from the canopy, he almost landed on top of a young woman carrying a basket. The woman turned and frowned. Tarryn did not have the time to worry about being seen at that point. If he was not back at the hospital within the next few minutes, Lady Leersac would be free to wander the streets unsupervised. There was no telling what that could entail.

"Oh, hello..."

It took a minute for Tarryn to recognise Paulette without the hat. He had been so used to seeing her in it at the house. She looked different in the daylight. There were freckles across the bridge of her nose. It took a moment for him to realise that he was staring.

"Sorry, I didn't recognise you."

"It's alright, I'm used to it."

Tarryn realised that, for Paulette, it was not unusual for a man to see her once and forget all about her entirely once their transaction was completed. They could walk right past her on the street and not know they had ever met.

"I'm sorry – I can't stop."

Paulette looked around confused. "Where is your mother?"

"At the hospital, I'm going there now and I'm late, which is a shame because I had plans."

"I could go and mind her if you need to run errands?"

Tarryn looked at her curiously. "Why would you do that? Have you forgotten what I said to you the other night?"

She shook her head. "No, I haven't forgotten. What you said was true, no point in being angry about the truth."

It was an interesting perspective. Tarryn generally found the truth made him nothing but angry. "Well, I'm sorry that I said it. Do you really not mind? I wouldn't be very long."

"I don't mind, I've got nowhere else to be and I'd like to see her again."

Paulette assured Tarryn that they would perfectly fine and would wait in the tea shop across the lane from the hospital. Tarryn thanked her and watched as she walked away. Paulette was nicer to him than he deserved. She was nicer to everyone then they deserved. He would never be able to see her for anything other than what she was, but as whores went, she was the only one he had ever felt sorry for. Not that sympathy was a worth a thing to anyone.

Focusing on the task ahead, Tarryn walked in the direction of the Butchers. There were few people around. Even in the daytime nobody strayed too close to the barricades. Tarryn slipped by unnoticed. A few of the sentries lay about the streets, legs spread in front of them as they sat on the kerbsides. They scratched and yawned idly.

A muscular dog with brown and white markings pulled at the chain it was tethered to, growling and snapping at the air. A sentry looked up and, on seeing nothing, threw an empty bottle at the dogs head. The animal yelped in alarm. Tarryn held one finger up to his lips and held the creatures gaze. The dog sat back, tongue hanging from its mouth and panting. After a moment it lay down in the dirt.

At the other end of the street Mandego was sitting on a fold-out chair that had been brought outside. It had been placed on the opposite side of a small wooden table to Catherine Crass. They were playing a board game of some sort, which Mandego was clearly winning. Catherine did not look particularly invested in the game. Mandego did not like to lose, so it was wiser not to try. She sat with her legs spread, swigging from a gin bottle. Elegant was not a word that one would use to describe Crass. They did not notice anything until the moment that Tarryn slid the blade of the knife beneath Catherine's chin. She started slightly at the feeling of the cold metal.

Mandego remained still. Tarryn was pretty sure they could see him now. Mandego did not look up. Tarryn was not certain that he had done it properly. He ought to have known he was there.

Mandego eyed the board, thoughtfully, rubbing his chin. After a moment, he picked up one of the counters from the board and moved it in a diagonal motion to the empty space above it.

"So it turns out that John Vanguard isn't the only sneaky little fucker around."

Tarryn dug the length of the blade closer against Catherine's skin.

Mandego was unperturbed. "Where is Vanguard then? Mewling at the barricades? Sent you to do his dirty work did he?"

This was not the conversation Tarryn had anticipated. "I'm not here to talk about Vanguard."

The look of resolve on the boy's face sent Mandego into a fit of laughter. "You haven't got a fucking clue where he is do you? Oh dear, your friend has gone and dropped you right in the shit, hasn't he? Well, you and the rest of this city." Mandego clicked his tongue against the roof of his mouth. "You shouldn't have come here. That was a mistake."

"I'm not scared of you."

There was the sound of several pistols being cocked at the same time. Tarryn looked around. From all directions, sentries stood with their guns levelled at Tarryn's head.

Catherine grinned smugly. Mandego looked up from the game board and locked eyes with Tarryn.

"Boo."

Reluctantly, Tarryn pulled the knife away from Catherine's neck. She reached up and rubbed at the skin, looking at Mandego in irritation. He pouted and tipped his forehead down as if in apology. Catherine harrumphed and turned away in protest.

"Have you met my lovely companion?"

"We've met."

"Bloody delight she is, isn't she?"

Catherine did not look to be in the best of moods. "Alright pretty boy?"

Mandego slammed a fist on the table. Catherine smirked. He turned back to Tarryn. "You see, the thing with you and Vanguard is that you think just because you can do what you can do, you're bloody unkillable, which makes you a pair of cocky bastards. I, however, happen to know that you are not unkillable."

Mandego tapped the side of his head twice with two fingers. "It's like I've said to Vanguard, I don't need to know where you are, I just need to know where you're going. You set one foot wrong now and there'll be more holes in you than there are in a tart's tights." He flicked one hand and Catherine stood, leaving the chair opposite empty. "Now, would you like to sit down and have a nice conversation like a proper grown up?"

Tarryn slipped the knife back into the belt beneath his coat and sat. He did not appreciate being spoken to like a child. Mandego thought he was better than him. The crime lord had something he needed though. Tarryn slid a piece of paper across the table. "I need this."

Mandego picked it up and glanced at the scrawled writing. "This? You can get this from any pharmacist."

"Not in the quantities that I need and not as quickly."

"Are you planning on bringing down an elephant?"

"Can you get it or not?"

Mandego snorted. "Get it? There's probably some under the kitchen sink." He snapped his fingers. "Someone run to the cupboard and fetch this for me."

One of the sentries took Tarryn's prescription from Mandego's fingers. They sat on opposite sides of the table, waiting and watching each other. Mandego never seemed to blink. "Are you and Vanguard not friends anymore then?"

"We were never friends."

"That's interesting."

"Why, what's it to you?"

"I'm just very interested in what Vanguard is up to these days."

The sentry returned and deposited a small brown bag at Tarryn's feet. Reaching down, he opened it up. It was full of glass vials, enough there to keep them going for a month. He closed the bag again, drawing the string up tight.

Mandego looked amused. "You do know that a five-year-old girl could have gotten that, right? I get that you're new to all of this but promise me next time you'll ask for something a little bit more exotic."

"What do I owe you?"

"You owe me a favour."

"What sort of favour?"

"I'll tell you when I need one."

Mandego ordered one of the sentries to see Tarryn safely back across the barricade. As the boy walked away

Catherine cocked her head to one side. Chewing on a slice of orange, Mandego wiped away the juice from his bottom lip. "What'd you think then Cath?"

Catherine shook her head. "Looks like an arrogant little prick to me."

Mandego smiled and moved his counter across the playing board.

With his business concluded, Tarryn made his way back towards the hospital. The walk gave him ample time to think. It seemed that Vanguard was a man who interested many people from all parts of the city. Being the only person in the city who could find out where he might be could bring certain advantages.

It might not have been the way that he had planned it, but it was starting to look like one way or another, Vanguard would be the one to restore their fortunes after all. All he needed to know was who wanted him found the most.

⚘

PAULETTE AND LADY LEERSAC WERE SITTING AT THE table in the window of the tearoom. His mother was happily watching the carriages passing by outside. Approaching the table Tarryn held out his hand for her. She took it and gave him a kiss.

"Hello, dear. Just look who I ran into on the way out of the hospital!"

"That must have been a nice surprise."

"Oh, absolutely, it's Thursday."

It was Tuesday. Tarryn did not bother to correct her; the conversation had no meaning anyway. Lady Leersac stood and put her hat on. It was not the same hat she had been wearing when she had left the house that morning.

"We have to go now. Do you need me to pay for the sweets?"

Paulette shook her head and rose from the chair. "No, I've already paid."

Tarryn walked Paulette to the corner of the street where she declined the offer of an escort back to the market. Lady Leersac stood looking out over the barriers that edged the waterways snaking through the lanes. There was a disgruntled looking swan poking around in the weeds. She shrieked with delight each time its head disappeared beneath the water.

Tarryn looked at the back of Paulette's neck. The skin was smooth and unblemished. It almost looked clean. "Would you like to go to dinner with me tomorrow evening?"

There was a look of surprise on her face that, given their recent previous encounters, was not a shock. In all likelihood, she would refuse. Tarryn had not given her any reason to want to spend any time with him.

"Alright then."

The swan, irritated at the lack of prospects, began to paddle away. There was a quiet squeak of disappointment from Madeline. Paulette bid them both goodbye and made her way back to the square. Tarryn took his mother by the arm. They walked along the waterway together. Lady Leersac chatted away animatedly. Tarryn was only half listening. A dinner with Paulette would not be the most unpleasant thing to endure. She was at least interesting to talk with.

One thing that Tarryn had learnt over the course of the last few weeks was that knowing what others did not was valuable. Power was something that Tarryn had not felt for a long time. Now he had been given a taste, he was hungry for more. He wanted to know who John Vanguard was. He wanted to know what he did, how he thought and what he loved. Tarryn wanted to know every intimate detail about the clothes that he wore, the bag that he carried and the way that he looked at the world. Tarryn wanted to know because knowledge was power. It was better than money. It was better than sex.

Paulette knew Vanguard. So they would go to dinner, and Tarryn would eat up every word that poured from her kind-hearted lips. Then, when the time came, he would know exactly how to strike Vanguard where it hurt the most.

CHAPTER 25
A TALE OF TWO DEMONS

As a younger man, Argent Cooke had not been at all interested in politics. Nor had his family long been established within the aristocracy. The Cooke family had not come from money. Nothing about his fortune was a birthright. As relative newcomers to high society, Cooke knew that his status was down to the sweat and grit of his forefathers.

Generations before Argent had been born, his great-grandfather had taken everything he had earned and invested heavily into the growing city. They had built foundries and businesses. By the time that Argent was a boy the Cooke family were one of the biggest employers around. They built the library and the theatres. Ernest, his father, was a patron of the arts. It had been a good time.

But it did not last. As more industries began to lose traction, many doors began to close. There were riots, the stirrings of civil war beginning to rumble through the streets. Many a rich house was crippled by debts built in the years that followed.

Kosic gestured towards Cooke. "My friend, this is..."

Vanguard stood unmoving. "I know who he is."

Argent remained seated. He nodded towards Kosic who exited the room, dutifully leaving them alone. Argent waved towards a chair. "Please, sit down."

"I'll stand up."

Vanguard paced the length of the room, taking in their surroundings. It was little more than a cell, albeit a slightly better furnished one than those he had experienced himself. Cooke did not seem in anyway phased by his movements.

Vanguard stopped a few feet away. "You know that anyone that walked through that door could put a bullet through the back of your head?"

Cooke leaned back in the chair. "Any man who has come this far with the intention of shooting me without question would do so regardless of where in this room I chose to sit." He turned slightly. "As it seems you're not going to shoot me, what do you want to know?"

There were many things that Vanguard wanted to know. He wanted to know why Carmen had lied to him about the pin. He wanted to know why one of Ludnor's cousins had been in a photo with Cooke. Mostly he just wanted to know what the hell was going on. In the end, he opted for the question that was bothering him the most. "Who was the woman, the one with the pin?"

Argent smiled. "You would have liked her. She had an exceptionally strong mind – a keen strategist, a business woman, a devotee to civil rights – she could have propelled this city into the future had she had the good fortune to have been born with the right anatomy."

"She sounds impressive."

"She was my mother, and yes, she was." The door opened slightly and Mira appeared. He greeted her with an amiable wave. "Could you bring us some coffee please...and some sandwiches, if it's not too much trouble?"

Vanguard reached up and pinched the bridge of his nose. It felt like Kosic had left a dent in the bone. "There's half an army out there looking for you and you've spent this whole time sitting beneath the feet of the one man in D'Orsee that *hasn't* been ordered to find you."

Cooke snorted affably. "Funny how these things work out isn't it?"

After a few minutes the door opened and Mira walked in carrying a pot of fresh coffee, two mugs and a plate of sandwiches filled with a thin paste that smelt like fish. Vanguard's stomach growled. Argent picked up one of the bread rolls.

He peeled the top half up and sniffed at the contents. "Their food is a little strange, but you get used to it." Argent placed the sandwich back on the plate. "There's a revolution coming. But I suppose you already knew that didn't you?"

"I've heard rumours."

Cooke nodded. "They're more than just rumours. Some of us have been preparing for it for a long time now. All across D'Orsee, people from the old administration - or what's left of it - and others too. It won't be long now before we're at war again. I've personally spent the last few years building an extensive network of supporters."

It suddenly made sense as to why the ash-haired man was in the photo. Planning a revolution was not an easy task. It would take a lot of people to communicate messages back and forth across the zones. Cooke would need to use someone he had known for a long time, someone he could trust. There were only three networks big enough in the entire city to manage it. One was

Mandego's army of cut throats and criminals. The second was Sanquain's Red Badges. The third was a group of men known only as 'cousins'.

"So why go into hiding? Why now?"

"Because we are almost ready for what must come, but for me that means I have made enemies as well as allies. There are not many people I can trust. I have money, I have resources and soon I will have enough men willing to fight back. What I do *not* have are men who are seasoned soldiers; men who can be relied upon to do what must be done when the time comes."

Vanguard paused for a moment. "Why am I here?"

Sliding from the table, Argent crossed the room to a large chest secured by a padlock. Turning the key in the lock, he lifted the lid and pulled out a lengthy scroll of paper. It had been rolled up and secured with a band. Argent unfurled the document and laid it out on the surface of the table. There was a golden crest in the top right corner.

Vanguard had not laid eyes on it in a very long time. "Where did you find that?"

Cooke placed a hand over the document, wiping away a few flecks of dirt. "I remember reading about it in the papers, the great battle at Lycroix. It was one of the turning points of the war. What was it people called you again?"

Vanguard said nothing.

"Ah yes, the Gentry. A good nickname, it suited you. This document lists the names of the soldiers that recaptured Lycroix. Isn't this your name, right at the top?"

"That was a long time ago."

Sometimes, when Vanguard thought back over his life, it was easy to forget who he had been before Bellitreaux. It was like reading back the story of another man's life. It was a story that had not been told for many years.

"The Ninth Company were legends. Everyone said so."

"Nobody ever said it to me."

"Perhaps they should have."

Vanguard felt the pain gnawing at the inside of his stomach. It was one that he had felt before, and had spent the better part of the last few years trying to ignore. It was an emptiness that he had learned to live with. Most of the time, he simply pretended that it was not there.

Argent rolled the paper back up. "I need an army, and this city needs men like the Ninth again."

The statement was almost enough to make Vanguard laugh. As far as he could tell, the city barely even remembered that the Ninth Company had existed at all. Nobody whispered their names or told tales of the things they had done. The world had forgotten them all. Only Vanguard remembered. The Ninth had given everything to him. Arnauld had plucked him from obscurity and given him a brotherhood to belong to. Vanguard had returned their loyalty by abandoning them to their deaths. Cooke might think that his name alongside theirs made Vanguard a survivor. As far as he was concerned, it made him a traitor.

"The Ninth are dead."

"Not all of them; you're still alive."

"What difference does that make?"

"If I'm right about you, Vanguard, it may make all the difference."

Vanguard was not sure he agreed but as the next hour passed, he listened to what Cooke had to say. They drank the coffee. The sandwiches did not taste as bad as they smelt. All the while, Vanguard took in every detail of Cooke's great plan. As far as industry and economy went,

Argent was a veritable trove of knowledge. He certainly spoke with the confidence of a man ready to lead a revolution. During the last rebellion, Vanguard had witnessed many a man think the same. Now they were dead. It was all well and good to talk; it was another thing entirely to take action, and then live with the consequences.

Along with the document bearing the emblem of Vanguard's former company, Argent also had in his possession a large selection of plans, blue prints and diagrams.

"This country cannot operate if every major city remains closed off." Argent trailed his finger across the paper. "We must reconnect with each other, re-open the shipping canals. There will be jobs and trade, not just for the nobility but for everyone."

"And *this* is your great plan, to rebuild the canal?"

"Part of it − I want you to see my vision for the future. First I need to ensure this city *has* a future. In order for that to happen the current regime must be brought to an end."

"So how exactly do you think I'm going to help?"

Cooke sat down on the chair and leaned back, fingers stroking the stubble on his chin. He had not had opportunity to shave for several days. "I'm a smart man Vanguard, but I'm not an arrogant man. I know that I make for a better politician than I do a general." He smiled to himself. "That's not to say I don't know how to wage a war. I'm quite well read on the subject."

"Books teach you nothing about war. Nothing worth knowing anyway."

"Perhaps, and perhaps not. I know that I can show this city what a good leader can be, what power can do when it is used for the good of the many and not the few. But before I can do that, I have to show them what the right side looks like. You can help me remind them. People think of an army now and they think of the Red Badges. The Ninth were different. I remember how they spoke of them dragging people from the flames as Lycroix burned whilst others ran - not because they were ordered to but because it was the right thing to do."

Vanguard felt his jaw tense. He felt the puckered scars tighten. Part of him almost swore that he could still feel the heat prickling at his skin. The smell of burning flesh was not one that anyone soon forgot. The people had forgotten though. They had all forgotten.

"We need men like that again."

"And so far you have one person?"

"I have Kosic as well. Did you know he hasn't lost a fight in over twenty years?"

"Have you seen the size of him?"

"I'm not saying he doesn't have an advantage." Cooke paused. "Do you know what the difference between you and Kosic is?"

"About one hundred and fifty pounds?"

"The difference *is* that when Kosic thinks about where he comes from, he thinks about what he *had* and not what he has lost."

"How is that different?"

Cooke looked at him. "Because one thing you mourn for and the other you *fight* for."

Vanguard felt every bone in his body aching. A decade or so ago he could have gone days without rest, these days his body told him otherwise. Time was catching up with him. He sighed. There were two things that no man could escape. Time and death were the two constants that could not be avoided.

Vanguard had spent most of his life running just ahead

of the sunset. Now he felt it creeping over his shoulders. He was old. There was not much more he could offer the world. The chances had always been slim that Vanguard would die an old man. To make it this far was something of a miracle.

Standing, Cooke reached out and placed a hand on Vanguard's shoulder. The strength of his grip was surprising. Cooke might have been the academic type, but he was not a weak man.

"I took a chance allowing you to find me here. I hope it was not a mistake. Stay with us tonight, think about it. We'll talk again in the morning."

Argent did not wait for Vanguard to respond. Instead he resumed his place at the desk, poring over his plans and barely flinching as the door closed behind him.

THERE WAS AN ARMCHAIR IN THE APARTMENT ACROSS the street. Carmen was in the cot, under the blankets, lying on her side. Mira perched on the end of the bed, reading aloud from a book. Carmen had her eyes closed. Kosic leant against the wall, listening to the story.

It was a good one. When they were children living in the camp, Mira's mother had read it to them often. Kosic did not have a mother. They had all been family though, so he had never felt like anything was missing. Mira turned the page, fingers running along the words.

The story told of two demons that lived in the darkness. They were cursed to bring suffering to the world. Their skin was the colour of death and their bodies were made of stone.

One day, one of the demons walked to the centre of a

village and spat into a well. It made the water toxic. Without it, the village could not survive and, as the people began to fall foul of the demon's poison, the weeping of children awoke the other demon from his sleep.

He walked to the well and looked down into it to see what the first demon had done. Because he lived in the darkness, he had never seen his own face before.

As he looked into the water, the sun rose behind his head and revealed his true image. He reached his hand out, the fingertips bloody, and he felt the warmth of the light burning at his back. The demon did not feel any pain. In fact, he was so enraptured by the sunlight that he let himself be consumed by it. When the rays started to envelop him, he lifted his face toward the sky. Tears streamed down his cheeks and into the well. It cleansed the water. The stone began to crack, flaking away like dust.

The demon cried out as he was reborn. When it was over, the skin shed from the demon's body and left in its place an angel with eyes of fire.

Somebody traipsed noisily up the stairs. Kosic opened his eyes. Vanguard had a pained look on his face. The corners of his mouth twitched, expression regretful. Staggering forward, he grabbed the banister with one hand. The room was filled with the sound of a long, exaggerated fart.

He knew he shouldn't have eaten the sandwiches.

CHAPTER 26
A CHANGE IN THE AIR

Some mornings you'd wake to find the world exactly the way you left it. Other mornings, you'd wake to find that it had somehow changed overnight. The sunlight would creep through the cracks in the walls and, as you felt any dreams you might have dreamt fade away, you would come to realise that nothing was the same as it had been before.

The armchair was not the most uncomfortable place that Vanguard had ever spent the night. He still woke up with a crick in the side of his neck. On the other side of the apartment, Kosic lay on a rolled out mat. There was very little movement from him. He was clearly a deep sleeper. Vanguard could not imagine the sort of man that would be stupid enough to wake something that large without good reason, so he left him to it. Carmen was awake. She stood at the window peering through a small gap in the shutters at the street below.

She lifted one foot and used it to scratch the other. "How's your face?"

Vanguard wrinkled his nose, wincing. "Sore."

There was a loud rumbling from across the apartment like someone trying to move heavy furniture across the floor. Kosic rolled over, lifting his arms so they came to rest behind his head. Carmen shifted around, obviously trying to disguise her discomfort. Vanguard was impressed. Her wounds were still relatively fresh. A lesser person might have taken the opportunity to languish in bed, complaining about the pain.

"I've never been a revolutionary before." She said matter-of-factly.

"Is that what you are now?"

"I think I might be."

They stood for a few minutes together, listening to the sound of Kosic breathing and the stirrings of life on the street below. "Why didn't you tell me the truth about the pin?"

Carmen twisted a strand of hair around her finger before putting it between her lips and chewing thoughtfully. She seemed to know what she wanted to say but, for once, was giving consideration to how she might answer. At first the sight of Carmen thinking before she spoke was a little unnerving. Vanguard had grown accustomed to the shrugging. However he soon came to the conclusion that given how often he found Carmen's perspective on the world intriguing when she hadn't given it much thought, it was likely whatever she said next would at the very least be interesting.

"I didn't know if I could trust you back then."

"And now?"

She looked Vanguard hard in the eyes. There was a seriousness to her that he had not seen before. He realised after a moment that this was the Carmen that existed after Bleath. Vanguard saw it in her expression. She was different now. "What really happened to your face?" She studied the scars carefully, her gaze roving over every inch of skin.

Vanguard turned away. "One day I'll tell you all about it."

"Cooke says you were a hero once but you never talk about it."

"Do you think I'm a hero?"

"I'm not sure I believe in heroes. I think it all depends on which side you're on."

"Everyone seems keen for me to pick."

There was movement from outside the window. Vanguard saw the occupants of the Splinters beginning to go about their morning business. Remy hauled a sack of flour across the street to an open door where Mira was waiting. Carmen stood at his side by the window, pulling the blanket tighter around her shoulders. It was still difficult to tell how old Carmen really was. Her body didn't give much away. With short hair, she could have easily passed for a boy.

"What do you think of Cooke?"

A small smile curled across her lips. "You know he thinks I might be rather clever?"

Vanguard could see why Carmen had been so drawn to Cooke's cause, despite the inherent dangers that it involved. There wasn't another man alive who had taken the time to look past the external to see if there was any potential lurking beneath the surface. Vanguard included himself in that. Experience had taught him that looking for potential was like searching for the start of a rainbow. You could see it all you wanted, but you were never going to do anything with it. The more you tried to chase it, the further away it got, until eventually it just disappeared.

Carmen leaned back so that her rear end touched the ledge of the window. There was really no position that she could be in, other than standing that did not hurt. She looked as though she were thinking about saying something. Vanguard could sense that there was something rolling around on the tip of her tongue. "Well spit it out then."

"Why do you pretend to be something you're not?"

"What do you mean?"

"I know you're a good person, deep down."

"I can name hundreds of people who would disagree."

"Henriette wouldn't."

"She's not here."

"Have you and Henriette ever...?"

"No."

"Not even once?"

"No."

Carmen considered something. "But you do love her, don't you?"

"I don't see how that's relevant."

She rolled her eyes. "Aren't you afraid it's going to dry up and fall off?"

"That's not how it works."

She snorted. "Not what I've been told."

Kosic stirred, sitting up. Glad of the distraction, Vanguard coughed loudly. The strongman groaned, clearly displeased at having been roused at such an early hour. "What are you talking about? This is a lot of noise to make."

Carmen gave Vanguard a sly wink. There were footsteps on the stairs. Demetrio appeared, clutching a pile of papers. He placed them down on the table. Carmen walked over and peered at the words. She scrunched her nose up, turning the paper one way and then the other in an attempt to make sense of the letters. "Would you like me to teach you?" Demetrio asked.

Carmen tucked a strand of hair behind her ear. "Nobody ever saw the point in me learning to read."

"There's always a point to reading. How else would you ever learn anything?"

Vanguard watched Kosic make his way through a hearty breakfast of several bread rolls, what appeared to be most of a pig and the half a dozen boiled eggs provided by Mira. Vanguard, whose system still hadn't quite gotten over the effects of the sandwiches yet, politely declined to partake.

A short while later, he and Kosic left Demetrio to explain the finer points of literacy to his newly recruited student. As they walked down the stairs, Vanguard caught a glimpse of Carmen, brow furrowed as she held a pen between her fingers.

As far as hiding places went, the tunnel was far from being the worst they could come up with, but it was hardly the best. Vanguard wondered how many people knew of its existence. He suspected it was far more than he would have liked. Cooke was pacing up and down the cell, looking like a prisoner of his own making. Vanguard stepped inside and the pacing ceased temporarily.

"Did you sleep well?" Cooke did not sound like a man who was particularly worried about whether or not Vanguard had enjoyed a good night's sleep. He sounded like a man who had more important things to discuss but was asking out of politeness.

"I've never been much for small talk."

Vanguard watched as the amiable expression on Cooke's face quickly turned into something altogether more serious. "In that case we have little time and a lot to talk about. Have you thought about what we discussed last night?"

"What do you want me to say?"

"I want you to say you'll join us."

Vanguard opened his mouth. People liked to think that there was always a right side and a wrong side to everything. They needed to believe in something good. Cooke thought he was offering Vanguard just that - the opportunity to become a part of something good. Vanguard's opinions of whether or not his plans were likely to succeed were neither here nor there. Cooke wanted something that he could not give him. There was too much blood now on his hands for Vanguard to ever be on the right side of anything. "I'm not the man you're looking for."

"May I ask why you think so?"

"Why does it matter? You have my answer."

Cooke sat back in his chair. "I'm curious; indulge me."

"Because you want some bloody martyr – that's not what I am and we both know it. My name on some shitty piece of paper doesn't make me a hero, it never did. I haven't been a soldier for a long time. The Ninth are dead and I'm only here because no bastard's had the good fortune to kill me yet." Vanguard pressed a finger to his face, pushing the skin where the scars lay. "You think this is going to make anyone follow you?" He snorted. "Men like you; they always think they know how to make things better and it's stupid bastards like me that pay the price. Trust me when I say the man you want died a long time ago." He gestured to himself. "All of this? It's just what got left behind."

Cooke nodded slowly. For a minute he did not speak. He seemed to be thinking. Vanguard watched as his whole body slumped forward. A loud, extended sigh preceded his response. "Good God, get *over* yourself."

Vanguard took a step back, body bristling. "I'm sorry?"

"*Poor Vanguard,* did nobody throw you a parade when you got home? Did the city forget to pat you on the back and say thank you?"

"What? I didn't..."

Cooke looked at Vanguard with the expression of man whose mouth had just turned sour. "You know I really thought there might be more to you." He shook his head. "I'd guessed you would be a cynical old bastard but I had hoped there could be something in you that might still be willing to fight back."

Something about the way that Cooke looked at him sent a chill running down Vanguard's spine. He couldn't explain it, but he had the feeling that somehow Argent knew more about Vanguard's past than he had originally let on. Images of gnarled black trees flashed before his eyes.

"I know what you think you are, and I know why you think it. But the truth is the world never made a monster out of you Vanguard – *you* made one of yourself because it was easier to let yourself believe that than it was to accept you couldn't stop it – that you weren't able to save any of them."

Vanguard heard the words come from his lips before he realised he had spoken. "What makes you think that you know anything about me?"

"Because I know what *really* happened to the Ninth."

The familiar ache in his stomach churned. Hearing the words aloud only made it worse. Vanguard did not know how but, somehow, Argent Cooke knew of Bellitreaux.

CHAPTER 27
WE MEN OF ASH AND SHADOW

"That's not possible. How could you know about Bellitreaux?"

"Because I met the only other man to survive it."

Memories flickered in Vanguard's mind. He remembered the men dying, starved and shot like animals. He heard the gunfire, remembered the open gates as the castle was flooded by rebels. Faces swam through Vanguard's consciousness, a swarm of ghosts passing by just as they had done everyday for the past half decade. They spun in an endless cycle, their lifeless eyes staring out at nothing. They were cold, grey. Every one of them was long since dust.

Vanguard shook his head as though doing so would wipe away the images. "The Ninth are all gone."

Cooke looked at him as though he were waiting for the weight above their heads to fall. Vanguard could almost feel it, hanging in the air between them. "I'm not talking about the Ninth." Cooke paused. "Tell me, does the name Lieutenant Eustace Duvinpot sound familiar to you?"

It had been a long time, but Vanguard remembered the name. He had not known the man long enough to know much of him and scarcely thought to remember him since. A young officer of the Twentieth, he had left Bellitreaux not long after they had arrived. They had all presumed him dead. He had in fact, returned to the city to much fanfare and been congratulated on the successful securing of the fortress. As the men of Bellitreaux starved, he was filling his belly up with as much food as he could stuff into his face.

"Tell me, Vanguard, how many times do you think Duvinpot thought of the men that he left behind? How much guilt did he carry? His name spared him. Sanquain made sure of it. Sanquain knew that the Ninth would never stand for his regime. He also knew that if you opposed him, others would have the courage to do the same. He couldn't afford for any of you to come back. Bellitreaux was never a mission, it was a death sentence."

Numbness crept across Vanguard. He couldn't tell if it came from simply standing too long in one place, or if it was some sort of latent self defence mechanism. He knew that what Cooke was telling him was the truth.

There had been no confusion over orders being sent to the fort. Sanquain had stopped provisions long before the rebels had ever made camp outside the walls. He wanted to be sure that the men inside would be too weak to defend themselves as he pushed the enemy towards them. He couldn't be seen to murder an entire company of heroes, but there was a whole legion of angry revolutionists more than willing to do the job for him.

"You might have blood on your hands Vanguard, but I can promise you that it is nothing compared to the blood on the hands of Felix Sanquain."

Cooke crossed the room and opened a chest, retrieving a fresh shirt from the pile of folded clothes. The one that he was wearing was pulled over his head. Cooke placed the old shirt over the arm of a chair. There was a vertical scar, about four inches long that ran down his back, perpendicular to the shoulder. Vanguard had seen many scars. It was the mark of a surgeon – a good one, it would seem. Cooke sensed his eyes on him.

"Did you know, fifteen years ago over ninety percent of patients to have the surgery they performed on me died within a month? I was thinking of that as they held me down on the table. Of course, it is quite common now." Cooke carefully buttoned the shirt up to the neck and straightened the collar. "I like to think that sometimes we survive for a reason, that the world has a greater purpose in mind for us."

Cooke took a pile of material and unfurled it. It was a cloak with a heavy hood, the sort that obscured the face. Cooke had not been outside the cell for weeks. It would feel good to get out, even if it was only for a few minutes.

Gesturing for Vanguard to accompany him, Cooke opened the door and together they walked in silence through the tunnel. Remy stood sentry outside of Kosic's apartment, leaning against the railing that ran along the length of the staircase. Cooke patted his shoulder as they walked by.

Demetrio was sitting at the table reading a book, glasses pushed down his nose. Kosic was taking his turn to watch the street below. Behind them, Carmen sat cross legged on the bed. A strand of hair kept falling across her face. Scattered across the mattress were screwed up balls of paper, the pen still in her hand. She paid no attention to Vanguard or Cooke. Instead, she pressed the nib to the page and slowly ran the ink across the pages until she had written a word.

"Sometimes we anticipate that the things we do will elicit great changes." Cooke smiled softly. "Tell me, what chance do you think she has in this world if things remain as they are?" Cooke placed one hand against his back. "This isn't about us, it never has been. The chances are nobody will ever thank us for what we have done, because nobody will ever realise all the things we had to risk and sacrifice just so that a girl like Carmen could one day sit and write her own name. We are men of ash and shadow. We endure the darkness so that others might see the dawn."

They watched for another minute or so. Vanguard felt a great weight pressing on his shoulders. Eventually Cooke felt the call of his cell and the work that was still to be done. Each second that they were outside ran the risk of the Red Badges passing through the Splinters and exposing them. They had already spent too long above the ground. He turned and descended the stairs, stopping briefly to drink in one last moment of sunshine before he returned to the tunnel.

Vanguard came to stop just behind him. "You were very confident I was going to come around, weren't you?"

Cooke grinned. "I'd say *hopeful* was more apt a word."

Watching as Cooke made his way across the street and into the back of the club, Vanguard found that a strange and long forgotten feeling had crept up and taken hold of him. Even back in his soldiering days, Vanguard had never been one for speeches and poems. Words were easy. But some people had a knack for getting you to see things in a different way. Since the day that he had left the Hole, Vanguard had been trying to atone for Bellitreaux. In the time that it took to climb a single flight of stairs, one man had made him realise that perhaps his survival had never been meant as a punishment. Just maybe, there was a purpose to it all.

Cooke still had no real idea of what war really was. He couldn't soldier worth a damn as far as Vanguard could tell. He'd been too privileged for too long to understand that all the flowery speeches in the world wouldn't stop men from dying. Sanquain had enough power to crush an uprising. Even to the untrained eye, Cooke's chances were slim. Yet Vanguard found that for the first time in a long time, he thought that maybe, just *maybe* it might be worth the chance.

Argent had been right about one thing. If by sheer dumb luck they somehow managed to survive what was to come, someday he was going to make a bloody good politician.

CHAPTER 28
PAULETTE

Paulette carefully pushed a morsel of food around her plate with what she presumed was the correct fork. Nobody had taken the trouble to tell her and she didn't like to make a fuss.

It had turned out to be something of a day of firsts for many people. While Carmen had spent the morning learning how to painstakingly write her own name, Paulette was spending the evening enjoying her first taste of fine dining.

A pianist played music from the corner as waiters seemed to dance around one another, silver trays filled with champagne glasses held aloft. Tarryn had chosen a good table. It allowed for a good view of the floor, sat tucked behind a thin screen that afforded a little privacy. He also had selected the wine and food. Paulette was relieved that nobody had asked her what she wanted, not wanting to reveal her lack of experience in Golden Quarter gastronomy. The food didn't taste half as bad as she had imagined. Back at Henriette's house the food was generally denser and mostly sweet. Chicken veloute and braised asparagus were things that happened to other people. The last actual vegetable Paulette had eaten had been in a soup and had been questionable at best.

"Don't you like it?"

"It isn't that." She paused, the fork hovering. "I'm just not sure why you brought me here."

Tarryn had not put much consideration into the venue that he had chosen. It was quiet, conveniently located and more importantly was pretty much the only place left in the city that would accept an account bearing the Leersac name. He had been before some years ago with his mother. The wallpaper had since faded and the furniture was outdated. Most of the patrons had long since abandoned it for more up and coming venues. "We can leave if you're unhappy."

"No, no, it's not that." Paulette's cheeks flushed. "I've just never been in a place this...*nice*."

The more time he spent with her, the more Tarryn found Paulette curious. She thought that they were in a respectable establishment. She did not realise that it was a place for the sort of people who weren't fit to be seen at the more exclusive eateries. It was the sort of venue that married men brought their low breed mistresses to whilst their wives held book clubs and charity luncheons.

"So are you living back at...that house?"

Tarryn wished that the floor would open up so that he could fall through it. No amount of information was worth this. Paulette had been quiet throughout the first course and entrée. It had been left entirely to Tarryn to steer the conversation. Behind the helm of small talk, he was directionless and lost.

"We don't need to talk about that."

Tarryn felt his leg twitching beneath the table. He wanted

to ask about Vanguard. He wanted to bring the subject up as if it were natural. Unfortunately he lacked the finesse or social experience for that kind of manipulation. Paulette lifted her hand and tucked a strand of hair behind her ear.

"What's the matter?"

"It's nothing."

"You can tell me."

Paulette let the fork rest on the side of her plate. She looked as though she were deciding whether or not to let Tarryn into her thoughts. "I think that Vanguard might be in trouble."

It would seem that manipulating the conversation was not necessary. "What makes you think that?"

Paulette leant over the table. She spoke softly. "You're his friend, aren't you?"

Tarryn held her gaze. He nodded. "Yes, I'm his friend."

"The Red Badges came to the house; they said they were looking for John and that if he came back we should keep him there. They seemed very concerned that they find him. One of them, he offered Henriette money. She told them she didn't know where he was, none of us do."

"Did he say anything else?"

"Only that they were going to some club and that if Henriette changed her mind she could find him there. I don't think she liked him very much."

Quietly contemplating the opportunity before him, Tarryn reached out and ran one finger down the stem of a glass. It was filled with a crisp, dry white that paired perfectly with the chicken. Tarryn preferred red.

Paulette took a bite of the chicken and chewed on it slowly. Tarryn always seemed to be thinking. She found it best to let him get on with it.

"Would you recognise him again?"

Paulette nodded, holding a hand to her mouth as if she were worried the food might fall from it. Tarryn pulled his napkin from the table and dabbed at his lips. The other hand reached into the air, his fingers snapping to garner the attention of a passing server. Standing, he offered a hand to Paulette. "Come on, let's go."

"Where are we going?"

"To the club. I want to see if we can find this man."

"I'm coming with you?"

"I need you to show me which one he is."

"Oh."

It was not the most enthusiastically offered invitation. Paulette was willing to take it though. She had met a lot of men in her time and none of them had been very nice to her. Some were better than others. They had still all got their money worth out of her. Most of them would have had her bent over the table before the waiter had even read the specials out. She was tired of being treated like a farm horse. Tarryn was unusual and quiet. Paulette was used to unusual and she enjoyed quiet. Other people thought that he was strange. Paulette was willing to overlook a lot of things if it meant getting out of the Black Zone.

She reached out and took his hand. On the carriage journey to the Splinters, she gripped his arm a little tighter. The more that Paulette was close to him, the more that Tarryn felt his resolve not to like her just a little wavering. Tarryn had never spent any real time with a woman other than his mother before. He had tried in his younger days, but inevitably after an hour or so they would find some reason to excuse themselves. Something he said, or something he did, would upset or offend them. It did not take much.

Tarryn remained fixated on the road ahead. Paulette was used to him being silent. It didn't trouble her. She often found it was not necessary to talk at all. She wondered what he was thinking about. Tarryn stole a glance at the side of her face. He was wondering if, beneath her green eyes and smooth skin, something about Paulette was rotten inside.

Arriving at the club, Tarryn paid for two tickets. Paulette had been jealous when Carmen had been taken to the show. Everything about it had sounded glamorous. Now that she was there, it did not seem to be quite as wonderful as Carmen had described. The crowd seemed lacklustre. There were a few girls in exotic costumes carrying trays of nuts and sweets around, offering them to disinterested patrons.

As they ventured further in it became more apparent as to why the place was almost completely devoid of customers. A large table had been laid out in a corner of the hall. Several of the Red Badges sat around it, smoking cigars and playing a card game. Beyond that, Lucien Herveaux stood in conversation with the red-bearded man. He seemed unhappy at the current state of affairs.

The Red Badge seemed to care little for his concern. "Watch your tone Herveaux; you'll get your freak house back tomorrow."

"I'm the one losing money here. This isn't your club-house. This is a business. I pay my taxes just like everyone else."

Sanderson uncrossed his arms and straightened to full height. He stood a clear head taller than Herveaux and had no qualms about standing extremely close. Unnerved by

Sanderson's pointed invasion of his personal space, Herveaux blustered and shook his head a few times before stalking off. Sanderson rolled his eyes and turned his attention back to the card game.

Tarryn purchased a bottle of lemonade for Paulette and found a seat for her at a table. She took a sip of the drink and agreed to wait for him to come back.

Sanderson was surprised to see anyone approaching. Most people kept out of the way of the Red Badges. What surprised him even more was the way that the man walking towards him was directly in his line of sight one moment, and then gone from it the next. By the time Tarryn was a few feet from Sanderson; he had disappeared and reappeared several times over, certainly enough for him to get the idea. Sanderson kept one hand on his pistol.

"Nice trick."

"I think you might have seen it before."

"I may have seen it once or twice."

"Then we have a mutual friend."

"He's not my friend."

A cold smile spread across Tarryn's face. "Then I think I might have an offer for your employer, if you could arrange a meeting."

Sanderson's top lip curled. "Why would I do that?"

Tarryn glanced back across the hall at Paulette who was sipping on her lemonade. "Because he wants John Vanguard, and I'm the only person who can see him."

From across the length of the club, Kosic stood watching from behind the curtain. Far beneath his feet, Cooke sat working on his plans. He did not like it. There had been too many Red Badges around the past few days. There was a rustling behind him. Carmen appeared, a quilted throw wrapped around her shoulders. Placing his hand on her stomach, Kosic pushed her back into the shadows. "What are you doing here? You should be in the apartment."

"Vanguard snores like a mule. Why are the Red Badges here?"

Kosic looked back at the card game. "I don't know but it is not good. Demetrio tells me they are everywhere. Sanquain uses them like spies."

"Do you think he knows?"

"I think he may suspect."

Carmen peered out from behind him, seemingly puzzled. Kosic turned back to the tables, trying to work out what it was she had seen. A woman stood on the other side of the hall, her back turned to the curtain. Carmen narrowed her eyes, squinting to get a better view. The woman turned and Carmen's mouth fell open. "I know her, that's Paulette – we lived together at the house."

"Does she know you are here?"

"No, nobody does, apart from us and Henriette."

Paulette was holding on to the arm of a young man with angular features. There was something unsettling about him. Carmen felt like they had met before but she could not place from where.

"Do you know the man?"

Carmen shook her head, pulling the blanket a little tighter around her shoulders. "I thought for a moment, maybe." She looked again. "I don't think so."

Kosic kept his eyes trained on Tarryn. "Tell Vanguard, tell him exactly what you've seen and tell him not to leave the apartment. Shut the doors and do not stand by the window. Nobody must know you are here."

Carmen nodded and left without saying a word. A moment later, Demetrio appeared behind him.

"I think she likes you." His voice was teasing yet there was a hint of warning to it.

"Don't make fun, she is a tiny girl."

"I'm just saying."

"I think you are imagining things."

"Maybe. Maybe not. You should be careful there."

Together they watched Tarryn and Paulette circling the club. There was a roar of satisfaction from one of the seated Red Badges as he relieved his counterpart sitting across the table of his wages.

"How many do you think we have?"

Kosic knew what Demetrio was asking. It was a question he had been asking himself more and more over the recent months. What concerned him was not how many people would sooner see Cooke presiding over D'Orsee than Sanquain, but how many of them would be prepared to make the sacrifices needed to see it happen. "Not enough."

It had taken some time for Kosic himself to come to terms with what Cooke was asking of him. At first the idea of fighting side by side with a man like John Vanguard had made him sick to his stomach. It was men like him that had taken everything from his people, shot and hunted them like animals. But Cooke had persuaded him that often the only way to prevail was to forgive those that had wronged you.

Now he saw that he and Vanguard were not so dissimilar. They were both built for destruction – Kosic with his strength, and Vanguard with his skill. Both of them had been judged and marked as outsiders by the very people they were set to liberate. They had both spent their lives as pawns in a game played by rich men. Now all Cooke had to do was persuade the rest of the people that their many differences ought to be outweighed by the need to rise against their one common enemy. It would not be easy. The network of Cousins was hard at work delivering the message. Kosic could only hope that they would hear it.

By the time Tarryn had walked back to the table where Paulette sat waiting, Sanderson had sent word to the Golden Quarter. A meeting would take place the next morning. He took Paulette by the hand, assuring her that all was well. Paulette smiled, happy that the matter was resolved.

It was getting late. Tarryn found them a carriage. As the wheels sped over the cobblestones he felt a slight movement next to him. He looked down to see a small hand on the top of his knee. Paulette bit her bottom lip. Tarryn looked at the hand, uncertain as to whether or not he enjoyed the feeling of it there. In the end he put his own over the top. He wasn't sure if it was supposed to feel comforting, or pleasant. It didn't really feel like anything at all. Paulette seemed content with the response. She twisted her hand, curling her fingers around his palm.

"Would you like me to take you home?"

Paulette looked at him, her voice barely more than a whisper. "I don't want to be alone anymore."

Paulette was never alone. What she wanted was not to be lonely anymore.

Tarryn was used to being alone. He had long ago dismissed the idea of any woman wanting him. It did not mean he did not crave what all men craved. What he could not abide however, was the thought of it being shared with anyone else.

He kept his eyes on the back wall of the carriage, feeling the gentle sway of the vehicle as it turned down a narrow street. "If you come with me tonight, you can never go back to that other place again. That life is over for you."

He felt the squeeze of her hand in silent agreement. Paulette leaned back in her seat, watching the road go by. A little while later, she lay on a mattress looking up at a dark ceiling.

She was cold. Pulling the blanket up, she rolled over to look at his bare back. It hadn't been terrible. It hadn't been good either. Running a finger down his spine, she watched the rise and fall of his shoulders.

"It's late. Go to sleep."

Tarryn waited until Paulette had settled and he felt the cadence of her breathing change. He did not want to turn around. It would mean facing the reality of what he had done. He lay awake, staring at the walls, the bitterness festering in his chest.

The next morning when she woke up, Paulette stretched out her arms. When they found nothing, she rolled over onto her side. The other side of the bed was empty.

CHAPTER 29
ROTTEN FLESH

I t seemed that an uneventful night for Felix Sanquain would turn out to be the precursor to an interesting morning. He had left the offices the previous evening just after eight, whereupon he had been driven back to his townhouse under the usual escort. He had read the evening paper, finished up some paperwork and drank a single cup of black coffee.

The staff bustled around the house. He largely ignored them. Sanquain had been sitting at his desk in the study when the housekeeper had knocked at the door. The captain did not accept visitors at home without prior arrangement and the rest of the household was well aware of this fact. He was informed that it was someone visiting on urgent business. When you had an entire city to run, everything was urgent business.

He had intended to give the guard who stood on his doorstep a lecture on the importance of boundaries and privacy. It would be followed in the morning by a more intensive form of retraining. The guard handed him a folded slip of paper. Turning it over, he found a short message scrawled in Sanderson's barely legible chicken scratch. Sanquain shut the door without dismissing the guard. Unsure as to whether or not he should stay or leave, the messenger remained standing on the doorstep for several minutes before backing slowly down onto the street.

It was nine o'clock exactly the next morning when Tarryn arrived at the chambers in the square. Sanderson was conveniently elsewhere. Sanquain had not bothered to send for him. Whatever discussion he was about to have, Sanderson did not need to be privy to the details. He knew more than was good for everyone already.

Tarryn entered the room and took a moment to take it all in. He could not help but wonder how many times he might have sat in meetings in that room had his father not been cast out of high society. The fate of the city was decided within those four walls and up until that moment, entry had been blocked to him.

"Please take a seat." There was a level of formality to the captain's voice that suggested it was not a request.

He took a seat across the desk. Sanquain considered him carefully. As far as physicality went, Tarryn left much to be desired. There was little in the way of mass or strength to him. He did not have the same gnarled indifference that Vanguard had nor the muscled bulk of Sanderson and his thugs. The boy was pretty, which could be an advantage under the right circumstances. Sanquain shook his head. "I fail to see how you could be of any use to me."

There were two ways that Tarryn could have reacted to the captain's disinterest. Either, he could cut his losses and walk away, chalking the experience up to a poor decision and false confidence, or he could see it not as a dismissal, but as a test. Sanquain was the sort of man to whom actions were worth more than words. Tarryn had been prepared for that. He was not well equipped for elaborate speeches or persuasion. He lacked the talent for it. There was something that he could do however, that would speak louder than words ever could.

Ever since reading the note that Sanderson had sent the night previously, Sanquain had been doubtful as to the authenticity of the boys claim. Unlike some of the less worldly people in his employment, he had never considered Vanguard's skills to be magical or supernatural. There had been rumours to that effect several times. It was a skill, an attribute – intrinsic but honed and mastered over time. Up until that moment he had never found another person who could do what Vanguard did with the same level of success.

Tarryn reached over, depositing a small package wrapped in cloth onto the desk before Sanquain. Lifting the material slightly, the captain found himself looking at a severed thumb. It had been detached from its owner, Jonathan Flake, several days previously. Sanquain recognised the small diamond shaped tattoo below the knuckle. Flake's name was one of those on the most recent list given to Vanguard.

Sanquain remained stony faced. "Are you here to make a confession?"

"I'm here to show you how I could be of use to you."

"Alright, you have my attention. I suggest you be very careful not to waste it."

"I need to find a way to restore my family name; you need someone to replace John Vanguard."

Leaning forward on the desk, Sanquain turned his head towards Tarryn. Tarryn tensed. Perhaps he had been too hasty. The silence between them was laboured, suffocating. Finally, Sanquain nodded slowly. "I'm listening."

Tarryn knew that if he were able to secure the employment of Felix Sanquain, he would no longer need worry that he could not afford to live as he deserved. He would be able to afford decent doctors to care for his mother and belongings more befitting their status.

More than that however, he would deprive John Vanguard of his living, his purpose and the only thing keeping him from utter destitution.

"If I understand you correctly, you're telling me that Vanguard has been allowing you to run around my city for weeks slaughtering citizens and taking credit for it?"

"Only the names on the list you supplied."

"*Interesting.*" Sanquain removed the pen from the ink pot on the desk. He took a scrap of paper with the other hand and scratched out a name with curled, flourished handwriting. It was brief, as execution orders went, but it served the purpose for which it was meant.

"What's that?"

Sanquain handed the paper across the desk. "A trial."

Tarryn felt the familiar tingling sensation spreading across his skin. It was the feeling of someone else's impending death. This time there would be nobody to hold him back. "What did he do?"

Sanquain looked at him for a moment. "Does that matter?"

Casting his mind back, Tarryn thought of the lessons that Vanguard had tried to instil in him. The importance of knowing who your mark was before you killed them. The fact that there were people in the world that deserved to die and there were those that did not. Months of self-righteous dogma that served only to help Vanguard sleep at night. The answer that he gave, when he finally gave it, was precisely the one that Sanquain had wanted to hear.

"Not to me."

After Tarryn had left, Sanquain sat for a little while rolling a small brass key between his fingers. It was interesting how things sometimes worked out exactly as you needed them to just by sheer chance alone. Nobody could have anticipated Tarryn Leersac. It was doubtful that anyone passing him on the street would even register his existence. In fact, Sanquain had proof they didn't.

Vanguard had been useful. At times he had even been interesting. But he had outlived his purpose.

Reaching into the drawer at his right hand side, Sanquain pulled out a metal box and pressed the key into the lock. There was a soft click. Inside a stack of letters and documents sat hidden. Sanquain unfolded a document and laid it out on the table. It had not been easy to find. A golden crest sat in the right hand corner. There were very few copies in the city. One of them, he suspected, was in the possession of Argent Cooke.

Sitting back in the chair, Sanquain sipped at a glass of water and looked down at the copies of the blue prints to Cooke's plans for rebuilding the canals, procured for him by one of his little spiders. They were good, he could concede that. If things had been different, Sanquain would have quite liked to talk with Cooke about his ideas for the city. Unfortunately, Cooke would not live long enough for that. None of them would.

Revolution was inevitable. It had been for a long time. But, more importantly than that, it was necessary. D'Orsee craved violence. A purge was long overdue. Sanquain's mind drifted back to the conversation that he and Vanguard had shared just months ago. The words he had used - *I'll say one thing for the war, it does leave a sizeable dent in the population regardless of the outcome.*

The spread of the lower classes was becoming a problem. The balance had shifted. As the city festered, the scum spread like a disease. Cooke believed that rebellion was the solution.

Sanquain knew better. So he would let them plan their coup. He would let them believe that they could beat him. Sanquain was a master of the game. In the end, he knew there was only one way to deal with rotten flesh. It needed to be cut away – swiftly, completely and without remorse.

CHAPTER 30
MY FALLEN COUSIN

I f it was a test of skills that Sanquain required, Tarryn was more than happy to oblige. The name Sanquain had given him was not one that he knew, but it was one that would be recognised by many people around the city. Far from being a criminal, or the type of low life that Vanguard would have been sent to dispatch, he had been chosen for a very specific reason.

The task was completed not long after their initial meeting. Sanquain was not the sort of man you wanted to keep waiting. There was however a certain amount of preparation required. Vanguard had taught him that. The environment needed to be right. There was an element of artistry to delivering a death blow to a man walking the streets, and then leaving without being seen.

On the first day of the hunt Tarryn had walked the Black Zone, cautiously waiting to see if anybody saw that he was there. This was Vanguard's territory and people had seen his face before. He did not want to take chances. Nobody noticed him at all. By the second day his confidence had grown. Unbound from the rules, Tarryn found it easier to study his target. For one thing, he did not trouble himself with concerns over the man's innocence or guilt. Tarryn's time was spent watching his movements, observing his weaknesses.

Each day a different person would enter the Ring O'Bastards through the front door and appear a short while later with a large sack which they carried out into the streets. They alternated their routes, each day changing at random the direction they would walk.

There was, however, one notable exception. He did not appear everyday, but one man in particular was a more regular visitor than any of the others. Sometimes he would emerge with the sack, sometimes without it. Other days he would not emerge at all. Tarryn watched, waiting.

Ludnor's cousin was an older man with a long, jagged scar running from brow to chin down the left hand side of his face. Lighter in weight than Tarryn, the ash colour of his hair made him easily identifiable.

Gregor Tamsk had lived a long and interesting life. As with so many others like him, those who saw him would never realise the extent of his service to the people. He received no recognition or reward, and asked for very little in way of recompense. Employed for many years in the service of Adelaide Cooke, he had kept more secrets over the years than most would ever know about. He was prepared to take them to the grave. Gregor was a man who collected more than just debts. He was a gatherer of information and a purveyor of news. The sacks that Ludnor sent from The Ring O'Bastards were filled with more than just counters. They were the system by which Argent Cooke conveyed his great message to those who wanted to hear it.

Unaware that his movements were being observed, the

man went about the business of collecting debts. At one point, there was a lively exchange between the collector and one of the debtors over the amount owed. Tarryn noted the speed and dexterity with which Ludnor's cousin brandished the pocket knife up his sleeve. Ludnor's cousin wasn't an amateur.

With the debts settled and all payments made, Gregor turned and made for the tow paths. He was a cautious man, never taking the same route twice. They were all careful. The network of Cousins had been established for a long time. None of them had great expectations of long, healthy lives but now, more than ever, they knew the importance of caution.

WATCHING THE COUSINS, TARRYN HAD LEARNT THAT there was one similarity in each of the routes they used. All of them would walk through the Black Zone before ending up at an old warehouse on the west side of the Tanners. They would walk into the building with a bag full of money and walk out empty handed.

The first time he noticed it, Tarryn had scoured the building. Several hours later and no stone left unturned, he had found nothing. The sack had simply disappeared, along with its contents.

The old man was fast for his age. Survival instincts kept him moving constantly. A high wall lined the periphery of the estate where the old warehouses were located. Gregor kept a wary eye on his surroundings, eyes constantly flickering from left to right. Several feet above the ground, Tarryn moved with light-footed steps along the bricks.

This time he would need to control himself. Sanquain

had been very specific as to how and when Gregor should die. Tarryn was to stay his hand until he had procured something useful from the old man. He would need to use restraint.

A few feet from the entrance of the warehouse compound Tarryn dropped from the wall. Gregor sniffed the air like a dog. His shoulders tensed, sensing something wrong. Tarryn swept the blade through the air just inches from Gregor's back. Moving like a seasoned survivor, the old man stepped out of the path of the blade.

He turned, unsure of where his attacker was but knowing that they were there. The agility of the older man took Tarryn by surprise. Taking his own blade from his pocket the man cursed and spat venomously. Tarryn had underestimated him. There was a reason that Ludnor's cousins had never once been robbed of their valuables.

"Come on then, let's have it, you prick."

Tarryn had been determined that this time his urges would not get the better of him. Sanquain needed proof that he could be a valuable asset. The captain did not want the insides of Gregor Tamsk to decorate the Black Zone like red confetti. He wanted what was inside his head. But as the old man fought to survive, Tarryn began to feel the familiar rush. Adrenaline surged through his muscles and he felt alive once more.

Dropping the bag to the ground, Gregor snarled. "Come on then, I'll cut you fucking open."

The blood boiled in Tarryn's veins. He did not have the time or inclination for a long drawn out fight. He wished that just for once someone would simply lie down and die quietly the way they were supposed to. Grasping at the knife, Tarryn twisted away from Gregor's counter attack. Resentment surged through every muscle. It was almost offensive, that this old creature should believe he could resist. Tarryn's desire to purge the anger rose, his control slipping.

"I'll gut you like a rabbit."

Upon hearing those words Tarryn's last shred of restraint evaporated. Caught up by a whirlwind of slashes and cuts, Ludnor's cousin did not go meekly to meet his maker. Tarryn felt the material of his sleeve tear, the ash haired man landing a lucky strike across the coat.

It did not matter how reluctant Gregor was to die, in the end, Tarryn had the advantage. He was younger, fitter. The old man was fighting a ghost. Gregor's breath became shorter, arms weakening as the muscles began to shake. The grip on his weapon loosened. There was no more resistance, no more fight. There was only the glint of the knife as it flashed backwards and forwards. Sharp steel plunged and was drawn back out of the tattered flesh over and over.

By the time Tarryn was done, the old man was long since dead. Wiping his face with his sleeve, Tarryn's mind slowly came back into focus. The rushing blood in his ears calmed. Sanquain had been very specific that the final blow should not come before Tarryn had extracted the information the captain required. It was going to be hard to get any information out of Gregor now. The contents of his throat were scattered across the concrete.

For a moment, Tarryn felt angry with himself. He shook the feeling away. It was not his fault. Vanguard had abandoned him before he could teach him all he needed to know. Vanguard had never shown him how to control it. All he had done was suppress him. Free from the cage, Tarryn was an animal. He was not to blame. Nobody had ever shown him how to be anything else.

The sack that Gregor carried was still on the ground. Hoping that he might find something of use to the captain, Tarryn opened it up and rummaged through the contents. There were splashes of blood on his fingers that stained the coins. It was by no means a fortune, but it would serve as a small, well earned bonus. Something in the bottom of the sack caught his eye. He fished out the trinket, turning it over in his hands. A little silver pin sat in his palm.

A few hours later, Tarryn stood in Sanquain's chambers. The captain was less than pleased. "You were supposed to extract the information before the job was finished."

"It didn't go to plan."

"I can see that. Now I'm left with nothing but another bloody mess to clear up."

"I can do better. Give me another chance and I'll prove myself."

Sanquain looked Tarryn up and down, taking in the measure of him. There was still blood beneath his fingernails. He had expected that the boy would not be able to curtail his urges. What he had not yet worked out until that moment was how Tarryn could be used to best effect.

The captain was a great believer in adapting to new circumstances. A leader who did not look for the advantages in a situation was one who would not remain a leader for long. Tarryn lacked control. Sanquain however was well practised. If the boy could not kill without causing chaos, then chaos was what Sanquain would use.

Years ago, when James Sanderson had informed him of the whereabouts of the last man who had been alive at Bellitreaux, Sanquain's interest had been piqued. Part of him knew that the best course of action would be to have the man killed immediately. Curiosity got the better of him. The captain wanted to see what sort of man he had sent to die. It turned out Vanguard was barely a man at all by then. Whilst he had been left to rot beneath the earth, Sanquain had purged the memory of the Ninth Company from the minds of the people. By the time Vanguard was above ground again, they had all but been forgotten. And, should they ever remember, Vanguard would provide a cautionary tale - a reminder that the Ninth were to be reviled rather than revered.

Sanquain had few concerns about Cooke's attempts to align the Splinters to his cause. The people would never unite with them. A few months of liberal propaganda could not wash away the decades of distrust and fear. The Ninth however, were a different matter. When he had taken power at the end of the war, Sanquain had been staunchly aware that there would be opposition to the new regime. There were people who would not see it as a necessary division of the classes, but as a system of oppression. He had worked hard to make sure that when the men returned from the fighting, they would be ready to come around to his side. For the most part they fell in line and from the remnants of the old guard, the Red Badges emerged.

Cooke had always been destined to meet Vanguard. Sanquain may have been able to delay the inevitable until a solution to his problems presented itself, but it had always been an unavoidable inconvenience. He could not afford for the idea of the Ninth to be reborn. The lower classes might not have been likely to band with the people of the Splinters, but the Gentry were a different matter. These were their sons, their own people. No matter what he had become by the time Sanquain had found him, John

Vanguard had once been the sort of hero that people followed.

Even if he had never believed it himself.

Cooke intended to resurrect the memories of the Gentry. There were already whispers on the streets that spoke of a man who stalked in the night, cutting the throats of baby killers and rapists. But reputation was a precarious thing, easily built and easily broken. Aside from Sanderson and Vanguard, nobody else knew of Tarryn Leersac outside of that room. They did not know who he was. They did not know what he could do. As far as the rest of the world was concerned, there was only one man who could move without being seen, leaving death in his wake. John Vanguard had a history bathed in red. Perhaps it was time for the people of the Black Zone to be reminded of that.

"Very well. I will allow you one more chance."

"Give me the name and it'll be done."

Sanquain smiled. "Excellent – and this time, I expect you to follow my instructions *very* closely."

Paulette was a little surprised to see Tarryn return home a few hours later. Normally she would not see him until the early hours of the morning and often not at all. They had barely spoken over the course of the week. During the day she would keep his mother company, administer her medicines and stop her from banging her head against the walls. At night she would either sleep in the spare room or in his bed. It was a convenient arrangement. She missed Henriette and the other girls although she did enjoy the fact that, for the first time in her entire life, she could sleep in a room without anyone else in it.

At first she had wondered if perhaps Tarryn was not interested in women. It wouldn't have bothered her in the least. She was just happy to quietly remain in the background.

Tarryn was just as confused by their relationship as she was. There were many occasions where he found Paulette genuinely satisfying to be around, maybe because she was so compliant and easily pleased. The women of the Golden Quarter were demanding creatures. Paulette didn't expect anything. On other occasions, he found even the sight of her abhorrent. Her presence made his skin crawl, the scent of her turning his stomach.

From a practical point of view it was beneficial to keep her around. It made his mother happy. It gave him the free time he needed to go about his business and it made him look a little less strange to others. As far as the world could tell, they were just one big happy family – the whore, the murderer and the mad woman screaming in the corridors. The thought amused him.

Paulette stood. "I didn't expect to see you so soon. Should I go to my room?"

"No, no, I'd like you to stay here. I have a gift for you."

"What sort of gift?"

"An apology for being so uncivil to you."

"You didn't need to do that."

Tarryn took a small package from his pocket, the item shrouded in white tissue paper. He gestured for her to come closer. Paulette walked across the room. Reaching up and sliding something into the fabric of her dress, Tarryn felt the point of the needle scratch at the skin of her collarbone. She flinched slightly. The pin was rather attractive now that Gregor's blood had been cleaned away.

"Thank you, it's beautiful."

He pressed his mouth to her cheek. Paulette felt little more than a slight pressure on her skin. It was strange - of all the men that she had been with, and there were many, she had felt something of them with each kiss and touch. She felt their anger, their hunger, and their desire. At times she felt their sadness. With Tarryn she felt none of it. Wherever the anger, the sadness and the resentment he so clearly felt was going, she wasn't made to suffer it. In the end, she was happier with that. After over a decade of feeling things, she was glad of a little nothing.

CHAPTER 31
MADNESS IS A MATTER OF PERSPECTIVE

Had the world been a better or fairer place, Tarryn would have been spending the cold, late hours in the comfort of his own bed. There would have been a fire glowing in the hearth. He would have slept soundly, dreaming of great ships lurching into the docks and the adulation that came with success and wealth.

But he was not. Instead he was waiting in the shadows, crouched on the rooftops of the Black Zone, watching the patrons stumbling out of the Rabbit.

Pathetic, drunken figures - they were barely alive and yet somehow, they were all better connected to the world than he was. They felt something - happiness, pain, regret, shame, intoxication. It was something. It made them real.

Tarryn didn't really feel much of anything other than anger. It distanced him from the world, set him apart. He felt as though the rooftop might as well be a thousand miles above the ground.

For as long as he could remember, Tarryn had longed to find a way to connect to the world. He had hoped, in vain as it had transpired, Vanguard would be the one to help him to do that. If he could not find a value in life, perhaps he could have found one in death. Seeing them now, Tarryn knew that his mistake had been to think that it was worth connecting to at all.

Vanguard had been right in one aspect – there were men that deserved to die and men that did not. His error had been to think that the conditions of either were dependent on that man's actions. Death did not come first to those who sin the most. It did not bypass those who lived good lives.

Tarryn had never been one of them. Deep down, he knew that he would never be one of them. He was something more now than they could ever be.

The last man stumbled out of the tavern a little less than twenty minutes later. There was a cloth bandage wound around his hand. Several people had asked Sam Wick what had happened. Not wanting to disclose the true nature of his injury and, more importantly, not wanting to be in Vanguard's bad books, he had lied and told them that a dog had bitten him. After a while they had lost interest. A dog bite was neither exciting nor news worthy.

Wick had spent much of the rest of the evening being ignored. After a full night of drinking, he wanted nothing more than to crawl into the scratchy covers of the cot in his cabin. He needed to sleep until the churning in his stomach dissipated. He had known it would be a mistake to eat the pie. Staggering down the street, he made more noise than a whipped dog.

Wick was close to the waterside when Tarryn dropped to the ground a few feet behind him. He turned; startled by a cat who had decided that it would be an appropriate moment to pounce on the rat that had scurried past. He saw nothing in the street behind him. Wick heard a whooshing sound and felt the impact of something heavy and blunt on the side of his head. Everything went black.

A short while later, eyelids fluttering, he woke to a pounding in his temple. There was a lump forming beneath the skin of his forehead, pressure stabbing behind his eye. Wick had suffered through many a hangover in his life, but nothing like this. Eyes slowly adjusting to the darkness, he came to realise that he was not in the cabin on the boat.

He was somewhere that he did not recognise. There was a smell of damp and a dripping from somewhere above his head. Craning his neck upwards, Wick saw a metal roof and realised that he was in a large shed of sorts. The sound of the lapping water outside suggested they were near the docks. Wriggling around, his senses honed in on the ropes that bound him to the chair. Panic and bile rose in his throat. There was a man, standing at the far end of the shack. He had one foot pressed against the wall and the other on the floor. There was something in his hand, turning around with each flick of his fingers.

Tarryn rolled the penny between his thumb and index finger, feeling the rough indentations of the markings. He was thinking about Paulette. He found that he was doing that more and more. It had become an illusion that he could almost believe. If he tried hard enough, he might eventually find himself capable of caring about her. He ought to buy her a present. It was what people did when they wanted to do something nice. Women liked gifts, his mother always had. He did not know what sort of thing Paulette might like. Flowers were nice, or so he had been told. She could put them in a vase and the scent would remind her whenever she walked into the room where they had come from. She would remember him.

"Do you know much about flowers?"

Wick croaked out a response, words trembling and lips dry. "What?"

"Flowers, what do you know about them?"

"Where am I?"

"That doesn't matter; there are more important things to think about right now. You're not being very helpful. Do you know anything about flowers or not?"

Wick searched his memory, trying to think of any latent knowledge of floristry that might be lurking in the recesses of his mind. There was a rumbling sound, Wick's stomach turning over and sending vomit rushing to his lips. Tarryn waited until he was done.

"Roses...roses are always nice."

"Are you trying to make me look like a fool? Roses are everywhere. There's nothing special about a rose, think of something else. Come on, I haven't got all night."

"Why...why are you asking me these questions?"

"Who else am I going to ask? You're the only person here."

"Please don't kill me. I don't want to die."

"Well then be useful."

Wick started to cry. Tarryn was not used to seeing a grown man weeping like a child. He watched him wailing and pleading. It was nauseating. There was nobody around to hear any of what he was saying, but if there had been they would have assumed that the old boatman had finally gone completely mad. There was not one useful suggestion amongst any of his ramblings.

Tarryn stood straight, an idea emerging. "Do you know

where I could get those white flowers? You know the ones that look like stars?"

"Are you talking about lilies?"

Tarryn clapped his hands together. "Yes! Thank you, lilies; those are the ones I was thinking of."

Satisfied that the decision had been made, Tarryn began to unbutton his jacket. There was too much restriction in it when it was done up. Tarryn was done being restricted. Wick realised that he was going to die. The smell of urine filled the container.

Crouching down next to the chair, Tarryn ran the blade across the gauze that covered the hole in Wick's hand. Slicing it across the material, he unbound it, layer by layer to reveal the hole that had been left by Vanguard's knife. It was red and tender around the entry mark. Tarryn pressed one finger to it. Wick made a noise that sounded like a cat being skinned. Tarryn retracted his finger. Tears rolled down Wick's face and landed in the vomit. "Who did that to your hand?"

"A dog bit me."

"Don't lie to me."

"I wouldn't, I promise."

Wick searched for a hint of compassion on his tormentors face. There was nothing.

"Tell me why Vanguard did that to you." Tarryn leaned closer, breath cold on Wick's face. "Tell me *everything*."

Sam Wick was not a brave man. There had really been no need to take him anywhere or tie him to a chair. It would not have taken much for the words to start pouring from his mouth. Tarryn listened with great interest as Wick revealed the reason behind the injury to his hand. Wick was hoping that there would be some piece of information; some secret revealed that would help his cause. It was human nature to cling to whatever small hope there was left. It would not help.

When he was finished, Tarryn rose to full height and cracked the bones in his neck. "The people deserve to know what sort of man John Vanguard truly is."

Wick's mouth opened and closed. "Yes, I mean no, I don't know what you want me to say."

"He tortured you."

"Please..."

"The truth must be revealed."

"I'll tell them, I'll them the truth about it."

"No, you won't, but you will help me to show them."

Wick's bottom lip trembled. "Are you mad?"

Tarryn could concede that it was a possibility. When it came down to it, madness was really just a matter of perspective. Perhaps the whole world had gone mad and he was the only sane one left.

"I've been asking myself that question a lot recently. This whole thing has been something of a question from the start. I suppose what I've been asking myself really, is what kind of man *am* I?"

Wick said nothing. It was alright. Tarryn did not need an answer. Taking the blade with one hand and clamping his fingers around Wick's jaw with the other, he squeezed until Wick's mouth fell open. Wick's eyes crossed as the tip of the knife found its way into the cavity. "You see, the truth is I've never been a man." The sound of anguished gurgling filled the air. "I was always a monster. I just didn't know it until recently."

Outside, the world slept as Sam Wick was taken apart slowly piece by piece. After a while there were no more noises. Even then, Tarryn did not emerge until sometime later. His type of artistry was not something that could be rushed. It was often said that a picture could speak a thousand words.

Sanquain fulfilled his promise to keep the streets clear. Undisturbed, Tarryn dragged the corpse of Sam Wick across the cobblestones until they reached their final destination. Once he was satisfied that the message had been delivered, Tarryn walked out of the Black Zone and back home.

There was less than an hour before dawn and he had lilies to buy. Perhaps he would take his mother with him. They could stop and have tea somewhere nice. He had not been good to her recently. The drugs had left sallow marks on her skin. She needed new face cream. He would buy her that as well. That would make her happy.

⊗⊁⊛

OF ALL THE THINGS THAT THE LAD THOMAS HAD expected to see on leaving the house in the early hours of the morning, a body was probably only about third on the list. At the age of ten, he had seen a number of corpses. It was not an unusual sight in the Pits. Normally though, they were face down in the gutter, their condition a result of either too much liquor or owing a debt to the wrong person.

It was still dark. Thomas was not afraid of the dark. There was not time enough to be afraid; he had forges that needed to be lit ready for the start of the work day. He pulled his jacket tightly around his chest against the cold, head bowed against the rain. If he didn't get a move on, he would be late again. Thomas didn't want to lose his job. He was the only one in the family who still had one.

Turning the corner close to the Rabbit, Thomas felt

the wind biting against the skin of his cheeks. There was a gas lamp ahead. Thomas noticed the feet first. They were pale, bare and frozen in the morning chill. The wind caught the baggy hem of the trousers at the ankles, pressing the material against the cold skin. A rope swung back and forth, creaking. The corpse of Sam Wick dangled from it, illuminated by the glow. Thomas stopped and looked up, arms at his sides. Cheeks bulging and face twisted, Wick looked down at him with vacant, glassy eyes. A purple black mass of semi-congealed fluid spilled from blue lips. Wick's jaw hung open, his tongue gone. Thomas blinked. He did not move. He simply watched the body swaying back and forth.

Eventually, his eyes trailed down the length of the cadaver until they came to rest on the thing that hung from Wick's neck and rested against his exposed chest - a white card emblazoned with a single letter. Behind the body, the walls had been daubed with red, a message scrawled across the brick still slick with rain and dirt.

Thomas could not read, he had never learnt. But there were those in the Pits that could - not many, but a few. They did not take kindly to Thomas waking them up by beating on their door in the small hours, small fists smashing against the wood. Thomas received a swift clip around the ear. "What kind of time do you call this, you little prick, why aren't you at work?"

He never received any apology for the clip around the ear. It was not in the nature of the men in the Pits to apologise for anything. However, as they both stood in the presence of the swinging corpse, he did feel the strong grip of a hand on his shoulder.

The old man looked down and nodded. "Alright, Thomas, be a good lad. Wake them up."

There were very few reasons that an alarm would be sounded in the Pits. If they rang the bells for every stabbing or mugging that occurred the entire population would hear nothing but ringing in their ears seven days a week.

Thomas barely felt the rain as he ran from the Rabbit to the church. The door was unlocked. There was nothing left in there worth stealing. Lungs bursting, Thomas climbed the stairs two at a time until he reached the top. The sprawling expanse of the city stretched out all around. Taking both hands, grubby and damp, Thomas gripped the thick rope and pulled with all his strength.

The old man stood alone in the street, the first rays of sunlight emerging over the rooftops. He scratched his chin, staring in quiet contemplation at the words on the wall as the bells rang. They did not bode well for anybody. Quietly under his breath, the old man opened his mouth and mouthed the words to nobody in particular.

'*What rises will fall.*'

CHAPTER 32
THE SPOILS OF WAR

Tarryn had not long closed his eyes when there was a loud, officious knocking at the front door. It was immediately followed by the sound of his fully conscious mother, still locked in her room, loudly announcing to him that there was somebody on the front step.

Glancing at the clock on the wall, he noted that it was just before eight which meant that whoever was standing outside was there on business. Even on the rare occasions when somebody did come to call, they did not come until well after midday. Paulette was asleep. Tarryn heard his mother yelling once more that there was somebody at the door. Rubbing his head with one hand, Tarryn replied to confirm that he had, in fact, realised that.

Hauling himself from the mattress, he padded barefoot along the length of the room to the window. There was a woman standing on the step, hands patiently folded across her front. Tarryn could not see much other than the top of her hat.

Exhausted from his encounter with Wick, after his

return Tarryn had taken off his dirty clothes and placed them into the basket at the foot of the bed. He would wash them later. There was no point in worrying about his mother seeing the blood. She wouldn't know what it meant anyway. As far as Paulette was concerned, Tarryn was just like Vanguard, dispensing justice to those who did wrong to the world.

It was a shame for her really. In a way Vanguard had abandoned Paulette in an even more callous way then he had Tarryn. He had known what sort of man Tarryn was when he brought her to the house. Tarryn doubted that he had given Paulette a second thought. He had just thrown her to the wolves.

Taking the robe from a hook, he wrapped it around his waist and went to see who was at the door. A pair of brown eyes lined with crow's feet looked up from beneath the hat. There was a slight downturn of the lips at the sight of the robe. Tarryn didn't care much about propriety. He wanted to go back to bed; his bones ached and his mother was still screeching.

"Can I help you?"

"May I come in, please?" The woman was shorter than average. The brim of the hat was as wide as her body and it was a large hat. The white collar of her blouse had been buttoned up as high as it would go. Everything about her was neat and proper.

"Who are you?"

"Someone who doesn't make a habit of introducing themselves whilst standing on a doorstep."

Tarryn stepped back, allowing the woman to bustle into the house. She looked up and down the hall, glancing into the room that contained the fireplace and armchair.

The woman removed the hat to reveal a tidy pile of mousy grey hair. "My name is Mrs Brown. I'm the housekeeper."

"We don't have a housekeeper."

"We shall agree to disagree. Is this the sitting room?"

Mrs Brown marched into the room, eyes roaming over everything. She walked to the armchair and took a seat, spreading the folds of her skirt neatly across her lap. "I will require a place to sleep preferably close to the front of the house."

"I'm sorry, but...why are you here?"

Mrs Brown reached into her bag and pulled out a piece of paper. She handed it to Tarryn. Unfolding it, he saw the mark of Sanquain's office in the corner. She waited patiently as he read the letter. When he was done, she took it back and replaced it. "The captain has paid me wages for the next month. As long as you remain in his employment so I shall remain in yours. I am here to cook, clean, and attend to the residents of the house. You will find I am very good at my job."

There was a banging from upstairs. Lady Leersac had taken to smacking the floor with a slipper in order to get attention. Tarryn looked up at the ceiling. Mrs Brown remained fixed in place. "Your clothes from last night, where are they?"

"Upstairs. I'll wash them."

"You will give them to me. Later you will find what you need folded in the closet." The banging continued unabated. "The captain will see you at nine o'clock. Your breakfast will be ready at quarter past eight. I suggest that you wash, dress and strip the sheets from the bed. There will be blood on them. A driver will knock on the door at eight forty and you are required to be punctual."

"Are these orders coming from you or Captain Sanquain?"

Mrs Brown sniffed. "I am simply a housekeeper. I don't give orders."

The creaking of footsteps on the stairs caught her attention. Mrs Brown cocked one eyebrow. Paulette appeared in the doorway still wearing her nightdress. "Who is this?" Her voice was a little quieter than normal.

Mrs Brown barely hid the disapproval on her face. "You may call me Mrs Brown. I am here to take care of the house."

Paulette felt herself flushing. "That's what *I* was doing." She mumbled, biting her lip.

"Well, now you don't have to concern yourself. I think it best that from now on we each stick to utilising the skills which we have been blessed with..." Mrs Brown paused, words lingering as she took in Paulette's appearance. "...of which I am doubtless you have many."

Lady Leersac continued banging on the floor.

Mrs Brown's eyes rolled upwards. "Is she locked up?"

Tarryn nodded.

Mrs Brown held out one hand. "I shall take the key now. You should go and get dressed."

As he stood in the bedroom, Tarryn stared at the racks of clothing in the closet. There was nothing in it that was not black. It had not been deliberately done that way. Black was simply easier to maintain. It was cheaper and it lasted longer. It was a uniform of sorts. Soon the wardrobe would be filled with garments more appropriate to his status.

Sanquain was pleased with his work; the arrival of Mrs Brown was proof of that.

The smell of food cooking caused his stomach to

growl. Paulette couldn't boil water without burning it. There was no more banging. The house had become, within five minutes of the woman arriving, efficient and orderly.

Tarryn felt the corner of his mouth flicker upwards. The skin around the corners felt tightened. Vanguard had promised so much and yet had delivered nothing. Within a matter of days, the captain had given him more than Vanguard had been able to in months. These were the spoils of war. They were long overdue.

"Will that woman be staying in my room?" Paulette enquired.

The arrival of Mrs Brown had left Paulette understandably concerned about her role in their arrangement. Tarryn did not need her any longer. Most of the time he did not even care to have her around. There was no reason that she could not simply go back to the Black Zone and return to lying on her back for a living. But his time with Vanguard had been full of promises that had not been kept. He had little to show for the efforts he had made. Paulette was the only thing that Vanguard had left him with. For some reason, Tarryn was reluctant to return her.

"This is your room now."

Downstairs he found his mother sitting in the parlour with a tray on her lap. Mrs Brown was bent at the waist, pouring tea from the pot into his mother's cup. Lady Leersac bid him good morning and enquired after his health. Tarryn took a seat and Mrs Brown served them both as if she had been doing it for years. They enjoyed a peaceful breakfast together.

Mrs Brown retrieved the dirty clothes from the wash basket as they ate. She peeled open the sleeves of the jacket to find the shirt bundled up inside. There were thick smears of blood across the front. A hair was caught around the button of the sleeve. Mrs Brown bundled them up and wrapped a sheet around them. Tucking the pile under one arm, she bustled back through the house and into the kitchen, dousing the washing water with detergent. Blood stains were always a pain to shift. She wondered if people knew how troublesome they could be. A simple wipe down leather coverall was always a preferable garment for a kill. It was a combination of youthful pride and lack of experience. Young people these days were always more interested in style than substance. Still, Mrs Brown did not question the captain. She simply cashed her cheques.

The boy was a psychopath. She had known it from the moment that she had seen him. Sanquain had a good eye for them. Mrs Brown was an organized and smart woman. She had worked well with many a psychopath over the years. They all needed a little help to reach their full potential. It was her job to ensure that they were fully prepared.

Tarryn did not remember the last time that somebody had cooked breakfast for them. In fact, he did not remember the last time they ate a proper meal together at all. The last memory he had of food was of some kind of attempt at a sandwich Paulette had made. He wasn't often hungry.

"Are you ready?"

The timing of Mrs Brown's question coincided perfectly with a knock at the door. The driver stood patiently outside whilst the housekeeper retrieved Tarryn's coat for him. As he pulled the cuffs of his shirt sleeves straight, Lady Leersac smiled broadly. "Where are you going?"

"I have to go to work, I'll be back later." He leaned over and pressed a kiss to his mother's cheek. Tarryn plucked one of his mother's hands from her lap and held it in his. Her skin was warm against his cold. "Have a lovely day."

With that, Tarryn left Lady Leersac in the competent hands of Mrs Brown. He kept his head pressed against the window during the carriage ride to the square. The road sped beneath them as they kept up a steady pace. There were people walking along, heading towards whatever mundane tasks they had planned for the day. They paid no attention to the carriage going by. It did not matter anymore. They were insignificant.

Arriving at the offices, Tarryn walked in and announced his arrival to the clerk. The man returned moments later and gestured towards the stairs. Lifting his head, Tarryn looked up at the ceiling of the great towers stretched up ahead of him. Tarryn was now officially in the employment of Felix Sanquain. The money, the carriage, the housekeeper – this was all just the beginning. There were no limits to what could be achieved with Sanquain behind him. Tarryn was going to do more than simply restore the name Leersac to its former glory. Finally he saw a future in which his father's legacy would die and his would be born. There was no amount of bodies that he would not leave in his wake to achieve it.

Sanquain was waiting in the office. This time the captain sat in a large leather chair that faced a matching counterpart. There was a tray on the table between them and two glasses had been filled. He invited Tarryn to sit down. "How are you finding Mrs Brown?"

Tarryn sat. "Efficacious."

"Good. She is an excellent housekeeper both in ability and discretion. She is also extremely loyal."

The context of Sanquain's statement was not difficult to understand. Tarryn knew that whilst working in the service of the captain came with certain benefits, it also came with certain conditions. Mrs Brown belonged to Sanquain in terms of both employment and allegiance.

The captain took a sip from his glass and exhaled. He lifted the glass so that it was level with his eyes and looked at the liquid inside. "I never liked Vanguard much, but he was a means to an ends. There was work to be done and he had the skills needed to achieve it. Now, I have you."

Leaning forward, Tarryn took the other glass.

"Your work with Samuel Wick was exactly as I wanted it."

"Thank you." Tarryn let the taste of the liquor roll around on his tongue for a moment.

Sanquain turned in his seat to look at the empty hearth. There were a few burnt logs in it from the last time that the fire had been lit. "What do you remember of the last civil war?"

"Not much. I was younger then."

"You know, there are many people who believe I rose to power because of what I achieved in those years. They're quite wrong. They fail to see the many years spent before that, working my way to the top simply to get people to understand the way that things must be. Success does not come without sacrifice. There are those who believe I enjoy causing them to suffer. Not the case. I simply understand that sometimes to do what must be done, we need to go to war."

The captain took another sip of whisky. It was not hard for a man with the right motives to stir dissent. All it took was a few acts of industrial sabotage, the right words whispered in the wrong ears. Sanquain had seen the effect that a crumbling economy had on a country. He had always found it strange. Slaughter thousands of people without cause and you were a murderer. Slaughter thousands by sending them to war and you were a strategist. When he had started the last war, many years before, he had done so with the intention of moulding the world into a better, more efficient place. The farmer did not concern himself with the fate of the rats he caught in order to protect his valued stock. It was a necessity.

"Is that we're doing here?"

Sanquain ran one finger around the rim of his glass. He always had a plan. For everything that had happened, for every secret and lie that had been told, he had always been one step ahead of everyone else.

"The masses are predictable. They grow discontented with their lot and they look for someone to blame. Cooke would have them turn against the upper class, the *true* benefactors of this city. *We* shall show them that the real cause of their trouble lies within their own neighbourhoods. And we shall watch them tear themselves apart."

There was a document lying on the table. Tarryn had not noticed it before. Sanquain did not say anything as he leant forward and picked it up. Opening it, Tarryn realised the nature of Sanquain's plan. The document was a warrant for the arrest and execution of John Vanguard.

Cooke anticipated that people would rally to his side, fight for justice. Sanquain knew them better than that. They were not an army, nor would they ever be. They were a mob, ready to march into the streets with their forks and torches. All he needed to do was provide them with a monster.

CHAPTER 33
LILIES

One benefit of Mrs Brown's unanticipated arrival was that Tarryn now found himself with an abundance of time in which to complete personal tasks. There was one in particular that felt like it was of utmost importance. Somewhere in the city was the perfect bouquet of flowers and he intended to find them. Or at least, that was if he could remember what the hell they were called.

Wick had said something about them but the name had since escaped his mind completely.

Flowers were not a particular speciality of his but it was not as if the species were uncommon. It bothered him that the word seemed to roll on the tip of his tongue but could not be caught. Tarryn had an excellent memory. He did not simply forget things. Walking through town he pictured their smooth white petals, but could not remember the word. There was a good florist in the centre of the market district. The man who ran it knew his varieties well and would no doubt have an excellent recommendation.

Tarryn hoped that Paulette would like them. He could give them to her when he returned home. His wrist was itching. Scratching at it, he wondered how many other men had bought her flowers before, realising it was probably none. She was lucky he had kept her, really.

A bell rang out as Tarryn entered the shop. The walls were adorned with colour. Delicate petals infused the air with sweet perfume. It was heady, the depth of the aroma seeping into his skin. He would smell like flowers for the rest of the day. The shopkeeper acknowledged his arrival whilst tending to the cuttings that were spread across the surface of the counter. "Good morning."

"I need a bouquet."

"A gift for a lady I presume? Does she have a signature bloom?"

Tarryn explained to the shopkeeper the specific type of thing that he was searching for. The man nodded, glasses sliding with each movement down the bridge of his nose. He pushed them back with one finger to hold them in place. "The white lily... an unusual choice, if I may say. Might she prefer something else?"

"What do you mean?"

There were many things that Tarryn did not understand about the world. How women worked was one of them. In his mind when he thought of Paulette, he thought of the delicate white flower. It was something fragile, easily damaged.

"We usually only supply them for funerals and memorials, such like. I'm afraid they have a bit of a reputation as a symbol for death. Are you sure you wouldn't prefer something more traditional? Roses, perhaps?"

Tarryn shook his head. It was exactly what he was looking for. "No, it must be lilies."

Still unconvinced, the shopkeeper brought forth a large bucket containing two dozen of the flower, stems half submerged in water. Tarryn looked at each one in turn, examining it carefully before returning it to the bucket. Growing increasingly concerned that he would not find a single one that was right, he began to panic. Each of them was tarnished in some way. The petals were bruised and out of shape. There were ones with some petals larger than the others. They had to be exactly the same. The shop-keeper noticed his hesitance. "Can I show you something else?"

"No, don't show me anything else. It has to be these, nothing else."

The shopkeeper had seen many young men brimming with nerves enter into his store before. They often had a very particular thing in mind for whatever flimsy young tart they were lusting over that week. This man was more than nervous. He flicked through each of the flowers, peering over every inch of each individual bloom. "She must be a very lucky lady to have someone pay such careful attention to detail."

"Yes, yes, I suppose so." Tarryn was not listening. He had found it. It was one of the last three left. The petals curved slightly, each of them exactly the same. It was unblemished, unspoilt. Handling it with the utmost care, he placed it on the counter in front of the shopkeeper. "I want this one."

"As part of the bouquet?"

Tarryn shook his head. There only needed to be one. It would ruin it if the flower were hidden within a cluster of substandard blossoms. There was not another one in the store to equal it. After the shopkeeper had diligently wrapped the single flower and placed it into a box for protection, Tarryn paid what was owed and left. The bell chimed as the door closed behind him.

There was a mild breeze washing across the Golden Quarter. It was pleasant and refreshing. He took his time walking to the Black Zone, breathing in the air and feeling the shift in the energy of the city. The closer that he drew to the boundaries, the more he felt it. There was a shuddering to the vibrations of the cobblestones that only he could feel. It was the thundering approach of a mob that had not yet formed. It would, soon enough.

If there was one thing that you could rely on, it was that news travelled fast. Information regarding the state in which Sam Wick's corpse had been discovered would have been well beyond the Pits by now. Sanquain would have made sure of it. Tarryn did not need to get far out of the Golden Quarter before he came across the first of the rabble rousers. They were just getting warmed up.

"And how are we meant to sleep when there are men with their tongues being cut out right beneath our noses? How do we keep ourselves safe at night?"

The man slammed a fist against his open palm. He stood on the pavement, spouting his opinions to anyone who walked past. Whoever the man was, he was no public speaker. He was just another angry voice blowing into the wind. But it only took one person to listen.

Tarryn had a suggestion to put to Sanquain. It was one thing to murder a man like Sam Wick. He was well known, but had never been particularly liked. He had certainly never been respected. If they truly wanted to turn the Black Zone against itself, they needed to strike a blow against that which they revered most – one that the people would not soon forgive.

WHILST TARRYN CONCLUDED HIS BUSINESS IN THE Golden Quarter, Vanguard was trying to work out what it was exactly that Kosic had put on the plate in front of him. It looked like some sort of meat, but it wasn't identifiable. He picked it up and sniffed it. No sooner had it been put back, Kosic pierced it with his fork, dragging it from one plate to another. "You eat too slow, it will be cold. No good for you."

There was a crashing from the ground below. Kosic stood, edging towards the window and looked through the crack in the shutters. The Red Badges were swarming the street, sending crates and boxes flying in their wake, at least a dozen of them, heavy boots clattering against the floor. The door opened and Demetrio slipped inside, pushing the hair from his face. "The Red Badges are outside, they're searching everything."

Vanguard had anticipated this. "Are they looking for Cooke?"

Demetrio shook his head. "No, they're looking for you; they say you murdered a man last night."

The announcement came as something of a surprise. Vanguard had murdered a lot of people. Nobody had ever come looking for him because of it. More to the point, this time, he actually hadn't done it.

Once Demetrio had relayed the details of Wick's untimely demise however, he was certain he knew who had. There was more shouting from downstairs. They could hear Herveaux's voice as he argued with the Red Badges, furious that his property was being treated with such disrespect. He had a much higher opinion of his business than Sanquain did.

"I need to leave; if they find me here, nobody will join your cause. Not if they think I'm the one that's murdering them. There'll be a pack of baying wolves at your door before sundown."

Kosic looked perplexed. "Why do you not do that thing that you do, where they cannot see you?"

"I can't, not all of the time. That's not how it works."

Carmen, who had been sitting on the bed with her notepad and pencil, glanced up. She was looking paler than usual. She had not been outside the apartment for several days.

She put down the book. "What should we do?"

"You should go back to Henriette; you can't be caught with me. Tell her to shut the doors of the house and to keep them shut."

"What if she says no?"

"Tell her that if she doesn't there won't be much of a house left to have soon. Once the fighting begins there won't be a looter or thief in the city that doesn't crawl out of the gutters."

"You think there'll be riots?"

Vanguard turned to Kosic. "You should tell Cooke. As soon as the street is clear I'll go."

Carmen scrambled from the bed. "I'm coming with you. I'm not scared." The corners of her eyes flickered. After all she had seen, she gave no mind to fear even though she ought to have done. Part of Vanguard wished he could be so sincere about something. But revolution was all well and good in words and speeches. The reality of it was a little grimmer.

Lifting his hand to the side of her face, he rubbed his thumb against her cheek. "That's why I need you to go to Henriette, there's nobody else I can trust." He paused for a moment. "You know, you shouldn't let them change you too much. Not the good bits anyway."

She hesitated for a moment, not moving.

"What?"

"I have to get dressed."

"Yes."

"Well, get out then."

Vanguard had spent the last few months watching Carmen parading around wearing little more than her underwear and sometimes less than that. He wasn't arguing with the request, it was just a little unexpected. As he descended the stairs, one hand gripping the banister, he glanced back and saw the bare skin of her back, spine curving as she sat on the bed.

It struck him then that Carmen had never been shy about her body because it had never occurred to her before that it was hers to do with what she wanted. Truthfully, she probably wouldn't have cared if Vanguard had stayed there. What she wanted was the right to want him not to be. Turning away, he walked to the bottom of the stairs and did not look back.

CHAPTER 34
NATURAL CAUSES

Making his way across the city, Vanguard felt something he had not felt in a long while. He felt exposed. Maybe it was the thought that somewhere out there was a man who could see him. It was not a pleasant sensation. He stuck close to the alleys and back passages that led through the Black Zone towards the border of the Golden Quarter.

Sanquain was a man with many secrets - most of which he kept hidden in his chambers. Vanguard could not be sure that he would find anything there of value but it was worth the risk. The captain was driving them all towards something and it would be a great advantage to know exactly where the end play would be made.

By the time the offices were empty it was way past dark. Vanguard opened the door to the room that Sanquain presided over and walked in, brushing his hand against the desk. Without the bustling of people and the constant scratching of pens, the chambers seemed desolate.

The top drawer of the bureau slid open. Vanguard

picked up the pistol and put it on the desk. There was a compartment beneath the drawer bottom. He pressed down on it and heard a clicking sound. Slipping the tips of his fingers beneath the wood, he tried to lift it upwards. The compartment was locked with no key in sight.

Vanguard could pick a lock, but that would take up valuable time that he didn't have. Sanquain was not the kind of person to leave a key stuck to the underside of a desk. Vanguard looked at the lock for a moment, considering the best course of action. "Fuck it." He took the butt of the pistol and smashed it against the wood.

The cracking echoed across the room, the sounds bouncing from the walls. Prising up the lid, Vanguard looked in the compartment below. It was empty. Whatever had been in there before, it had been removed. He was about to check the next drawer when he heard a door open and close down the corridor. Realising that he was not alone; Vanguard took the pistol from the desk and stood with his back against the wall. Too late, he realised that he had left the bag lying on the floor in the middle of the room. The door swung open.

Sanderson found himself looking down the business end of the pistol. He did not need to look into the shadows to know who held it. Vanguard kept his finger on the trigger, teeth pressed firmly together. Neither of them moved a muscle. Finally, Sanderson spoke. "Are you going to shoot me then or not?"

Part of him very much wanted to. Vanguard had always known however, that until the time came when he was able to put a bullet between Sanderson's eyes without thinking about it, it was not time for him to die.

Lowering the barrel slightly Vanguard aimed instead at Sanderson's knee cap. It wasn't his time to die but that did not make them friends. Neither did it mean that either of them was guaranteed to make it back out of the chambers in the same condition that they went in. Vanguard took in a breath. Above them, the sounds of the rain pattered against the tiles of the roof.

Eventually Sanderson walked over to the window and stood staring out across the city. Sanquain had a good view from up there during the day. It was different at night. It was hard to tell where the sky began and the city ended. "You've really gone and fucked us all this time."

The aftermath of Wick's run in with Tarryn was all over the streets. Sanderson was not a squeamish man. The sight of blood neither excited nor frightened him. So it said something that even he found the manner in which Tarryn dispatched his marks to be discomforting.

"I'd have thought you'd be happy to have me out of the picture."

"Funnily enough, so did I, until that mad bastard turned up." Sanderson took a seat at the desk, lifting both feet from the floor and placing them on the surface.

Vanguard wondered how many times they had both stood with the captain in that room. He wondered how many lives had been ended by decisions made at that desk.

"Why are you here, Sanderson?"

"I'm here because, unlike those dumb fucks out there, I know you. I knew you'd come here."

"Congratulations. Are you going to arrest me?"

"No, and neither are they. Sanquain doesn't actually want anyone to arrest you at all, not yet. The order's been given but he knows they won't find you. Shit, it's half the reason he put up with you in the first place, all that creeping about you do."

"So why bother to send out the Reds?"

"Looks good on paper, doesn't it? As far as half this city is concerned, you're a deranged murderer. It wouldn't look very good if they weren't at least trying. Where have you been, anyway?"

Vanguard said nothing.

Sanderson continued. "Doesn't matter. Don't you want to know why I've been looking for you?"

"Why?"

"Because Sanquain's gone and given your little psychopath his own list of names."

Vanguard felt a prickle rolling up the back of his neck. Sanderson put his feet back down on the floor. The list had not been easy to copy. The handwriting was barely legible, the names taken from a stolen glance of the copy on the captain's desk. "He's out there now slitting throats all over the place and I've not been called to clear up a single body. Want to know why? Because the poor bastards getting gutted aren't the same sort of sad little shits you used to play around with."

"Who are they then?"

"Any poor bastard that's had dealings with you."

"Why? Why bother with all of this? If Sanquain wants me why doesn't he just send the boy?"

Sanderson shrugged. "Don't know, don't care. Maybe he wants you to suffer, he wouldn't be the first. Doubt he'll be the last."

"If you're on his side, why are you telling me all this?"

Standing up, Sanderson rubbed his elbow with one hand. "If that little prick is out there with a list of people that have had dealings with your sorry arse how long do you think it's going to be before he comes for me?"

"What makes you think I give a shit if he comes for you?"

"Because you don't want to let anyone else kill me before you get the chance."

Sanderson was correct. His name did appear on the list that the captain had handed Tarryn. It was not however, a priority. There were others who would die first. The name Gregor held no meaning for Vanguard. Sam Wick was already dead. The third and fourth names however, were ones that he knew well.

As Sanderson and Vanguard stood in the offices of Sanquain's chambers high above the city, below them on the streets, Tarryn marched with steadfast purpose towards the Tanners. It was going to be a busy night.

Sanquain was pleased with the boy's progress. The city was already on a knife edge. Cooke's letters sat in a neat pile in front of him on the table in his townhouse. There was a fire crackling in the hearth. He had requested it be lit specifically. There was no need to keep the letters anymore; they had told him all that he needed to know.

The last name on Tarryn's list was not one that the captain himself had originally added. He had to admit it was a bold move. Sanquain's intentions had been simply to paint Cooke's supposed hero as a cold blooded killer. What Tarryn planned would elevate Vanguard's reputation to something far beyond that of a mere murderer. Taking the letters and throwing them into the fire, he watched the flames licking at the edges of the paper. They turned brown and crisp, shrivelling away to nothing. The clock chimed midnight. It would be done soon.

By the time the sun rose in the morning, John

Vanguard would never again be able to walk the Black Zone without a target on his back.

THE RING O' BASTARDS WAS CLOSED. LUDNOR STOOD AT the bar and counted out each of the counters from the evening's business. It had been a busy one. The taverns were always the first to profit when times were bad. They were always bad. This was worse. Usually at that time of night there would still be several customers draped across the bar, too drunk or too miserable to go home. The bar was deserted. Outside the streets were empty. Nobody wanted to risk not being at home to protect what little they had when the looters came.

There was a rattling at the door. He had locked it for once. The opportunists had already started to appear, picking off the weaker businesses and taking what they could. Ludnor would be damned before they'd get their hands on his wares. "*Fuck off.*"

The rattling ceased. Ludnor watched the door carefully. Slipping one hand beneath the counter, he felt for the handle of the cleaver and brought it out. Setting it down on the bar, he continued with his counting. Ludnor shook his head and snorted. Gossip and rumours were abounding. The old bar keeper was well aware of the death of Sam Wick, he kept his opinions about the matter to himself. The door rattled again. "I said *FUCK OFF.*"

It stopped abruptly. Ludnor was about to seal up the bag when he heard a clattering coming from the kitchen. The back door was locked and bolted. There was however, a hole in the wall beside the stove that he had been meaning to fix. Ludnor had given up trying to keep the cat out. One of these days he was going to put it in the pot and make a soup out of it.

There was a door between the kitchen and the bar. Its installation had been deemed necessary after the fourth attempt by one of his patrons to make a hasty exit through the back without coughing up their counters. It opened, the sounds of the hinges creaking. Ludnor's back straightened. Eyes narrowing, he looked at the man standing in the doorway with the knife in his hand.

Taking the cleaver from the bar and letting it hang from his fingers, the oldest man in the Tanners took his stance. "I knew you were a vicious little cunt the minute I saw you."

Tarryn stared at Ludnor. Slowly he reached up and put one hand into his pocket, retrieving from it a single counter. He placed it down on the table next to him. Scratched into the face of the counter was a single V. He cocked his head to one side. "You're a little old, for a revolutionary."

Ludnor gripped the cleaver a little tighter. "We both know you don't give two shits about any revolution. You'd be here even if none of this were happening. You stink of death and now you've come for me. Well, better men than you have tried - I've been a part of this since before you were even a twitch in your father's balls. Fuck Sanquain, fuck this city and *fuck you*."

Tarryn did not disappear. He did not want to - not for this one.

Tarryn held respect for one thing and one thing only and that was death. Ludnor had out run death for decades, more so than any other man in the city. Now that it had finally found him, he had earned the right to see it coming. Darting forward, Tarryn leapt up, bringing his body to the surface of the bar and sliding along the counter to the other side where the old man swung the cleaver through the air. Anybody walking past the tavern at that moment would have seen the panes of the window smeared crimson.

❧

LESS THAN AN HOUR LATER, VANGUARD STOOD TAKING in the scene that lay before him. It looked like the aftermath of a battle. Chairs lay upturned on the floor. Counters had rolled across the wooden boards, creating a crunching carpet of red, blue and black.

Ludnor was behind the bar. He was also under the tables and on the shelves. There were little bits of Ludnor scattered across the length of the Ring. The old man had not gone quietly.

Vanguard stepped over the mess, coming to a stop at the counter and looking down at the barkeeper's body lying beneath the pumps. The cleaver was still gripped in his hand.

In the corner of the room, the piano sat unblemished by blood or sinew. Vanguard plucked a bottle from the shelf along with a glass. This was no time for sobriety. Henriette would have been unhappy about it, but she wasn't there to tell him so. The liquor burned just the way he remembered it. Footsteps ran across the street outside. It would not be long before the body was discovered. He needed to leave as quickly as possible.

Instead he placed the glass on the top of the piano. Ludnor had been one of the few people in the city that Vanguard had genuinely respected. The old man had always been a curiosity to the neighbourhood. There were plenty of rumours as to his origins. He would have liked the time to mourn his death. Or at least have one drink with him. Pressing a finger to the key, the note rang out slightly off tune. Vanguard closed both eyes.

All across the city, people were starting to turn on one another - rich against poor, zone against zone. This was no revolution. It was chaos. There would be riots before the next time the sun set over the skyline. Cooke sat on one side of D'Orsee and Sanquain the other. In the end all it came down to was who could tell the best lies. That was all it had ever been, both of them weaving a spider's web of stories and rumours, spun across the streets and woven through the fabric of the city.

They were stories in which John Vanguard was both villain and hero, two sides of the same coin spinning in the air. Carmen was right; it was time to choose a side once and for all.

For more than half a decade, Sanquain had been the architect of misery. All the lives that had been destroyed, all the bodies that lay beneath the ground - all of them led back to Sanquain. Cooke might not have all the answers yet, but it was better than what they had now. Anything was better than this. Vanguard poured himself another drink. He might as well have two.

Vanguard had intended to go directly back to the apartment. That night however, his body had different plans. He didn't try to fight it. He'd been doing that long enough.

Henriette had been surprised to see him walk into the parlour at the house. He did not say anything about it; instead he leaned down and whispered something in her ear. The parlour door was rapidly closed. When it opened again, Vanguard left both the house and Henriette, her face flushed slightly, hands still gripping at the table edge.

Vanguard would never speak of what occurred in the parlour that night, not to anyone. He would however, regardless of how many years there were or were not yet to pass, fondly remember it as the most satisfying six minutes of his life.

It had been an interesting life. Vanguard had never been under any illusion that he would die a peaceful death. Tarryn would see him coming of course but by then it would be too late. The time had come for the coin to land where it may. Felix Sanquain had to die.

CHAPTER 35
THE DEATH OF CATHERINE CRASS

Mandego heard the pounding of a fist against the door. He sat up, the bed covers sliding away to reveal his bare chest, a smattering of grey hair covering the skin from nipples to navel. Falling back against the pillows, Mandego groaned as the thudding continued. Placing both hands over his head and closing his eyes, he felt a pair of soft, warm hands running over the length of his body. They slid up the outside of his leg to his stomach, fingers circling. Slapping the hand away, Mandego heard a giggle from beneath the sheets. He peeled them back and looked down at the girl who bit her lip. "A very good morning to you too, now please, kindly fuck off."

She pouted, rolling over and stretching as if to indicate how very comfortable she was.

"I'm sorry, was I whispering? I said fuck off."

The pout changed from one of teasing coquettishness to actual irritation. Vacating the bed and flouncing across the room to retrieve her clothes, the girl muttered under her breath. Mandego rolled his eyes. There was a pleasant jiggling to her naked buttocks. She glared at him before opening the door and cursing at whoever was standing on the other side.

Mandego pulled the covers back over himself. "Fucking whores."

He had no sooner closed his eyes when the pounding started again. "FOR THE LOVE OF FUCK, WHAT IS IT?"

The sentry that had been posted outside his door for the night came in. His face was ashen. Mandego sat up. "Well?"

MANDEGO GOT DRESSED SLOWLY. THERE WAS A FROCK coat in the closet made from burgundy velvet. She had always liked him in that one. He put it on and buttoned it all the way up to the top. Lifting his hands, he adjusted the silver chain that he wore around his neck. Satisfied that it was hanging correctly, he went to the door and opened it. The sentry was waiting outside.

The streets had already been lined. Mandego had a lot of people; they were all thieves and bastards. Not one of them would hesitate to kill the other at the slightest provocation if it were not for the boundaries of the barricade. They were the scum of the earth. This was their sanctuary.

Each head turn to follow the undisputed king of the Butchers as he walked down the middle of the street. There was one person and only one person that they held an iota of respect and admiration for and that man was Hector Mandego. It was a respect built out of fear, not love, but it was a respect nonetheless. The street was silent as he approached the end of the Butchers.

Stopping at the barricade, Mandego lifted his head and cast his eyes upwards. Perched on top of the splintered wood and twisted metal, eyes wide and mouth open, was the severed head of Catherine Crass. Mandego looked at it. Carefully placed on the surface of her tongue, was a card. The rest of her was nowhere to be found. Not a single person moved. Not one word was spoken.

Hector turned away. "Take it down."

One of the men began to climb the pile of debris to retrieve the head. He picked it up carefully, making his way awkwardly down once again. He presented it to Mandego who took it in his hands.

Lifting it to his lips, he whispered something into Catherine's ear. Mandego had a lot of lovers. Catherine had always been his favourite. She doled out black eyes and broken jaws just because the mood took her. She was vile, hot tempered and not above stabbing a man in the guts if she felt so inclined. Others had come and gone. Catherine had been there for years. She had deserved a better death.

"Who watched the barricade last night?" There was no answer. "I said who was watching the barricade last night?"

A voice called out from the masses. There was no honour amongst thieves.

Magnus, the sentry who had been in charge of the barricade the night before, did not have time to offer a counter argument. Before he could so much as utter a word, Mandego crossed the street and pressed a pistol to the front of his head. There was a crack and a spray of blood, brains exploding from the back of his skull. He dropped to the floor, leaving whatever was left to dribble into the gutter.

Mandego turned so that he looked at the residents of the Butchers. He still held Catherine's head in his hands. "We know who did this. I want him found. He's out there somewhere. Find that bastard, find him and bring him to me, I want to put a bullet between his fucking eyes."

Nobody moved at first. "Well? Get a fucking move on."

Tarryn watched from the rooftop. He saw the look on Mandego's face when he realised that what the sentry had told him was true. Catherine Crass had put up her last fight. She had fought too. There was a scratch mark on his face to prove it.

There had been many people fall beneath his knife since things had begun. Catherine had been the only one so far to leave any sort of mark on him in return. It was a shame that he could not tell Mandego about that. He probably would have liked to have known it.

CHAPTER 36
A HEAVY PRICE

The clock tower in the middle of the square rang out nine times. Sanquain looked down from the window, watching the last of the preparations being added to the stage. Harried looking workers hung the flags across the platform.

Nobody knew exactly what it was that Sanquain was going to announce. There had been flyers displayed across the city stating that there was to be a public address. The square would soon be filled with people keen to hear what news would come. They would pack themselves in, eagerly craning forward to find out what was to be done about the monster rampaging about their city. He wondered if any of them knew that the monster would be walking amongst them.

Vanguard would come; there was no question of it. The captain looked back over his shoulder. Tarryn was sitting at the desk, nursing a glass of fresh water. Sanquain could have almost sworn he saw the side of the glass freeze as Tarryn touched it.

It looked as though if he held it long enough it would shatter.

"Are you ready? There must be no mistakes today."

Tarryn seemed unfazed. "There won't be."

The boy had changed significantly over the last few weeks. The presence of Mrs Brown, the freedom that came with knowing the city would protect him from retribution; it had all given him a cold confidence that had not been there before.

"You and Vanguard have a history. Can I trust you to do what needs to be done?"

"I won't let you down."

"You're not to kill him, is that clear?"

"Crystal."

"I've spent too long waiting for the right moment to cleanse this city; I won't have that derailed because you can't control yourself."

Tarryn placed the glass down on the table, wiping one finger up the side. "I'll be good."

It was almost time to leave. There was a knock at the door and a Red Badge appeared. He was freshly shaven, clean and alert. This was good. Sanquain needed them to be alert. Nothing could go wrong. "Get the guard ready. I want to be on stage in five minutes."

The Red Badge nodded obediently and closed the door. Tarryn stood. With one hand he reached up and did up the clasp on the neck of his jacket. Mrs Brown had starched the collar. It gave him even more sharp angles than nature had already gifted him with. Tarryn looked as though he could cut a man just by looking at him.

Sanquain adjusted his cuffs. "Shall we go and create a new world?"

There was an elevator at the end of the hall. It was

usually reserved only for the use of Sanquain. Tarryn entered, hands clasped behind his back. The rest of the guards filed in. One of them, a gruff looking man with a bald head, turned and met with Tarryn's gaze. His top lip curled slightly. Tarryn said nothing as they descended. The elevator door opened and Sanquain stepped out, followed by his guards. The bald man turned to look back, opening his mouth to speak with Tarryn. A cold shiver ran up his spine. There was nothing there.

Vanguard was accustomed to working under the shadow of night. That morning the sun shone so brightly on the square that he thought it might blind him. Maybe he was imagining it. There had never been any sun there before. Without the cover of darkness, Vanguard felt exposed. Not vulnerable exactly, but somehow more aware of everything.

The stage had been erected in the centre of the square. The city clock provided an impressive backdrop to the wooden platform. The crowd would be packed in tightly. Still, Vanguard was experienced and capable enough to find a way to the front regardless.

He could approach from the left or the right; either would provide the opportunity to get close enough to Sanquain for the job to be done in a matter of seconds. Ideally, the strike needed to come from the left. There was a small set of steps that led up onto the stage on the right hand side. They were narrow, big enough only for two men at a time to ascend. Sanquain would be at his most vulnerable in those few seconds. That was all he needed.

Vanguard sniffed the air. Tarryn was nearby. He knew it because he could smell death. The air was heavy with it.

He had never had much in the way of good fortune. It didn't matter now. He would have liked to have said that he had no regrets, but it would have been a lie. He had plenty of those. There was not much about the world that Vanguard would miss. He supposed he would not miss much at all if he were dead. That was a sort of comfort.

He would have liked to have lived to see what Carmen would make of herself. He suspected that whatever it might be, it would come as surprise to the rest of the world.

Vanguard had forgone the bag for this occasion. It was cumbersome to manoeuvre with, at least with so many people around. Plus, he had some personal possessions that held no worth to anyone, but that he should like Henriette to have. At least that way, there was a chance that someone would remember him. All of his belongings, save for the clothes on his back and the knife hidden in the sleeve of his jacket, were neatly folded and left on the floor of Ludnor's shed. No doubt by now the cat had probably claimed them for a new bed.

Vanguard kept his head low. Merging into the crowd, he flickered in and out of view. The odd person would catch a glimpse of a collar pulled high, or a low hood, but then it would disappear once again.

It was a varied assembly, old and young alike gathering to hear the address. Flirty young girls made inviting faces towards the soldiers standing around the periphery of the square. An occasional eye would wander, only to snap back into place when faced with the bellowing roars of their officers.

A noise sounded from the stage, a fanfare to announce Sanquain's arrival. The doors to the tower opened and a number of guards filed out. They formed two lines and proceeded forwards until there were twelve of them, six on each side. It was most likely the captain would take four with him up the steps. He would go first and they would follow, two abreast. Glancing from side to side, Vanguard saw no sign of Tarryn. He knew that he would see him sooner or later.

Captain Sanquain made his way across the square for what would be the final time. The people did not applaud; they simply stood quietly and waited. The stage loomed before him, the banners depicting the red and white colours of his sigil catching the breeze. Vanguard pushed his way through the crowd. The people parted, rearranging and reassembling around him. The guards kept their eyes open, seeing nothing. Sanquain was half way across the square as Vanguard reached the front of the audience.

Sliding the knife forward, he touched the blade with his fingers and thought of Henriette. He thought of the parlour and cake, the oil slicked puddles outside and Vince standing at the door. Stepping forth from out of the crowd, Vanguard used his right leg to propel himself forward, rising up to stand on the step between the ground and the stage.

He just needed one moment – one moment for his knife to find the soft skin of Sanquain's throat and it would be over. Vanguard's knife did not find the captain. It was halted in mid-air, the tight grip of Tarryn's arm reaching around his chest and pulling him back.

The captain felt a rush through the air. There was a cry of alarm from the crowd, a woman's voice screeching out like the cry of a mouse seized by an owl. There was the whisper of a blade, cutting the air just a breath from his neck. Sanquain had never been so close to death. Not his own at least. To feel it come within a fraction of his own self was an experience that he would not soon forget.

Anger and regret instantly churned in Vanguard's stomach. Tarryn stood behind him, cold breath on his neck. He heard quiet words whispered into his ear. "I see you, Vanguard."

The people watched, unsure as to whether what they thought was happening was in fact, happening. They had seen the captain approach the stage to make an address. Now they were watching three men standing on the stage, two of whom had not been there a moment previously.

Across the crowd, James Sanderson stood with his lips pursed together. Sanquain looked like a man who had been mildly inconvenienced, not one who had just escaped death. He suspected it was because Sanquain had known that death was coming for him. "Stupid arsehole."

Vanguard had made a hack job of it even by his usual standards. The knife had never been destined to meet its target. This was what happened when you stopped killing for money and started killing for purpose. It got you killed instead. Sanderson reached out and grabbed the boy in front of him by the scruff of the neck.

"Let go of me." The boy snarled, showing his little yellow teeth.

"You know Herveaux's place? The one full of freaks?"

The boy struggled against his grip. "Yeah I know it, what for?"

"Go there now; run as if your life depended on it which, incidentally, it probably does. Find the giant, the one with the dopey face. Tell him the mob is coming for them. Go now!"

"Why? You can't tell me what to do, you ain't a'officer."

"Go now or I'll tan your arse so hard you'll shit sideways for the rest of your life."

Relinquishing his grip, Sanderson watched as the boy stumbled away, feet clattering against the pavement.

Turning his attention back to the centre of the square, he saw the rest of the guards file up onto the stage, pistols pointing directly at Vanguard.

Stomach churning, Vanguard saw the people staring up at him. He saw their disgust and horror. They looked at him and saw a monster. Sanquain pointed at him, arm outstretched. "You see this man? This man who has spent so long stalking the streets, murdering good people like yourselves? He comes here today as an agent of the insurrectionist Argent Cooke."

Vanguard let his head hang. It was over. He could feel the resentment rippling across the square. The people shuffled and murmured. Heads began to turn, first one way and then the other as the whispers built in volume to crescendo like a thunderstorm.

Sanquain marched across the stage, words echoing across the gathered crowd who quieted at the sound his voice. "You have suffered unjustly, afraid to walk the streets at night. Why should *you*, the decent, hardworking people be forced to live in a city full of killers and criminals? Even now, Cooke cowers in the Splinters, with the people set to steal your homes and your livelihoods. Too long you have hoped for justice; today you shall have it."

It was a good speech. If Vanguard hadn't known better he might have been convinced himself. Back in the Splinters, Kosic and his people were preparing to fight back against Sanquain and the Red Badges. Instead the very people they were prepared to fight for would march to their door and break it down.

Vanguard felt Tarryn's grip against his arms tighten. The boy was savouring the moment. He was basking in the glow of Vanguard's defeat. Vanguard would have been able to feel his heart beating, if there had been one there to feel.

Sanquain turned, jaw squared and tone victorious. "John Vanguard, you are under arrest for desertion of duty at the fortress of Bellitreaux, for causing the deaths of two hundred and thirty six soldiers of this city, for the murders of countless residents of D'Orsee, for aiding and abetting a known and wanted fugitive and for intention to incite rebellion."

The gathered crowd watched in hushed awe as cuffs were placed on Vanguard's wrists. There was a slow ripple of applause. Sanquain lifted both arms into the air as the guards marched Vanguard to the waiting wagon. The crowd cheered.

Taking one last look over his shoulder, Vanguard saw Tarryn watching him. There was no flicker of remorse, nothing to indicate there was anything left of the little humanity he had once had. He simply stood, looking down from his platform at those below him.

Sanderson watched as Vanguard was bundled into the wagon, bound for the Hole. There was no telling how long Vanguard would last once Sanquain had him below ground. He wouldn't be surprised if he simply had him killed immediately. It was what Sanderson would have done.

If the boy had run quickly enough, Vanguard's friends in the Splinters would soon know what was coming for them. They could watch their own backs. Sanderson needed to take care of some business of his own. As the crowd still reeled from the shock of what had happened, Sanderson put his hands in his pockets. Waiting for a moment, he rolled his eyes, cursed himself for what he was about to do and turned off in the direction of the Butchers.

CHAPTER 37
DEATH WITHOUT PURPOSE

Tarryn had not been expecting a warm greeting when he arrived home following the incident in the square. News travelled fast. Paulette might not have been the most forthright person in the world, but Vanguard had been her friend. She ought to have something to say about his arrest.

He was interested to see just how upset she might be; whether she would cry about it or not. Often he found her prettier when she was crying. Sometimes he would say things just to see the tears rolling down her cheeks. There was something beautiful about it, a peacefulness that it brought. One day he might try to explain it, to make her understand that he didn't want to hurt her. It just came naturally to him.

If Paulette had been at all smart, she would have realised that her predicament was entirely Vanguard's fault anyway. She had been like a lamb to the slaughter, following behind him and bleating at his request. Being with Tarryn would make her tougher.

Tarryn had been very pleased with her reaction to the

flower. Paulette had told him how much she enjoyed it. She had put it in water and placed the vase on the windowsill in the bedroom.

Mrs Brown did not like Paulette. By now, even Tarryn often forgot that before she had arrived at the house she had been a Black Zone prostitute. The house keeper did not forget.

Taking off his coat, Tarryn saw Mrs Brown come through the house with a large basket of his mother's clothes. There was a slight sheen to her face. She had been steaming the dresses in the bathroom. Tarryn was glad he no longer had to worry about things like that. "Where is everyone?"

"Your mother is taking a rest in her room."

"And Paulette?"

"Gone to see her friends in the Black Zone, she said."

"Who?"

"She didn't say." Mrs Brown pursed her lips. "I expect she has a lot of friends."

Mrs Brown watched him ascend the steps, a sly smile curled upon her face. She turned and continued carrying the basket through the house, a cheerful whistle on her lips.

In the quiet solitude of his room, Tarryn took off his boots and lay back on the bed. He tried to quell the anger he felt. Paulette would be back. She would not abandon him. He told himself that it was nothing more than a simple errand. Perhaps she had returned to fetch some clothes. Tarryn had not given her enough dresses. That was his fault. His muscles ached. There would be tasks to take in hand later, but first he needed to close his eyes just for a moment. Tarryn crawled across the mattress, slumping down into the soft pillows.

He tried to sleep but each time he did, he saw visions of Paulette. The image of her, laughing and smiling as he stood out of sight, ignored and unheard, an endless parade of faceless men passing by. Pressing his face into the pillow he tried not to let the thoughts consume him. The more he tried however, the more he knew that she had gone back to the Black Zone for one reason only. People did not change. The itch on his wrist had returned. Pulling his hand from under the pillow he stared at the skin. It was raised and blotchy. This was not the first time it had happened. Tarryn stared at his arm. A thought began to form in his mind. It filled him with revulsion.

Nothing like this had ever happened before Paulette had arrived in the house. She had poisoned him, infected him with something, just as his father had done his mother. He clawed at the skin, trying to dig out whatever part of Paulette was burning through his veins.

Tarryn caught sight of the lily sitting in the vase. There was not enough water in it. The sunlight had dried it almost to nothing. The leaves had curled and begun to brown. The petals had lost their lustre. Rising from the bed, Tarryn stormed over to the window and grasped the vase from the sill. Throwing it against the wall, he watched as it smashed into a hundred tiny fragments.

A few moments later Mrs Brown heard the door slam. She glanced into the hallway and saw his coat had been taken from the peg. Smiling, she returned to the washing and continued about her work.

FELICIA CREPT DOWN THE STAIRS OF HENRIETTE'S house. The front door was closed. She pulled it ajar, pressing her face to the gap. Vince remained steadfastly unmoving. Henriette had closed for the day. It did not mean the house could be left unguarded.

"We've got no tea left."

"What do you want me to do about it?"

Felicia pouted. "Can't you go and get some? Nobody has even so much as knocked the door in hours. It'll take five minutes. You'd be back before anyone even knows you've gone."

The answer came in the form of the door shutting in her face gently. Felicia flounced back down the hall thoroughly disgruntled by the whole situation. It was like being under house arrest. It was one thing for Henriette to want the girls kept safe but the lack of tea was a different thing entirely. The last person who had been allowed entry was Paulette.

The girls had been surprised but happy to see her. Paulette had craved the comfort of her family. If they had known she was coming before hand they would have requested she bring tea with her. She had almost reached the parlour when the door creaked open. Vince might have given the impression of being silent and stoic, but he had a definite soft spot if you knew where to look for it. "Did you change your - "

Vince lurched into the hallway fingers trembling as he tried to hold together the split skin of his stomach. Blood oozed from beneath one hand as he grappled at the wall with the other. Unable to stand, he crashed to the floor. Clawing at the air, he desperately tried to push the door shut.

"Go upstairs!"

Felicia stood frozen to the spot. Face glistening, Vince tried to kick at the wood, attempting to block the entrance with his foot as the blood pooled beneath him. It did not work. A figure loomed in the doorway. Groaning, Vince struggled to his feet and thrust the full weight of his bulky body against the attacker. Gut meeting with the knife for a second time, Vince's eyes flickered. Saliva frothed at the corner of his mouth. He went down and did not get back up again.

Felicia's feet moved involuntarily. Darting around the two men, a hairsbreadth from the knife, she took the stairs two at a time.

Nobody followed her. The front door closed and as the girls waited behind the locked door of their room, they heard the sound of Vince being dragged through the hallway. Felicia and Annabelle pulled what furniture they could in front of the door, barricading it.

Felicia looked back at the other girls. "What do we do?"

There was very little in the way of items that could be used as weapons. Henriette limited the number of things that could be turned on the girls as a precaution. Opening the drawers and rooting through them, Paulette searched desperately for anything that could help. She found nothing.

The sounds of footsteps walking slowly up the stairs and across the hall came to a stop outside the door. A familiar voice drifted through the wooden pane. "Paulette, don't you want to see me?"

"Tarryn! Why are you doing this?"

He slid a cloth along the length of the blade. Lifting his head and sniffing the air, Tarryn could taste the fear behind the door. "Why am I doing this? Why do you think?"

Lifting one leg, he thrust the flat of his foot against the

door. It held firm. Tarryn cracked his neck. It wouldn't hold for long. With each thud from the other side of the barrier, the girls moved further back until they felt the wall against them. "I gave you a home." The door shuddered once again. "I kept you when nobody else would have done."

Paulette looked at the other girls, eyes red with tears. "I'm so sorry, I'm so sorry."

There was a final smash and the door burst open. Tarryn saw them in the corner, bundled up in each others' arms. There was nowhere for them to go. Paulette stepped out in front of the other girls, raising her arms as if to provide a blockade. Tarryn almost looked as if it amused him.

Her voice shook. "You don't need to hurt them, you only came for me."

Tarryn smiled. After everything that they had been through, Paulette deserved to know the truth about what he was. He could show her now. It would be the only bit of real honesty between them.

"True, but it is in my nature."

It was valiant of her to want to save her friends. It was about the bravest thing that Paulette had ever done. Unfortunately Paulette's death would be like the rest of her life – it would serve no great purpose.

CHAPTER 38
WHAT GOOD COMES FROM
NOTHING

Henriette stared at the open door. There had always been noise coming from the house. Now as she stood at the bottom of the steps, she felt the stillness all around her. There was no laughter. There was no arguing or screaming. The smell of Vince's cigarette still hung in the air.

She already knew what awaited her when she crossed the threshold. There were smears of blood across the wood.

All she had ever wanted to do was protect the girls, to offer them what little sanctuary she could. She had failed them. Lifting her skirt up so that the hem would not smear more blood across the tiles, Henriette walked into the house. Vince lay where he had fallen, arms still outstretched. There were puncture wounds across his body. The gold band around his finger glinted in the light.

Placing one hand on the banister, Henriette took each step with as much dignity as she could muster. Her home had become a slaughterhouse. She would not further sully it with histrionics, no matter how much her heart ached.

The girls had already lived their lives stripped of their class, their dignity and their pride. She would allow them quiet dignity now in death. There was no more she could give them than that.

She could not stop the tears from falling, or the breath from catching in her chest as she looked upon the floor of the second floor bedroom. They lay still, eyes wide and mouths open, faces contorted in horror and sadness. The world had been cruel to them until the bitter end.

Kneeling down, Henriette stroked Annabel's face with one hand. She was still warm. Henriette stood back up. She lifted her face to the ceiling and closed her eyes. When she opened them again, she realised that there was one body missing. Sickness lurched in her stomach. Paulette was not amongst them.

Descending the stairs once more, she stopped on the first floor and looked down the corridor. The doors to the rooms were all closed, save for one. It was the snow queen suite.

The room was decorated in white and blue tones, a crystal chandelier hanging from the ceiling. Crisp satin sheets in silver and white had been laid freshly pressed only the night before. The hues of the room had always made it seem colder than it was. Carmen sat on the edge of the bed, a bowl of warm water on her lap and a wash cloth in her hands. She did not turn around, nor look up from her task. Taking the cloth, she wrung out the water and wiped it slowly across Paulette's face. Paulette stared at the wall opposite with glass eyes, although she did not see anything. She was gone, like the rest. There were angry red marks around her throat.

"I tried to close her eyes, but they wouldn't stay shut."

Henriette sank to the floor, one hand against the boards.

Carmen continued. "He put makeup on her, I don't know why. I didn't think she'd like it. She knew how you felt about make up. I think he did it to be cruel."

Carmen had arrived at the house far too late to fall victim to Tarryn's bloodlust. She had come across Paulette; her body lying on the bed and propped up by cushions. He would not be back. He had done what he had set out to do.

"I think that Paulette always believed if she showed the world enough kindness, that eventually it would show her a little in return. But it doesn't work like that, does it?"

"No, it doesn't - at least not often - not for us."

Gathering herself, Henriette walked across the room. She stopped and placed a hand on Carmen's shoulder. Carmen reached back and placed her fingers over Henriette's.

"We should go, we'll call someone to come and care for them properly. There's nothing more we can do now. Paulette is gone now. They're all gone."

Carmen placed the bowl on the nightstand, next to the pile of coins that Tarryn had left – one last payment for services rendered. Slowly, she shook her head. "No. No, not really. Paulette was never real you see, she never existed. It was all just pretend."

Henriette could barely comprehend this as being the same wild, scrawny young girl that had come into her house several months ago. She was grown now, moulded and shaped by the world. It had made her into something harder, something stronger than it had ever intended for her to be. Carmen took Paulette's cold hand in hers. "Her name was Penny, do you remember that?"

"Of course I remember."

"Paulette never existed, but Penny did. She might have been gone a long time ago, but Penny was real. Paulette was just the mask that Penny wore when she forgot who she was. Do you understand?"

Carmen stood and turned away from the bed. Pulling the girl towards her, Henriette held onto her tightly. She felt the tears running down her neck as they both cried together. They were tears mixed with sadness and anger. They were tears that mourned the loss of their friends. Mostly, they were tears that grieved for the world that they lived in.

The moment was interrupted by the sound of clattering downstairs. They exchanged glances. Henriette pulled the gun from her bodice. Creeping down the stairs and peering over the banister, the two women saw a head topped with a shock of ginger hair leaning over Vince's body.

Sanderson looked up and saw the women, pistol pointing at him. "You can either shoot me or you can come down here and help me save your man."

Henriette shook her head. "He's dead."

Sanderson grimaced. "Well thank fuck you're not a fucking doctor, now either come here and help me or I'm leaving him to die on the floor."

Carmen and Henriette hurried down the stairs and into the hallway. Sanderson instructed Carmen to fetch him needles, thread, cloths and anything else she could get her hands on. The puncture wounds on Vince's body had come quick and fast. Tarryn's mind had been consumed by the thought of death, but it had not been Vince he wanted to satiate his blood lust. The doorman had simply been a lumbering obstacle. There were four puncture marks deep enough to have been potentially fatal, but he had missed most of the vital organs.

"This is one lucky son of a bitch, the knife cleared right past the liver. No rupture to any of the major arteries, although given the state of him I'd say he doesn't have much blood left."

Carmen returned with the items, passing them to Henriette who knelt beside Sanderson. Reaching his fingers into the blood soaked material; Sanderson tore it away from Vince's chest. He took the needle and thread from Henriette with the other hand.

"What can I do?" She asked.

"Hold him together; this is going to be messy."

Henriette placed her hands on Vince's stomach and tried not to let her fingers slip. Sanderson worked quickly. Carmen hovered over them both. "Will he live?"

"Probably not thanks to you, while you were upstairs crying over the already dead your man was just bleeding to death on the floor. Lucky for him I showed up."

Henriette felt her jaw tighten.

Sanderson coughed. "Look, I'm sorry that your girls are dead. If it's any compensation, I'd like to kill the little fucker that did it myself - that bastard is half the reason I'm having such a shitty day."

He pulled at the thread, tearing it with his teeth. Vince was barely warm to the touch. There was so much blood on the floor that Carmen wondered if Sanderson were lying to them, if it was some sort of cruel trick. "Thank you."

Sanderson stood up and wiped the blood down the leg of his trousers. "Don't bother thanking me he still might die yet. I've asked a friend to come here. I was expecting everyone to be dead so it'll be a surprise to them, but there it is. They'll take him back to the city guard and see if they can perform some sort of miracle."

Henriette looked at Sanderson. "Why would you help him? Why would you come here?"

By the time Sanderson had relayed to Henriette and Carmen what had happened in the square at the Golden Quarter, two men had arrived to cart Vince away. They carried him out, a little less carefully than they should have done. Henriette reached out and touched his arm as they took him from the house. She glanced up the stairs. They would take the girls too.

"What will they do with them?" Henriette could not bear to think of the girls being left at the bottom of the canal.

For once, there was sincerity in Sanderson's voice. "They'll bury them."

"What do we do now?" Carmen asked.

"We need to go to the Hole. How many shots do you have?" Sanderson looked at Henriette, who quickly checked the chambers. There were three bullets left.

"Some, not many."

Carmen shook her head. "I still don't understand why you're doing this."

"I'm certainly not doing it for you or the good of the people. I'm done, I want out of this city and as much as it pains me to say it, John Vanguard is my best chance of getting out. As long as the murderous little bastard that did this is alive I've got a target on my back."

Henriette nodded to Carmen. Taking the stairs two at a time, she disappeared into the bedroom to retrieve a few practical items. As Carmen walked past the empty bed that Paulette had been lying on, a flash of silver caught her eye.

It was impossible not to notice the grim expression on Carmen's face as she came back to join them. The silver pin was held tight in her palm. There was only one man in the city that gave pins like that.

When Carmen had first met Gregor Tamsk on the night that Vanguard had taken her to Herveaux's club, he had been meeting with several prominent members of Argent Cooke's secret network of supporters. The other girls behind the door had told Carmen that he was a man who could help her find the new life she craved. It was he who had given her the pin, an unspoken promise that when the time came, Cooke would ensure that girls like Carmen would never have to sell themselves for the benefit of others again.

Gregor was the vessel by which Cooke would send his call to arms. If Tarryn had taken the pin from Gregor, it meant that the messages had been intercepted. Cooke was relying on his supporters to rally to him when the uprising began. None of them were coming.

Sanderson cleared his throat. "We need to go." He looked Henriette square in the eyes. "Another few hours and this whole city will implode. There's nothing worth saving here anymore. So, all that's left to decide is - do you want Vanguard back or not?"

Henriette swallowed. She thought of Paulette and the other girls. She thought of Vince fighting for his life as his children wondered where their father was and why he had not come home. She felt the aching inside her chest. She did want Vanguard back. She wanted to hit him, to scream bloody murder at him. She wanted him to be angrier than he had ever been before. Henriette wanted more than anything to hear his rough voice whispering promises of vengeance. She wanted him back so that they could get the kind of justice that only comes with blood.

She tucked the pistol into the top of her bustier and nodded towards Carmen. Taking the keys from her pocket, Henriette led them out of the door. She closed it behind them, the blood stains still smeared across the wood. She locked it. It would not open again. The house was not their home anymore.

CHAPTER 39
FROM OUT OF THE PITS

There was a great blackness.

Usually when people regained consciousness, the first thing they saw was a bright light. It was the reason that so many claimed to be certain there was a life after death. They were sure they had seen God. The chances were always higher that it was nothing more than a flickering lamp above their heads.

Vanguard didn't see any light. It was just as well, for he had long since abandoned the idea of there being any sort of heaven for him. He did not see the light, because there was none. Far beneath the ground, the sun was nothing more than a distant memory.

The first thing that he did notice was the noise. It had a steady, repetitive sound, like a drum beat that crept around the sides of his head. The dripping pipe - just as he remembered it. A groan escaped his lips. He was sitting on a stool, back pressed against the wet stone. Drops of water landed on his shoulder, causing a damp patch to spread across the arm of his shirt. Taking in a deep breath, he felt a familiar pain ‑ cracked ribs, certainly one but maybe more.

"Is it just as you remember it?" Walking into the cell, Sanquain placed the lamp down on the table and turned it up high. Vanguard blinked, the sudden glare hurting his eyes. "This must be like a homecoming for you." He took a seat on the stool on the other side of the room. "I want you to know that if nothing else, I always admired your conviction. I don't suppose it matters anymore, but it takes a lot to maintain any sort of principle in this place. You did your best."

Sweat beading across his brow, Vanguard croaked. "You always knew, didn't you?"

"About Cooke? Yes, I knew. If all of this was just about Cooke I'd have had a bullet put between his eyes long ago. It's always been about more than that."

"How many more people have to die for you to get what you want?"

Sanquain looked at him. "This isn't about what I want. This is about what is best for this city, perhaps even what is best for this country. Sometimes the weak have to die so that the strong can survive. I thought you of all people would understand that."

"He's going to kill you one day."

Sanquain seemed unconcerned. "Who? The boy? I'm well aware that he'll try at some point. I'll deal with that when it becomes necessary. Let's face it; Tarryn Leersac is just John Vanguard without the dubious moral compass, and look where John Vanguard is now."

Standing up Sanquain tapped twice on the door. The grate opened and a pair of eyes appeared. Vanguard heard the jangling of keys in the lock. As the door opened he let his dry lips part one last time. "If you kill enough of them, one day they'll rise up. One day you'll have to answer for what you've done."

Sanquain stopped. He shook his head. Taking a few steps towards the stool, the captain leaned down and brought his face to within a few inches of Vanguard. "You may be right, but it won't be today."

He left. The grate snapped closed, blocking out what little light had been able to get through. Vanguard looked up, squinting through the darkness towards a ceiling that he could not see. Instead he felt it, looming overhead. He heard it. Smelt it. Shuffling, he moved the stool a few inches to the right. The dripping water that had been rolling down his back now splashed against his face. The water pushed the hair from his eyes, just enough so that they would not itch anymore.

There was something oddly calming about it. You would think that returning to that hell hole would have been a fate worse than death. Somehow it felt as though it had always been inevitable. The darkness enveloped him like a pair of welcoming arms. He was ready for it.

A while passed; he could not tell how long. At one point the guard reappeared and removed the shackles from his wrists. Vanguard rubbed at the sore skin. Able to stand up once more, he paced the room, fingers scratching against the walls until he located the cot. Lying back, he heard the sounds of hopelessness. It was the dripping of the water, the jangle of keys from the hands of the guards walking past. It was the muffled groans of his unseen neighbours. At least this time he would not have to listen to it for long.

Vanguard took in a breath. Pain caught in his side. Lifting one hand, he placed it over the tender skin and thought about what it might be like to die. He thought of the black and white landscape, the frozen trees of Bellitreaux. Sanquain would most likely not let him survive the night. At some point, whether it was a minute from then or an hour, someone would come in and press the barrel of a gun to his head.

Vanguard had always assumed his death would be slow. It would come from a wound received in battle or starvation and sickness. Being shot, after all that had happened, seemed so short and devoid of interest. He had not hoped for pain, but after having delivered so many into the hands of death himself, he should have liked the time to feel it a little for himself before it took him.

"Seven long years, and you still haven't figured any of it out."

The voice rang out, crisp and low from out of the darkness. Vanguard sat up. It was a voice he knew but did not care to hear. He had spent years learning to block it out. Vanguard was not alone in his cell. The truth was that he had not been alone for a long time. "Leave me alone, I don't want to hear it."

"No change there then."

"You're not real; you're just in my head."

Arnauld pitched forward on his chair, grey face emerging from out of the walls like a fog. There were two empty spaces where his eyes ought to have been. His blue lips cracked and flaked. He reached up and scratched at the bullet hole in his temple with one bony finger. "I'm dead, John; where else am I going to be except in your head?"

"If you're just in my head then why can't I get rid of you?"

"Maybe you don't really want to." He leaned close. Vanguard felt the chill of his breath. Arnauld sniffed, looking around the cell. "Nice place you've got yourself here. Very cosy." The ghost of his former mentor looked down at the bruises forming beneath the open material of Vanguard's shirt. He sighed. "What were you thinking, John?"

"What can I say? I make bad choices."

Arnauld cast his face to the floor and snorted. "Is that what you think you do? You see, from where I'm sitting, it seems as though your problem isn't making bad choices. It's *not* making the right ones. Because you know better than anyone that sometimes the right choice hurts. So much so that you've spent years punishing yourself for the one good decision you ever made." Lifting his head once again, he picked a cobweb from his bony shoulder. "So what will you do now?"

"They'll shoot me probably, sometime before dawn if Sanquain doesn't have me tortured first. Not much else I can do now, is there? At least then I might get some peace. I'll be dead and that'll be that, the debt will be settled."

"How so?"

"Two hundred and thirty six men died and I should have been one of them."

Arnauld shook his head, the tattered paper skin around his neck shuddering. "You know what? He really does have you pegged."

"Who?"

"Cooke - he's got you absolutely right. I barely recognize you anymore. All this weight you've been carrying – the guilt, the shame. You wear it like a millstone around your neck. You're afraid to give it up, because you don't know what you are without it anymore." The dead man reached out and placed a hand against Vanguard's burnt cheek. He still remembered pulling him from the flames.

Arnauld thought of the first time they had met, long before Lycroix. All the years they had spent together; all of that time watching as John Vanguard fought to find some tiny shred of meaning in the shit show of a world they found themselves in. It was a fight he felt his friend was losing. "*I* remember."

The touch of his hand was not cold, nor did it bring fear to Vanguard's heart. It filled him with a loneliness that he could not rid himself of no matter how hard he tried.

"It is time to let go of the blame. The balance of debt extends to more than just two hundred and thirty six men. You feel you betrayed us all those years ago, but you are betraying us now. You are betraying our memory."

Vanguard's eyes stung, bile rising in his throat. He felt the terrible pain in his stomach, the great ball weighing him down. It was grief. It was guilt. He did not know how to let it go.

"Walking away from that place was the one smart thing you ever did. We were all doomed men, from the moment we arrived. You're not one of us anymore. *We* are dead, John Vanguard; Bellitreaux is a place for ghosts. It's time you left us behind."

"I can't, I've tried." Silent tears streamed down Vanguard's cheeks. They made no noise, the only movement the shaking of his shoulders. The floor beneath him was damp and dirty. He could not look up, could not bear to look Arnaud in the face.

"Greed killed us. Corruption put us in the ground. Don't let it take you too. You *must* choose life, or none of this means anything. We will have all died for nothing. The living need you now, not us." Arnauld laid one skeletal hand on his shoulder. "You must understand, the dues owed were never yours to pay...but they were always yours to see paid."

There was the sound of crashing from beyond the walls of the cell. Vanguard heard voices shouting and the sound of pistols. The noise of the thudding intensified, rattling the walls of the cell. There was the sound of a pistol being fired just a few feet away. The dripping water splashed against the stone floor. Vanguard felt the ground shaking.

Arnauld looked back to him. "Have faith Vanguard. There is a peace for you out there - but it won't come from dying in this dank hole. You'll find it one day, I know you will."

Vanguard lifted his chin. "Easy for you to say, you're already dead." The words cut short, choking him. He regretted saying them instantly. "I'm sorry, Arnauld."

The last remnants of his old friend had almost disappeared. As the spectre melted into the background of the cell, Arnauld gave him a smile. "We know you are, John." The remnants of his face faded, leaving only his voice behind. "We know."

The cell door slammed open. Splintered and twisted wood hung from the frame. Sanderson stood, red-faced and speckled with sweat. "Well? Are you pleased to see me?"

Surprised was more apt a word. "*Sanderson?*"

"That's another one you owe me."

"Are you alone?"

Sanderson leaned back, peering back down the corridor. Henriette and Carmen were clumsily dragging the guard into one of the adjacent cells. The man stirred slightly. Henriette cracked his skull with her boot. Behind them a group of sentries from beyond the barricades dealt with the remainder of the guards still left alive. "Don't ask."

Scrambling his way out of the cell, Vanguard lifted one arm to shield his eyes from the light of the torches. Sanderson loaded another round of shots into his pistol.

Carmen called to them from the other end of the empty corridor. There was blood smeared across her face. There had clearly been more than one obstacle to their rescue attempt. She looked an entirely different person to the one he had seen lying in the cot in Kosic's apartment. "We need to go, now!"

"Why are you here? You shouldn't be here."

Vanguard felt the strike of a palm hit him sharply across the cheek. It hurt. Henriette stood glowering at him. She had been angry with him on many an occasion, but never had there been such frustration in her eyes. "I told you once I can't abide a stupid lodger, and I certainly won't be told what to do."

Vanguard had known for a long time that he loved Henriette. It wasn't the sort of love that led to a happy life. Things like marriage and a contented dotage would not suit either of them. But it was love all the same. She had already slapped him once. It wouldn't make any difference now if he did something really foolish. It was unlikely he'd live long enough to reap the consequences. Vanguard placed a hand either side of Henriette's face and kissed her lips. For the smallest fraction of a second she didn't protest. Then she pushed him away. "Stop being ridiculous."

Carmen made a disgusted face. She was still of the age where the sight of two middle aged people kissing repulsed her. Sanderson stood, pistol in hand and eyes rolling. "Yes, well, this is all fucking lovely, but can we get out of here now before we all end up stuck down here and miss the entire revolution?"

Vanguard's eyes darkened. "There won't be a revolution. Sanquain will have the entire Black Zone burned to the ground before the night is over. Cooke and the others will be trapped in the Splinters with an angry mob and a few hundred Red Badges to finish the job."

Carmen reached out a hand. "Come with us."

Vanguard stood as straight as his body would allow. The remnants of Arnauld's voice lingered in his ears. With each step it got a little quieter. Every inch closer to the daylight, Vanguard felt the ghosts of Bellitreaux fading further into the background. He kept his eyes on the exit ahead, focusing his mind on the feeling of Carmen's pulse. The light flickered at the opening of the tunnel.

Vanguard heard it calling out to him.

The air outside smelt of rain and ash. There was already smoke on the horizon. Vanguard looked up at the sky and felt the water splash against his cheeks. He held out one hand, letting the dirt slide from his skin. He half expected it to turn to stone.

Hector Mandego stood at the entrance of the prison. At his back were the men and women of the Butchers. Sliding the strap from his shoulder, Mandego held Vanguard's bag in his hands. With a cocksure grin, he tossed it across the gap. "You'll be needing this."

Vanguard didn't bother to ask how Mandego had found it. He was just relieved to see that nothing had been taken – or at least, nothing that mattered.

"You always were full of surprises, Hector."

"Are we to be allies then?"

Mandego moved from side to side, feet dancing lightly across the wet mud. Vanguard caught a glimpse of the pistol at his side. At any other time, he would have been just as likely to start a war as to end one. His involvement was not likely to be an act of benevolence. "A temporary alliance; you and I wouldn't do well on the same side."

Mandego grinned. "I told you that when the fighting started I'd be there to carve myself a slice. Wouldn't be much of a slice if half the city is burned to the ground. Plus, I wanted to be the one to slit the throat of the little cunt that killed Cath."

"I didn't do it Hector; not Catherine."

"I'm well bloody aware of that."

"So we'll see you in the Splinters?"

"You'll see me alright." Without hesitation, Mandego gave the order to his crew. They scattered across the Pits like a swarm of locusts heading in the direction of the Splinters. Mandego took the knife from his belt and clasped it between his teeth. Lifting one hand, he gave a mock salute before turning away.

Vanguard inhaled deeply. Carmen slipped into place on his right-hand side, Henriette on his left. She pulled a pistol from her bustier and checked the chamber. Sanderson rolled his eyes. Vanguard reached down and touched the material of the bag at his side, the knife in its usual place.

He turned to face Henriette. "There's something I need to do."

She searched his face, brow creasing. It looked like she had something to say. Vanguard waited, knowing that these would possibly be the last words he ever heard from her lips. There was a momentary flickering of softness in her eyes.

Then she spoke. "Don't do anything stupid."

He gave them a nod before melting away into the night and disappearing.

"What do we do now?" Carmen asked nobody in particular.

They were an unorthodox band - the prostitute, the madam and the thug. Looking from one person to another, Sanderson could not help but think that his involvement with their plan was destined to end in disaster. Still, for reasons unknown to himself, he said the words no man would ever dream of hearing him say. "Now? Now, we go and save this city...like a big bunch of fucking heroes."

CHAPTER 40
MAN RESURRECTED

Kosic could smell the paraffin rags tucked inside the glass bottles. Even before the boy had arrived carrying the news of Vanguard's arrest, the people had started to gather in the streets. What little hope Kosic and his comrades had of convincing the residents of the Black Zone to join Cooke in his rebellion were fading to nothing.

Remy and Demetrio kept watch at the door. There were more people gathered outside with each second that passed. They heard the mob calling out, taunting the occupants of the club with insults and accusations. There were few words exchanged between Kosic and those crowded inside. There was little to be said. Around seventy of them had gathered in the club, reaching the relative safety of the building before the hordes descended.

Kosic knew they could not keep them safe there for long. The doors would not withstand much. He looked around at the people gathered inside. The majority of them were young; far too young in Kosic's opinion to be faced with such terrible choices.

"Come out, freaks!" The voices in the street grew both in volume and aggression.

Herveaux, uncertain as to what was happening and why so many people should be there stomped angrily about. Pointing the riding crop at Kosic, he snapped like a turtle. "What the hell is going on here? I demand you tell me!"

Kosic rolled his eyes and finally said the words he had longed to say since the day they had met. "Shut up tiny man, before I break your skull."

Herveaux's mouth opened and closed a few times. His face went red, moustache twitching. "You signed a contract, you *belong* to me."

"We belong to nobody."

A few moments later Herveaux found himself bound and tied with ropes. It was hardly a fitting punishment for the man but it would have to do for the time being. Kosic turned his back to him, ignoring his protests. Cooke appeared; his fine clothes in stark contrast to Kosic's own patched together ensemble. Peering through the gap, Kosic looked out across the street. The people stood shoulder to shoulder, staring back at them. There was a yell from within the crowds.

"Show your faces, bastards!"

Sanquain's lies had worked. The residents of the Black Zone had heard how the people of the Splinters had sheltered the murderer of Sam Wick and Ludnor. They had been told of men who spoke in secret languages and conspired to steal their jobs and homes. It was easier to believe that their enemy was made up of the strangers from another world than it was to face the fact that the true enemy was the one they had chosen for themselves.

"Murderers!"

Kosic glanced down at Cooke. "And these are the people you wish us to fight for?"

There was a smashing of glass as a bottle hit the wall a few feet from the door.

At the end of the street, Tarryn stood watching the people gather from every direction. They flooded in from the alleys and side streets; angry men with their clubs and sticks. The city guard stood at his back. A small flicker of a smile curled across his lips. There would be a lot of death - more than enough to satisfy his craving for it. Through destruction and chaos, Tarryn would become recognised. By this time tomorrow, he would be celebrated and hated in equal measure. He wanted it. He needed it. He would never go back to living in the darkness again.

Kosic felt a strange sensation in his gut. Something was not right. There was something he was missing, something that he knew was there but could not quite find. Pressing his hand to the wall and pushing one eye to a small gap, he looked across the crowds. "Something is wrong."

Demetrio stood back, his face contorted. "What do you mean? All of this is wrong, they were supposed to be coming to fight *with* us, not burn us to the ground."

"I don't mean that, something else is wrong."

The streets were filled with people. In addition to that, the Red Badges now lined the alleys and winding paths that connected to the road. They stood in tight formations, blocking off any escape route. Still more people poured in. It was as though they were being ushered like lambs into a pen. At first, most of the crowd seemed to be made up of younger men, armed with sticks and bottles. A second glance and Kosic saw women, men too old to be standing for so long out in the cold and bare-footed children, grimly holding on to their siblings. They were packed so tightly they could barely move. "Why are there so many people?"

"Because they want to kill us." Demetrio grew more frustrated each time Kosic spoke.

"But there are children..."

Unseen, Tarryn wound his way through the crowd. He moved between them like a ghost. Looking down at his hand, he grinned, tossing the small stick into the air and catching it again. Vanguard had always preferred knives. Tarryn couldn't understand why. There was something so much more convenient about powder and shot.

A balcony overlooked the open square of land directly outside the club. Climbing the stairs, Tarryn ran his thumb over the smooth surface of the package. The Red Badges stood exactly as instructed, a wall of pistols and bayonets ready to stand firm against the fleeing crowd. Tarryn took a moment, basking in the smell of sweat and hatred. He felt it seeping from their pores and contaminating the air. Sanquain was right, they were no better than animals. He placed one hand on the wooden post to his left, climbing up so that he stood on the ledge. Cool rain brushed at his face, the droplets clinging. Above the people, he struck a match against the side of the post and touched it to the fuse.

It twisted in the air, sparks dancing around like fireflies.

From within the club, Kosic saw the explosive silhouetted against the white circle of the moon. There was a loud clap as it hit the ground. The sound of it bounced from the walls, shaking the buildings. Inside, the floor rattled beneath their feet.

A herd of driven people by fear and confusion surged towards the club. Chaos ensued, the crush of bodies pressed together like a tidal wave. Embers caught on the wind floated down and settled on the barrels and wagons all around. Flames licked into the air. As the people tried to push their way past the soldiers, they found the guns turned on them. A portly Red Badge turned to one of his subordinates. "Send word to Captain Sanquain, tell him that the lower breeds have begun to riot."

The guard nodded, turning away and running through the streets. "Make sure that every street is sealed off, barricade them in." The guards glanced at each other. "Kill anyone who looks like a rebel."

As he watched from behind the closed door, Kosic saw the people as they ran, pressing into one another and searching for someone to show them the way out. He heard the air filled with screams as mothers lost hold of their children. He closed his eyes, picturing images of green fields and blue skies. He thought of the harelipped girl in her cage. He saw the bear, grunting and shuffling as it danced around with heavy chains at his ankles and the man who beat it until its spirit broke. He looked down at his fists, clenching them open and closed.

Kosic turned to Cooke. "We have to open the doors."

Cooke nodded. "You understand that we are outnumbered ten to one?"

"If we let them kill these people, the city will never follow you."

Cooke took the pistols from the holsters at his side. Kosic was right. It was not the fight that he had wanted, but it was the one they must have. He looked back over the small assembly that stood inside the hall. "If anyone wants to take the tunnel, we won't judge you for it."

Demetrio stepped forward, crudely fashioned club in

one hand. He still had the pencil tucked behind his ear. "If we fight, we fight together."

The door of the club burst open. The people of the Splinters barrelled forth into the path of the Red Badges, seventy against hundreds, in the defence of the people who hated them so much. Breaking rank, the Red Badges began to shoot indiscriminately. A young woman fell to the floor at Remy's feet, a bullet hole between her eyes.

In the midst of it all, Kosic roared and bellowed, leaving unconscious men in his wake. Bullets and fire whipped the air around him. He could taste smoke and blood. With every moment, his stone fists found more skulls to crack, more enemies to fell. From the corner of his eye he saw the glint of a barrel. There was a boy, maybe fifteen years old, in the path of the bullet. Kosic pulled the boy into his chest and turned his back. The bullet went wide, ripping through the muscle of his shoulder. Kosic roared as his flesh tore.

The boy opened his mouth, uncertain as to what was happening. His father had told him of the mad giant who lived in the Splinters. "What are you?"

The people nearby stopped as Kosic, face red with blood lifted his fists to the air. "I am Kosic; I am the undefeated, and I am not your enemy."

They watched as he pointed through the crowds. Out of the haze and smoke of the gun fire, the figure of a man appeared. Stepping across the rubble, puddle water and blood splashing at his ankles, Argent Cooke emerged before them.

"See? See how this man fights for you? *We* are not your enemy. The real enemy is all around you. They turn their guns on you. They burn YOUR home. See them now and tell me, what will *you* do?"

As his voice carried across the chaos, one by one people began to look around them. They clung to whatever weapons they had found, adrenaline rushing through their veins. The boy that Kosic had saved from the bullet stepped back, turning to the Red Badges who now seemed uncertain as to who was in control. The crowd began to stir with a new sort of energy and the dark clouds rolled overhead.

⚜

VANGUARD STOOD ON THE LEDGE OF A BUILDING, THE night air cold against his face. He had never been particularly bothered by heights. It had always been the view that he had disliked. The more of the world he saw, the more his bones ached and his soul grew heavy.

Below him, the tension on the streets outside Herveaux's club had begun to shift. As Cooke rallied them with his words, the people of the Black Zone turned. They began to face their enemies. Looking out across the square, past the crowds and the smoke, Vanguard found what he was looking for. Standing on the balcony with a blade in his hand, was Tarryn.

Separated by the blood and destruction below, they existed together for a brief moment in a world beyond the world, made of shadows and death.

A slow smile spread across Tarryn's face. Vanguard watched him drop from the balcony and into the crowds, disappearing into the chaos. He knew that Vanguard would follow. He had no choice. Vanguard already had enough things to regret.

This time, he could not walk away.

SHOULDER ACHING, BLOOD AND SWEAT ON HIS BROW, Kosic stood at the boy's back. He glanced up. There were grey clouds gathering overhead. They blocked out the moon. For a few seconds, the skyline of the city was bathed in darkness. When they parted once more, just for a moment, he saw the silhouette of John Vanguard standing on the rooftops. There was a bag at his side and the glint of a knife in his hand.

CHAPTER 41
THE END

The sound of gun shot and crackling fire filled the air. Mothers cradled their children, the ashes matting in their hair as the Splinters was set alight. Armed with little more than whatever they could lay their hands on, the people of the Black Zone fought to save themselves.

Unseen, Tarryn stalked through the street, his knife twisting between ribs and slicing through flesh as he struck down one person after another.

Sanderson adjusted the belt around his waist, feeling the weight of the sword and pistol. He had not worn them for a while. He had been done with soldiering a long time ago. Being a Red Badge was far from soldiering. "Better late than never I suppose."

Hector Mandego ran his tongue over cracked lips. Behind them, a small army of criminals and thieves stood at the ready. One word and they descended into the fray screaming bloody murder. Mandego watched them. Before he disappeared into the crowd, he removed the blade from his belt and looked at the others. "None of this makes us friends. This time tomorrow we'll either all be dead, or back to killing and thieving off one another - business as usual." Henriette glared at Mandego who gave her a sly wink. "I don't mean you, love, I *like* you."

Carmen said nothing. She looked down at the pistol in her hand. It had belonged to one of the guards back at the Hole. Nobody had said anything when she had taken it. Sanderson raised one eye brow. "Do you know how to use that?"

Carmen nodded unconvincingly. Henriette had shown her the basics. It would have to be a baptism of fire. There was no other choice. Nothing came for free. Even freedom had to be bought. Holding the pistol above her head, Carmen let out what would have passed for a battle cry had she been a soldier. She was not a soldier. She was just a girl wearing odd clothes and hungry for a life that should have been hers.

Sanderson sighed. "Bloody hell."

From the midst of the crowds, Tarryn looked out across the sea of scrambling bodies. The knife was all well and good, but Sanquain had wanted as many of the low breeds dead as possible. Nothing cleansed the earth like fire did. Crouching to the ground, he picked up a discarded torch. There were already fires burning everywhere, women and old men desperately trying to douse the flames with rags and puddle water.

Vanguard scanned the crowds for a glimpse of the one face he was searching for. Finally he saw him, torch in hand and coat splattered with blood and sinew. He watched as the people parted around him, seeing as Tarryn pulled his arm back and threw the torch through the air, the flame landing inside the open door of Herveaux's club and licking the walls. A moment later the crowds surged, pressing together and Tarryn was gone.

Sanderson had been surprised to find that he was not as rusty with the sword as he had thought he might be. It had been a while and even then his training hadn't been anything to write home about. Mandego and his men had honoured their word, or so it would seem. The men and women who would normally have the city quaking at the very mention of their names, for one brief and fleeting moment, became its saviours. They were survivalists, just as he was, doing what needed to be done to stack the odds greater in their favour. Sanderson fully intended on living to see the next day dawn. Unfortunately, the best laid out plans often never come to fruition. It would seem that it would not be Sanderson who would survive the night, but rather Henriette.

The bullet hit true. Sanderson fell to the cobblestones, his fall broken by Henriette's arms as she caught him. Gore slid through her fingers as she tried to stem the flow. There was nothing she could do to stop it. If Sanderson had not stepped into its path, the shot would have blown her brains out. "Why did you do that?"

Sanderson coughed up a lungful of black, sticky blood. "Don't...don't fucking go on about it."

It wasn't an act of love or friendship that made him do it. In the end, Sanderson was never able to tell anyone why he did it, although many would later speculate. Carmen suspected that it was because deep down, somewhere in the very furthest away part of Sanderson, was a part that was good.

Sanderson felt the energy drain from his body. Eyes rolling back, he pointed with a shaking hand down the street. Henriette looked towards where Vanguard ducked and twisted through the crowds. If Sanderson had the strength left, he might have told Henriette the truth. Instead, he took it with him to his grave.

Vanguard had always wondered how it was that Sanquain had found him. He never knew why the captain had plucked him from his prison cell. He thought he owed Sanderson for that. As it turned out, the balance of debt had always been in Vanguard's favour.

The day that Sanderson had been caught in the woods he had been carrying several items of a contraband and legally ambiguous nature on his person. Sanderson had been scheduled to go to Bellitreaux the same day that Vanguard and the Ninth Company had been dispatched to take the castle back from the rebels. Instead he was sent to the city to face a court martial. By the time he was released, Bellitreaux was surrounded. Vanguard had never known it, but by brawling in the trees that day he had inadvertently saved James Sanderson's life. Sanderson flicked his tongue across the chip in his front tooth.

Henriette saw his mouth move. She leaned forward to listen to his last words. She squeezed his hand tightly as the fighting continued around them, the only person Sanderson had ever met to give him just one moment of comfort. "Tell John..." Sanderson's eyes fluttered. "Tell John...he's an arsehole."

As James Sanderson was taking his final breath, a little further down the road, heading for an overlooked side alley, Lucien Herveaux pulled a young girl by the arm through the chaos. He had no intention of fighting for anyone, Red Badges or otherwise. His investment had gone sour and he was not about to lose everything he had. The girl tugged at his arm as he dragged her through the street. She looked to be barely thirteen. "Let me go!"

Herveaux's face grew redder as she struggled. "You freaks are mine! I own you!"

The girl would be far from as lucrative as the club had been, but perhaps he could use the money from her to buy more. He could rebuild his empire, one harlot at a time.

The glint of metal stopped him in his tracks. A small, skinny figure blocked his path. Carmen held the pistol aloft, eyes dark and void of sympathy. She had none to give. The barrel of the gun came into focus. There was the soft click of the barrel primed.

She lifted her chin. "Let her go."

Herveaux snarled. "This isn't your business. I *own* her."

"I said let her go."

Contempt spread across Herveaux's face. He saw the way that Carmen's hand trembled. "You're nothing but a scared little girl. You won't kill me. You're just another low breed whore."

The trembling stopped. Carmen's expression became composed, almost serene, as she came to an important realisation. Head tilting to one side, she smiled slowly.

"You're wrong." She stepped forward, the colour draining from Herveaux's face as he felt the barrel pressed to his forehead. "I'm not a whore..." Carmen pulled the trigger. Herveaux hit the ground with a thud. She took a moment, one brief second to stand over the club owner, considering his corpse. "I haven't decided what I am yet."

⚜

BRANDISHING THE KNIFE, TARRYN TWISTED ON THE balls of his feet, coat tails cutting the air. Dozens of bodies lay strewn across the cobbles, none of them the ones that he wanted to fell. Tarryn stalked, slicing and searching across the square.

Finally, he saw him.

Vanguard stood across the way, their eyes meeting. Tarryn's eyes flickered, the club behind him ablaze. The wood burnt red, spitting out embers. The posters that hung had blackened to a crisp. Vanguard saw the ashes falling around his head.

The city had always been its own sort of hell. Now he had unleashed a demon upon them. That was why he saw him. It was why they saw each other. Vanguard had never been destined to save Tarryn. He had been destined to rid the world of him.

Tarryn called out. "What do you think, Vanguard? Am I everything you thought I would be?"

Vanguard felt his grip tighten on his blade. "Everything - and much more."

"So what now, old friend, where do we go from here?"

Ribs sore and body beaten, Vanguard lowered his head. "Now I end it."

Face fixed, Tarryn kept moving back until he was standing almost inside the building. With that, a smile crept across his face. "In that case..." Disappearing until only the blue of his eyes could be seen, his voice echoed through the smoke. "*Come find me.*"

The club was empty. The stage was a splintered wreck, velvet curtains burnt away. Glass and stone crunched under foot. Vanguard kept both eyes open, watching for movement in the shadows. He caught a glimpse of a black coat, a figure moving through the smoke. A sudden rush of air and Tarryn appeared, knife slashing the space between them. Vanguard stepped back. The blade struck the collar of his jacket, slicing through the material.

From the right, the knife came again. Tarryn was smart. The boy was not invisible to Vanguard but then again, neither was Vanguard invisible to the boy. They could not deceive each other the way they could others. Instead Tarryn used the smoke, the darkness of the shadows to camouflage his every turn. He had grown, learnt. Around them the blackened rafters groaned. Tarryn appeared like a ghost from out of the smoke. Vanguard reached out, grabbing hold of the pale wrist, stopping the knife in mid air. Undeterred, Tarryn lifted his leg to slam his foot against Vanguard's calf. It jarred, the bone shuddering.

Pushing back, Vanguard and the boy battled across the room, the heat of the fire burning as though they stood in the seventh circle itself. Spit frothed and foamed at the boy's mouth. Tarryn bent his head low and pushed forward. His skull connected sharply with the bridge of Vanguard's nose. Vanguard staggered back, dazed. He felt something heavy hitting him in the back of the head. A second blow hit him across the back of the shoulders. Vanguard stumbled, falling to the floor.

Tarryn circled, the wooden stake gripped with both hands. He had lost the knife, but it would not matter. Vanguard would meet his end the way O'Keefe had. Tarryn would see his brains sprayed across the floor. "You can't beat me, Vanguard! I'm better than you. I'm more now than you could ever be."

Lifting the stake above his head, he bore down with an almighty force into the floor. Vanguard rolled away, the impact of Tarryn's makeshift club sending a vibration across the ground just inches from his face.

This was not how he intended to end his days. Vanguard had survived the streets, he had survived

Bellitreaux, and he had survived the Hole and Sanquain. Unlike Wick, or Ludnor, or Paulette, he had survived the city. Nothing on the earth was going to see John Vanguard end his days lying on the floor of some cheap show house, blood and sand in his mouth.

Tarryn was still raving, eyes blazing. "You're nothing anymore."

Seeing an opportunity, Vanguard took his knife and drove it deep into the side of Tarryn's leg, between the ankle and calf. Tarryn roared into the flames. With unbridled anger, he brought the full weight of the club down onto Vanguard's stomach. Vanguard tried and failed to roll away once more, vomit expelling from his lips.

What stood over him now was all that was left after Tarryn's humanity had been stripped away. It was primal, uninhibited. It was what lurked beneath the surface and had ached to be released for all those years.

At his angriest, at his most dangerous, Tarryn Leersac was nothing more than a vengeful child. He was a bitter, hateful boy blaming everyone else for his failings. His father, his mother, Vanguard. The strikes came swift and hard.

"You made me what I am - I am your legacy."

"*No.*"

Tarryn paused, hands still clutched at the weapon. Shoulders heaving, he looked down at Vanguard. The old man was struggling to breathe. He would not last much longer. The fire raged on around them. Tarryn barely felt it. He barely felt anything at all. Vanguard lay, beaten and bruised on the floor. "I never made you. I just see you now for what you always were. *The wrong choice.*"

Rage exploded inside Tarryn's chest. Eyes aglow, he lifted the club one last time. Vanguard braced himself for the impact. There was a thundering noise, like the charge of a great beast coming across the earth. Vanguard turned his head; face pressed against the sand and saw the blur of brown on white skin. Tarryn was swept from his feet. Kosic had the size and strength of a battering ram. They rolled across the club together, coming to a stop a few feet apart.

Vanguard tried to stand, but his body had other ideas. He was done. Kosic searched the flames, looking through the smoke for a glimpse of Tarryn. "Get up, we have to go."

Vanguard coughed out a weak response. "Get out of here, find Cooke and go."

Kosic glanced around them, the heat burning at his face. The flames, the smoke, the destruction - the building was crumbling. There was a crash, the sound of footsteps barely perceptible across the floor and the flash of ice blue eyes. Kosic could not see death coming, but he felt it.

It was not Kosic that Tarryn needed to kill. He could die later. First, Vanguard needed to pay for what he had done. Tarryn emerged from the smoke, the length of the club the only thing between him and his former mentor.

It was in that moment that Kosic saw him for just a fraction of a second. He saw Tarryn standing across the room. Vanguard was using the last of his strength to get to his feet. He scrambled up, body black and blue.

The sounds of fighting dulled in Kosic's ears, the heat giving way to a pleasant coolness that only he could feel. He closed his eyes and thought of home, of the people and the soft coastline breeze that he had always enjoyed.

Kosic hoped that one day Cooke would find a way to fix their broken world. The muscles in his back tensed - the blood and sweat still dripping from his skin. He glanced at Vanguard, who met his eyes and returned his look with a single nod.

With everything that he had left in him, Kosic the Undefeated levelled his shoulder at the beam that stood central to the stage and ran. There was a loud cracking as the weight of his colossal mass hit the charred wood. It splintered, but stood firm. The noise of the ceiling groaning stopped Tarryn in his tracks. He looked up, the dust and debris from the beams catching in his eyes.

Clenching his teeth together, Kosic pushed as if he were trying to fuse with the beam, feeling the weight of the ceiling bucking and breaking. There was a shaking, an almighty rumbling like the sound of the gods awakening. Kosic, pushing his feet against the ground, roared out in unison with the sounds of the building. The walls sank down and the ceiling above them crumbled. The last thing that Vanguard saw was Tarryn Leersac, his pale face peppered with dust as he disappeared beneath a mountain of charred wreckage and debris.

CHAPTER 42
AM I DEAD YET?

F ar beneath the ground, where the stage had once
stood in the middle of Herveaux's club, under the
earth and rubble, John Vanguard felt himself lifted
from his grave and taken out of the wreckage. There was
no pain, no feeling or sense of time. All he felt was the
cool air around him. Blackness consumed him, until finally
he saw a flickering light in the distance.

Kosic took one weary step after another. Vanguard was
heavier than he looked and Kosic had sustained injuries
that a weaker man would have succumbed to long before.
He had made his peace with death, but it seemed that
death was not quite ready for them yet.

Had the tunnel not been beneath the theatre, they
would have been nothing more than crushed bone at that
moment. Instead, the beam had crashed through the floor,
and it had taken both Kosic and Vanguard with it.

The tunnel was quiet. There were no more gunshots.
Above him was only silence. The heat of the fire had
cooled, the wreckage still smouldering. When he had

regained consciousness, Kosic had searched for Tarryn in the tunnel. There had been no sign of the boy.

Carrying Vanguard towards the light of the street outside, he felt his weight shift. There was a subtle flickering to his eyes. Kosic dropped to his knees, trying to put Vanguard down with as much care as was possible. Leaning against the damp walls, Kosic watched Vanguard lick his lips. "Why aren't I dead?"

"Maybe it is not your time yet."

Vanguard groaned. He felt as though he might still die yet. "It was my time a long while ago."

Kosic leant back, bones cracking in ways that he knew they should not be cracking. He lay there, shoulder to shoulder with Vanguard. They sat in mutual silence for a few minutes. It was oddly calm in the tunnel, almost peaceful.

"Do you think many survived?"

Kosic shook his head. "I don't know."

"You should go and find the others."

They sat for a few moments more. Vanguard felt the aching in his bones. He wanted nothing more than to close his eyes and let the world drift away. Kosic's voice sounded distant. "Will you come with us?"

"You should go. I need to rest."

"Will you be alright?"

"I've walked away from worse places."

Kosic grinned, despite the pain. The giant looked down and nodded. It was time for them to go their separate ways. The uprising had been put down for now, but it was far from over. Sanquain's time would come to an end and they both knew it. They each had their own battles to fight in the meantime. "What should I tell your friends?"

Vanguard paused for a moment. "Tell them that I made

a choice. Tell Carmen that now she can make hers." He thought for a moment. "And tell Henriette something for me too."

⚜

Mrs Brown was not a sympathetic woman. It was one of the things that Sanquain valued most about her as an employee. Her complete lack of empathy made her a woman well equipped to do a job with remorseless efficiency. She wrung out the wet cloth, the blood dripping from her hands and down into the wash bowl.

Tarryn stirred. Opening his eyes, he saw a golden chandelier above his head, a moulded ceiling that he did not recognise. There was something soft beneath him, a velvet material that felt crisp and new. "Don't move or you'll bleed on the chaise longue."

The curt sound of the housekeeper's voice drifted down from above. Tarryn immediately went to move. A pair of strong hands held him back. "You will do as Mrs Brown tells you – that is an order."

Sanquain sat across the room on a plush armchair. An unknown soldier held Tarryn firmly in place as the doctor examined him. Mrs Brown handed him some sort of metal instrument. A fire crackled in the hearth. Tarryn heard the sound of a log falling. The whole house smelt clean and new.

"Where am I?"

"In the Golden Quarter about a mile from my chambers. You sustained several injuries. Mrs Brown and the doctor here will see that they are treated properly. When you are recovered, you will report to me." Sanquain took a sip from a glass of whisky.

"Where is my mother?"

"Admiring her new armoire I expect; that was where she was the last time I saw her."

Tarryn felt the cloth being wiped across his face. The skin had started to harden. The scars would be there permanently. Tarryn wondered how his mother would feel about them. She barely recognised him as it was. He would be a stranger to her now more than ever.

Sanquain rubbed his chin. It had been disappointing to learn that the bodies of neither John Vanguard nor Hector Mandego had been found amongst the embers. It was some little consolation to know that Sanderson now rotted in a pile of low breed scum. The body count had been high, but hundreds had escaped the flames and bullets. Still, it was enough to deter any further thoughts of rebellion for now.

Cooke had escaped, as had a few of the other perpetrators. Sanquain would find out which of the men at the city gates had betrayed him, but for the time being, he had damage control to oversee. "Mrs Brown, would you be so good as to clear the room?"

The housekeeper stood up and took her bowl. The doctor and guard followed suit, offering a curt bow to the captain as they left. Sanquain walked slowly over and leaned down until his face was level with the chaise longue. He had not expected the boy to live after they had pulled him from the rubble. Perhaps it was true what they said; perhaps he was part demon after all.

Sanquain reached out with a gloved finger and pressed it to the side of Tarryn's cheek. The scar puckered and twisted. Tarryn felt it like the jab of a knife into the side of his skull. He heard Sanquain's voice hissing in his ear. "Your work is not yet finished."

With that, the captain left Tarryn lying on the chaise in his new home.

Mrs Brown went upstairs to check on Tarryn's mother who was, indeed, still flitting from room to room, admiring the furniture and goods that had been bestowed upon them. She could not believe their good fortune. They had generous friends. The housekeeper took the cloth and placed it by the wash basin. She smiled; satisfied that she was doing her job as well as ever.

The captain had shown no interest in Paulette. Her death was not one that was necessary for the purpose of Tarryn's work. It was, however, necessary to Mrs Brown. She would not have another woman meddling with her business. It had not taken much. Tarryn was as jealous as a child. Mrs Brown had known that the smell of other men on Paulette would seep into his pores and fester under his skin. Reaching into the pocket of her apron, Mrs Brown took out the bottle of cologne and watched the remaining contents sloshing from side to side. It had cost a few pennies, a drop or two on his pillow each night. Mrs Brown would lose no sleep over the matter.

Lying on the chaise, Tarryn felt that if he had a soul, that he had perhaps sold it to the devil. But he had none and so he had no better sense now of his great purpose in the world then he had when this had all begun. Turning his head to the side, he watched the glowing fire. It was hypnotic. A moment later, his eyes rolled up to look upon the marble mantelpiece that ran across the length of the hearth. There, staring back at him from beneath the glass was the damned squirrel in its jar.

OUTSIDE THE CITY WALLS, HENRIETTE STOOD WITH HER back to the horizon, feeling the rush of the wind on her face. The leaves of a tree rustled behind her. She could not remember the last time she had seen a tree that looked like a real tree. Somebody had strung a rope from the bough of it, a thick branch attached to the end, forming a makeshift swing. It had probably been a long time since someone had sat on it.

Demetrio sat upon the grass running his fingers across the soft, green blades. There was a thick length of gauze wrapped tightly around his arm. He had fared much better than some the others. Remy would be mourned, as would the rest of the fallen. For now there was still work to do.

Cooke placed a hand on Carmen's shoulder, squeezing it as she watched the road. It was the first time she had been outside the walls. It was not as it should have been for her.

"I don't understand what happened. What did we achieve?"

It was a good question and one he wished he had an answer for.

Demetrio stood up, swinging a sack over his shoulder. It was the same sort of sack that Gregor had used each time he had collected the counters from the Ring O' Bastards. People had always wondered where the money had gone. Revolution was a costly business. Ludnor had always been a most appreciated donor to their cause. "Nobody else is coming. We're the only ones left."

Carmen shook her head. "We should wait a little bit longer."

She squinted, eyes scanning the road that led back to the city. Across the distance, a large figure appeared, walking towards them. Carmen held her hand to her forehead. Her heart beat a little quicker. The figure grew closer, battered and bruised but still very much alive.

A wide smile spread across Cooke's face. Demetrio punched the air. As he drew level Kosic opened his arms to them. Carmen ran forward. He held her so tightly she felt that she might be crushed. Eventually he let go and she stepped back, face flushed. "Hello, tiny girl. I am pleased to see you." Kosic greeted the others with a nod. "Are we all that are left?"

"All that got out."

Henriette looked at him thoughtfully. "We thought you were dead."

"Not yet, and neither is Vanguard. I think he is like cat, with nine lives."

Carmen looked back towards the walls of D'Orsee. There had been small acts of rebellion all over. The word of Cooke's revolution was spreading. Soon it would reach the other cities.

Cooke noted the expression in her eyes. "Will you come with us?"

Demetrio reached down into the sack and fiddled about for a moment. He withdrew a large wad of notes. Placing the money into Carmen's hand, he wrapped the girl's fingers around it and held them tightly for a moment. She looked at Cooke who gave her a simple nod. "It's your choice. Nobody can tell you what you must be anymore."

It was enough money to walk away. For the first time ever, she was completely free to make her own decisions. Carmen could find her own way in the world and become whatever it was she was destined to become. She bit her lip. "Where do we start?"

Demetrio pointed north. "Lycroix. We'll start there."

Carmen took one last look at the city and turned away.

As she walked down the open road, Demetrio and Cooke followed suit. Kosic lingered for a moment, watching Henriette hesitate.

She was looking at the wall, scanning it, remembering all that had happened. "He was never going to come, was he?"

"Vanguard? No, I don't think he was."

Henriette didn't seem surprised. "Did he say anything to you before you left?"

Kosic's face fell, a red blush creeping over his already darkened skin.

"What? What was it?"

Kosic turned to Henriette. Reaching out, he took one of her hands in his and pressed his fingers over hers. She steeled herself to hear what John Vanguard had to say to her.

"I would rather not say - it was very vulgar."

CHAPTER 43
ASHES

Vanguard picked his way across the charred remnants of the Ring O'Bastards. It was little more than a burnt out husk. The looters had been in, and had then been subsequently cleared out by the Red Badges. No doubt they took their share too.

Sitting amongst the rubble, half askew and legs broken was the old piano. Reaching out, Vanguard pressed down on one of the keys. In another life, maybe he would have learnt to use his hands for something other than taking life. Perhaps he would have made beautiful music. But this was not another life.

Making his way to the back of the wreckage, Vanguard stepped into the yard and looked at the door of the shed. It was still padlocked. As he turned the key in the lock, Vanguard found everything as he had left it. His clothes left in a bundled pile, an assortment of personal items in a box. They knew he would be coming for it.

They were out there somewhere, hidden amongst the shadows and twisting backstreets of the city – the downtrodden and the mistreated, a network of Cousins ready to rise up against Sanquain and his like.

D'Orsee was a sleeping beast, awakening from a long night and rumbling with discontent.

War was coming. It was unavoidable, whether it was a week from then or a year. Mistakes had been made and lessons learned, with countless more still to come. Cooke would find his army. The man had a way of making you want to fight back. But it would take time. Until that day, Vanguard would remain in D'Orsee to do what he did.

Slinging the bag over his shoulder, he tossed the padlock to the floor and shut the door behind him. The crudely painted V stared back at him from the metal. He ran his fingers over the letter.

It turned out that Carmen had been right that day sitting on the edge of the bathtub. Over the years Vanguard had been many things to many people – a soldier, a deserter, a murderer, a monster. But that didn't mean that was all he was, or all he could be.

He still carried the Ninth with him, as he did Paulette, Ludnor, even Sanderson. But the ball of grief no longer weighed him down. It was no longer the chain that kept him shackled to the past. John Vanguard was a man who knew the cost of war. At times he saw the necessity in death. And now, finally, part of him was beginning to believe that perhaps there was a reason he was still alive.

Three times Vanguard had found himself buried beneath the earth, and three times he had risen up from the dead. But what Sanquain had merely exhumed, Argent had revived. That was the difference. Cooke, Kosic, Carmen and Henriette – what they offered, with their spirit, their hope and endless will to survive was more than just a second chance. It was a resurrection.

There was a rustling in the debris, a small creature darting out from beneath the wood and metal. He glanced down. Vanguard was a man who appreciated the ability and skill to survive. There were few that had it, even fewer who achieved it.

They had a long road ahead of them. It was time to begin.

The old ginger cat, snaggle-toothed and singed of all its fur, mewled angrily at his feet.

CHAPTER 44
THANK YOU

Thank you for choosing to read this book.
If you enjoyed your time with Vanguard, please consider
leaving a review on Amazon, Goodreads or your social
media

You can get updates and news about upcoming releases via
my website https://htinsleywriter.wordpress.com/

Or you can follow me on Twitter

9 781527 288942